A
KILLER
APP

A
KILLER
APP

AN HOA MYSTERY

LINDA LOVELY

LeVel
BEST BOOKS

For Tom Hooker, my husband
My steadfast partner
in life's many adventures.
I couldn't ask for a better friend.

Praise for the HOA Mysteries

"An excellent mystery written with charm, appeal and wry humor - and ex-Coast Guard Kylee Kane is a great main character."—Lee Child, International bestselling author of the Jack Reacher Series

"Author Linda Lovely gives Kylee Kane a mission in keeping with today's fast-changing technological times with a cadre of colorful characters that keep you guessing what could happen next...and to whom."—C. Hope Clark, award-winning author of the Edisto Island Mysteries & the Carolina Slade Mysteries

"In *A Killer App*, Coast Guard retiree Kylee Kane, now an HOA security consultant, faces her toughest opponent. The sinister Chameleon will take any steps to sideline enemies. But how can Kylee track down an opponent who only seems to exist in cyberspace and uses Artificial Intelligence to influence, intimidate, and kill? A chilling preview of potential AI perils.—Gregory Stout, author of the Jackson Gamble Mystery series

"I was spellbound by the interweaving of treachery, artificial intelligence, and the effectiveness of the human brain. Between well-drawn characters and a story told in a linear fashion through different character points of view, the reader is consistently engaged in this well-paced novel."—Debra Goldstein, award winning author

"Lovely excels at balancing the life-and-death stakes of her well-paced narrative with the character developments of her robust and memorable cast... A delightful, page-turner of a mystery, not to be missed."—*Jonathan*

Haupt, coeditor, *Our Prince of Scribes: Writers Remember Pat Conroy*

"Another masterful mystery by Linda Lovely. Filled with twists, turns, and interesting characters. Being part of an HOA can be dangerous business."—Dana Ridenour, award-winning author of the Lexie Montgomery FBI undercover series

"*Neighbors to Die For* is filled with kidnappings, coastal intrigue, adrenaline-pumping action, and an intelligent sleuth—everything I need in my mysteries. Loved it!"—Melissa Bourbon/Winnie Archer, National bestselling author of the Book Magic & Bread Shop Mysteries

"Linda Lovely delivers another twisty mystery with the perfect mix of wry humor and quirky characters. Anyone looking for a fun, fast page-turner, here it is!"—Tami Hoag, #1 *New York Times* bestselling author

"… a distinctive setting, a tenacious female sleuth and captivating suspense." —Katherine Ramsland, bestselling author of *How to Catch a Killer*

"Low Country murder, intrigue, and even a little romance… Kylee Kane is a welcome addition to the genre, and author Linda Lovely knows how to stir the pot with crackling dialogue and a tidy little mystery. Highly recommended!"—Richard Helms, Derringer & Thriller award-winning author of *Brittle Karma*

CHARACTERS & HOMEOWNER ASSOCIATIONS
(No worries. You'll meet them gradually.)

Welch HOA Management Company

- Ted Welch, owner *(retired U.S. State Dept.)*
- Kylee Kane, security consultant/*retired U.S. Coast Guard*
- Grant Welch, Ted's son
- Myrtle Kane, Kylee's mom
- Frank Donahue, construction & maintenance
- Robin Gates, IT & website
- Mimi Jones, intern

Rand Creek HOA

- Jocelyn Waters, board president
- Andy Fyke, opposes rentals
- Sherry LeRoy, board member
- J.T. Landreth, AI dupe
- Connie Beck, gossip
- Jeannie Crooks, J.T.'s friend

Lighthouse Cove HOA

- Dr. Amanda Holder, Artificial Intelligence expert
- Ed Hiller, YV chef
- Leona Grimm, dog lover

Hullis Island HOA

- Cliff Jackson, board president
- Chief O'Rourke, head of security
- Bill Clark, security officer
- Byron Kisker, disgruntled owner

Satin Sands HOA

- Steph Cloyd, board member
- Donna Dahl, board president
- Chad Norton, Steph's friend
- Aaron Cloyd, Steph's brother

Law Enforcement

- Sheriff Deputy Nick Ibsen
- Sheriff Deputy Josie Muschel
- Coast Guard Lt. Alysha Carter

Other

- Kay Barrett, B&B owner
- Xander Pringle, attorney
- Hank Mitchell, marine repair
- Bubba Quarles, nativist cult
- Claude Appleton, teen incel

ARTIFICIAL INTELLIGENCE

- Artificial Intelligence (AI)—Programs structured like the brain's neural network are given access to vast stores of information via the internet and other sources. This allows them to predict how to respond to queries or commands. The responses can take a variety of forms—text, spoken language, images, or videos.
- Deepfake—High-quality, polished videos or audios that can convincingly insert people into settings they've never visited, and make them appear to say or do things they haven't said or done.
- AI Whisperer—A person talented in creating language prompts to cause an AI program to produce the desired results, whatever they might be.
- Hallucinate—When an AI program delivers a bizarre response to a question or command.
- Training—Feeding an AI program information it needs to perform a specific task or set of tasks, such as mimicking a celebrity's speaking style, voice, and mannerisms.

Chapter One

The Chameleon

Wednesday Evening, June 28

I critique my fifteen-second video. Deepfake Andrew Fyke looks as wrinkled and decrepit as the real-life old fart. Virtual Fyke just needs to blink a bit more as he teeters at the top of the stairs. The deep shadow I placed behind him suggests someone or something lurks there.

I add a few more blinks and close the video to craft my text to J.T. It needs to achieve the perfect balance between outrage and pathos to convince J.T. to do what her social media pal, me, can't—push Fyke down the stairs.

Rand Creek's Home Owners' Association office sits on the second floor of the clubhouse. Earlier, I spoofed an email from the HOA's lawyer asking Fyke to meet him there at nine tomorrow morning to review covenant change procedures. When Fyke finds the office locked and no lawyer waiting, he'll leave by the back stairs. Always uses them. That's where J.T. comes in.

My minion believes I'm a wheelchair-bound oldster, who shares her outrage about sexual perverts allowed to roam free. Our shared mission? To protect grandkids visiting Rand Creek from pedophiles like Fyke.

Is Fyke a pedophile? Beats me. Never met the man in person. Have zero interest or knowledge of the old codger's sex life, past, present, or future. Simply need him to disappear—incapacitated or dead—doesn't matter.

I use AI—Artificial Intelligence—to prepare a text that touches on all of J.T.'s hot-button issues, then attach the video clip of Fyke at the top of the stairs. A like-minded friend supposedly captured the video.

"Look how easy it would be to give this perv a deserved shove. He'll be there all alone at nine a.m. tomorrow. How I wish I could give that push. Dear Lord, no telling how many children would be saved."

If J.T. had a brain, she'd realize the Fyke video is fake. A photographer would have to be Spider-Man to get that camera angle. Luckily, deep thought isn't one of J.T.'s attributes.

Did I need to create the deepfake video? Probably not, but it offers J.T. a nice mental rehearsal. Shows her how easily she can become that vengeful shadow, give Fyke a fatal push.

All my correspondence with online idiots is encrypted and delivered via burner phones. I've even arranged for the attached Fyke video clip to vanish soon after J.T. views it. My somewhat hokey homage to *Mission Impossible*. Too bad I couldn't incorporate a burning match and theme music.

To pull off the disappearing trick, I sent J.T. a free app to open videos. Told her it was much better than what she'd been using. Didn't mention I added an instruction to the app. It knows to delete video files with my custom tags after they're opened.

How many times will the real Fyke blink before he plummets down the stairs?

I'll never know. Like the puppeteer voicing *Mission Impossible's* off-screen assignments, I'll be far away from the action. I prefer to direct God-like from the ether.

Should the mission fail, I'll disavow any knowledge.

Then again, should the mission succeed, I'll disavow any knowledge.

Chapter Two

Kylee

Thursday 10 a.m., June 29

As I drive along Hilton Head Island's bustling main drag, Grant and Mimi, my nineteen-year-old passengers, argue about a dystopian movie's outer-space aliens. Grant thinks they're flawed heroes. Mimi disagrees.

Their passionate debate makes me smile. Not that I've seen the flick or ever will. My taste runs to romantic comedies and mysteries with hopeful endings. Working for Welch HOA Management, I have enough close encounters with folks who could be mistaken for alien lifeforms.

Grant is the son of my employer, Ted Welch, who's also my lover. That's a recent, unexpected complication. Growing up, Ted and I were Keokuk, Iowa, neighbors. Back then, Ted was my late brother's best friend and a pest. Who'd imagine we'd reconnect in the South Carolina Lowcountry four decades later.

Since the teens have quit chatting, I glance at Mimi in the passenger seat and peek at Grant in the rearview mirror. Want to see if they're hypnotized by their latest hobby, calling up the newest AI chatbot on their smartphones and competing to prod the AI to hallucinate. That's what the industry calls it when an interactive AI goes off the rails and spouts nonsense, threatens a user, or declares undying love.

3

From what I understand, the one thing these AI chatbots never do is speak in tongues or misuse punctuation. Their command of whichever language they're asked to employ appears flawless, even if the content is gibberish.

"Time to quit playing with your smartphones," I say. "We're almost to the Rand Creek gate. I'll ask the guard to prepare security passes so you two can come and go as needed."

Grant speaks up. "Better let security know I'll be taking aerial photos. Drones freak some people out."

"Good idea. Show your commercial drone license to the guard when I introduce you."

Grant worked for his dad last summer, but Mimi's been on board less than a month. Both students are rising college sophomores on summer break. Grant's a cadet at The Citadel in Charleston, while Mimi's studying ornithology at Cornell University. The two began dating last summer and bonded in earnest during last Thanksgiving's kidnap ordeal.

Given the unpredictable course of young love, I had qualms about Ted hiring the pair to work side-by-side all summer. But they're great kids, and Ted's having a devil of a time recruiting good—okay, any—employees. His woeful pleas about being short-handed are the sole reason I'm still on the payroll. Not how I envisioned spending my days after retiring from the Coast Guard. My seventy-nine-year-old mother, Myrtle Kane, is another Ted pushover. He's sweet talked Mom into part-time receptionist duties.

At the Rand Creek gate, a friendly guard prepares security passes for Grant and Mimi and alerts the in-house TV channel to stream a message that any new drone sightings are authorized.

Mimi oohs and ahhs when we pull up at the Rand Creek clubhouse. "Wow, it's Tara on steroids."

A fair appraisal of the mega-mansion's impractical Old South plantation vibe. Most owners in the 3,000-unit complex for the fifty-five and over crowd would never dream of huffing and puffing up the building's front twin curving staircases. A sedately sloped handicap ramp around back gets ninety-nine percent of the traffic.

Mimi pauses to frame a photo of the ornate entrance. A birder, she's honed her photo skills, capturing the aerial antics of our feathered friends. Taking still photos of Rand Creek buildings and amenities to revamp the community's website should be a piece of cake.

"Who are we meeting?" Grant asks as Mimi snaps off more shots.

"Jocelyn Waters, the president," I answer. "Haven't met her, but based on the Island Packet's profile piece, she's a big-shot Realtor. Owns Be Shore Realty & Rentals and has an interest in several local restaurants and bars. She's a major player in local politics."

After we enter the main floor of the mansion from the back ramp, I lead the way down a wide, marbled corridor to a nondescript door. If you're not averse to a little exercise, the door hides a back stairwell that offers a quick route to the top floor. Its well-concealed existence harkens back to servant passages, installed to ensure the master's retainers come and go unobtrusively.

As we near the stairwell, a faint keening sound puts me on alert. *An animal in pain?* I cautiously crack open the door, letting light filter inside the dim vestibule. It takes a second for my eyes to adjust.

"Good Lord!"

An elderly man's body is crumpled in a fetal curl. I fumble for the light switch, and harsh, green-tinged fluorescents react with staccato blinks before they hum at full power.

The garish lighting doesn't improve the ghastly scene. Blood oozing from the man's scalp looks like ketchup on his frizzy white hair. While the thin, pretzeled body doesn't move, fluttering eyelids assure the oldster's alive. A miracle considering the body-size crater in the drywall behind his stooped back. Bile rises in my throat as I notice a whitish bone peeking through his scrawny right wrist.

I kneel at his side. "What happened? Did you fall down the whole flight of stairs?" I babble. "Don't worry. We'll get help."

Grant opens his ever-present cellphone. "We need an ambulance. An older gentleman has fallen. He has a head injury and broken bones."

Mimi, tapping away on her own cell, holds up a finger to signal Grant. "We're on the first floor of the Rand Creek clubhouse near the back entrance," she says. "The address is 710 Rand Creek."

The injured victim moans. I gently sweep the back of my hand across his forehead. He's super-hot. Feverish? A concussion? Does he even know we're here?

There's no midpoint landing in this stairwell. The steps march in a straight line to the second floor. The man must have tripped at the very top and hurtled below like he was sliding down an icy chute without a luge. Given the drywall carnage, he hit with the force of a sledgehammer. He's lucky to be alive.

"EMTs are on the way," Grant says. "What should we do?"

"Go outside to direct them," I suggest. "I'll call the gate and keep this gentleman company until they arrive."

Mimi starts to follow Grant, then pauses, wedging her camera bag between the stairwell door and the doorframe to keep it open. *Good thinking.* Oxygen feels at a premium in the coffin-sized space.

"So…dizzy," the man mumbles.

"No wonder," I reply. "You had a nasty fall and banged your head. Stay still. EMTs are on the way."

The man's thin lips twist as he labors to form words. Each syllable escapes on a breathy whistle of air. "Think teeth…broken. Feels sharp."

"Don't exert yourself. Don't talk if it hurts."

While I'm dying to go into interrogation mode—*Who are you? Do you remember falling? Any idea how long you've been here?*—I restrain myself. The man's jaw may be broken. Asking him to chat isn't a kindness.

I'm finishing my call to the front gate when a door creaks open at the top of the stairs.

"Who's down there?"

The alto voice is brusque, demanding.

A tall, broad-shouldered newcomer is silhouetted in the door frame atop the stairs. Even though her stylish silver pantsuit looks nothing like a toga, her stance reminds me of a classic Roman statue.

"There's been an accident," I answer. "A man fell down the stairs. We've called an ambulance."

The woman's heels click on the uncarpeted wood as she descends a few steps to get a closer look. "Is Andrew conscious...coherent?"

She halts midway, waiting for my answer.

Is she afraid she might get bloodstains on her outfit?

Not fair. The cramped stairwell barely offers enough room for me and Andrew, whoever he may be.

"He's conscious but dazed," I answer. "I'm Kylee Kane. Here for a meeting. We found this gentleman a few minutes ago. Do you know him?"

"Yes, that's Andrew Fyke, a resident."

I hesitate, deciding how to describe Mimi and Grant. Since they're with me as Welch employees, I don't want to refer to them as teens or kids. "Two of my associates are waiting outside to direct the ambulance."

"Nothing more to be done then." The woman's voice is cold, matter-of-fact. "I'll wait for you in the conference room as long as I can. I have an important Realtor meeting in an hour. We may need to reschedule."

Jocelyn Waters. Given her tone, she's either an emotional iceberg or doesn't care for Andrew. Since she feels no need to introduce herself, Ms. Board President must expect all us peons to know who she is—and feel honored to be graced by her presence.

She reverses direction and briskly climbs the stairs. At the top, Jocelyn firmly shuts the door.

Staring at the closed door, my brain cells finally fire.

There are light switches at the top and bottom of the stairs. That door at the top was shut when we found Andrew sprawled in total darkness. I've trekked up and down these stairs a few times. I can't imagine a single scenario that would prompt someone about to descend the stairs to close the door behind him before turning on the lights. This man's fall is no accident.

Someone shoved Andrew.

Then, once the deed was done, his attacker shut the door. If Andrew did have a chance to switch the light on, his attacker turned it off, leaving his victim to suffer and perhaps die alone in the dark.

Chapter Three

Kylee

Thursday, morning, June 29

Once the EMTs arrive, I climb part way up the stairs to give them space, but remain within eavesdropping territory. The victim is Andrew Fyke, age seventy-five. The confused gentleman has zero memory of the actual fall or how it happened.

I follow the medics when they carry him outside. As an attendant reaches for the ambulance door, I ask, "Are you taking him to the Hilton Head Hospital?"

"Yes, but he may be transferred to Beaufort Memorial or MUSC in Charleston for surgery."

"Thanks," I reply. "I'll contact the hospital to find out how he's doing."

Since it looked like an accidental fall, law enforcement wasn't called. Should I take the initiative to share my misgivings with the Beaufort County Sheriff's Department? No. Not given my reign last year as Miss Unpopularity. I need some concrete evidence.

At least Nick Ibsen, my main nemesis, isn't the sheriff. Too bad he decided to stay on as a deputy after abandoning his campaign to become the head cheese. I'm pleased to say Ted and I had a hand in Nick's election campaign debacle.

As the ambulance departs, Grant and Mimi join me.

I sigh. "Guess we go inside. Jocelyn Waters may or may not be waiting for us. Saw her on the stairs. Says she's expected at a more *important* meeting, so don't be surprised if we're dismissed."

Once the sarcasm escapes my lips, I wish I'd bit my tongue. I'm a poor role model for Mimi and Grant when it comes to client diplomacy. I suck at disguising my feelings or keeping un-asked-for opinions to myself.

In the conference room, Jocelyn is typing away on her iPad. I clear my throat. Still, her head stays bent as her fingers dance over the keys. I take the opportunity to study the woman's face. Based on the magazine profile, her children are in their early thirties. That probably makes her a couple of years my senior. Well-preserved mid-fifties? No threads of gray in her auburn hair. Probably dyed, but nicely done. No reading glasses, even for computer work. Contact lenses? Subtle makeup. Glowing skin. Firm neck. *Yeah, I hate her.*

"Take a seat," she finally commands, still not looking up. "Decided I might as well get some work done since you weren't on time."

Jocelyn's dismissal prompts Grant to roll his eyes in a silent exchange with Mimi.

Uh, oh. Need to suggest Grant mimic his dad's diplomacy and leave the eye-rolling to me.

Jocelyn shuts down her iPad, and we lock eyes. Her irises are an arctic blue. Yep, the unnatural, but apropos, color suggests tinted contacts.

"Could Andrew sue Rand Creek for his injuries?" Jocelyn asks. "What can be done to limit potential liability?"

Not the greeting I expected. The president appears to have zero curiosity about the extent of Andrew's injuries or what's become of him.

I don't mention my belief that Andrew's the victim of an attack. *Due diligence prevents foot-in-mouth disease.*

"While I'm no expert on liability, I think there would need to be evidence of negligence—something like a cracked stair tread, a missing handrail, or a burned-out light bulb."

She nods. "Good. Andrew's a troublemaker. File a report with our insurance company to document that our stairwell, lighting, etc. were in good repair on this date. Include photos. Now, let's talk about the website."

I attempt a smile. "Let me introduce Grant Welch and Mimi Jones. They'll be photographing Rand Creek and all your amenities. Grant has a commercial drone license and provided aerial coverage for several Welch properties last summer. Mimi's photographs of birds have been featured in several national publications."

"Birds?" Jocelyn's eyebrows shoot up. "That seems a weak recommendation for styling and shooting interiors. It takes a discerning eye to capture what appeals to the mature, upscale owners we hope to attract. We're paying Welch HOA a handsome fee for a new website. I hope you're not trying to do it on the cheap."

I want to strangle the woman. Had her body been discovered at the bottom of the stairs, I'd be even more certain the fall was no accident.

"I'm sure you'll be happy with the results," Mimi interjects, saving me from myself. "If you're unhappy, Welch HOA will arrange added photography."

Jocelyn frowns. "Yes, and it would delay the new website. We gave you a deadline. What progress has been made to modify the website so owners can vote online for covenant and rule changes? Mailing paper ballots is a pain and expensive."

I hoped Jocelyn wouldn't bring this up. Ted's much better at verbal tap dancing. Several Rand Creek owners have told Ted they worry what might happen if Jocelyn can see how they vote. They're afraid of retaliation or even vote count chicanery.

"What's the answer?" Jocelyn prods.

"Ted's exploring options," I begin. "Ways to ensure owners will feel confident their votes remain private. Owners might feel intimidated if they believed board members could check how they voted. There's also the need to ensure owners the votes they cast can't be altered electronically."

"Tell Ted we hired your company to perform assigned tasks, not to revisit board decisions. This is a cost-cutting measure. We're not debating policies or philosophy."

She glances at her watch, then slides a paper across the table. "I listed the photographs I want by next Friday, July 6, at the latest. Before then, the board expects a preview of the proposed website structure and features, including the voting module. I'll text you a meeting time."

Jocelyn stands. "I'm out of time. Get that report to our insurance company with photographs. Good day."

I'm stunned mute. Don't even repeat her "Good day." A ding signals the elevator has arrived. Grant, Mimi, and I stay mum an extra minute. Want to make sure the elevator doors have closed on Jocelyn's fashionably-clad butt.

"Yikes," Mimi says. "I've met a few Welch HOA clients on the haughty side, but that woman is a walking rude meme."

I nod my agreement. "Thank heavens, we don't have to deal with the likes of her every day. I actually like most of our clients."

Our clients? When did I start thinking in terms of "our" clients? Past time for me to exit. What began as a temporary security consulting gig has morphed into a lot of client hand-holding. Not a job suited for a retired Coast Guard investigator.

I stand. "Have fun shooting Jocelyn's photo list. Remember the back staircase. Take several close-ups of the stairs. Let's meet at the car at noon. I'll try to park near the same spot. Meanwhile, I'll see if Mr. Fyke's arrival at the clubhouse was caught on camera, and I'll call on Sherry LeRoy, a *nice* Rand Creek board member. Curious to see if Sherry agrees with Jocelyn's verdict that Andrew Fyke is a troublemaker. If so, I want to find out who he's antagonized."

"Why?" Grant asks. "Think it'll help you determine if the man will sue?"

I shrug. "Guess I could ask Sherry about that, too. Mostly, I want to know if Andrew's angered anyone enough to push him down those stairs."

Grant chuckles. "You can take the investigator out of the Coast Guard, but you can't remake suspicious minds. What makes you think it wasn't an accident?"

"I'll tell you at lunch."

Chapter Four

Kylee

Thursday, morning, June 29

My short stroll around the clubhouse finds only one security camera focused on the seldom-used front entrance. While there's only a slim possibility the camera captured any worthwhile activity, I head to the Security Office to check it out.

The Welch HOA Management relationship with Rand Creek is new and limited. Since it doesn't currently involve any security oversight, I carefully rehearse how I'll word my request to view camera footage. Want to avoid giving the impression I'm checking up on Rand Creek security, or looking for excuses to put us in charge.

I introduce myself and explain Jocelyn asked me to prepare an incident report for the insurance company. I suggest the camera footage might help pinpoint Mr. Fyke's arrival time.

"I'll show you what we have," the woman on office duty says and directs me to a computer console. Her fingers are a blur as she rapidly presses a sequence of keys. Think she's done this a time or two.

"How about I set the start time for seven a.m.?" she asks. "That's when security unlocks the clubhouse doors. They're locked at ten p.m. every night unless there's a special event."

"Works for me," I answer.

She nods. "I'll fast forward to advance the images. You tell me when you spot something of interest."

"Okay. Thanks."

Not a single soul approaches the clubhouse front door after it's unlocked at seven. Not even Mr. Fyke. The first arrival is Jocelyn, who shows up a few minutes after nine. If I were suggesting security improvements, I'd add a camera to monitor the clubhouse's back ramp since that's how most folks access the building.

With video surveillance a bust, I opt for a more certain source of intel about the victim—Sherry LeRoy. Hope she's home. I've never visited her condo. In the past, we've met in the clubhouse or lunched at a local restaurant. But I know she lives in the first building Rand Creek opened.

Inside her building's vestibule, I press a buzzer beside the name LeRoy. Sherry answers before the sing-song tones can repeat the melody.

"Come on up," she invites. "Fourth floor, end of the hall. Good timing. Just pulled a blueberry coffee cake out of the oven."

My taste buds stand at attention. I tell my brain they need to stand down. I'm going out to lunch.

But wouldn't Ted advise against hurting a client's feelings when she's playing hostess?

Having justified my calorie surrender, my taste buds celebrate.

As I exit the elevator, Sherry's cheery voice booms from the end of the hall. "This way to award-winning coffee cake." Her tanned arm snakes out from an open door and beckons me with a crooked finger.

Can't help but smile.

"What a view!" I exclaim as I walk into the living room.

Picture windows showcase a panorama of white sand and sparkling ocean. The interior décor is equally stunning. The white upholstery is dazzling but would never survive in any Kane household—let alone inside my floating abode, the River Rat. I named my thirty-eight-foot Island Packet sailboat after the dinghy Dad and I sailed on the Mississippi River.

Sherry waves away the décor compliment. "Thanks, but I can't take credit. The decorating's all Alice. I'm sorry she's not here. I know my wife would love to meet you. So, tell me what brings you here, while I rustle up coffee and cake."

My petite hostess vibrates with energy. Makes me wonder how many cups of coffee she's already downed. A retired dental hygienist in her late fifties, Sherry worked in her husband's dental practice until his death. She expresses no regrets about her prior life and speaks fondly of her late husband. Yet, Sherry also proclaims Alice is the love of her life.

"I have some sad news," I begin. "En route to a clubhouse meeting with Jocelyn, I discovered a badly injured owner at the bottom of the back stairs."

"Good Lord, what happened?" Sherry's facial expression signals alarm, then concern. "Who was it? Will they be all right?"

I nod. "Hope so. His name is Andrew Fyke. He definitely broke some bones and probably has a concussion. When we found him, he was conscious but dazed. Still, he was able to answer the EMTs' questions before they whisked him to the Hilton Head Hospital."

Sherry's straight, super white teeth—courtesy of her late husband?—worry her lower lip. "I chair the Welfare Committee. Andy's a widower, lives in one of the townhouses down the street. Hope he provided an emergency contact."

She grabs a community directory from the kitchen counter and leafs through the booklet.

She frowns. "Andy lists a son in Seattle. No way his boy can be at the poor man's bedside today. I'll visit the hospital before I call his son. Don't want to alarm him if his dad's condition isn't serious." Sherry folds down a corner of the directory page to keep her place.

"Say, did Jocelyn ask you to tell me about the accident? Can't believe our president even remembered we have a Welfare Committee, let alone that I'm the chair."

I accept a coffee mug from Sherry and obey her "sit, sit" instructions. A cozy kitchen dining nook is positioned a few steps from the stove.

"Afraid my visit has nothing to do with the Welfare Committee, and Jocelyn didn't mention you. She asked us to prepare insurance company documentation to show Andrew's fall wasn't the result of negligence—a precaution should he decide to sue. She described Andrew as a troublemaker. I wanted a second opinion before I report to Ted."

"Troublemaker?" Sherry scoffs. "Bet Jocelyn would describe me as a troublemaker, too. Andy was a member of Rand Creek's first batch of owners. His townhome was built less than a year after they completed this condo building and two years before the patio homes and assisted-living facility were added. Since his arrival, there have been a gaggle of rule changes. Andy always speaks his mind if he thinks a new rule proposal or capital expenditure is plain silly."

My hostess sets a dessert plate in front of me. The heavenly scent of cinnamon wafts from the warm coffee cake slice. I use the furnished fork to corral a crumbly bite complete with two plump berries. Chewing gives me time to consider where this conversation might head.

Sherry's funny, bright, and a dear. She loves to regale friends with stories. To put it plainly, she's not averse to embroidering facts to boost a tale's entertainment value. While she's never malicious, the resulting stories can wander far afield.

If Sherry hears over breakfast that a newcomer is flirting with a divorced neighbor, by lunch, she might announce they're dating. By the time dinner's served, Sherry might even hint wedding bells could ring soon.

To avoid feeding the powerful Rand Creek rumor mill, I don't share my suspicion that Andrew was shoved down the stairs. No sense providing starter fuel for panic about a murdering fiend attacking elderly residents. Too easy to trigger terror in a tightly-knit, over-fifty-five community.

"Sounds like you're fond of Andy," I probe. "Is Jocelyn his only detractor?"

"Afraid not. Rentals, especially short-term rentals, are the new bee in Andy's bonnet. He's been soliciting signatures to force a vote on a covenant change to eliminate all rentals. He's not the only owner to complain about renters blasting loud music, partying into the wee hours, trashing common areas, and ignoring pool and fitness center rules. Of course, the folks who own rental property hate Andy."

I'm surprised. "Are rentals truly a problem? Don't most Rand Creek residents own their units?"

"Yes, but a growing number of buyers are 'younger' folks—mid-fifties—who plan to retire here, but still work and live elsewhere," she replies. "They rent the units to cover Rand Creek fees. Rand Creek has no limit on what percentage of homes in the development can be rented, and owners need not occupy properties at closing. It's quite different from my HOA experiences on the West Coast."

"How many rental units are we talking about?"

Sherry shrugs. "Twenty possibly thirty?"

"Is there any age criteria for renters?" I ask

Sherry laughs. "Yes. Supposedly at least one person who signs the rental agreement must be fifty-five or over. Doesn't mean the double nickel who signs ever shows his face at Rand Creek."

Wonder if Ted knew about this donnybrook when he put his hat in the ring to take over Rand Creek management. Redoing the website and creating an electronic voting system are part of a trial engagement. If Ted gets the overall contract, he'll have to deal with unhappy people no matter who loses a vote on a proposed covenant change.

I glance at my watch. "Wish I could stay longer but I have another meeting. And, like you, I plan to stop by the hospital later to see how Mr. Fyke is doing."

Since I ate every crumb on my plate, I don't mention my next 'meeting' entails taking Grant and Mimi to lunch.

Chapter Five

The Chameleon

Thursday, Lunch Hour, June 29

Leona's mutt is driving me crazy. You'd think its little throat would seize up after a seemingly endless barking jag. How does she tune it out?

Dammit, wish I could afford to move. Not possible until I finish my app and it starts selling. Mom's fatal heart attack was perfectly timed. Gave me a place to land when the university handed me my walking papers. Though Mom had purchased a Rand Creek condo with plans to downsize, she hadn't gotten around to putting this Lighthouse Cove McMansion up for sale.

Its gaudy architectural pretensions aren't to my taste. Too bad I can't move into Mom's more contemporary Rand Creek condo. Not an option. At fifty-two, I'm a mere child according to the senior community's demographic.

Suck it up.

I'll lose money if I try to dump this mausoleum while the real estate market's in a slump.

Glad I can at least escape to Rand Creek for exercise. As the owner of Mom's condo, I am entitled to use the community's recreational facilities even if I'm too young to live there.

I believe strongly in taking care of my body. I weigh each morning and take immediate action should my weight climb more than two pounds. I don't understand how people let themselves get fat and flabby as they age.

My exercise routine is as important to me as intellectual challenges. I plan to live a long, healthy life and make enough money that I'll never have to wonder if I can afford anything I desire.

* * *

I change clothes in the Rand Creek locker room, then head to the weight machines. I'll work out on them for half an hour before I start my aerobic conditioning and run an hour on a treadmill. I listen to podcasts while I run. Multi-tasking lets me keep up on tech developments, and I have a lot on my plate.

I'm thinking about J.T., wondering if she took my bait, when fingers dig into my upper arm.

"Have you heard?" Connie Beck's huffing like she's finished a marathon. Since she's in street clothes, I surmise exercise isn't the cause.

"Andy Fyke's in the hospital," she wheezes. "Heard sirens and ran right over when I saw an ambulance parked outside the clubhouse. They found Andy at the bottom of those back stairs. Fell and crashed like a ton of bricks. Conked his head and broke bones. Who knows how serious the internal injuries are at his age?"

I want to whoop for joy. It appears J.T., my AI-guided human experiment, acted on my suggestion. I order myself not to smile. Need to show concern, compassion.

Had to be J.T. Would be too coincidental for Fyke to accidentally trip and tumble this very morning. Wish I could have seen it. Wonder how closely the scene resembled my rehearsal video?

"That's horrible. An awful place to trip," I comment. "Those stairs are steep. Has the gentleman talked? Did he say how he fell?"

Connie shakes her head. "The EMTs spirited him away before I got there. I only have headlines, no details."

I work hard to keep a neutral, concerned expression. How long before I find out what happened? Did pillow-soft J.T. plow into Andy's spindly legs?

I envision the impact in cartoon style—a roly-poly bowling ball hitting a human sweet spot for a strike.

I'm dying to text J.T. or check to see if she texted me. Impossible. I did away with that temptation by erasing the existence of my crippled alter ego. The phone used by my avatar to egg J.T. on to violence is toast, and all my fake's social media accounts have been closed.

Must admit erasing social media accounts takes persistence. Am amazed how often I'm invited to wish happy birthday to an online friend whose ashes were scattered two years ago.

Continued contact with J.T. would be beyond stupid. What if Andy did see who shoved him? If J.T. is ever identified and alleges she had an online accomplice, the authorities will find no video evidence to back up her claims thanks to my *Mission Impossible* zeal. They'll simply assume J.T.'s another Looney Tunes character with imaginary voices telling her what to do.

Yet I do need to find out what Andy thinks caused his fall. Does he know he was pushed? While I've never met the old man, there's plenty of paper to document we're adversaries. No way for me to gin up an excuse to make a bedside sympathy call.

Social media chatter should tell me all I need to know. Andy's injuries will be a hot topic on the Lowcountry's most popular chat site—The All-Seeing Ear—better known among locals as Earful. Homeowners rely on Earful to spread gossip, post selfies and grouse about vendors, neighbors, and their HOAs. Spreading conspiracy theories is a competitive sport.

The All-Seeing Ear promotes itself as the only trustworthy source of community information, since the local app lets neighbors share unvarnished, unfiltered, and uncensored opinions. The heavy conspiracy component has been a godsend. It's helped me recruit a half-dozen individuals into what I think of as my personal ROTC—Reserve Officer Training Corps. I've carefully groomed these minions. They view me (*whoever they think I am*) as more than a friend. I'm their wise mentor. With the right triggers, I can activate these reservists to help me accomplish a variety of goals.

Connie touches my arm. "You here for Tai Chi?" Her question brings my focus back to the here and now.

Since Connie's reported her breaking news, she's ready to reenter her retirement regimen—prunes, Wordle, and Tai Chi. The combo keeps her poop moving, exercises her brain, and helps her bend over far enough to pull up her dowdy, elastic-waist britches.

"No, only using the fitness equipment today," I answer. "Have fun at Tai Chi."

After I finish with the weights, I set the treadmill incline to ten degrees to increase the burn and keep my mind off Andy and J.T. Need to give the gossips time to post. There will be plenty to see in an hour or two.

I'm confident I left no virtual fingerprints. J.T. was molested as a child and hasn't been able to jettison her emotional baggage. That primed J.T. to buy my tale of a perverted Andy, who regularly gives in to sinful impulses. I also whispered the man finances all manner of evil. Took me almost an hour to create a deepfake video clip that purports to show Andy proclaiming kiddie porn as a First Amendment right. Made that video disappear, too.

I smile. Does anyone really make such First Amendment claims? Who cares? I also doubt the real-world Andy, a tightwad, has ever given a dime to any cause, liberal, conservative, or out-in-left-field.

Though Andy escaped death this morning, it should be weeks, if not months, before he can traipse door-to-door with his stupid anti-rental petitions.

Now, I can concentrate on other matters. I want my new app ready to market by fall. I'm counting on holiday sales to make a killing.

I smile.

A killing. Yep, it'll be a true killer app.

Chapter Six

Grant

Thursday, Lunch Hour, June 29

Mimi suggests Delisheeyo for our lunch break, and I go along. I can tell Aunt Kylee is less than enthusiastic, given Delisheeyo's menu is strictly vegetarian. Whenever Kylee gets to pick a lunch spot, she makes sure it offers either cheeseburgers or Reubens. Hey, they're two of my favorites, too. But Mimi's talked me into eating at Delisheeyo before, and it's okay.

Once we're seated, I watch Aunt Kylee frown as she studies the menu.

"Why don't you order the Acai Bowl," I suggest. "You'll like it."

Mimi quickly endorses my recommendation. "It not only tastes good. Acai berries are loaded with antioxidants. The dish is good for your whole body. Not sure if it can erase wrinkles, but I've heard Acai berries help old people look more youthful."

Mimi's cheeks color, turning almost as red as her hair, as she glances at Kylee, who never tries to camouflage the wrinkly creases around her eyes. Mimi's remark prompts a wry smile from my aunt. *Oops.*

"Oh, Kylee, I didn't mean to imply you should worry about wrinkles," Mimi fumbles. "You look great."

My aunt laughs. "Afraid I lost my epidermis battle decades ago. In my teen years, I couldn't wait to start a tan as soon as spring arrived. No sunscreen.

21

Lots of sunburns. Especially the summers I worked as a lifeguard. But let's talk about Rand Creek, so I won't be fibbing when I write this off as a Welch HOA business lunch. How did the photo shoot go?"

"Like you suggested, we stayed together," I say. "Started at the clubhouse, scouting for appealing interior shots."

"I took lots of pictures but without people," Mimi adds. "I brought along model release forms, but the clubhouse was deserted. To my mind, photos of empty rooms are sterile. After we pick the best locations, can we invite models? Would certainly make the place look more welcoming, if we showed people actually using the facilities."

I chuckle. "Jocelyn would want veto power over who you photograph. I'm sure she'd nix anyone overweight, wrinkled, frail, or too ethnic-looking."

Aunt Kylee pauses between bites of the sweet Acai Bowl and waggles her spoon in agreement.

"You're right on the money, Grant. Maybe we shouldn't bother Jocelyn with recruiting or approving models. After all, she did let us know how *terribly* busy she is. Ted knows several owners. Bet he can suggest willing models. If the resulting photos are unveiled at a full board meeting, it'll be tougher for Jocelyn to disparage her neighbors' looks."

"Good thinking," I say. "I already have most of the drone photos. Captured great aerial overviews of the clubhouse and fitness center. They show the condos, townhouses, and single-family homes fanning out from the center like spokes on a wheel."

"We went inside the fitness center," Mimi adds. "Had to laugh. Six men, squeezed into exercise spandex, were sitting at a table between the racquetball court and a room stuffed with exercise bikes, treadmills, and weight machines. The men were snarfing down snacks and playing poker. Wondered if they poured themselves into spandex to hoodwink their wives about how they spent the morning."

Aunt Kylee smiles. "Could be. Haven't been inside the fitness center. Is it nice?"

"It is," I answer, "and we did spot two jock types playing a spirited game of racquetball, as well as one woman running on a treadmill like she had a pack of wolves on her heels. My guess is they were all near the fifty-five-minimum age. They'd win Jocelyn's approval as models."

Mimi wiggles in her chair. "Kylee, before we split up this morning, you promised to tell us why you think that old man was shoved down the stairs."

I'm as curious as Mimi. "Do you still think someone pushed Andrew?"

My aunt nods. "My gut says yes."

She explains how the closed door at the top of the stairs made her realize how odd it was for the stairwell lights to be off when we found Andrew.

"I paid a visit to Sherry LeRoy, another Rand Creek director, to see if someone other than Jocelyn thinks Andrew's a troublemaker," Kylee adds. "I asked Sherry if she thought Andrew was likely to sue Rand Creek.

"She pooh-poohed it. Sherry likes Andrew, but admits he has enemies. He's been collecting signatures to force a covenant change that outlaws the rental of any Rand Creek properties. Since Jocelyn owns rental units, she wants to nip his initiative in the bud."

I pause between bites, wondering if Kylee plans to share her suspicions with the authorities.

"What's next? You'd be loco to tell the Sheriff's Office you suspect a crime. They'd show you the door before you could finish a sentence."

Kylee shrugs. "Agreed. Maybe Andrew's memory will come back, and he'll recall what happened in excruciating detail. Meanwhile, I'll drop you two back at Rand Creek to finish the day's photo shoot. Mimi, if you're looking for a condo that screams style, call Sherry LeRoy and ask if you can photograph her unit."

"We have one more chore," I add. "Jocelyn is sure to check that we documented the stairwell's *pristine* condition for the insurance company."

I turn to Mimi. "How long do you think we need to finish today's photo list?"

Mimi tilts her head as she goes through a mental list. "Maybe two-and-a-half hours."

"You going to hang with us?" I ask Kylee, though I figure I already know the answer. Standing around playing observer isn't compatible with her DNA.

"Nope," Kylee answers. "I'll find something useful to do."

I grin. "Where do you plan to start snooping?"

Kylee treats me to an eye roll. "Never you mind. Let's meet back in the parking lot at four-thirty."

Chapter Seven

Kylee

Thursday 2 p.m., June 29

Hilton Head Hospital is relatively small. For that reason, it seems more friendly and welcoming than urban healthcare complexes. I tell the front information desk volunteer I'd like to visit Andrew Fyke.

She checks a patient roster. "I'm sorry. We don't have a patient by that name."

"The paramedics brought him in this morning," I explain. "He fell down a flight of stairs. He definitely had a compound fracture of his wrist. I could see the bone protruding. He also may have had a concussion and a broken jaw."

"Oh," she answers, "that explains it. After evaluation in the ER, he was probably transferred to Beaufort Memorial for multiple surgeries. We don't have all the surgical specialties."

"Would you mind calling Beaufort Memorial to see if he's there?" I ask.

"No problem."

Minutes later, I get my answer. The patient's still in surgery. They operated on his wrist first, now a plastic surgeon is tackling his broken jaw.

"The anesthesia will probably keep him under or groggy for quite a while post-surgery," the volunteer adds. "Doubt you'll be able to see him today.

Hospital visiting hours end at six o'clock."

I thank her and return to my car. Now what? I retrieve my cellphone to call Sherry and let her know Andrew's been transferred. As a matter of principle, I keep my cell switched off until I need to phone or, heaven forbid, text someone. Once I power on, I find Robin Gates, Welch HOA Management's IT guru, has left me a voicemail. Robin knows better than to text me, given that Mom and I share top honors as Welch HOA's reigning communications dinosaurs. We only send and receive texts under duress. I listen to Robin's voice message:

"Kylee, log into The All-Seeing Ear. There are at least two dozen Earful posts about a Rand Creek accident at the clubhouse. Since you're there, you may already know someone was injured, but you need to take a look at the wild conspiracy theories it's generated."

I heed Robin's suggestion. Welch HOA Management monitors posts on what we cynically agree is an "earful of crap" to see what information—or, more likely, misinformation—the jungle drums are pounding out.

If a client HOA becomes the target of Earful misinformation or slander, Ted informs the HOA's directors and recommends the best way to counter. Ted learned early on that replying to Earful posts only excites and encourages outrageous trolls. We only lurk. No member of the Welch staff ever posts or replies to a post—even if we're the subject of personal attacks. And, believe me, I've been a target.

Scanning message traffic about Andrew Fyke, it's clear he has both online friends and foes. A few friends suggest his fall may not have been an accident. They theorize one of Rand Creek's rental property owners shoved him. A couple of the posts mention the "Ice Lady"—a moniker I figure applies to Jocelyn—and hint she could be the shover. Yet, so far, Fyke's friends have refrained from sharing real names.

Andrew's foes poo-poo the idea he was shoved. They paint Fyke as a mental case, who fell because he was raving about some renter's pissant rules infraction instead of watching where he put his feet.

I phone Robin to let her know I got her heads-up.

"Hey, Robin, thanks for alerting me to the Earful posts. If you have time, could you scan the posts and make a list of Andrew's presumed friends and foes?"

"Sure. Want me to see if Rand Creek has contact info for them in its database?"

"That would be super. I have the uncomfortable feeling I may need to talk to several of them. I assume Ted doesn't know about the incident."

"Correct, when he left this morning, he said not to bother contacting him unless it was a real emergency. Said you could catch him up on the rest at dinner."

"Okay, thanks."

Ted, the boss man, is in Atlanta. He and Frank Donahue, the company's maintenance and construction expert, are meeting with an Atlanta structural engineering firm.

Frank recently found signs of serious structural defects at a client's condo complex. The condo's reserve funds are not even close to covering the cost of needed repairs. Ted and Frank are trying to negotiate the best remediation deal they can. The necessary special assessment will be very painful for owners.

With two hours to kill before I pick up Grant and Mimi, I know exactly where to head. Satin Sands. That's if Donna Dahl is in. In my mind, I often think of Donna by the Freckles nickname Ted gave her when he described the HOA's board members before I met them.

Donna answers my call on the second ring. Doesn't even give me a chance to say hello. Caller ID makes it hard to surprise anyone these days.

"Hey, I didn't call you about some new dust-up," Donna says. "That means you must want something. It'll cost you the usual. Meet me in the clubhouse and buy me a drink."

I laugh. "I'll buy. But only if you can deliver a Cliff Notes summary of Lowcountry HOA conflicts related to rental property."

"Better plan on two drinks then, or maybe I should order a pitcher," Donna answers. "See you in a few."

Chapter Eight

The Chameleon

Thursday Afternoon, June 29

My killer app will need a sales pitch. Something that makes it sound fun and therapeutic. "Irritating people getting you down? You need this delightful Artificial Intelligence mood lifter."

Or maybe: "Transform anger into joy. A mentally healthy, fun way to banish enemies."

Okay, time's a wasting. Need to quit daydreaming about how to promote my killer app and think about adding modules or spinoffs to broaden its appeal.

When the university canned me, I focused first on creating an app that made it easy to upload any face and substitute it in videos. When such apps became a dime a dozen, I enhanced my app to simplify uploading individual audio and video samples for Artificial Intelligence training. This lets my users create facsimiles of their enemies and prompt their creations to spew any nonsense they choose. The results come with appropriate facial expressions and gestures.

Of course, users can upload their own images and voices, too. This way, they can construct make-believe conversations in which they demolish foes with their superior intellect. The app lets them craft the perfect comebacks and put-downs. Things they could never dream up in real-time in the real world.

To help lazy users achieve maximum satisfaction with minimal effort, my customers can drop their enemies into their choice of several pre-set scenes. Initially, I favored porn-lite scenarios that debased or humiliated the customers' deepfake enemies. However, once AI amateurs flooded the market with deepfakes of celebrities frolicking in crude porn, I knew the luster had gone from porn-lite.

When I asked myself how my app should evolve, I began work on my current project, a far more versatile and satisfying deepfake app—a real killer.

My app lets ordinary folks channel their anger and frustration into make-believe violence, thereby obtaining relief and staying out of jail. Users only need the ability to point and click on their computers or tap to select options on their smartphones. The app will do the rest, and it'll cost less than an AR-15 style rifle.

Instead of slugging that next-door neighbor, who cranks up his leaf blower at seven a.m. every Saturday, my user can punish him virtually. Load an image of Mr. Blower Dude's face—and his voice, if they wish—and use a drop-down menu to select gender, age range, and body type. Then, the user decides whether to watch his target die quickly or suffer over an extended period.

I'm confident the market is huge. I figure at least half the population, like me, would want to see Mr. Blower Dude blown to bits, decapitated, or staked by a lagoon with a hungry alligator prowling his way.

Creating pre-set death scenario videos of the most hackneyed fatalities was a snap. The two I label "Instant Relief" let the user upload faces and voices for both the victims and themselves. That way, users can become the Samurais who poke bloody holes in their victims and ignore their pleas before decapitating their Mr. Blower Dudes with a powerful swipe of the sword. Or, they can verbally castigate their enemies before throwing a switch to blow them to smithereens.

My "Extended Gratification" offerings let users toss the man—or woman—

onto a lagoon bank with a nineteen-foot alligator lurking in the weeds. With this option, users can watch the monster gator toss his ultimate lunch about in his powerful jaws until it drags the pitiful chump below the green algae slime of the lagoon.

I gave my Artificial Intelligence brainchild access to thousands of documentaries and scenes from B-movies to model the blood-curdling scenes. Then, I blended and tweaked the results into composite, make-believe options.

I have yet to perfect my "Delayed Gratification" options. One lets users check in periodically over a day or two to taunt enemies as they die of thirst amid endless desert dunes. Another leaves injured victims in the wild, where they're harassed by snarling wolf packs.

I sigh.

A much greater challenge is figuring out how to broaden my revenge app's appeal to the world's namby-pambies. I'm aware some folks would shrink from such gruesome retribution, even if it's make-believe.

So, instead of fragging Mr. Blower Dude, they might prefer the leaf blower to disturb a hornet's nest. Then, they could chortle as he runs off screen, slapping himself silly and screaming, "Help!"

The image suddenly conjures up a source of childhood joy. Cartoons. Yosemite Sam. Bugs Bunny. Porky Pig. Tweety Bird. Mighty Mouse. The geniuses who created those cartoons knew how to make mayhem fun!

That's it! I'll offer a cartoon module. It would definitely bring in a whole different PG13 audience. Who wouldn't want to see a cheeky varmint outsmart a neighborhood asswipe or an arrogant university dean?

Speaking of neighborhood asswipes, Leona Grimm, the old biddy who lives next door, is out walking her Chihuahua-Yorkie mix. I hear that hairy little monster yapping day and night. Comes right through the walls, practically rattles the windows.

You'd think a neighbor's barking mutt wouldn't be a problem in a neighborhood with huge lots. You'd be wrong. On deep lots like Leona's and mine, the sprawling McMansions often crowd setback lines. My home office sits only fifty yards from where her hairy rat likes to exercise his vocal cords.

If I hadn't complained to the HOA about her freakin' dog's constant barking, I might consider motivating one of my minions to do the woman in.

Poisoning the damn dog would be a simple matter. But that's impractical, too. Leona would only buy another yapper. And if Leona or the dog died, I'd be a prime suspect.

But what if Leona moved—voluntarily?

Hmm. What would it take to convince Leona she needs to hastily pack her bags and leave Lighthouse Cove? Naturally, she wouldn't leave Ginger, her stupid dog, behind.

Chapter Nine

Kylee

Thursday 3 p.m., June 29

My car can practically motor to Satin Sands on autopilot. Before I began working for Welch HOA Management, I'd only visited the ungated, three-hundred-home community a few times to play league tennis.

Then, last October, I became a regular Satin Sands caller. First, I was asked to investigate the bizarre possibility that someone planted a poisonous snake in a resident's screened blueberry patch. Soon after, I was tasked with evaluating a laundry list of security upgrades championed by Roger Roper, then president.

Roper claimed his costly measures would keep out all manner of riffraff and improve Satin Sand's prestige. My analysis suggested the changes would do zippity-do-dah to enhance security. That's when Roper talked his cohorts into firing Welch HOA.

Post-Thanksgiving, however, Satin Sands got a new president, Donna Dahl, who rehired us. Donna and I have also become good friends.

Satin Sands occupies a skinny peninsula with a generous shoreline that's sometimes sandy. The quantity of sand and the size of the beach depend on the whims of annual storms. While they sometimes deposit sand, a year or two down the road, a new storm reneges and scours the sand away.

Parking in front of the clubhouse, I hear the thwonk of tennis balls. Sounds like all four clay courts are occupied. The pool's busy, too. The sunny day has brought out more than a few kids to practice cannon balls.

Inside the clubhouse, I head to the bar. Donna is at her favorite back booth, hoisting a daiquiri. I assume the spare glass on the table has my name on it. Though I always call Donna by her name, I often think of her as Freckles. Ted gave her the apt nickname when he provided me with a who's who playbook. The plump Irish lady has a generous dusting of freckles across her nose and cheeks. She's also saucy, unpretentious and fun.

Well, at least that's the side of Donna's personality I usually see. The other side is a shrewd business lady. Donna and her late husband owned and jointly managed a multi-million-dollar fast-food franchise.

"Since you asked about rental conflicts, I figured you could use a drink as well," Donna says as she slides a sweating daiquiri toward my side of the table. "What's up?"

While I seldom drink, at least before sundown, Donna knows I'm fond of daiquiris. And it's not like one alcoholic beverage will lessen my ability to do my job this afternoon. Hell, it might help.

"Thanks," I say. "Guess my boss won't fire me for sharing a cocktail with a client."

Donna laughs. "Can't imagine anything you could do to get yourself fired. Lord knows, in a normal company, you'd have long since been pink-slipped. Let's see, you've been caught sneaking into gated enclaves, stealing horses, and decking a colleague."

I smile. "Hey, my boss was right beside me," I protest. "But, back to rental properties in HOAs. Apparently, Rand Creek owners are fighting tooth and nail about rentals. I don't get it."

"What's not to get?" Donna asks. "Renters can be real pains in the butt. If you own your house, you may not want 'tourons' across the street. In fact, now that our beloved ex-president, Roger Roper's off the board, he's leading a group of rule lovers clambering for severe rental restrictions."

"Sounds like Roper," I say. "Sometimes Mom complains about tourist morons, too. But she's friendly with Hullis Island owners who have bought properties for eventual retirement and need rentals to help cover mortgage and insurance expenses until they move in. For others, the units are investments, expected to appreciate in value, even if rental incomes don't actually cover annual expenses."

I shrug. "Mom figures the occasional idiotic renters are an acceptable tradeoff. The exorbitant fees tourists pay to golf and dine at the club subsidize club memberships for residents. And Mom enjoys golf, tennis, and eating out."

My friend nods in agreement. "You're right about Hullis Island. And I think Roper will have a hard time selling tighter rental restrictions in Satin Sands. But Rand Creek is a different animal. It's a fifty-five-plus community marketed to folks who could pay a thou to golf at Pebble Beach without blinking an eye. With all the retired attorneys and former judges living there, I foresee a huge lawsuit. These are folks who always fight to defend their interests, whatever they may be."

Donna thinks owners in resort-oriented communities are unlikely to nix rentals because they understood the tradeoffs when they bought. "They know the pros and cons. That's less true in HOAs marketed as retiree havens. These owners expect their neighbors to be their clones. You know, elderly folks who define a madcap, late night as an eight o'clock dinner reservation. When they discover the rental property next door subjects them to a merry-go-round of loud music, overflowing trash bins, and blocked driveways, they're pissed."

I'm still puzzled. "But I read through Rand Creek's covenants last week. It looks like Rand Creek already prohibits rentals for periods of less than three months. Doesn't that eliminate weekenders?"

Donna chuckles. "You military vets are so naive. Welcome to capitalism. If there's money to be made, rules are inconveniences, not barriers. Here's one workaround. Rand Creek only allows three-month or longer rentals, right? So, what does Lou Short-of-Funds do with the hard-to-sell house he inherited in said HOA? He converts the ownership to an LLC; then he offers one-percent shares to weekend renters. The shares make them *official* owners. Who cares if the *owners* forfeit their shares the minute they vacate the premises?"

"Wow, wonder who thought that up? Who'd go to such extremes to rent a property? Wouldn't it be a paperwork nightmare?"

Donna shrugs. "Nah. Simple computer program. Create the form, then press a few keys to insert new names and repeat the transaction."

I sip my drink and wonder if it's kosher to ask the president of one client HOA her opinion of another HOA pres. Since Donna's involved in an unofficial roundtable of Lowcountry HOA presidents, I'm sure she's met Jocelyn Waters.

Donna tips her glass up for a long drink and meets my eyes. "Given that you've just come from Rand Creek, can I assume you had the pleasure of making Jocelyn Waters' acquaintance?"

What? Is Donna reading my mind now?

"Uh, yes," I fumble. "Met Jocelyn this morning for the first time. Only spent a few minutes together. Just long enough for her to make photo assignments for Rand Creek's website makeover."

"She's a piece of work." Donna makes a rude noise. "Tries to take over every meeting. She's super ambitious. I hear she's planning to go into politics. But surrounded by other HOA presidents, she has too many egocentric competitors to bat anything close to 500 on keeping the floor. Have to admit I'm one of the loudmouths who sticks out a vocal shepherd's hook to yank her off stage."

"I know she owns a real estate and rental company," I say. "Has she voiced her opinion on rentals in any of your meetings?"

"Oh, yeah. She's a huge proponent of individual property rights. She raves that nobody has the right to tell owners they can't rent their properties. Of course, she sings from a different hymnbook when she champions an architectural review committee's right to tell property owners their shutters were painted an unacceptable shade of green."

"Jocelyn owns rentals in at least five HOAs and makes a good buck managing units she's sold as investment-rental properties," Donna adds. "She and her hubby were among the original investors in Rand Creek. Guess that's why they built a big home there. Scored a really nice piece of waterfront. They've been there at least five years."

"That surprises me. Can't believe she's sixty. But she'd have to be if she bought there five years ago."

"Wrong," Donna replies. "Take another gander at those Rand Creek covenants. Only one family member needs to be fifty-five or above. There are no age restrictions on other household members, so long as they're over eighteen. That leaves plenty of leeway for rich old men and their trophy wives. Jocelyn's hubby is at least a decade her senior."

I glance at the big clock over the bar. "Wow, I need to get going. Don't want Grant and Mimi to be arrested as underage loiterers in the Rand Creek parking lot. Thanks for the rental tutorial."

"My pleasure," says Donna. "Say hey to the rest of the Welch crew."

Chapter Ten

Kylee

Thursday 5 p.m., June 29

After I pick up my teen colleagues, we head to Ted's office on Highway 21. He bought the building for its Port Royal location, a central hopping-off spot to visit HOAs anywhere in Beaufort County.

The office, a former convenience store, has benefited from a half-hearted makeover. Once grocery aisles were removed, carpet-covered walls were brought in to divvy up the wide-open space. The second-hand cubicle dividers came in a variety of mix-and-don't-match colors. What can I say? The office isn't a style showcase.

My boss saves his renovation energy for the dilapidated white-elephant mansion he calls home in Beaufort's Historic District. A lover of architecture, Ted says he couldn't bear to let the "unique" treasure decay. Since his office entered the world as a hard-luck convenience store, I guess he feels it's preordained to remain homely.

Who am I to judge? Mom thinks my floating home is an abomination. Of course, Mom thinks all boats are pug-ugly. She's deathly afraid of the water and seizes any excuse never to come aboard.

Both Mom's and Robin's cars are still parked in front of the office.

As soon as I switch off the ignition, Mimi starts fumbling for her camera bag, preparing to bolt.

"See you tomorrow," she says. "Gotta run. Mom's having folks over for dinner, and I promised I'd be home early."

Grant sneaks a look sideways at me before he gives Mimi a kiss.

"Okay, text you later," he says.

Ah, young love.

When Grant and I enter the office, Robin and Mom are hunched in front of Robin's computer. The door's squeak makes Mom jump.

"Ted needs to put a bell on that door," she snips. "Startled the crap out of me."

Grant laughs. "That's a lot of crap to startle."

"Don't sass your grandma. Come here and give me a kiss, or have your lips gotten too strenuous a workout spending the day with Mimi?"

I shake my head and groan. Mom always tries for the final word, but Grant gives her a run for the money. When Ted, Grant's dad, was nine years old, his mother died. Mom immediately took Ted, my younger brother's BFF, under her wing. Growing up, Ted spent more time at our house than across the street at his own.

He's always been family, which initially made our late-blooming romance feel sort of weird and incestuous. Grant not only calls my mom Grandma, he calls me Aunt Kylee. Confusing, huh? But I'm getting over it. Have to admit Ted's become an addiction. One I don't want to fight.

"What computer nonsense have the two of you so entranced?" I ask. "Must have been mighty good for our arrival to make you jump out of your skin."

Grant mimics one of Mom's shame-on-you finger-stroking gestures. "Did we catch you watching porn?"

"Could be," Robin answers. "I'm beginning to think reading Earful posts qualifies. Once someone hints there's a secret conspiracy afoot, dozens of tag-alongs expand on the theory."

"What started the latest conspiracy wreck, and does it involve a Welch client?" I ask.

"Afraid so," Mom answers. "Hullis Island, where yours truly is a director.

According to Suzy Martin's post, 'Our board is putting the final touches on a secret proposal to ban the household display of all flags except the Stars and Stripes.' She adds we're even establishing specs on how big Star-Spangled banners can be."

"Where the heck did this come from?" I ask. "You've never mentioned the board considering any such thing."

Mom sighs. "Think I've tracked it down. The Covenant Review Committee, which I might add doesn't include a single board member, discussed ways to enhance our sense of community and ease the political divides. To get us all singing Kumbaya, one woman suggested either banning political flags or limiting their display to two weeks before an election.

"Apparently, someone on the committee blabbed about the discussion. Though there never was a proposal, assumptions became accepted facts, and we were off to the races. There were fifty Earful responses to the initial post. Within hours, owners were outraged by the board's insidious plan to prohibit all outdoor displays from Christmas lights to garden statues."

I adopt a pretend outrage expression. "Oh, Mom, how could you trample all those people's rights to free speech?"

When I chuckle, Mom gives me the stink eye. "It's no laughing matter. Why the heck did I agree to stay on the Hullis Island board until the next election?"

Robin closes down the app. "Some of the Hullis Island neighbors are calling Myrt a two-faced traitor," our young IT expert adds. "They're demanding an immediate owners' meeting to voice their objections to the proposed covenant changes."

"What do you plan to do?" I ask.

"Well, what I'm not going to do is duke it out on Earful. I've talked with the other directors. Even Cliff Jackson, our president, agrees we should schedule an open board meeting ASAP. Of course, he wants the meeting to begin and end with a statement that the board has not seen or discussed such a proposal. He expects security, including you and Ted, to act as sergeants of arms to enforce order and decorum."

I groan. The Hullis Island rumor avalanche isn't quite so funny when I'm among the villagers to be trussed and burned at the stake.

"Ted may not want to come home." I groan. "Let's not tell him about any new conspiracy—at Rand Creek or Hullis Island—until he and Frank pull into the drive."

"Have you heard from Dad?" Grant asks. "Is he planning to be home for dinner?"

Mom arches an eyebrow. "I can always trust you to fret about when you'll get fed," she quips. "The answer is 'yes.' Ted says he'll deliver Frank by six-thirty at the latest. So, you won't starve. Got a pot roast and veggies in the crockpot."

Mom looks at me. "You're coming, right?"

I want to say no. I'm bone-tired, and I'd like a little quiet, alone time. But I'm expected, and I need to bring Ted up to speed on Andy Fyke and the Earful chatter suggesting his fall was no accident.

I'm fifty years old and never married. While I experienced a fair share of enforced togetherness in the Coast Guard, I always had time to myself. Now, I seem to spend every waking moment with family—blood or otherwise.

These days, a good many of my sleeping moments aren't alone either. When Grant spends the night with his granny, I'm in Ted's bed, or he's in mine. Grant and Mom both know the deal. Still, I'm hung up about us unmarried old folks sleeping together when Ted's son is snoozing under the same roof.

"Sure. Count me in for supper," I answer. "I'll provide dessert. Grant and I will stop at Publix en route to Hullis Island. Grant can pick the cake, and I'll choose companion ice cream."

Chapter Eleven

Kylee

Thursday 6:30 p.m., June 29

As we pull up to the Hullis Island gate, Bill Clark, the amiable fellow on duty, waves and chuckles. "Merry Christmas," he calls.

Huh? We're only a few days away from the Fourth of July. Guess I missed the joke.

Turning off the center road that bisects the Hullis peninsula, Bill's season's greetings suddenly make sense. The first house on Mom's street is decked out with Christmas lights and a blow-up snow globe in the front yard. Two doors down, a neighbor has paired Christmas lights with a Halloween witch and an Easter bunny. Across the street, an oversized political flag flaps in the breeze. The flag champions a politician soundly defeated in the last election.

"Holy sh...sugar!" Grant catches himself. "What's going on?"

I groan. "Got it. Hullis Island neighbors are protesting against the alleged ban on outdoor displays. You know the proposed ban the board has never seen."

Wait till Ted gets a gander.

* * *

Grant and I are setting the dinner table when we see Ted's Lexus pull into the driveway behind my Camry.

"Dad and Frank are here," Grant calls to Mom.

"Just under the wire," she replies. "Told Ted we'd eat without them if they were late."

As Frank steps inside, I smile at his rumpled appearance. He's wadded his blazer into a wrinkled ball. His dress shirt's unbuttoned at the neck, allowing his white cotton tee to show its stuff. Like me, Frank is allergic to "professional" attire. Frank says in all the years he owned his own roofing company, he never got "gussied up" to meet clients. Figured they'd be less likely to question his prices if his worn work boots had holes.

Frank sniffs the air. "Smells mighty good in here, Myrt. He offers a smart salute to Grant and me as he tosses his balled blazer onto a chair and walks toward his kitchen. Mom's been living with Frank ever since an arsonist torched her Hullis Island home on Thanksgiving Day.

A widower, Frank's a few years younger than Mom's seventy-nine, and he's definitely sweet on her. He insisted she stay with him until her housing situation got sorted out. "My house is way too big for one old man. Silly for you to stay in a hotel or pay to rent a place."

Despite—or maybe because of—potential island gossip about unwed old codgers shacking up, Mom agreed. I sense the living arrangement won't change once the rebuild of Mom's home is completed next month.

Hmm. Wonder if she'll sell or rent her replacement house.

After Dad died, Mom repeatedly claimed she would never remarry. "Why should I? Certainly don't have plans to have more kids, and I've seen how finances can torpedo senior-citizen relationships. Keeping control of my own pensions and Social Security benefits are powerful incentives to stay single."

Frank snags a baby carrot out of the bowl Mom's loading with veggies and gets his hand gently slapped. For a moment, I picture Mom smacking Dad's hand for similar pilfering. The memory makes me smile. I'm glad Mom has Frank in her life. Since Ted and I became a couple, I realize how much joy's to be found in everyday sharing, be it jokes, new recipes, a hug, or baby carrots.

Ted's arms wrap me from behind as he nuzzles the top of my head. "Can't wait to hear what's up in the neighborhood," he says. "I've heard of Christmas in July sales, but I didn't get the memo about Hullis Island decorating for Christmas, Halloween and Easter in June."

I turn around and hug him back. "Maybe you should wait till after dinner to hear why. Don't want to ruin your appetite."

Of course, the updates don't wait. Before dessert's dished out, Ted and Frank have answers to all their Hullis Island décor questions.

"Myrt, has the board set a date for an open board meeting?" Ted asks.

"Yes. We considered doing it before the weekend, but we decided there wasn't enough time to notify everyone. We finally agreed on Sunday afternoon. That should get the holiday fireworks off to an early start."

Frank pushes back from the table. "I'll get the cake while I consider which decorations to put out for the weekend. I made some nice, full-sized reindeer out of scrap lumber."

Mom rolls her eyes.

"I'm afraid it's time to move on to another potential HOA problem," I say.

It takes me a good ten minutes to describe how we found Andy Fyke's broken body at the bottom of the stairs, my suspicion that he was pushed, and the Earful conspiracy theories about who might be the pushee.

"I thought I'd visit the hospital tomorrow morning to check on Mr. Fyke," I conclude. "Maybe he'll remember something more that will help establish whether he tripped or someone attacked him."

"Good idea," Ted agrees. "If anyone can coax him to recall a detail to help solve the mystery, it's you. Of course, you can't hint you suspect he was shoved. Might prompt him to try and remember something that never happened."

I nod. Definitely have no desire to cause Mr. Fyke more grief.

Chapter Twelve

The Chameleon

Friday morning, June 30

I close down the local Earful app for lonely whiners. Damn that Leona Grimm. She's using the app as a megaphone to lobby owners to buy the vacant Lighthouse Cove lot next to me and turn it into a DOG PARK.

Right this minute, I can hear her chihuahua mix's high-pitched yips as the hairy rat runs circles in her side yard. Drives me crazy. Just imagine the audio soundtrack if her mutt had twenty playmates growling and howling next door.

Can't believe how many empty-nesters like Leona lavish their affection on mongrels when their kids move out. Not that the *parents* train their four-legged *children* any better than they did their two-legged offspring.

I will not...not...not...tolerate a dog park next door.

Think. What do you know about the old biddy? What would prompt her to move away?

I've only been in Leona's house once. I paid one of my dutiful daughter visits not long before Mom croaked. My mother needed to return a book Leona had loaned her, and she dragged me along on the house call. The borrowed book ballyhooed multiple examples of paranormal activities with no apparent scientific explanation.

As we walked across the lawn, Mom whispered the widow was having extreme difficulty coping with her husband's sudden death. "Leona's been visiting palm readers and she's talked about hiring a medium to conduct a séance," Mom said. "Leona is convinced her husband was preparing to share something very important with her when he dropped dead. It was probably, 'I want a divorce.'"

Hmm. It's definitely time for the pompous stiff to return and plead with Leona to vacate her house before she's killed in some macabre manner.

The how of the stuffed shirt's reappearance comes to me with absolute clarity. Can't help but giggle. While Mom and I were at Leona's, she forgot the name of an author she wanted to recommend. As a memory aid, she spoke the name of her always-on digital answer machine and asked, "What author wrote The Ghost Chronicles?"

A second later, a mellow female voice answered, "Marlo Berliner."

Since Leona knows diddly about digital protection, it should be a piece of cake to hack into the widow's Wi-Fi. Then, I'll tell her about a weather app for her know-it-all sphere and offer to provide it free of charge. My doctored app will give me programming access.

Yes. It'll take a little effort, but it won't be long before her dead hubby's voice replaces the dulcet-toned answer woman. The stiff will command Leona to get out of Dodge. He'll say he's been granted a vision that something horrible will happen to Leona unless she exits her house before the Fourth of July.

I clap my hands. If I don't have to sell this place, I don't care how long the current market dip lasts, not with my rental income stream. It's keeping me comfortable without tapping into any other income sources. Amazing how much money vacationers and couples willingly plunk down for short-term rentals. Gotta love the big spenders who visit for weekend getaways and pre-retirement research excursions.

After Mom's Rand Creek condo proved a rental cash cow, I began checking daily for distress-sale properties in popular Lowcountry communities. That reminds me, haven't looked for potential Rand Creek bargains today.

I open my backdoor to the HOA's software. Nice thing about a fifty-five-plus community is its relatively quick turnover. Once the well-heeled mothers and fathers who own the property shuffle off this mortal coil, their offspring want to wrap things up quickly and liquidate. No patience.

Terrific. Two more condos will soon go up for sale. I copy the names of the heirs inquiring about selling restrictions, given the community's age limits on occupancy.

Don't worry. I'll help you cash out faster than I can say SUCKER!

I contact the heirs, pretending to be former friends of the freshly deceased. Need to initiate a dialogue before they talk with real estate agents and list the properties. Easy to convince greedy patsies they'll net more if the sales are just between us *friends.*

A flicker of a thought brings a smile. Maybe I should research which properties might offer the best rental returns and cross-check for cash-strapped heirs. Then, I could program my minions to knock off the folks who own the most profitable units.

A little too ambitious.

I stand and begin one of my stretching routines. Sitting too long in front of a computer screen doesn't do my body any favors. Maybe I'll take an hour to zip over to Rand Creek. I prefer its fitness center to the one down the road at Lighthouse Cove.

Avoiding my own HOA's facilities lets me remain a mystery to my wealthy neighbors. I always use my Dr. title when I introduce myself. That seems to impress the owners who fell into money pits without the need to exercise a single brain cell. They accept me as an eccentric genius. One who prefers solitude in my oversized mausoleum. Definitely not a coffee klatch candidate.

Chapter Thirteen

Kylee

Friday morning, June 30

Beaufort Memorial Hospital may be bigger than its Hilton Head cousin but the vibe remains small-town friendly. Even though visiting hours haven't officially begun, I get a go-on-in wink from a nurse on Andy Fyke's floor. "I'm sure he'll appreciate some company."

I pause at his room's open door and knock on the doorframe. "Mr. Fyke, are you up to chatting with a visitor?"

Fyke's bed is cranked up and a food tray's been wheeled into position. Only thing on the tray is a giant sippy cup. He shakes his head no, and I start to apologize for intruding when he points at his jaw. Then he waves me inside and picks up a steno pad and pen sitting on a bedside table.

Can't talk. Left-handed, he scrawls on the paper in big looping strokes. *Jaw wired shut.*

Okay, this conversation is going to zip along. Not aided in the least by Mr. Fyke's atrocious penmanship.

Hey, give the guy credit. Andy didn't order me out of the room so he could sulk in silence about his broken jaw and the cast on his right wrist. The poor fellow's probably trying to write left-handed when he's a righty.

"Hi, I'm the one who found you in the stairwell yesterday," I begin. "Wanted to see how you're doing—if there's anything I can do to help. Do you remember what happened?"

Remember U, he writes. *Dark. Dizzy. Then U. Lights.*

Hmm, he remembers the stairwell lights were out. "Did you fall before you had a chance to turn on the lights?"

He frowns as he shakes his head. *Who U? Jocelyn send U?*

Okay, fair question. Wonder if Sherry snuck in after-hours last night and spilled the beans that Jocelyn's worried he'll sue Rand Creek for negligence.

"No, Jocelyn didn't send me. I'm Kylee Kane. Jocelyn doesn't know I'm here. I work with Welch HOA Management. Rand Creek hired us to build a new website and tie in the HOA's back-office software so owners can use the website to update their contact info or pay fees online. I was there yesterday to introduce the folks taking photos for the website."

U manage rentals? Fyke still looks suspicious, though maybe his grimace merely reflects pain.

"Uh, no. That's not a service Welch offers."

Geez, the Chamber-of-Commerce rhetoric is killing me. But I'm not about to admit my main jobs are investigating crimes and funny goings-on inside client HOAs and identifying safety and security issues that need fixing. Admit that, and Andy might make a small leap and conclude I suspect he's the victim of a crime.

Fyke's pen scratches over the paper. *Sherry says U OK. What U really want? Friends think I pushed.*

"Is that what you think?" I ask.

Maybe. He quits scratching on the paper when a cough bottled up behind his wired-shut jaw rattles his chest. Broken ribs? Once the pain subsides, he pens two more words. *Heard someone.*

"What about the lights?" I repeat. "Did you turn them on when you opened the door to the stairwell?"

He blinks. The skin between his eyes forms a knot as he considers. He shrugs and writes. *Murky. Mind's a blank after open door.*

I turn at a nurse's cheerful singsong. "Time to clear away that tray and take your vitals. Were you able to get down any of that protein drink? You need to keep up your energy since you can't eat solid food."

The nurse scowls when she notices me. "Sorry, Miss. You need to leave. Mr. Fyke must rest."

I squeeze the patient's good hand. "I'll be back, Mr. Fyke. Do you have a laptop or tablet? Maybe I can retrieve one to make communicating easier."

He vigorously shakes his head and tugs on my sleeve to make me delay long enough to see what he's writing.

Don't have laptop only desktop. Rent me 1?

I pat his shoulder. "Welch HOA will spring for a loaner. No problem."

Need to ask Robin to set up a tablet.

Chapter Fourteen

Kylee

Friday morning, June 30

Parking at the office, I notice Robin's beat-up VW bug doesn't have a single-vehicle neighbor.

"Morning," I call to Robin. "Looks like you're the office Lone Ranger today."

"Yep, Ted and Frank are at Sea Bay, hoping to convince the board to accept the Atlanta engineering firm's bid to fix the condo's structural defects. The price tag is two million dollars more than what's in the HOA's reserves. But, for safety's sake, Frank thinks renovations can't wait, and he says the bid's reasonable."

Don't envy Ted and Frank their morning.

"Is Mom coming in today?"

"Later." Robin chuckles. "Think Myrt's having second thoughts about serving on the Hullis Island board. Right now, she's in an executive meeting. They're nailing down the agenda for the Sunday gathering. They're expecting an angry owner mob."

"Should be a doozy," I agree. "Guess Mom filled you in about Christmas coming early on Hullis Island?"

"Didn't need to." Robin laughs. "Loads of snapshots were posted on the Earful site this morning."

"Speaking of which, did you see any new social media chatter about Mr. Fyke's fall?"

Robin's hands leave her keyboard, and she tilts back in her swivel desk chair. "Noticed one puzzler post. Some woman wondered if Fyke's pants were unzipped. Seemed to hint the gentleman might have been paying attention to the wrong part of his anatomy when he fell."

I frown. "Good Lord. Earful gossips will be the end of civilization as we know it. Have Grant and Mimi checked in?"

"Not yet. But I don't think they plan to come in the office today."

Inside my compact cubicle, I fire up my PC to search for Rand Creek units marketed as rentals. Doesn't take long to find a slew of ads on VRBO—Vacation Rentals By Owner—and Airbnb sites.

Sherry's estimate of twenty to thirty rental properties is pretty close. I copy the contact info for each ad. Six rentals list Jocelyn's real estate office as the contact. While that doesn't mean Jocelyn owns the units, all of the rentals fatten her coffers. Rental managers are sort of like bookies. They get a percentage regardless of the rental's actual profitability.

Can see why Jocelyn pegs Fyke as a troublemaker.

"Robin, you're working on tying Rand Creek's back-office software into the new website, right?" I call out. "Does that mean you can access the HOA's owner database?"

"Sure can. The existing code's pretty good, though I'm going to suggest some tweaks before it's integrated into the website. A number of owners complain they can't log in unless they enter a cellphone number. Whoever wrote the code made the cellphone number a required field. And, as Myrt frequently reminds me, assuming everyone owns a cell makes the assumer an ass. If I want to avoid her lecture, that ass had better not be me."

I chuckle. "Mom's right, but I'm hoping you can postpone making that fix long enough to lend me a hand. I want to send you a few addresses of Rand Creek properties advertised as rentals. If it won't take too much of your time, can you look up who owns these units and their contact info?"

"Sure. Easy."

I head to the breakroom for a cup of coffee. By the time I'm back at my desk, Robin's emailed me contact information for thirty-two owners of rental property. A quick scan disappoints. At least half the properties are owned by trusts or LLCs.

Will take a little more work to ID the actual humans who might object to Fyke's anti-rental campaign. Maybe I should start by discreetly chatting up the man's friends. They haven't been shy about suggesting that some rental property owner shoved Andy down the stairs.

"Robin, can I ask one more favor? Can you crosscheck the Rand Creek owner database with the Earful posters who believe Fyke was attacked? I'd like to have a conversation with some of the residents in Fyke's anti-rental camp."

Yeah, it's risky. Jocelyn will go through the roof if she finds I'm nosing around to see if something other than Fyke's carelessness caused his fall.

Chapter Fifteen

Grant

Friday morning, June 30

I call Robin to confirm Mimi and I will be at Rand Creek most of the day.

"What are you up to?" I ask. "Playing video games or trying to solve WORDLE?"

"Funny boy," Robin replies. "You get to play with your drone all day while I'm stuck at a computer doing actual work. Kylee's here, but I think she's leaving soon. Then, I'll be all by my lonesome."

"You've always got Earful gossip to amuse you," I joke. "Any new tales of alien invasions?"

"No, but I'm looking at Earful posts as we speak. Getting Kylee the names of Fyke's Rand Creek friends—at least the ones publicly suggesting he was pushed. Think Kylee plans to grill one or more of them, hoping they'll name names."

Bet they'd be more likely to spill if they weren't actually asked, just shooting the breeze.

"Robin, I have an idea, and I'll bet Kylee will love it. Can you figure out which, if any, of Fyke's friends belong to Rand Creek social clubs?"

"Sure, will search back issues of the community newsletter. I've been scanning them for a digital archive on the website. The newsletters always include updates about bridge nights and book clubs. Why do you care?"

"For the website, Mimi wants to take photos of real owners having fun, enjoying the facilities. See if you can find an activity shared by at least three friends of Fyke's. You know, playing cards in the clubhouse or doing yoga at the fitness center.

"If we can coax some of Fyke's friends to be models for a photo shoot, I'm sure they'll gossip while we're setting up. Won't be able to stop themselves from dishing about who they consider as prime suspects in Fyke's attack. Kylee won't even have to pose a question."

* * *

It turns out several of Fyke's friends play bridge. I've spent the last half hour phoning prospects and asking them to come to the clubhouse card room at two o'clock for a photo shoot. So far, six have committed.

They assume I called because their names appeared in newsletter articles about bridge. That's true. No reason to suspect I cherry-picked Fyke buddies—people who share his opposition to rental properties.

I call Kylee to tell her what I'm up to. Pretty sure she'll be psyched.

She laughs. "You're devious, Grant. Good idea. Wind 'em up and let 'em gossip. You know I want to be there. Guess I can be one of Mimi's grips. She can order me to move furniture or adjust lights. If we're lucky, the models will pay no attention to us. Figure we have no reason to be interested in what they're jabbering about."

I'm proud of my brainstorm. "Maybe you should talk to Dad about giving me a raise?"

"Ha, ha," Kylee replies. "I'd say it's more likely he'd fire both of us. But we know he's short of replacements."

Chapter Sixteen

The Chameleon

Friday Afternoon, June 30

I phone Lighthouse Cove's security office to ask if they've followed up on the panicked call I made yesterday. Though it's hard to imagine I'd ever be suspected of foul play in Andy Fyke's tumble, it seemed prudent to have a rock-solid alibi for the time of his *accident*.

So, at nine o'clock yesterday morning—about when I primed J.T. to act—I phoned security. "I think someone's trying to break in my back door," I whispered. "Please send someone right away."

In less than three minutes, two Lighthouse Cove security officers were at my door. Assured me I was safe and that they were investigating. Around the back of the house, the officers found wet bootprints on the patio and a dent in my sliding glass door's metal frame.

Not exactly a shocker. A little earlier, I wet the bottoms of a pair of men's boots and stomped around outside to manufacture the prints. Then I attempted to jimmy the sliding door and purposely dinged the metal panel. The in-person security visit proves I was home yesterday morning— nowhere near Rand Creek.

I'm following up with the security office today because I think that's what a frightened, single lady would be expected to do.

"There haven't been any reports of strangers," the officer on duty tells me.

"But we've got your house on a watch list for extra patrols."

"Thank you, Officer," I gush. "That makes me feel so much better."

Indeed, it does. They'll know I'm tucked safely inside my house when the next *accident* happens. An accident I hope to arrange for Steph Cloyd.

Bubba is the only one of my avenger recruits who lives outside an HOA. He proudly calls himself a Lowcountry native. Ha! First Nation people populated this region long before his trashy ancestors staked a claim on a few acres of swampland. His hovel's a bit upstream from Satin Sands on one of the Lowcountry's many estuary fingers.

I discovered Bubba in a TV documentary about disgruntled "patriots" who belong to a nativist cult. Not sure what else to call the assembly. Not organized enough to be classified as a militia. Anyway, the cult members blame any and all of life's daily irritants on Lowcountry newcomers.

Bubba and his buddies view new arrivals, especially retirees and second-homeowners who hail from Yankee-land, as evil communists. The nativists are convinced we're all present-day carpetbaggers out to destroy their freedom and way of life.

While I haven't quite grasped the group's whole victimhood worldview, they somehow think newcomers are barnstormers for UN Agenda-21. Bubba and his fellow travelers firmly believe the United Nations' hidden, top-secret mission is to eliminate all private property rights and force people into vertical communes.

Hey, what can I say? Bubba's a whacko, but a useful one.

While at least five men featured in the documentary were potential candidates for my reserve corps, Bubba quickly became my number-one pick.

I was delighted to learn Bubba's father is in prison. Once I found video of the patriarch's arrest, I knew I could use the jailbird's voice samples to fake calls to the son. Bubba's comments about his dad in the documentary indicated he viewed the man as a persecuted hero—though Bubba never actually bothers to visit him in prison.

Then I discovered Bubba already had a personal set-to with Steph Cloyd, giving me a starting point to ratchet up his hatred.

Steph, who lives in Satin Sands, is a devotee of coastal rowing. Every dawn, he ventures out in his sleek rowing shell. One morning, about three months ago, Bubba revved up the four-hundred-horsepower motor attached to the butt-end of his fishing boat and screamed down the narrow waterway. At that same moment, Steph was sculling around a bend. Bubba capsized him. Then he circled Steph, laughing and churning the water so he couldn't get back in his shell.

Steph reported the incident to the Coast Guard and the Beaufort County Sheriff's Department. With no evidence to support Steph's claims, Bubba merely got a visit and a stern warning.

To fan the flame of Bubba's hatred, I had his imprisoned "dad" use a contraband burner phone to tell him Beaufort County bureaucrats were coming for him. Supposedly, the prison grapevine had it on good authority that Steph reported Bubba for violating Beaufort County outdoor burning restrictions.

Actually, I acted as the anonymous tattletale. I didn't witness Bubba's unlawful torching up close and personal. Didn't have to. The idiot bragged about it inside a private RebSocial group. Said he refused to abide by the ridiculous rules imposed by bird-watching-butt-in-o-crats.

"Who's stupid enough to limit a burn pile to plant stuff when you need to get rid of other junk," Bubba raved. "And, who in hell, besides some rich fat cat, can sit staring at a fire until the last coal farts out? If they don't like how us native Lowcountry folks deal with trash, they should pack up and go back North."

Casting Steph in the role of fire snitch was easy. He's on the board of FACE, Friends of the Atlantic Coast Environment, a regional environmental protection group. Hey, I'm a FACE member myself. But Bubba will never know that.

So, what's my beef with Steph? I'm convinced he truly is a goddamn snitch. He must have blabbed to his fellow Satin Sands' directors. Told them my university departure wasn't exactly voluntary. I wouldn't have signed the damn separation agreement if the university hadn't promised to stay mum about kicking me to the curb.

Knew I shouldn't have trusted those bastards. Steph's sanctimonious brother Aaron was on the university tribunal that condemned me. Before my fall from grace, Aaron introduced me to Steph at a faculty party. At the time, Aaron and the university were happily bragging about my genius abilities in the Artificial Intelligence field.

I had a sense of foreboding the minute I learned Steph Cloyd was joining the Satin Sands board. That meant he'd have a say on my proposal to do a bit of freelance software consulting for the HOA.

I figured Steph would wonder why the Artificial Intelligence genius he'd met—a professor at a prestigious university—was pitching a nothing HOA entity to handle a simple software coding job. No doubt Steph called his brother, Aaron, who spilled the beans. Then, Steph told the board to stay clear of me, an "unethical" person.

Unethical—because I'm a woman. A man would never have been censored.

I framed my Satin Sands consulting proposal as a favor rather than a money grab. Said I understood Satin Sands normally couldn't afford my services, but, as a new owner of a rental property, I wanted to contribute to the community. Steph put the kibosh on my offer. Can't fathom another reason for the board to take a pass.

Of course, the actual pay-off for my services would have been a personal backdoor into Satin Sands software. One I could use long after my consulting gig ended to view emails and confidential financial information. My backdoor to Rand Creek software is paying off nicely. Gives me early alerts about owners behind in paying their HOA fees and heirs asking questions about selling their dead folks' homes. Knowledge that lets me make preemptive, low-ball offers.

My Satin Sands consulting deal seemed clinched until one of the directors died, and Steph was appointed to serve out his term. Overnight, I was notified another vendor, Welch HOA Management, had been selected to handle the software update.

While I doubt Steph can cause me more harm at Satin Sands, I can't allow him to badmouth me beyond his HOA. That's something he could easily do. As a director of FACE, he comes in contact with a wide cross-section of

Lowcountry movers and shakers.

I settle in to study aerial imagery of Steph's coastal rowing route, one he generously shared online with his rowing club. I'm searching for the perfect spot for Bubba to permanently sink Steph and his loose lips. Then, I'll use Artificial Intelligence to script a phone call from Bubba's jailbird dad to his son. It must fire up Junior's rage. I need him super eager to rev up the four hundred horses that muscle his motorboat. The objective: Steph's vulnerable rowing shell.

Chapter Seventeen

Kylee

Friday afternoon, June 30

D*ang it. Another red light. Another backup.*

    Once people are ensconced in their green, inviting Hilton Head Island communities, they're treated to a relaxed, small-town vibe. But the island's busy main arteries can be subject to maddening, bumper-to-bumper traffic snarls, especially during tourist season. That's why I'm running late.

The dashboard clock in my car tells me it's 1:50 p.m. as I pull into the Rand Creek clubhouse parking lot. Need to hustle.

Grant's pacing as he waits for me outside the door to the clubhouse card room.

"Wanted to warn you," he says. "To fill two bridge tables, we let the Fyke friends we nabbed recruit three more folks. Bottom line, some of the card players could be pro-rental. Who knows? They might even own rental properties."

I shrug. "Shouldn't be a problem. A little verbal back and forth might even help. Is everyone here?"

"Not yet," Grant replies. "Six came early. Mimi's waiting for the remaining two to decide how to pair them at the tables. The early birds are milling about."

Inside, I introduce myself to the six cardsharps. Jocelyn won't be happy with the selected models. All appear to be seventy-plus. Not the fifty-five to sixty-year-old demographic she's eager to target. The age of our models doesn't surprise me. They're Fyke's friends, and he's part of Rand Creek's older clientele.

"Hope all of you avoid those back stairs when you leave," I casually comment as I adjust a window shade. "I understand the gentleman who fell down them yesterday is still in the hospital."

That ought to get their tongues wagging.

During the entire photo shoot, I don't utter another word. Just keep my ears open. I can tell Grant's doing the same. I collect the names of two rental property owners the card players seem to agree are potential suspects in the Fyke attack.

Jocelyn is their number one candidate. Why am I not surprised? Motive and opportunity. The other name they bandy about—Xander Pringle— means zip to me.

* * *

As soon as the elevator doors shut on the last card player, Grant comes over to give me a high five.

"That was fun," he says. "What names did you get? Wasn't surprised to hear them mention Jocelyn as a suspect. Two of the card players also talked about another woman, Amanda Holder. Sounds like she and Fyke have been squabbling, and the board has done a poor job of running interference."

I smile. "Well, that gives me a third name to check out. One gent was adamant the culprit had to be a man, and he nominated Xander Pringle as the likely shover. He didn't think a woman would or could physically attack Fyke. His knowledge of women is obviously limited."

Grant and Mimi both laugh.

"So, what's next?" Grant asks.

"I'm hoping Ted knows Xander or Amanda. Will wait to see what he has to say about our potential criminals."

I'm both dreading the evening and looking forward to it. Ted asked me to join him at a Marshview owners' meeting. The meeting is what I dread. This one's an informational meeting about a proposed pickleball complex. Ugh. The six o'clock start time sucks, too. HOA management companies are required to attend way too many evening and weekend meetings.

In this case, the timing will delay the promising portion of the evening. I'm invited to spend the night at Ted's house. Since Grant's staying with Mom and Frank this weekend, I'll have plenty of time to pick my boss's brain.

Of course, I have other plans for Ted, too. Like seducing him in the two rooms he's finished renovating. I figure Ted's historic fixer-upper ought to be home to a few moans of pleasure as a counterbalance to the constant racket of nail guns.

Ted believes he's saved an architectural treasure from total decay. Could be, but he's also opened a bottomless money pit.

Chapter Eighteen

The Chameleon

Friday early evening, June 30

I f I still had students, I'd delight in sharing some—though not all—of my secrets to extract sublime performance from my customized AI programs. My understanding of the technology and structure makes me a champion Artificial Intelligence whisperer. That's the tech world's term for individuals skilled at determining—and meticulously fine-tuning—language prompts to get AI programs to yield high-quality responses.

Mr. Lester Grimm's online obituary gave me all the clues needed to resurrect Leona Grimm's dead hubby. Before retiring to the Lowcountry, the Grimms lived in a medium-sized Ohio burg, where he owned a business that manufactured toys for pets. Not a shocker, given Ginger's cornucopia of fake bones and squeaky rubber mice.

More importantly, I discovered the civic-minded and rather humorless Mr. Grimm served his county as a councilman, and he loved to pontificate. Thank you, internet, for preserving such inconsequential ramblings for posterity.

Tonight, Leona will wake to her husband's voice—somewhat tortured but still sounding like a humorless snob. His voice will whisper through one of the digital spheres she chats with all day to make her feel less alone. In his ghostly desperation to reach Leona, Mr. Grimm has latched on to a high-tech way to warn her.

But warn her of what?

It's not hurricane season. No big Lowcountry earthquakes since the 1886 Charleston shocker. Maybe a house fire or a gas pipe leak?

No, if my dead stiff offers specifics, old Leona may try to foil the possibility. Tell neighbors about a threat, or report it to security. The danger must be vague but directed solely at her house. I urge my Artificial Intelligence app to create a threat that's ominous and personal yet ambiguous. I feel fairly confident the result will work.

"Leona…Leona…Leona." My app suggested Lester's nasal voice should intone her name in the middle of the night to wake her. It determined Lester should repeat the name invocation at least three times, each entreaty a few seconds apart. Leona needs to be awake and alert to grasp the warning.

And the message is?

"You must leave this house. Listen to me. I was granted a vision of the future. You and Ginger, both dead, side-by-side, on the living room floor. So much blood. I wasn't permitted to see how you died, only your bludgeoned bodies. I begged for this chance to warn you, to let you escape this horrible death. There's only one way you can cheat fate. You must move out of Lighthouse Cove before the Fourth of July and never return. Do not fail me. I couldn't bear for you and Ginger to be tortured."

I decided mentioning the dog by name would be a nice touch. Since Ginger was given a line in Lester's obituary, he must have been as nuts about the pooch as Leona is.

God, how I hope my parapsychology experiment works. Good riddance to annoying barking.

Next, I need to do some advance planning for the call Bubba's jailbird dad will make to his son. The conversation's goal? Urging Bubba to ram Steph's rowing shell at dawn.

Within my AI inventory, I've created what I think of as individual buckets for each of my potential avengers. Bubba's AI bucket contains all the words, phrases, opinions, and prejudices voiced by Bubba and his nativist extremists on private social media. It also contains everything I've learned about his father and their relationship. To this treasure trove, I added selected input from like-minded internet posters.

For the call from jailbird dad's presumed contraband burner cell, I dip into this bucket's memory bank for the right vernacular and syntax. This ensures I avoid any highfalutin or cancel-culture vocabulary that Bubba might realize would never pass his illiterate dad's lips.

Okay, so what word prompts should I use to forge a bombshell that fires up Bubba's paranoia and sense of victimhood? He needs to think Steph is about to do something to cause him irreversible harm. Bubba needs a provocation to act, not sometime, but immediately.

What should it be? Got it. Bubba's dad has overheard a prison guard talking about Steph Cloyd's plan to sue Bubba on behalf of FACE—the environmental group Bubba hates. The lawsuit will seek foreclosure of Bubba's land to compensate for the ecological damage he's caused by burning tires, depositing the hulks of rusting cars in the marsh behind his trailer, and dumping used motor oil into the estuary.

The foreclosure lawsuit is utter nonsense, but not if Bubba buys it.

I've worked hard to coax Bubba into believing his dad really cares enough to phone and text him. I also had his deepfake father introduce Bubba to *me*—well, to one of my fake identities.

I'm a local gal, sympathetic to nativist causes but scared to reveal my real name and identity. That's because I unknowingly wed a bastard, communist Yankee, who keeps me under his thumb by threatening to take my kids away.

It so happens that this downtrodden native lass has a husband, who's a rower and one of Steph's friends. How handy? The two men chatter endlessly about their routes.

Making this crap up is really fun.

I tweak an AI-generated text from my cowering nativist gal. To it, I append notes on the timing of pre-dawn and actual sunrise, as well as a weather forecast of light winds and a minuscule chance of rain. I include a map of Steph's water exercise route with two big X marks. One shows where Bubba can hide unseen; the second pinpoints the prime ambush spot. These spots should ensure there are no witnesses to Steph's and Bubba's catastrophic collision.

Chapter Nineteen

Kylee

Friday early evening, June 30

"Why don't we ride to Marshview together," Ted suggests when we meet up at the Welch HOA office. "We'll come right past the office on our way back. You can pick up your car then."

"Not a chance," I answer. "I plan to flee Marshview the instant the crack of a gavel signals adjournment. It'll take you an extra hour to vacate the premises. I'll use the time to run a few errands."

Ted doesn't dispute my timing estimate. From experience, we both know he'll hang around to answer questions or address concerns from folks reluctant to speak out before the entire assembly. Plus, Ted's a champion schmoozer. Guess the saying "opposites attract" has some truth to it. I hate social chitchat with people I barely know.

In the parking lot, Ted gives me a chaste kiss on the cheek. "Drive safe. If I can start the meeting at six on the dot and run it in a reasonably orderly manner, we might have a prayer of sitting down to supper by eight. I'll be sitting up front with the board."

He lifts an eyebrow. "Can I assume you'll hang at the back of the room?"

Ted knows me, too.

"Right, you are," I answer. "The meeting's at the club, right?"

"Yeah, they moved all the tables out of the large banquet room to squeeze in as many chairs as possible. They expect a large turnout."

As I drive to the Marshview subdivision, I marvel at how quickly the Lowcountry landscape changes. Driving this same route a few years ago, I passed lots of tree-studded vacant parcels. Now, most host shopping meccas, medical and professional buildings, and entryways to brand-new residential neighborhoods.

The transformation shouldn't surprise me, given Beaufort County's popularity as a landing spot for retirees and well-to-do second home owners. The last decade's twenty-percent growth rate means all the newcomers need to live somewhere, and solid land represents less than half the county's 468,000 acres. Open water, bays, inlets, and estuaries claim the rest of our geography. That makes vacant parcels a real prize.

I slow as I approach Marshview's gated entrance. The golf-course community caters to single-family homeowners but includes several clusters of townhomes and condos. The mature HOA has been in existence for thirty years. Today's owners seem almost equally split between early buyers, now in their late sixties to early eighties, and newbies in their forties and fifties. The generational divide is one reason I dread this meeting. Don't expect it to be a love fest.

The parking lot is packed. I pass the club and pull into a side street. I drive a fair piece before I can find an open space that doesn't block a driveway.

After I hoof it back to the club, I join a long queue that snakes around the corner of the building. The line moves at a snail's pace, which only ups the anger of a big woman behind me.

"For God's sake, what's taking so long?" she bleats. "You'd think we're at a Coachella rave."

The loudmouth is beefy but mostly solid, not fat. I put her in her early forties. Her makeup is far from subtle. Must use a painter's trowel to apply that much foundation. A push-up bra forces her boobs front and center like a ship's prow. I grin, imagining her using them to plow through the queue.

I search the line ahead for Ted. He's nowhere in sight. Either he was waved ahead, or he knew the location of secret door number two. Briefly, I wonder if the hold-up's due to a metal detector brought in to scan for weapons. Hope not. My Glock's in my purse, nestled next to my concealed carry permit. Since last year's attacks, I tend to keep my gun handy.

As I inch closer to the portal, I see they aren't checking for weapons—though it wouldn't be a bad idea based on the Amazon gal's ugly mood. The hold-up? The HOA Secretary is making everyone sign in, before he checks their names off an owners' list. Not sure why that's necessary at an informational meeting where no votes will be taken.

I show my Welch HOA identification and get a pass on signing in. As Ted predicted, I make a bee-line for the back of the room. Few empty chairs anywhere else. I opt to stand.

There's a low hum of conversation as the impatient audience waits for the show. According to my watch, it's a minute after six. Latecomers are still searching for seats, though I can't help but notice Amazon gal's occupying an aisle seat in the second to last row.

Come on, Ted, start the meeting.

Good, he's walking to the podium.

"Thank you all for coming," Ted greets the crowd. He introduces himself and explains why he's acting as MC before he gets to the reason for the meeting.

"Usually, Marshview has only one owners meeting a year—its November annual meeting. However, as you were notified by mail, an August meeting has been scheduled to vote on a special assessment to finance a new recreational complex. This meeting is purely informational. Its intent is to answer all your questions about the proposed complex and assessment before the vote."

A woman sitting on an aisle a few rows ahead of me huffs, "Like the old fogies here will listen. Nothing's going to change their votes. They oppose all efforts to improve Marshview property values."

A gray-haired gentleman seated a row ahead of her turns and glares. "If Marshview is such a dump, why did you buy here, honey? Plenty of other HOAs have pickleball courts."

I sigh. The owners are already sniping at each other.

Ted turns the mic over to one of the two Board members behind the push for a new recreational complex. Three of the five directors oppose it. That's why a group of younger owners decided to bypass the board. They cajoled a quarter of the HOA membership into signing a petition forcing the board to hold a special August meeting. The purpose? To approve clearing some commonly-owned wooded greenspace to build a pickleball mecca.

The director, who's all-in for the half-a-million-dollar transformation, tells the audience the complex will include fourteen pickleball courts with grandstand bleachers for viewing, a new building to house men's and women's restrooms, shower facilities, and storage space, and an adjacent lanai for social after-match gatherings.

The presenter goes on to cite statistics on pickleball's growing popularity before she motions her fellow collaborator to the podium. Apparently, it's his job to cover in excruciating detail the architectural plans, site drawings, and costs. Can't believe how slowly he talks. Wish I could put him on a time clock, with a maximum number of minutes per slide. He repeats each cost figure justification at least three times. Same goes for his favorite phrase in the Marshview covenants, which references "enhancing" the value of the community.

The dour expressions of the three anti-pickleball HOA directors are hard to miss. Ted tells me they feel the splinter group's forced vote will further divide the HOA. They also resent that the full board wasn't party to the research, the plan's creation, or the bidding process. But at least a vote for or against by all the owners is required.

That's why Ted has emphasized that he must act as a neutral third party, even though his management contract was signed by the directors opposing the assessment.

Why am I here? Security concerns have popped up among folks opposing the complex. While a single, gated road enters Marshview, the site chosen for the pickleball complex backs up to a wildlife preserve. In theory, the unwashed public can stroll into Marshview through this opening to access the pickleball courts or restrooms. If questions arise about possible security add-ons, like cameras, I'm here to answer.

When the presentation of construction details finally concludes, the perky female director reclaims the mic to proclaim the assessment—a mere five thousand dollars per residence—is a steal and will pay off handsomely in higher property values.

"Bullshit." I hear more than one audience member grumble that opinion as Ted steps to the podium. He announces the meeting is now open for owner questions. At least a dozen hands shoot up, wanting to be recognized. Things are about to get a lot more lively.

Ted first calls on a gentleman around Mom's age, late seventies.

"When Marshview opened, the developer marketed it as a quiet residential community. While top-notch amenities were offered to golfers, tennis players, and swimmers, neighbors who simply wanted to enjoy the Lowcountry's natural beauty and serenity were promised protected, serene greenspace. This abomination will destroy that promise—the reason many long-time residents bought here."

Ted next calls on a woman in shorts, who waves a pickleball racquet in the air. "I'm one hundred and fifty percent behind the assessment. Go, pickleballers!" She goes on to heap praise on "the dedicated, selfless directors who found a way to champion this wonderful project despite out-of-date naysayers."

The pickleball enthusiast pauses to glare at the three directors opposing the project before she resumes slobbering over her heroes.

"We owe them a huge, huge round of applause for devoting their time and energy to this fabulous proposal. Let's hear it for Eva and Jeff!"

Directors Eva and Jeff stand and bow as half the crowd claps. Owners in the opposing camp sit on their hands and scowl.

Ouch.

The next speaker, a woman I place somewhere in her sixties, states she lives next to what's now the greenspace enclave.

"We fell in love with our property because it was bordered by these lovely woods. This monstrosity of a project will destroy the value of our home. Can you imagine living next to the noisy racket from fourteen pickleball courts?"

"Just turn down your hearing aid," comes a jeer from across the room.

I'm always shocked by such ugliness in a community where well-off residents have so little to complain about. These people must be successful to afford their homes. Yet they squabble and name-call like kindergartners.

The next speaker's an older gentleman seated in a wheelchair at the end of the last aisle. His voice booms despite whatever disability prevents him from standing. He begins by acknowledging that some fellow homeowners call him a "tightwad."

"I'm a retired widower, and I have enough money to live comfortably. If forced to throw away five thousand dollars for this donnybrook, I won't land in the poor house. But being frugal is why I have a comfortable nest egg. The way I was brought up, a person doesn't throw money away just because he has it."

"Yadda, yadda," a male voice interjects, "we don't need old farts like you lecturing us on finances."

Ted bangs the gavel. "Please, everyone who wants to speak will have a turn. You owe each other the courtesy of not interrupting."

The widower clears his throat and continues. "I simply don't see a good return on this investment. Is pickleball a fad? Maybe, maybe not. But owners who want to play pickleball have courts available in two county rec facilities less than ten minutes from our gate. How many of the owners asked to shell out thousands of dollars will ever step foot on a pickleball court? My guess? Less than half.

"Here's what I think. Those favoring pickleball courts should pay for them. I'd be quite happy to attach a codicil to my deed pledging that I and all future owners of my property will abstain from using the facility."

The Amazon woman I heard dissing older neighbors before the meeting frantically waves her arms.

When Ted recognizes her, she stands and rotates in a slow three-sixty like she's on a barbecue spit. Guess she wants to make sure everyone sees her angry, red face.

"My name is Bitsy Payne, and I've owned a home here for two years. People who bought decades ago are old, and their notions about everything are equally ancient. They mope around in wheelchairs and moan and bitch. No interest in making Marshview appeal to younger buyers. If these Methuselah cheapskates can't afford to live here, so be it. I don't care. Why should I? They're gonna kick the bucket really soon anyway."

Wow.

Bitsy receives a smattering of applause as well as boos. She's still standing when the young lady seated beside the wheelchair speaker pops up.

"How dare you!" she yells and illustrates her contempt by spitting at Amazon lady.

The goober meanders down Bitsy's bare skin from collar bone to deep, propped-up cleavage.

Oh, shit!

Bitsy retaliates with a wind-up slap that lands with enough force to echo through the banquet hall. Staggered by the blow, the irate spitter rights herself and shoves Bitsy.

Knocked off balance as her high heels twist, Bitsy staggers and grabs a healthy hank of her shover's hair. The spitter screams as she joins Bitsy in a free fall that drops them to the floor, where they roll down the aisle like a twined tumbleweed.

Good Lord!

A man in a nearby row claps and yells, "Cat fight! Cat fight! Get it on video." He laughs uproariously as he reaches for his cellphone.

I glance toward the front of the room. Normally, Ted's Mr. Decisive, but at the moment, he looks torn between using a mic to try and quell the disturbance and running up the aisle to pull the screaming women apart.

I decide to solve his dilemma.

"Stop it. Stop it, right now!" I bark as I shoulder past another spectator videoing the wrestling match. Stooping down, I try to wedge an arm between the writhing bodies.

Bitsy frees one of her hands long enough to reach up and rake her long claws down my cheek.

The sting is instant, and I smell blood.

For a moment, I consider leaving the struggle to claim my Glock. No matter how much I'd like to, I wouldn't shoot anyone. Yet, firing a round into the ceiling might get the combatants' attention. Somehow, though, I figure gunplay wouldn't be Ted's preferred method of resolution. And, who knows how many other audience members brought firearms and might feel obliged to join in.

"Hilda, honey, back away from the witch," Mr. Wheelchair pleads. "She's not worth it. If your mother could see you, she'd turn over in her grave."

Ah, the spitter is Wheelchair's daughter.

When Hilda tries to disengage, I use all my strength in an attempt to pull Bitsy away from her. It's like trying to wrangle a bucking bronco. She heaves up and knocks me off my feet. When I land, Bitsy forgets the spitter and jumps me.

She sits on me, straddling my waist. I'm still busy sucking in oxygen when Bitsy balls her right fist and punches my jaw.

Okay, no more Ms. Nice Gal.

I put my hands between us, palms out, to signal it's time to stop. Her glare tells me she's not buying. Since she's a righty, I'm pretty sure she'll hit from the same direction. I snake my left foot out to trap her right ankle and throw her off-balance.

As Bitsy's right fist arcs toward my jaw, I'm ready. With a simple hip hike, I use the momentum of her own punch to fling her on her back. And, what do you know, I'm now straddling Bitsy.

Gotta say, the Amazon isn't a quitter. But she isn't too bright either. When she tries to throw another punch, I trap her right arm against her chest. She may outweigh me, but there's no way she can bring that fist back into action.

When I see her balling her left fist, I sigh. Really? I grasp the meat of her thumb and twist her left hand away.

She flails for a moment before trying to bite me. Is she kidding? This woman needs Prozac. I torque her left wrist.

She whimpers and lays back. I back off her wrist until her creative insults turn to my mother. I torque the wrist again.

"You ladies having fun?" Ted's standing above us.

"She hit me."

"If she promises not to do it again, do you think you could get off her?"

Bitsy stares up at me but refuses to say a word.

I release her wrists and slide away. But I keep my feet between us as a barricade.

"You ugly, old interfering cow," she hisses as she rolls to all fours to face me. "You don't know who you're dealing with."

I long to scream back, "Bring it on, bitch!" However, Ted's calming influence prevails. Considering the circumstances, my response is remarkably demure. "I did no permanent damage. You're fine."

Bitsy stands and continues to glower at me. "I'm going to sue you!" she snarls.

"Better folks have tried," I reply as I pull up my shirt collar to dab at the blood oozing down my cheek.

Honey, I may sue you if you've knocked any teeth loose.

"Lotsa luck claiming she attacked you, Bitsy," drawls a bystander. "I'll be one of her witnesses, and there are probably six videos. The lady was only trying to stop you from beating the stuffing out of Hilda."

I'm on the floor on my butt, scooting clear of Bitsy, when Ted pulls me to my feet.

"Next time, maybe you should sit up front with me," he says.

Ted apparently ended the meeting while I was otherwise engaged. Everyone not in our little fight club is exiting the building.

Looks like we might get to eat dinner earlier than expected, unless Ted feels the need to stop at Kay's B&B first for a consult about a possible lawsuit. Good thing Kay Barrett, Esquire, a dear friend, has not forfeited her license to practice law.

Chapter Twenty

Kylee

Friday evening, June 30

An hour after the meeting broke up (literally), I'm parked on a couch in Ted's living room with an icebag to my rapidly swelling cheek. Before arriving at Ted's, I stopped by the River Rat, changed clothes, and cleaned and applied antiseptic to the scratches on my cheek. No telling what evil lurked under Bitsy's nails. Unfortunately, I had a close-up view of them—neon green with little smiley faces. *Give me a break!*

My medical first-aid and cool-down layover let Ted beat me to his house. When I arrived, he put his hands on my shoulders and assessed the damage. Turning my head one way and then the other.

"Bet it hurts," he said. "The scratches on your right cheek don't look real deep. Should heal quickly. But you're going to have bruises on the left side where Bitsy landed a punch. It's already swollen and discolored."

"Thanks," I quipped. "You look ravishing and sexy as hell, too."

Ted hugged me very gently. "Nothing broken, right? Jaw, ribs?"

"No," I answered. "I worried she might have knocked a tooth loose, but it seems fine."

Damage assessment complete, Ted ordered me to rest on the couch with the icepack until dinner was ready.

My eyes are closed when Ted comes in and gently kisses my eyelids. "May

I escort you to the dining room?" he asks. His soft, warm breath tickles my ear.

At the dinner table, Ted pulls out my chair. He obviously did some planning ahead of the Marshview meeting to make our evening romantic. Don't imagine he was counting on his lover having a shiner.

The table's set with flickering candles, roses from his garden, and real china. A big change from the paper plates and plastic utensils that have become standard since his kitchen is in disarray (to put it mildly) and Ted doesn't have a dishwasher.

Knowing I'm allergic to wine and champagne, Ted omitted the romance novel's fine vintner component of the evening spread, substituting sparkling apple cider. A good thing since I probably shouldn't mix alcohol with the painkillers I slugged down before my arrival.

Ted gets big brownie points for the festive setting. And I'm hoping he'll earn more bonus points post-meal. While his boudoir's antique wallpaper may be peeling, his king bed suits me just fine. Not too firm, not too soft, perfect for lovemaking.

Around clients, it's sometimes hard to act like we're simply professional colleagues or PG-rated friends. While we don't pretend around Mom, Frank, and Grant, it's still a little awkward for me.

Ted has no problems broadcasting we're lovers. I'll get there, but the relationship is still young. Before we shout our new status from the rafters, I want to make doubly certain it's long-term and not just two middle-agers knocking a little rust off their latent lust.

I love Ted. Don't doubt that for a minute. That will never change. But I'm still nervous about upsetting our family dynamic.

"The table looks lovely," I comment. "But since you don't have a working stove, I'm curious what's on the menu?"

"Ordered chef salads from Luther's plus an entire key lime pie." Ted grins. "Perfect for a warm summer evening."

I laugh. "Yeah, I think it's a little beyond warm in here. I'd call it sweaty. What do you suppose folks who lived in these historic Lowcountry homes did back when? It's not like there's a scarcity of muggy mid-summer evenings like this one—not a stir of breeze."

Ted smiles. "A lot of plantation owners traveled to the South Carolina Up-country for a little mountain relief. Don't worry, though. Air-conditioning is high on my agenda. While the Historic Foundation doesn't want folks messing with exteriors, interior updates are fine."

Ted retrieves our salads from the mini fridge that's temporarily stashed in the dining room, and I raise my sparkling apple cider in a toast.

"Here's to the Historic Foundation's wisdom and to you keeping enough HOA clients to afford the exorbitant HVAC fee a mechanic will charge to cool this crumbling gem. I hope my wrestling match tonight won't harm your reputation with the Marshview board."

"No, all five directors were glad you broke up the fight before it got any more out of hand. And how about leaving off with the decrepit-house insults? Your sailboat's bathroom is so tiny I have to back my butt in. At least my house doesn't require people to be contortionists to sit on the throne."

We pause the shop talk while we eat.

"This chef's salad's terrific," I say. "Love the sweetness of the grapes and the crunch of the candied pecans, and the chicken's so tender."

Once we finish our salads, Ted clears the dishes, opens the mini-fridge, and retrieves a gorgeous key lime pie. "How big?" he asks.

I debate a minute before moving my fingers a little wider. I do need sustenance to heal, right?

As he slides a wedge of pie onto my plate, he asks. "Did you have a good day prior to the ladies' World-Wide Wrestling event?"

I tilt my head and waggle my hand in a see-saw, maybe yes, maybe no gesture. "Well...guess I should give you a Rand Creek update."

I describe his son's brainstorm and my afternoon.

"We discreetly identified three of the people most unlikely to weep over Andy Fyke's tumble and resulting injuries," I sum up as I finish the last bite of pie.

Despite my injuries, I hope a romp in the boudoir will consume a few of the extra calories I inhaled.

"Jocelyn won't be happy," I add. "The bridge players Mimi photographed are all septuagenarian cronies," I add. "Of course, Rand Creek's president would be even more peeved to hear the residents bandied her name about as Fyke's most likely attacker. Just guessing here, but doubt she considers an orange jumpsuit to be haute couture."

Ted chuckles. "I'm trying to picture her in prison garb. Nonetheless, I doubt Jocelyn had anything to do with Fyke's fall. Not her style. She's slick. Far more likely to game the system to sideline Fyke. Find some reason to justify depositing his covenant change petition in a circular filing cabinet."

Ted pauses. "Tell me again who else Fyke's friends suspect?"

"Xander Pringle and Amanda Holder. Haven't had a chance to look up information on either of them. Not sure if they live in Rand Creek or are absentee owners. Only know both own rental property and are furious with Fyke."

Ted's forehead creases. "The names sound familiar. Xander's such an unusual name. I should remember the connection. Oh, I know. Xander's a real estate attorney, handles tons of closings. While I've never met him, his office often asks us to provide documentation to verify that sellers of HOA properties don't owe association fees, fines, or assessments."

"How about the woman? Think she might be a real estate professional, too?"

"Holder...Holder," Ted mutters. "I've got it. Amanda Holder was one of Ernie Baker's supporters. A widow who lived in a big, gothic-looking monstrosity in Lighthouse Cove. She lived down the street from Ed Hiller. But she died of a heart attack over a year ago."

"Well, this Amanda Holder is definitely alive and kicking. One of her Rand Creek rentals is located two doors from Fyke. He's filed formal complaints about her renters, and he asked the board to hold the woman responsible for damage the renters inflicted on common property.

"Fyke also contended not a single person in Holder's last group of renters met the HOA's age fifty-five requirement. He claimed they were all in their early twenties. According to Fyke's friends, the Holder woman denied everything. She called Fyke senile and insinuated he might have damaged the property himself. Since Fyke had no video to prove renters were to blame, his complaint went nowhere. That incident prompted him to start his campaign to eliminate rentals."

Ted pauses with his fork in mid-air. He's more disciplined about dining etiquette than me and has yet to finish his pie. I blame the Coast Guard and my time aboard ship—chew fast while you can.

"The two Amandas could be a mother and daughter," Ted says. "That's not a thing in the Midwest, but Southerners sometimes name baby girls after their moms and add the mother's maiden name as a middle name. That way, the daughter honors the mother's heritage. We can check the Lighthouse Cove owner list after supper."

"Well, if you'd hurry up and finish that pie, I have a different activity in mind. How about a race to see who can shuck their clothes the fastest? The door to your bedroom will serve as the starting line."

"You're on." He grins as his hand bobs up to his shirt's top button.

"No cheating," I warn. "Remember, the bedroom door is the starting line."

"But you can just yank your top over your head," he complains.

"Not my wardrobe problem."

Needless to say, I win the dump-the-clothes-the-fastest contest. But Ted's speed is impressive.

And he does win many bonus points over the next two hours.

Chapter Twenty-One

Kylee

Saturday morning, July 1

Sun pours through holes in the oilcloth shades covering Ted's bedroom windows. Hard to imagine any moths hard up enough to dine on the vintage oilcloth. Don't want to think about what other bugs might be inclined to chomp on the window coverings. Termites?

A side sleeper, I perform a one-eighty in the king bed to check if Ted's awake. His side's empty.

How late is it? Can't check the clock. Around midnight, I shoved the bedside alarm face down to keep its glowing digits from painting my pillow an eerie green. I fumble to right it.

Ugh. Seven-thirty. I slide from under the sheets naked as a jaybird and pick Ted's borrowed robe off the floor. The fuzzy loaner is secured solely by a soft belt. One tug, and I'm buck naked. Could be that's why Ted always loans it to me. No objection here.

I follow my nose to the dining room. The aroma of coffee. Smells like Blueberry Cobbler, my favorite roast. Unfortunately, my route takes me past a gold-leafed mirror. The image looking back at me isn't exactly gilded. My bruised left cheek's painted in unfortunate shades of green and bluish-black. A vivid red line down my right cheek is hopefully a short-term gift from Bitsy's painted claws.

Ted looks up from his seat at the dining table, coffee mug in hand. "Morning, sleepyhead. How does your face feel?"

"It looks worse than it feels," I assure him.

Hmm. He's fully clothed. Work duds. No going back to bed. Darn.

I wave a greeting, opting for coffee to lubricate my tongue before I engage in any more conversation. I notice Ted did a little rearranging in the dining room while I slept. Gone are last night's candlesticks and the room's make-shift kitchenette has expanded to include two TV trays. One holds a coffee pot, the other a microwave. Sort of looks like a student has jerry-rigged his dorm room for fast access to hot coffee and ramen noodles. Wonder how long it'll be before the remodel allows Ted to use his kitchen.

Not complaining. Ted's coffee pot holds ten cups. I pour a mug, take a welcome sip, then wander over to plant a kiss on Ted's cheek. He tugs on my belt, prompting the oversized robe to fall open.

"Hey, don't start anything you can't finish. You're already dressed. Got an early morning meeting on the docket? Hope Jocelyn hasn't summoned you to complain about your staff."

Ted folds the Beaufort Gazette he's reading. "No, but I might prefer that. Have a special ten o'clock membership meeting at Sea Bay to explain the extensive work needed to fix the aging complex's structural defects. Frank and I will be joined by a partner from the engineering firm we hope to engage to do the work. He's driving over from Atlanta. I'm due to pick both of them up in thirty minutes."

"Doesn't sound like I'll see much of you today."

"Afraid not. After the HOA hears the firm's proposal, I get to explain financing options. Don't expect to see many smiling faces. Two costly choices. Cough up one humongous special assessment or fork over a smaller assessment for a down payment and commit to a ten-year bank loan to fund the remainder. The loan would require membership approval to collect an additional annual HOA fee pledged to the bank."

"Good luck," I sympathize. "Nobody likes the bearers of bad news."

"What about you?"

"A little more sleuthing on Mr. Fyke's behalf," I answer. "Kay Barrett must have dealt with Xander Pringle on real estate transactions. I'll see if she has a few minutes to give her take on the possibility Xander attacked Fyke. I'll also call Ed Hiller, my favorite Lighthouse Cove chef, for the skinny on suspect number three, since the Lighthouse Cove directory says a living-breathing Amanda Holder resides on Ed's street."

Ted's phone buzzes, interrupting our back-and-forth. I take a chair and slide the newspaper over to scan the headlines while I wait for the call to end. Ted's "Oh, no" and hangdog expression tell me the news is bad. Ted's end of the conversation consists mostly of questions: "When did it happen? ... Is he dead? ... Who's investigating—the Sheriff's Office or the Coast Guard?"

Finally, Ted tells the caller he's sorry he can't change his morning commitments. Then, he adds, "Kylee's right here. I'll give her the phone."

He presses the phone against his chest as he whispers, "It's Donna Dahl. Steph Cloyd was killed early this morning while he was out rowing his scull. A motorboat hit him broadside, and a propeller finished the job. Deputy Nick Ibsen was first on the scene. He doesn't seem willing to entertain the notion that the fatality might be a murder. Ibsen says it looks like an accidental collision, and the motorboat driver panicked and left the scene. Donna vehemently disagrees."

An uncontrolled shudder follows Ted's mention of my nemesis, Nick Ibsen. Briefly a lover, he now goes out of his way to paint me and Ted as incompetent at best, slime buckets at worst.

After sucking in a big, calming breath, I reach for the phone.

"Donna, I'm so sorry about Steph. I know you were really fond of him. He was a terrific addition to your HOA board."

"Steph was such a good guy," she says. The catch in her voice signals she's still close to tears.

"I left a voice message on your phone," she continues. "Wanted to talk to both you and Ted. I need help. I can't seem to make Ibsen seriously consider that Steph's death was planned. That it's no accident—"

"Donna," I interrupt. "You know my history with Nick. Any sign I'm sticking my nose in will send him into orbit and harden whatever asinine stance he's taking."

"I know." Donna sighs. "But when I told Ibsen I felt sure Bubba Quarles rammed Steph on purpose, he shrugged. Said people always want to try and make someone responsible for accidents. Told me I needed to accept Steph's death was probably just that—an unfortunate accident."

"What makes you so sure it wasn't an accident?"

"Steph reported this Bubba Quarles to the authorities a month ago for recklessly driving his motorboat. Since there was only Steph's word—no other witnesses—Bubba only got a warning. But the warning angered the guy enough to threaten Steph. Said he couldn't wait to meet Steph on the water again when it was just the two of them."

"Okay, I'll see what I can find out. Maybe the Coast Guard can help. But I can't make any promises. Tell me the motorboat guy's name again."

"Bubba Quarles," she answers. "And I bet he has a criminal record, given Steph's encounters with him."

I end the call and hand the phone back to Ted, who is shaking his head.

"I know you're friends with Donna and want to help, but, please, keep your distance. Nick would love to find an excuse to charge you with obstructing an investigation."

"True," I answer, "but according to Donna, there won't be much of an investigation. So how can I be interfering? I'll simply ask a few questions."

Ted shakes his head. "Where have I heard that before? Be careful. Dinner at Myrt's tonight, right? Six o'clock."

Chapter Twenty-Two

Kylee

Saturday morning, July 1

Yes, I promised Donna I'd look into Steph's boating tragedy, but I've learned the hard way it's easier to make headway if the Sheriff's Department doesn't think I'm tramping on any official toes. That means I won't show my face near the crime scene until I'm sure all the deputies are gone.

That makes the first order of the day picking my friend Kay Barrett's brain about Xander Pringle. Fingers crossed, she has a few minutes to chat. Both Kay and I are in our early fifties, single, and have spent most of our careers in male-dominated fields—military, for me, law, for her. No wonder we became fast friends when I settled in the Lowcountry.

Recently, Kay launched a second career. While she still does legal work for former clients, she no longer takes on new ones. She's too busy operating a Beaufort B&B, an historic inn that sits three blocks from Ted's renovation project.

Since it's a sunny day and the temperature is still in the low eighties, I decide to walk over. Beaufort's Historic District is always a visual delight. While spring azaleas may put on the most extravagant show, summer isn't far behind, with tea roses, hibiscus, and hydrangeas providing colorful blooms and a floral scent that lingers after you pass the many wrought-iron gated gardens.

Of course, I'm not the only one out enjoying the day. Hearing the clomp, clomp of hooves behind me, I know the horse-driven carriage tours have already begun. The early start's no surprise on this busy tourist weekend.

I climb the stairs to the B&B's wide porch, where two of Kay's guests occupy rocking chairs. Prime seats to watch the parade of Saturday tourists following their walking maps of the Historic District.

"Good morning," I greet the ladies. "Beautiful day, isn't it?" As expected, they agree.

Inside the B&B's front foyer, I catch a glimpse of Kay chatting with a young couple in the breakfast room. The experience at her B&B includes a full breakfast with all the expected Southern comfort foods—eggs, bacon, sausage, grits, biscuits, and country gravy.

Kay notices me walking down the hall and excuses herself to greet me.

"Hey, Kylee, are you here to bum breakfast? I saw your car at Ted's house last night."

She pauses. "Oh, good lord, what happened to your face? Are you okay?"

I shrug and answer, "A livelier than usual HOA meeting. Tried to break up a fight between two owners. Video's probably on YouTube by now."

"So, did you come to see me because one of the combatants looks worse than you and is suing for damages?" she asks.

"Not yet. I came to pick your brain, but I wouldn't complain if that knowledge was delivered with a side of bacon."

Kay laughs. "The breakfast rush is over. Those newlyweds are the only latecomers. Go ahead, take a seat at that table by the window. I'll grab us some grub. I'm ready to sit a spell."

Between sips of coffee and nibbles on a blueberry muffin—the bacon was all gone, and I'm not a fan of biscuits and gravy—I ask Kay what she can tell me about Xander Pringle. "Figure over the past two decades, you've dealt with every Beaufort real estate attorney."

"Xander moved to town maybe ten years ago," Kay replies. "And, yes, I've dealt with the slimeball. Hope you plan to tell me he's under investigation for screwing over clients. Something he should have been disbarred for ten years ago."

"Can't accommodate you," I answer. "Yesterday, his name came up in a different context. When rumors started flying that Andrew Fyke might have been pushed down a flight of stairs, several of Fyke's friends nominated Xander as the pushee."

A snort signals Kay's derision.

"No way, Jose. Can't imagine Xander engaged in a physical attack. The giant sloth can't find doctors willing to replace his bad knees or hips until he sheds some weight. He walks with a cane, all stooped over. He couldn't sneak up behind anyone. He'd sound like an elephant using a tree trunk for a cane.

"Why did someone name Xander as a suspect?" she asks. "The guy steals clients blind. No need to push them down the stairs."

I explain the rental controversy, noting that Andy Fyke's been canvassing for petition signatures to outlaw rentals in Rand Creek.

Kay nods. "Yep, Xander certainly would have a motive to sideline this Fyke. He's put together a healthy rental portfolio. In large part, he's done so with underhanded tactics. One of his clients, AKA victims, confided how Xander recommended he should pass on the purchase of a condo. Handed him some gobbledygook about an unclear title. Next thing the client hears Xander owns the property. Tried to hide the purchase inside an LLC but messed up. Other attorneys know Xander's a louse. Unfortunately, he's cagey enough to avoid lawsuits."

"Okay, thanks." I sigh. "Will move him to the bottom of the suspect list. Have plenty else to keep me busy. Did you hear a FACE director was killed early this morning while out rowing his shell?"

"No!" Kay gasps. "Been too busy with the breakfast rush to listen to the radio. Please tell me the victim isn't Steph Cloyd."

"Oh, Kay, I'm afraid it is. How did you guess?"

"We're both on the FACE board," she answers. "Steph often talks about getting his coastal rowing in first light before boat traffic gets heavy. What happened?"

I tell her what I know, which isn't much. Though, I do explain why Donna thinks Bubba Quarles attacked Steph on purpose.

"Can you get the Coast Guard involved?" she asks.

"Already called a friend. She took a look at USG satellite imagery. Unfortunately, she couldn't find anything helpful during the relevant time period. The crash took place in a shallow tributary. There's some argument as to whether it's a navigable waterway and, therefore, within Coast Guard jurisdiction.

"While the Sheriff's Office could ask for Coast Guard help, the authorities think it was an accident, and the boater panicked. Deputy Ibsen doesn't believe whoever fled the scene represents any further danger to the public. He told Donna they'll ID him when he brings his boat in for repair. Then they can determine if he should be charged for leaving the scene."

Kay finishes chewing a bite of biscuit while she thinks. "In other circumstances, I could understand Nick's point of view. But his nonchalance is stupid if he's been told this Bubba guy threatened Steph."

I shrug. "He was told. Nick knows Donna and I are friends. Maybe that's why he's sticking with his accident theory. Probably dismissed Donna as another hysterical menopausal female. The guy's a misogynist.

"Then again, maybe Nick really is investigating Bubba. He could be taunting Donna. Making her mad by patting her head and telling her to go away like a good, little old lady."

Kay runs a finger along the rim of her mug as she stares into her coffee. "Quarles. Why do I know that name? Something about the family."

"I know," she says as the lifelong Beaufort resident's memory clicks in. "A man by the name of Quarles was convicted of manslaughter a dozen years back. Can't be your guy, though. He has to be in his mid-seventies by now, and he's probably still in prison. Might be the suspect's father, though."

Across the breakfast room, the B&B honeymooner guests leave their table hand-in-hand.

Kay tips her head in their direction. "My clue to get up and moving. Have three suites turning over today and need to get the breakfast mess squared away. Afternoon tea time will be here before I know it."

"Thanks, Kay. Will keep you posted about the Steph and Fyke mysteries."

Chapter Twenty-Three

Kylee

Saturday morning, July 1

As soon as I leave Kay's B&B, I call to see if my favorite—okay, only—celebrity chef buddy has time for a chat. Ed Hiller responds with an enthusiastic invite.

Ed, his wife, and two kids live in Chicago. That's where he started his restaurant chain and where he films his TV cooking show, *Eats with Ed*. Whenever he can, he flies out of the Windy City to take a breather at the Lighthouse Cove home he inherited from his dad.

Fortunately, the Hiller family's celebrating the Fourth of July in Beaufort County.

Ed answers the door in an oversized apron that's clearly needed, not some fashion accessory. Today, the apron's decorated with buttery, golden droplets. My guess is Hollandaise or a close cousin.

"Oh, my," Ed says when he sees my face. "Looks like you could use a hug—but not too tight."

While he snakes his free arm around my waist, he holds his other arm high and to the side to prevent the big whisk he clutches from dripping on me.

I met Ed late fall while trying to figure out who was behind a phony 991 active shooter call that prompted a SWAT raid on Lighthouse Cove's clubhouse. Hardly a prank, the SWAT team's startling arrival triggered an occupant's fatal heart attack.

Ed turns in the hallway. I know the way. A direct route to his gleaming kitchen.

"My wife, Lydia, took the kids to the swimming pool," he says. "Don't know if they'll be back in time for you to meet them. Meanwhile, come along. I'm testing a new seafood recipe that's ready to pop in the oven."

I follow in Ed's waddling yet energetic wake, telling myself not to giggle. Just as in our first encounter, the chef's backside view reveals chubby, churning bare legs. This morning, his sturdy appendages emerge from iridescent, floral swim trunks. Ed says he gets so hot bustling about the kitchen that he shuns long pants—unless TV cameras are rolling.

Ed flicks a hand toward a mammoth double-door refrigerator. "There's a pitcher of lemonade in the fridge. Why don't you pour us both a glass while I finish up? Then you can fill me in on whatever mysterious goings-on you're investigating."

He nods toward the kitchen's large picture window. "Look at that brilliant sunshine. Our oleanders are bursting with gorgeous pink and purple blooms, and there's a light breeze tickling the palm fronds. Yet, my intuition tells me you're about to report some crime is afoot in this beautiful paradise. Does it have anything to do with your bruised cheek?"

I chuckle as I pour the lemonade. "Must admit this *crime* may be entirely a product of my fevered imagination. Thursday morning, when I went to the Rand Creek clubhouse, I discovered a badly injured gentleman lying at the foot of a flight of stairs. Though he remembers nothing about his fall, my gut tells me he was pushed. Andy Fyke's friends tend to agree, and they're only too happy to suggest enemies who might want the gentleman dead or sidelined."

Ed holds up his now oven-mitted hands in mock surrender. "Hey, never heard of this Fyke guy, and, just like last time you interrogated me, I have a solid alibi. On Thursday morning, me, the missus, and our kids were shoeless at the Chicago airport, running the security gauntlet to board a plane."

I smile. "Don't need to verify your whereabouts, and I didn't imagine you'd be acquainted with Mr. Fyke. I'm actually looking for a little off-the-record intel on a down-the-street neighbor. Her name's Amanda Holder."

"Dr. Holder?" The rise in Ed's pitch suggests total surprise.

He strips off his oven mitts and takes a seat at the kitchen table.

"Hard to believe the doc's been here long enough to cultivate enemies. Also, my impression is the lady's aloof, a loner. Keeps to herself. Yesterday, Lydia invited her to a spur-of-the-moment block party this evening. Dr. Holder said, 'No.' Okay, there's nothing weird about someone turning down a last-minute invite. Yet Lydia felt Holder's curt, no-excuse reply was intended to relay a don't-bother-me message."

I twirl my lemonade glass while I think. "Sounds like you haven't had much face-to-face contact with the doctor. Did your dad ever mention meeting the woman when she visited the elder Amanda Holder?"

"No," Ed answers. "Before Dad fell ill, he told me the late Amanda risked wearing out her jaw bragging about her 'brilliant' daughter. Boasted she was some world-renowned professor at a prestigious New York university. Don't remember which one.

"Eventually, Dad started running for cover whenever Amanda popped outside her house. Felt the old lady tried to make him feel bad. Hinted how his son—me—must be a disappointment. After going on about her daughter's shining intellect, she'd imply it must be sad for a financial wizard like Dad to be saddled with an unambitious son. A son content to work as a 'cook.'"

I chuckle. "If only the lady had tasted your creations, she'd have traded in her brainy daughter in a heartbeat. Any thoughts on why this supposed genius left her university to hole up in Beaufort County?"

Ed tips back in his chair and sips his lemonade. "Dr. Holder moved into Lighthouse Cove less than a week after her mother's fatal heart attack. About a year and a half ago now. She barely had time to plant her mom six feet under before taking up residence.

"Seemed strange. It was smack in the middle of February. I thought universities frowned on professors exiting mid-semester. Decided the doc must have been on sabbatical and elected to spend it here in isolation to concentrate on her research."

"Do you know what Holder taught at the university?"

"Some sort of computer science. If she's asked, Holder tells neighbors she's developing a cutting-edge software application."

Given that Ed isn't a gossip and doesn't appear dazzled by Dr. Holder's genius, I decide there's no harm in explaining why I'm asking about the woman.

"Dr. Holder's name came up because she owns Rand Creek rental property and has been involved in a couple of disputes with Andrew Fyke. Andy was pushed down a flight of stairs this past Thursday. And his friends think it might be because he's heading a drive to prohibit rentals."

Ed nods. "Yeah, I can see the two of them would be on opposite sides of the issue. When the doc's mother passed, she asked Dad's opinion about selling a Rand Creek condo she inherited. He recommended postponing a sale and renting it until the market rebounded.

"Hard to imagine the doc being upset enough over the loss of income from one rental unit to physically attack this Fyke fellow. Now, if our neighbor Leona Grimm had been attacked, I'd nominate Dr. Holder as the prime suspect. I worried the doc might start foaming at the mouth when Leona launched her campaign to install a dog park in the empty lot next to Dr. Holder's house."

I roll my eyes. "Hope that dog park effort goes nowhere. I've heard Ted's tales about the vicious neighborhood feuds that can be triggered when dog owners insist it would be wonderful to turn someone else's next-door lot into a doggy playground."

Ed scoots his chair back from the table. "Hey, I've got an idea. Why don't I introduce you to Dr. Holder right now? I'll say we were visiting, and you happened to mention the Rand Creek rental debate. When I recalled she owns property there, I thought she might like to share her opinion on the matter as a non-resident owner."

I weigh the pros and cons. *Why not?*

"Let's do it."

Chapter Twenty-Four

The Chameleon

Saturday noon, July 1

I stretch and do some neck calisthenics. Sit too long at my computer and my shoulders ache. Time for a lunch break. Want to see if any local TV station's providing aerial coverage of what radio newscasts are describing as a tragic holiday boating accident.

It's a tragedy, all right. I wish Bubba had drowned along with Steph. Can't believe the idiot left the scene of the "accident."

The texts I sent Bubba—okay, the ones sent by his nativist gal pal—urged him to stay at the scene or head to a nearby dock to immediately report the incident. My stand-in carefully explained why Bubba should act broken up and cooperate fully with authorities. Told him it would help establish the collision was truly an accident. The logic escaped Bubba's tiny brain.

The TV news report on the boating mayhem starts just as I finish spreading low-cal mayo on a turkey and tomato sandwich. Excellent, the reporter says we'll see helicopter coverage after a short break.

Ring. Ring. Ring.

Dammit. Who's at my front door? I want to eat my lunch and watch the news. Maybe whoever's out there will go away if I don't answer. I check the Ring doorbell image on my phone.

Dammit doubled. It's that chipmunk-cheeked chef from down the street.

Thought I made it clear to his little wife that I had zero interest in wasting an evening at some schlock block party.

Wait. The woman with him isn't his wife. This woman's face suggests she just went a few rounds in a domestic squabble. Her curly white hair looks familiar. Got it. Saw her photo plenty on the news late fall. She has some sort of military background and works security for the company that manages Lighthouse Cove and Rand Creek.

Shit! Shit! Shit!

Guess I'd better find out what brings them to my door. I switch off the TV and head to the front of the house.

"Yes?"

As I crack open the door, I don my most annoyed expression, making it plain the interruption isn't appreciated.

"Sorry to bother you," the chef says. "But I wanted to introduce you to my friend, Kylee Kane. She works for Welch HOA Management, the company that manages our HOA. While we were chatting, Kylee mentioned her boss is trying to get a good cross-section of owner opinion about the push to end Rand Creek's rentals. Knowing you inherited your mom's condo there and are renting it, thought you might like to share your perspective. But, if you're in the middle of something..."

Try as I might, I can't force my jaw to unclench and fake a smile. Can't believe this introduction is some crazy coincidence. How did I end up on this snoop's radar?

Better let them in. See what I can find out.

"I'm very pressed for time," I say. "But you're welcome to come in for a minute."

I lead the pair into the living room. A space I haven't set foot in for at least a month. They take seats on opposite ends of the sofa. I perch on the edge of a club chair across the way.

"My perspective is probably no surprise," I begin. "I do own and rent two Rand Creek condos. Naturally, I oppose any covenant change. While I inherited the first unit, I bought the second as an investment property. Certainly, if any change is contemplated, owners like me who purchased

94

investment properties in good faith must be grandfathered."

The snoop doesn't take her eyes off me. Looking for some tell?

"Have you spoken with Andrew Fyke about the petition he's circulating?" she asks.

"Andrew Fyke?" I tilt my head, mimicking how I think I'd react if I heard a name that's familiar but can't be placed. "Oh, yes, I've never met the man, but I did hear he was trying to get names on some sort of petition."

Don't overdo it. Just act unconcerned.

I scoot forward in my chair, preparing to stand. "Afraid I can't provide insights about how other Rand Creek owners feel about rentals. Since I don't live there, I haven't met many residents."

The snoop and the chef don't shift their butts a single millimeter. Can't they take a hint?

"Mr. Fyke had a nasty fall the other day," the snoop adds.

Good grief, the woman acts like I've invited her to spend the afternoon.

"But the gentleman's recuperating," she continues. "From what I hear, Mr. Fyke's friends plan to continue his petition effort. Since the rental debate won't vanish any time soon, you may want to contact the board to make sure your opinion is heard."

Does she expect me to sob or have a tizzy fit?

"Sound advice. However, I'm afraid I have more pressing concerns. I'm immersed in a software development project that requires my full attention."

"Oh, what kind of software project?"

"Artificial Intelligence—AI. A new app." I hope my sharp tone and clipped reply will communicate that my visitors have overstayed what little welcome they had.

"AI…Are you working on one of those chatbots that can carry on conversations with users?" the chef asks. "I heard it won't be long before I can look in my refrigerator, list the ingredients nearing their expiration dates, and ask for a recipe to incorporate them.

"Is that right? Would it suggest tried-and-true recipes or try to invent one. Can't imagine—"

I clear my throat to cut him off and simultaneously study my watch. Not about to swap recipes with chubby Mr. Ed. I almost smile, remembering a re-run of an old television show that featured a Mr. Ed, a talking horse. Horse...ass—close enough.

I stand. "Sorry, but I *am* pressed for time. Hope you understand."

"Well, thank you for seeing us," the snoop says.

I don't reply, just usher my two unwanted pests out the door and close it firmly the minute their butts cross the threshold.

Need to give this nuisance visit some thought.

Wonder if I can convince J.T. to confess and commit suicide?

A succinct note in J.T.'s handwriting admitting she attacked Fyke would nicely tie up all the loose ends. If her note says she pushed Andy because he's a perv, it would end the feverish online speculation that Fyke's fall had something to do with his proposed rental ban. The gossip could then switch to Fyke. Is he really a perv? How did J.T. find out?

Is it harder to convince someone to do themselves in than it is to coax them to off another human? This could prove to be an interesting experiment.

Yet I shouldn't put all my eggs in a J.T. confession basket. Kylee Kane deserves some research. I have no doubt I can find ways to ensure she's far too busy to poke her nose in my affairs.

I smile. Based on her bruised face, it appears I'm not the only one who thinks she should mind her own business.

Hullis Island is one of Welch HOA Management's clients. Since I own two rentals on the island, I received a notice about Sunday's hastily-called owners' meeting. Based on the social media hysteria surrounding some idiotic rules about outdoor decorations, the gathering promises to be contentious.

Wonder how well the snoop and her employer handle adversity. I definitely plan to attend. If nothing else, it should give me ideas about ways to stir the pot and keep Kylee's feet to the fire.

Chapter Twenty-Five

Kylee

Saturday afternoon, July 1

"Well, Kylee, what's your read?" Ed asks. "Is my neighbor, Dr. Holder, just rude or is she pretending indifference and ignorance in regard to Mr. Fyke and his quest to nix rentals."

I chuckle. "My guess is the latter. While I never went to a private girls' school, Dr. Holder's looks made me want to squirm like a student who's been sent to see the headmistress. That is assuming the headmistress never smiles and enjoys rapping knuckles with a ruler.

"Not what I expected," I add. "She's not unattractive. Or at least she wouldn't be, if she lost the glare, and didn't look as if she were grinding her teeth behind those thin, sealed lips. She's not afraid to spend money on herself. Those blonde streaks in her dark hair aren't from the sun, and I'll bet her contact lenses are tinted to make her eyes that unusual emerald green."

Ed laughs. "She definitely works out, lifts weights," he adds. "Maybe she wrestles under the name Amanda the Anaconda. If she wrapped those arms around my neck, she could choke me out before I could squeal 'I give.'"

Ed and I seem to have launched a competition for who can best diss the doc. "Her nose is a little big, but maybe I think so because she looked down it the whole time she talked with us."

Ed laughs. "Together, we've painted her to a tee. Attractive face, ugly personality, and arrogant as all get out. Wonder why Dr. Holder didn't want to share more about her software development project. Most people love to brag about their accomplishments. D'you suppose she thinks we're secret agents for a rival software developer?"

"Doubt that. More like she decided we're too dumb to understand. And I certainly didn't buy her 'gee, who's that' act when I mentioned Andy Fyke. She knows exactly who he is. Fyke filed a complaint about her renters, and he's leading the effort to end rentals. Dr. Holder may be a computer genius, just like her mother boasted, but the professor's no actress. Bet she scared the crap out of her students."

"That's a safe bet. If I were a kid, I'd run from her class like a scalded cat," Ed comments as we reach his front yard.

"Come inside, and I'll treat you to lunch. At least, I hope my new recipe is a treat. We'll know in five minutes. That's when it's due out of the oven. I'm always happy to have unbiased testers."

"Ed, there's nothing I'd rather do. Your creations are spectacular, but I promised Andy Fyke I'd pop in the hospital to deliver a computer tablet. Robin texted she has one all set for delivery. I need to swing by the office and pick it up. With Andy's broken jaw and atrocious handwriting, he needs help pronto. Of course, playing delivery gal will give me a chance to ask Andy about his dealings with Dr. Holder."

Ed pulls a sad face. "Guess I'll have to lunch alone and rely on the missus for a recipe appraisal when she comes home from the pool. Let me know when you and Ted are free for dinner. Would love to have you over to meet the family. We plan to be here for two weeks."

"Can't imagine anyone turning down an invitation to dine with the star of the *Eats with Ed* TV show. I'll check when Ted's available. Promise."

* * *

The entrance to Beaufort Memorial Hospital is quieter than I expect on a holiday weekend. There are plenty of convenient parking spots and no ambulances queued to drop off ER patients. While the Fourth of July holiday isn't until Tuesday, Lowcountry vacationers tend to arrive early and start setting off fireworks as soon as they unpack. While many beach communities ban fireworks, it's legal to sell them throughout the state. I'm sure this hospital plans for the inevitable accidental burn cases.

The mid-summer celebration always puts the Coast Guard on high alert, too. Heavy boat traffic, inebriated skippers, and overconfident swimmers combine to ensure a heavy volume of calls for rescues and boat accident investigations.

Since I know Andy's room number, there's no need to stop at the reception area. This call is well within normal visiting hours.

Walking down the hall, I can tell the door to Andy's room is open. Oh, but he has company. Sherry LeRoy hunches over to study a clipboard in the patient's hands.

"Sorry, Andy, I just can't make out your writing," Sherry says.

"Sounds like I arrived in the nick of time."

I announce myself and hold up my gift. "Andy, I've got your loaner tablet, and our computer expert promises it's super simple to use. It'll let you type whatever you want to communicate."

"Oh, Kylee, thanks for coming." Sherry smiles. "It's really nice of you to provide a loaner."

That's when Sherry's smile slides into a grimace. She's noticed the damage to my face.

"It looks worse than it feels," I say. "Hey, I'm the victor. I successfully broke up a fight between two over-stimulated female combatants. Nothing to worry about."

Turning my attention to Andy, I give him a cheerful smile. Can't tell if he's glad to see me or not. Facial expressions are tough to interpret when a man has his jaws wired shut.

"Did you hear about that dreadful boat accident this morning?" Sherry asks. "The one that killed Steph Cloyd. It's really upset Andy and me. We both volunteer with FACE, and Steph was a real champion for the environment."

"I heard the news report," I answer. "A terrible waste."

I quickly change the subject. Don't want to give Sherry any hint I've been asked to poke around and see if Steph's death is something more sinister and tragic than an accident.

I offer Andy a few simple instructions on using the tablet. Once he's typed a few lines, I casually mention that I happened to run into another Rand Creek property owner this morning—a Dr. Holder.

Andy's reaction is immediate. His fingers practically punch through the tablet screen as he types. "THAT WITCH! I'LL STOP HER IF IT'S LAST THING I DO!"

Sherry pats Andy's arm. "Now, don't upset yourself. I'll give Kylee the lowdown on the foul doctor. Thank heavens she's a PhD and not a medical doctor, or none of us would be safe."

For the next five minutes, Sherry unloads nonstop about Dr. Holder. Here are the nuggets that stick in my brain. The bridge players' gossip is accurate. After Andy complained about Dr. Holder's renters damaging common property, the doc retaliated, calling Andy senile and suggesting he actually might have been responsible. While it's true Dr. Holder and Andy have never met face-to-face or communicated one-on-one, Dr. Holder absolutely knows who Andy is. No need to wrack her brain to place him.

Why did she bother to pretend when it's so easy to check the history?

Chapter Twenty-Six

Kylee

Saturday afternoon, July 1

I grab a takeout burger and fries at the nearest fast-food joint and call Donna while I'm wolfing down the meal in the parking lot.

"I should be at Satin Sands in thirty minutes," I tell her.

To forestall the shock that seems standard when friends first see my fresh bruises and eye-catching scratch, I give Donna an advance warning and assure her it's really nothing.

After she commiserates, the Satin Sands president instructs me to meet her at a beach launch area favored by the coastal rowers.

"Since Satin Sands doesn't have a gate, we attract a lot of coastal rowers," she explains. "This afternoon, members of Steph's rowing club and FACE friends are building a beachside tribute with shells and flowers. I want you to talk with Chad Norton, one of Steph's friends. He can fill you in on Steph's history with Bubba Quarles."

It takes a few minutes to find a parking spot near the beach. Along the shore, dozens of men and women wearing swimsuits and shorts have built a mountain of flowers. Given Donna's five-foot-one height, I worry about spotting her in the swarm. Good thing she has fiery red hair.

"Kylee, I'm over here," Donna hollers and motions for me to join her. "Been watching for you."

My friend hugs me. While an impish grin usually creases Donna's freckled face, there's no hint of a smile today. The tracks of recent tears mark her plump cheeks.

As soon as Donna releases me, she introduces the tall, lanky man towering over her. "Kylee Kane, meet Chad Norton, Steph Cloyd's best friend and rowing buddy."

A ball cap shades the top half of Chad's tanned face. Can't tell whether his light eyes are gray, green, or blue. Whatever the color, his swollen eyelids attest to recent tears.

"I'm so sorry for your loss."

As I voice my condolences—a phrase I've repeated far too many times—I feel the inadequacy of the words.

Chad dips his head in acknowledgment. "It's too late to save Steph. But I'm determined Bubba Quarles will pay for my friend's murder. His death can't be called anything else."

Surprised, I frown. "Has Quarles been positively identified as the hit-and-run boater? Did he turn himself in?"

Hadn't heard any updates on the radio.

"No," Chad admits. "But I know it's Bubba. Steph had a run-in with that raving lunatic four weeks ago. Bubba's boat came screaming around a bend and capsized Steph. The redneck's got a four-hundred-horsepower motor mounted on the back of a fishing boat that probably cost three times more than the rusting trailer he calls home.

"What did Bubba do when Steph went in the water? He drove his boat in circles around him. Creating waves and chop to prevent Steph from righting his shell. Whole time, Bubba was laughing hysterically. Yelled, 'Come and get it, gators! Fancy pants on the menu.'"

Chad shakes his head. "Steph reported Bubba, but since he had no evidence to corroborate his story, the guy only got a warning."

"I understand why you suspect Bubba," I reply. "Yet, from my Coast Guard days, I can safely say he isn't the only careless showboater gunning a fishing boat in these narrow inlets."

Chad sighs. "You're right. Believe me, as a rower, I've run into plenty of idiots with a hundred times more horsepower than brain cells. But, just last week, Bubba threatened Steph again. Told him his days were numbered for snitching and reporting him for fire violations. Said he'd add Steph with the other trash to his next burn pile. Just waiting for the right opportunity."

"Did Steph report the threat to the Sheriff's Department?" I ask.

Chad takes off his cap and runs his fingers through his hair. "No, given what happened the last time, he didn't see the point. But Steph told me, because he wanted someone to know about the threat in case anything happened to him.

"I told all of this to a deputy this morning. He discounted it. Said people posture and make threats all the time to scare people. Doesn't mean they ever plan to act on them."

Sounds like Deputy Do-Wrong, aka Nick Ibsen. Judging others by his own bluster. Can't believe I ever dated the man, no matter how briefly.

"Chad, I'm sure the authorities will pay Quarles a visit and look for damage to his boat."

"Lot of good that'll do," Chad replies. "I know where Bubba lives. So, another rower and I went to check out his dock. His motorboat is gone, nowhere to be seen. An inflatable dinghy is tied to the dock where the motorboat normally sits.

"Bubba was sitting on his dock, a shotgun in his lap. As soon as he spotted us, he raised the gun and started yelling obscenities. Told us to get the hell away, that the water near his dock was private property. Private, my ass. These tributaries are all public property."

"What do you think happened to the boat? The authorities should be able to get a warrant."

"Maybe they will, maybe they won't," Chad answers. "My guess is the boat was damaged in the crash, and Bubba stashed it somewhere for the time being. If deputies come by, he'll claim the boat sunk or some bull crap. Once again, no one will be able to prove otherwise."

"Not necessarily," I say. "I checked with Coast Guard friends this morning. They didn't have satellite imagery of the area at the time of the crash, but it's possible future fly-overs can locate the boat."

I pause. "You seem certain Bubba planned the attack. That it wasn't a chance meeting. How would Bubba know where and when to stage it?"

"Nobody's more predictable than Steph. Barring bad weather, he rowed out every morning. Followed the same course every day, starting at dawn. Liked to get his exercise in before any possible interruptions."

"Can you help?" Chad's fingers twist the ball cap in his hand. "Donna says you've helped solve crimes before when nobody with a badge seemed to care."

"I'll do what I can," I say, "but, as you note, I don't have a badge. That severely limits my investigative options. However, what I do have are a number of talented friends and dogged determination. How can I reach you if I have more questions?"

I tuck Chad's business card in my pocket, and he returns to the group, mourning Steph's death and sharing memories of better days.

Donna walks me to my car. "Thanks, Kylee. Couldn't let this drop, knowing how Nick Ibsen's biases can distort investigations. But I realize you aren't eager to start a turf battle with the Sheriff's Office. If you find evidence, I'll be happy to act as a go-between."

I smile. "You're right. I prefer to stay as far away from Nick as possible. While he's not the sheriff—thank heavens—he's done his best to poison fellow officers' opinions about me and Ted. Glad I haven't needed to deal with the authorities this year.

"That may have to change, though," I add. "Yesterday, when I asked for a Cliff's Notes summary on HOA rental controversies, I didn't mention a possible connection to a crime. Andy Fyke is the fellow leading the Rand Creek charge to ban rentals. Thursday, he was badly injured in a fall down a flight of stairs. While he has zero recall of how he fell, my gut tells me he was pushed."

"Got any suspects?" Donna asks.

"Not really. Andy's friends nominated a few Rand Creek owners who rent properties. Based on our prior conversation, you won't be surprised to hear Jocelyn headed the list. They also mentioned a realtor, Xander Pringle, and an Amanda Holder, a high-tech software developer. I understand that these folks are foes. Yet, it's hard to believe any of them would risk physically attacking someone over a little rental income."

Donna frowns. "You say they mentioned an Amanda Holder? Dr. Amanda Holder? Now there's a coincidence. A few months ago, Dr. Holder bought a Satin Sands house for a steal. The sellers wanted to unload it quickly since they live out of town. They were preoccupied with finding a good nursing home for their dad. He'd lived in the house for at least a decade."

I nod. "Sounds like the doc definitely has a vested interest in rentals. Have you met her?"

"Sure have," Donna answers. "She contacted me about updating Satin Sands software. Said she noticed some glitches, and, since she was a new owner, she'd help out for practically nothing."

I frown. "Didn't Robin just finish updating your software?"

"Yes, Dr. Holder made the offer before we signed off on the Welch HOA contract."

I cock an eyebrow. "Hey, I realize you count Ted and me as friends, but I know you'll jump at any opportunity to save Satin Sands money. Why didn't you take Holder up on her proposition?"

"Well...Steph strongly recommended we pass," Donna adds. "He wouldn't say what he knew or how he knew it, but Steph said he had a solid reason to oppose giving the woman access to our data.

"I didn't press Steph for details, because he was clearly uncomfortable," she continues. "Prompted me to do my own checking. Dr. Holder had bragged about her computer research at a New York university. Since I knew Steph's brother, Aaron, was a prof up north, I looked up Aaron's bio, then checked the faculty roster. Sure enough, Aaron and Amanda taught at the same university. I decided Aaron talked out of school and warned his brother against any association with the ex-professor.

"Plus, there was something strange about Dr. Holder's departure from academia. A year ago January, the school profiled Holder, making a big deal out of the fact she'd be teaching a course in Artificial Intelligence the next semester. A month later, she moved to Beaufort County. I bet she was sacked. While I don't know why, Steph thought it serious enough to pass on her offer."

Interesting, but probably unrelated.

I shrug. "Who knows? Could be Holder got fed up with the bureaucracy and quit. Or if she did get canned, it might have been for boinking a student. Whatever the infraction, it doesn't move her up the suspect list as Andy's attacker."

We've reached my Camry, and I give Donna a farewell hug. "Take care. I'll call if I find any hard evidence this Bubba Quarles is the hit-and-run boater who killed Steph."

Chapter Twenty-Seven

Kylee

Saturday afternoon, July 1

I t's Saturday afternoon. Why on earth am I inside the Welch HOA office staring at a computer screen. I thought when I retired, I'd be spending sunny days however I pleased. Taking a dip in the ocean. Sailing the River Rat up and down the Intercoastal. Reading a good mystery in a hammock.

But, no, here I am, cooped up in a stuffy office with anemic air-conditioning and windows painted shut.

Can't blame anyone but my obsessive self. Hand me a mystery, and I can't stop tugging at it. Did the same when I was a kid. Had to put the puzzle together, even if our dog, Brownie, chewed half the puzzle pieces into pasteboard mush.

I open the account Welch HOA keeps to do background checks on prospective employees and vendors. When I plug in the name Bubba Quarles with Beaufort, South Carolina, as a location, I get two hits. As Kay Barrett suspected, Bubba Quarles, Sr., is a jailbird. That makes Jr. my pigeon.

Oh, my, Bubba, you're almost as well acquainted with law enforcement as your dad.

While Bubba hasn't spent serious time in jail, he's been hauled in three times on drunk and disorderly charges, plus a more serious domestic violence beef. Too bad Bubba's ex-wife ultimately refused to testify. No doubt due to threats. His ex quickly left the county. Smart move.

After a few more clicks, I have a picture of Bubba's shaky finances. Six different construction companies have employed him, but he hasn't lasted at any job for more than four months. Currently unemployed, he owes back taxes on his property, and at least one of his payday loans is in default. Other than a deed to the couple acres of marshland his father signed over when he left for prison, Bubba's possessions include an aged trailer, multiple guns (he does have a hunting license), and a three-year-old motorboat.

I jot down Bubba's address along with the motorboat's make, twenty-four-foot length, engine manufacturer, and hull color. The model is advertised as being able to maneuver in relatively shallow water.

I know how Grant and Mimi planned to spend this Saturday. Loafing at the beach. Probably dividing time between body surfing Hullis Island's minuscule waves and roasting in the sun. I frequently remind them to lather up with sunscreen. The warnings tend to trigger eye rolls from both teens. While I hope they're not blistered, maybe they've had enough rays and are tired of the holiday crowds. Think I'll invite them on a boat ride.

Grant answers his cell on the fourth ring. "Hey, Aunt Kylee, what's up? You know it's Saturday, right? Now that you're working with Dad, I get nervous if you phone when I'm off the clock."

"Well, it's mid-afternoon," I reply. "So, asking a small favor doesn't really count as ruining your day off, does it?"

"Shouldn't have answered." Grant sighs. "What's the favor?"

"I'd like you and Mimi to join me for a short sail. I'll provide cold drinks and snacks."

"Un, huh, what's the catch?"

"You need to bring your drone for a little aerial reconnaissance."

"Heck, that's not a deal breaker. You know I like to fly it. Let me talk to Mimi."

I wait while Grant puts the proposition to his girlfriend.

"Mimi wants to know if the photography has something to do with Andy

Fyke," Grant says.

"No, but it's for a good cause."

"Okay, we need an hour. Meet you at the marina."

When I get to my boat, the River Rat, I'll map out the best route for our cruise. The tributary that skirts Bubba's property is too shallow for my sailboat. Can't chance my keel running aground. Need to find a deeper finger that runs parallel to Bubba's creek. With the drone's range, Grant can do a flyover from a fair distance.

A distance that's beyond the range of the redneck's shotgun.

Where would Bubba hide his stinkpot? Stinkpot being the derogatory term we sailing snobs apply to motorboats.

Bubba must have stashed it quickly. My guess is he beached it in a marshy area and covered it with palm fronds as camouflage. Since it appears to be the man's most expensive and prized possession, I'm betting it's stowed close by. He'd want it near enough to know if anyone messed with it.

Since I'm fifteen minutes from the marina and Grant and Mimi won't be there for an hour, I have forty-five minutes to kill. Might as well do a little more background research.

I enter Amanda Holder's name and her Lighthouse Cove address. No arrests for the lady—not even a speeding ticket. Interesting that she got a concealed carry permit as soon as she moved to South Carolina. Wouldn't imagine it being high on to-do lists for most folks who work out of their homes.

The doc's finances are solid. However, she's mortgaged the Lighthouse Cove mansion. Probably to fund her recent real estate splurges. The LLC she created owns four rental properties—one in Rand Creek, one in Satin Sands, and two on Hullis Island. For some reason, the Rand Creek condo she inherited from her mother remains in her name.

I copy the addresses of all five properties. Wonder how Frank and Mom will feel when they learn the mysterious doctor owns a Hullis Island rental just up the block from Frank's house.

Maybe worth a stroll after dinner to check it out.

After I finish the background check, I conduct a more sweeping online search with Amanda Holder and Artificial Intelligence as keywords. Too many hits to even begin to read them all. The doc apparently wasn't BS-ing about her celebrity in the Artificial Intelligence field. Lots of technical papers under her name. And she was once a publicity hound. Granted interviews to a dozen reporters covering AI advances and potential applications.

Interesting.

I bookmark several lengthy interviews to read later. Time to head to the River Rat.

Chapter Twenty-Eight

The Chameleon

Saturday late afternoon, July 1

I jerk awake with a start. Feel groggy, grungy. Naps never leave me feeling refreshed. I put my feet up for a sec when my unwanted company departed, and, bam, fell sound asleep. Shouldn't work so late at night, but hate to quit when I'm making excellent progress.

I yawn and stretch. Must say Lighthouse Cove's peace and quiet is a nice change from Manhattan's cacophony.

Yip, yip, yip.

Dammit. That's what woke me. Ear-splitting, high-pitched barks from Leona's ugly mongrel. Will arrange for Mr. Grimm to visit Leona tonight. Make him sound downright hysterical that she needs to flee Lighthouse Cove with precious little Ginger in tow.

As I push up from the easy chair, I glance at the oil painting of Dad that hangs over the fireplace. Mom commissioned an artist to paint it ten years after he died. Dad was maybe thirty in the photo the painter used as a reference. The portrait looks nothing like the father I remember. The one I begged not to die and leave me alone with Mom. Missing from the portrait are the extra thirty pounds around Dad's waist, the jowls that hung over his shirt collar, and the defeated look in his eyes.

I loved him. I was Daddy's little darling. The year after he died, I'd sneak to his grave whenever I could to tell him my dreams, my plans. The ones I never bothered to tell my self-absorbed mother.

Mother never asked what I thought or felt. Don't think she ever forgave me for inheriting Dad's build—tall, big-boned, broad-shouldered. She'd wanted a little girl who shared her petite, pixie physique. Unable to promote me as her China doll, she settled for bragging on my brain power. A straight-A prodigy she could tell friends about while hiding me away at private girls' schools.

Months ago, when I recalled the comfort my one-way graveside conversations once gave me, I realized Artificial Intelligence could deliver even greater peace. It could resurrect the dead. I had the power to restore Dad's vanished voice and reclaim his soul. Now, when I'm lonely at night, I speak to my father, and he answers.

I captured his voice from 8 mm reels and digital videos of family outings. Sure, deep down, I realize when Dad answers me, it's because I've pre-programmed his responses. The conversations still comfort me. A warm affirmation I remain his darling Wunderkind.

Because Dad's business partner insisted the company purchase mega key-man insurance policies, Mom never needed to do a lick of work her entire life. Dad's death didn't interfere with her bridge, golf outings, or afternoon teas. Plus, she had the money to send me away to private schools and off to summer camps.

Dad's death convinced me to grab any pleasure I want whenever I can. A lesson gleaned from the contrast between my father's face at thirty and his sad demeanor before he died. Life is short. Why make it hard? My epitome was strongly reinforced by my university colleagues and Ayn Rand.

I'm not wicked. I'm an Objectivist. The twin events of my university fall from grace, and Mom's simultaneous death plunked me into unfamiliar Lowcountry surroundings. No friends and nothing to do but fume. My so-called university colleagues vanished with my rebuke. Not a single one phoned to commiserate—even the ones I'm sure howled with laughter at my video prank.

That's when I noticed Ayn Rand's *Atlas Shrugged* on Mom's bedside table.

Her book club had been reading controversial classics. Before I started that novel, I had only a vague recollection of what made Rand controversial.

Once I devoured *Atlas Shrugged*, I read everything I could find about Rand's Objectivism philosophy. Suddenly, my funk evaporated. Screw those gowned university deans, who like to dress in ceremonial robes and act like tribunal priests certain of their righteousness.

It was as if Ayn Rand were speaking to me from the grave, telling me my happiness was my sole moral purpose. I memorized several of her quotes and recite them every morning when I wake. My very favorite? "There are no evil thoughts except one: the refusal to think."

I now see I'm part of the natural objective, a catalyst. I let my imagination picture possibilities. Like my life minus Leona and her mutt.

If I happen to share visions of death and destruction with individuals who make them real, it's on them. Their decision to kill or maim. Not mine. I didn't push Fyke down the stairs. J.T. did.

I think about my other interactions. The little game I'm playing with Leona may even be beneficial. She'll believe her husband's love extended beyond the veil, and he labored to return and save her and the damnable yapper.

Time to concentrate on J.T. What would prompt her to confess and then pull the plug? Should I resurrect my avatar who convinced her Fyke was a child molester? It's a bit risky, but it would certainly be easier than getting J.T. to bond quickly with a new online friend.

I can blame the sudden disappearance of J.T.'s buddy on identity theft. The thief took over the identity of J.T.'s friend and locked the online companion out of her internet accounts.

I have an epiphany. The old friend will suggest authorities are hot on J.T.'s trail. She'll bemoan the horrible publicity certain to accompany J.T.'s eventual trial. Just need to stress how news coverage will scar J.T.'s children and plague them the rest of their lives.

Chapter Twenty-Nine

Grant

Saturday late afternoon, July 1

I spot Aunt Kylee top side, polishing the River Rat's trim as she waits for Mimi and me. My aunt seems to lack an off button. Wouldn't exactly diagnose Kylee as hyper but she seems happiest if she can avoid sitting still for long periods. And, if she is sitting, her brain's on speed.

It was a little weird at first, when Dad and Kylee hooked up. What with me thinking of Kylee's mother as Grandma, it felt kind of like Dad was dating his sister.

Stupid. They're not blood relatives. I'm over it. They both seem happy, though Aunt Kylee still squirms if Dad attempts a lip-lock when I'm in the room.

Puzzles me how Dad could fall in love with polar opposites. Kylee never wears makeup, and she dresses for comfort. She prefers pizza parlors to fancy restaurants, and she loves outdoor adventures. My mother's another story.

Admittedly, I don't see much of Mom since the divorce and her marriage to His Honorable Moneybags. Still, even when Mom and Dad were hitched, it practically took a bomb threat to force her out of air-conditioned luxury. And she always kept Dad and me waiting while she put on her face.

I knew both Mom and Dad were unhappy long before the divorce. The breakup was sort of a relief. Glad they both moved on to happier places.

Since I'm carrying my big drone and related paraphernalia, it's impossible for Mimi and me to walk side-by-side down the pier.

"Lead the way, Mimi," I suggest. The bonus? A nice view of Mimi's tan legs from sandals to her bikini bottom.

"Hey, thanks for coming," Aunt Kylee says as she welcomes Mimi onboard. "Hope I didn't spoil your day off."

Mimi tries not to shudder when she sees the beating Kylee's face took last night. Dad texted me about the Marshview fiasco, and I told Mimi what to expect.

Kylee smiles at Mimi. "Yeah, I know. Maybe I should have you show me how to cover up the bruises with a little makeup."

"It's not that bad," Mimi lies.

After a strained pause, Mimi assures my aunt she isn't spoiling our fun.

"The beach was packed, and we were about to leave anyway," she adds. "Besides, I love sailing with you. Brought my camera, too. May get a chance for some unique views of marsh birds in their habitat."

"Hi, Aunt Kylee," I say as I hop down to the River Rat's wide deck.

I chuckle. "At least this time around, my drone reconnaissance will be under the watchful eyes of an investigator who packs heat. You have your Glock handy, right?"

Kylee doesn't laugh. My joke seems to fall flat.

She frowns. "The man we're investigating was last seen sitting on his dock with a shotgun in his lap. But I mapped out a water route that should prevent Bubba from ever seeing the River Rat, and even if he does, we'll be safely out of shotgun range."

"Do you want the drone to take pictures of this guy?" I ask.

"No, I don't need photos of Bubba. Already have access to his mug shots, and he's not my type for a pin-up poster. Steph Cloyd's friends think Bubba Quarles used his souped-up motorboat to mow down Steph's rowing shell and murder him. When the shell split, the motorboat's blades finished the job. Bubba, or whoever was driving the boat, left and never called the authorities. I doubt Steph could have been saved, but we'll never know."

Mimi and I are shocked silent. "How horrible," Mimi finally murmurs.

Kylee nods. "If Bubba's smart—a big question—he didn't stash his damaged boat within sight of his property. But he's lived in these backwaters forever. Knows all the hummocks and feeder streams. Steph was killed at high tide. So, if Bubba did it, I'm betting he high-tailed it to a marshy area that can only be reached by water at high tide."

I interrupt. "Wait a sec. If Bubba abandoned the boat at high tide, how'd he get back to his house? He couldn't walk."

Aunt Kylee nods. "Steph's friend Chad checked out Bubba's dock shortly after the body was discovered. A blow-up dinghy was tied to the dock in the motorboat's usual spot. When Bubba scuttled the stinkpot, he might have towed the dinghy along to paddle back home."

"Did the Sheriff's Office fly the area to check for the boat?" Mimi asks.

Kylee shakes her head. "When Donna spoke with Deputy Do-Wrong, he said their priority this busy holiday weekend had to be beach air patrols."

I start unpacking my drone. "Okay, let's go find Bubba's boat. Not that the Sheriff's Office will jump for joy if Welch HOA Management solves another crime while the deputies are sucking their thumbs."

"You're right about that."

I think about asking to captain the boat, but when I see the heavy traffic on the Beaufort River, I change my mind. The river's not as crowded as it will be when the annual Beaufort Waterfront Festival gets underway, but it's plenty busy.

Tough to dodge jet-skis, kayaks, and boats of every description. Even worse, the locals who party on river sandbars sometimes knock back a few too many and take siestas on floats. While they're snoozing, they can accidentally drift into boat lanes. Hard to see.

After I ready my drone, Mimi and I sit in the bow to scan for debris—and floaters (hopefully, live ones)—to give Aunt Kylee an early heads-up.

Glancing back at our captain, I try to imagine what she looked like when she was my age. Dad told me he had a crush on Kylee even then. Since her hair turned white before I was even born, I've always thought of her as older. But she never seems to age much. Just a few more crow's feet around her eyes.

She's always been up for any outdoor activity I wanted to try—hiking, skiing, skeet. Well, there was the one rollerblade fiasco. First time out, my aunt complained her stupid protection pads were cutting off circulation in her legs. I pointed and laughed. "No wonder. You mixed up and Velcroed the elbow pads around your knees. The knee pads are on your arms."

The great thing is Aunt Kylee hooted at her screw-up. She may be over fifty, but she hasn't lost her sense of humor or her taste for fun.

Once we leave the busy river, we head up a tributary with lots of bends, but it's apparently plenty deep. Kylee is keeping an eye on her depth gauge to make sure the River Rat's keel won't get stuck.

"Oh, my God," Mimi exclaims. "We have to stop!"

"What's wrong?" Kylee asks.

"Oh, sorry to scare you. Nothing's wrong," Mimi answers. "Just spotted a pair of Black Rails with four chicks. Can't believe my luck. The chicks are hardly ever seen. Have to shoot some photos."

"Sure, we can idle," Kylee replies. "If Bubba dumped his boat, he won't be moving it anytime soon. Hope our presence doesn't cause your birds to fly off before you get some pictures."

"They won't," Mimi answers. "Black Rails are called ghost birds. Very secretive. The South Carolina coast is one of the only places the endangered species still nests. They won't abandon their chicks."

Mimi grabs my arm and focuses my attention up the bank to a stand of marsh grass almost parallel with our shoulders as we stand on the deck. "Do you see them?"

"Nope," I answer.

"The chicks are all black. The adult's upper back is kind of rust-colored; the rest of the feathers are grayish with white speckles. They're tiny and spend far more time darting around the pluff mud than in the air.

"When we get really high tides, and their nests get submerged, the birds have to swim until the water recedes. Climate change and rising tides are destroying a lot of Black Rail habitat."

"Hey, I see them," I whisper, even though Mimi doesn't think us being so close will make them fly off. "Wow, their eyes are red."

Kylee and I watch as Mimi changes camera lenses and takes a series of close-ups.

She smiles. "Think I have all I need. Thanks for waiting."

"No problem," Kylee says. "It's July. The tide's high, and we've got plenty of light. Sun won't set until eight-thirty or so."

"Yeah, but Grandma Kane is expecting us for supper at six—and my stomach's already growling."

Kylee smiles. "I left a phone message for Mom, explaining why we'll be late and asking for her to plan on serving dinner a little later. She'll understand. Plus, I stocked up on snacks. They're below deck whenever you start to feel faint."

Chapter Thirty

Kylee

Saturday late afternoon, July 1

I spread out a map and show Grant where we're anchored. Then I outline the perimeter of the marsh area where I suspect Bubba might have stashed his boat.

"What kind of range do you have?" I ask

"With this new model, about seven miles, and I have forty minutes of air time. No problem scouting this whole area."

"Sounds good," I say. "Don't expect to see a whole boat. If Bubba is hiding his stinkpot, it's probably draped with palm fronds—maybe even camouflage netting. The boat's twenty-four feet long, and I expect he won't have totally covered its bright white hull."

"Okay."

Given the relatively small screen on Grant's drone control console, I avoid the temptation to peer over his shoulder. Since Mimi's happily watching for birds, I decide to occupy myself reading some of the Dr. Holder interviews and articles I downloaded.

Wow. Dr. Holder has little patience with interviewers who aren't grounded in the whole alphabet soup of tech abbreviations. When asked what GPT stands for, the doc's curt response—Generative Pretrained Transformer—seemed to imply anyone stupid enough to ask didn't deserve any added explanation. I pity the poor reporter. If she's like me, Generative Pretrained Transformer leaves me no clue about how GPT actually works.

Ha! In contrast to the short shrift given to explaining how AI works, Dr. Holder becomes almost erudite, describing rosy scenarios for AI's future. She predicts it will help battle climate change, save endangered animals from extinction, and make workers more productive.

As an example, she suggests AI will handle all online support in the near future. "And the AI helpers will answer questions in the caller's native language. Callers will no longer have to decipher the heavy accents of support workers in some foreign cesspool."

Dr. Holder scoffs at the notion the U.S. government should place restraints on AI development or use. "Every technology can be used for good or evil. You can't stop advancing. Someone will keep improving capabilities even if our government tries to straight-jacket the industry. Better that we pull ahead of China and Russia."

I get her point, but it doesn't erase my fear that AI will be used to target and dupe segments of the population into believing almost anything. In 1938, Orson Welles' radio broadcast panicked listeners into believing Martians had invaded the U.S. Just imagine how many more people could be suckered by cinematic newscasts featuring deepfake images of the U.S. president or the Pope being taken prisoner by those aliens.

The internet's already awash with deepfakes of politicians "saying" things they'd never say, while fake porn features not only celebrities but unknowing teens. The faces and bodies of naïve innocents who pose for friends are easy to capture. Producers are even talking about making movies starring long-dead actors. Elvis may indeed live again.

"I think I've spotted something," Grant says. "Come see."

I jump up to take a look at his console. Below crisscrossed palm fronds, the bright sun reflects on blinding patches of white. Whatever object is beached on this marshy hillock, it's definitely manmade. A little more than twenty feet behind the dazzling white splotches, I spot the ebony sheen of the molded motor casing. Has to be Bubba's motorboat.

"Great job. Think that's it. When you get back home, can you make a copy of that image with a time stamp and the GPS coordinates?"

I step away to give Grant some elbow room.

"Sure," he answers. "First, I'd like to fly just a little bit closer to Bubba's dock. Want to try for a wide-angle shot that'll show the beached boat's relationship to the dock. That could help authorities figure out which channels provide the best route for a salvage effort.

"Oh, shit! I see the cracker. The drone's closer than I intended. Bubba's still sitting on his dock, and he's raised his gun. Oh, no."

By the time I rush back to Grant and get an over-the-shoulder peek at his controller, the screen has gone black.

"Did he shoot it down?"

Grant swears. "Must have. The drone was within control range and had plenty of flight time left. I can hear Dad now. When I talked him into a more expensive model, I kidded, 'What are the odds some new terrorist will destroy my second drone?'"

"My fault." I sigh. "I'll tell your father and spring for a replacement. What about the pictures? Are they lost?"

Grant chews on his bottom lip as he considers. "Afraid so. During flight, the drone stores all images on a memory stick for later download. But I noted the GPS coordinates when the drone went down. Maybe we can salvage it if it landed in marsh grass and didn't sink."

"Would the images survive?" I ask

Grant shrugs. "Don't know. Depends. The images will be fine if no water gets inside the drive. Say, you know it's a felony to shoot down a drone. Even hobbyist drones are considered aircraft, and the charges of downing one are the same as attacking a 747. Maybe this Bubba can be jailed for that, too."

"Even if we recover the drone and the damage indicates it was downed by a bullet, we'd still need to prove Bubba was the shooter. If the last drone photo of Bubba raising his shotgun was destroyed, there's no hard evidence."

"Are we going to try and salvage it now?" Mimi asks.

I shake my head. "Can't tonight. The tide is starting to go out, and the River Rat has too deep a draft. We might be able to recruit help from one of the coastal rowers. But if Bubba's shotgun had enough reach to down the drone, it could pick off anyone he spots trying to retrieve it."

"Hey, maybe we can interest a Special Ops team in a nighttime mission," Grant jokes.

Chapter Thirty-One

The Chameleon

Saturday late afternoon, July 1

H *as to be Kylee Kane. Dammit.*
　　As soon as I powered up my computer, I received five alerts. They came from traps I'd requested at sites with sensitive information. Unfortunately, even I can't make some internet information disappear—at least not without creating bigger problems.

Since my little noon tete-a-tete with Kylee Kane, someone has checked my credit, banking, tax, concealed carry permit, and voting records. They also accessed info about my employment history, college degrees, and the university classes I taught.

Every one of my real profiles on platforms from Linked In to Instagram has new hits. Not to mention more downloads of papers I've authored and articles quoting me as an AI expert.

This has to stop! Time to turn the tables.

It takes less than an hour to compile an in-depth portrait of Kylee Kane.

The snoop is a retired Coast Guard investigator. *Crap.* Her marine and boating knowledge may mean Bubba's even more likely to get his ass handed to him for fleeing after his motor blades turned Steph into human sushi.

The good news is the snoop has enemies. News stories from last year reveal the woman and Welch HOA Management have few friends in the

Sheriff's Department or in Ernie Baker's right-wing media empire. Perhaps one of Ernie's TV talk show hosts can be persuaded to air creative deepfake videos that raise serious questions about unethical Welch HOA management practices.

Ha! I laugh when I see the Earful posts that show how the snoop got her almost-shiner and decorative cheek scratch. More than one attendee videoed the wrestling match at the Marshview HOA meeting. The investigator's apparently not afraid to mix it up. Jump into the fray.

Could I take her? She's what—five-foot-six at most? Looks fit. But so am I. I'm three-plus inches taller, and, I dare say, have more muscle mass. I should, for God's sake. Work at it enough. My nemesis doesn't look like she lifts weights. A runner, maybe? Not a lot of extra fat.

I replay the portion of the video where Kylee displays some fancy maneuvers to immobilize the bigger woman. On the basis of size alone, the snoop's opponent should have had the upper hand. If it should ever come to a physical confrontation, I know what not to do. Give her zero chance to use some martial arts crap. Take her out quickly from a distance.

I move on from assessing the snoop's strengths and weaknesses to looking at her family. The mother, Myrtle Kane, appears a particularly inviting target. The old lady got herself appointed to the Hullis Island HOA board last fall when a bunch of scaredy-cats resigned.

Some long-time residents are now skewering Myrtle as a turncoat. If the HOA is indeed poised to impose a slew of new restrictions, they think she has to be in on it.

Myrtle has hold-over enemies from last year, too. The directors who resigned—and their friends—resent Myrtle and the other appointed, un-elected replacements.

Potential there.

Might have an angle of attack on Myrtle's morals, too. Since an arsonist burned her house to the ground, she's been shacking up with widower Frank Donahue. *Tut. Tut.*

Myrtle's Facebook page tells me plenty about her extended "family." Posts of candid photos reveal just how close Myrtle and daughter Kylee are with the Welch men—Ted and his son, Grant. Should either Welch male become the subject of a smear campaign, I imagine Kylee would walk over burning coals to defend them.

Wonder if deepfake sexcapades could raise concerns about Ted harassing female clients or employees. Or maybe I could make it look like Grant uses or sells drugs. I'm sure the Citadel would then investigate the cadet for violating the school's honor code.

Anticipating some creative fun with the Kane and Welch households, I gleefully shut down the computer to take an exercise break. Since the investigator seems so eager to target me, I'll return the favor. Maybe I can even fine-tune features of my soon-to-debut killer app while I toy with my real-world headaches.

* * *

Sweaty from my workout, I relish the shower's soothing massage. New ideas and forgotten tasks often pop into my head in the shower. Guess it's the relaxation. I spent so much time pondering how to screw with Kylee's fate, I haven't made my daily check of rental properties. A neglect I'll remedy as soon as I towel off.

What do you know? One of my Hullis Island rentals is vacant. This one is practically across the street from Frank Donahue's house and his *roommate*, Myrtle Kane.

The couple who rented it for the Fourth of July holiday checked out early. A death in the family. Naturally, they won't get a refund. My contract's crystal clear. You rent for a week; you pay for a week. This is an unexpected bonus: I'll move in for a few days.

A stroll around Old Lady Kane's neighborhood may help me gauge Hullis Island owner sentiment. Maybe I can identify new ways to stir HOA animosity and keep the snoop and her fellow Welch busybodies fretting over something other than Andy Fyke's tumble or Steph Cloyd's death. Since I'll be in close proximity, maybe I'll hack Frank Donahue's Wi-Fi. My hunch is his password will be as simple-minded as Leona's. Her doggone password?

Ginger.

I have a few more online tasks before I can pack for my Hullis Island reconnaissance. First, I re-establish contact with J.T., texting from a new burner phone. My explanation for the recent silence? I apologize, saying someone stole my identity.

J.T. immediately responds, telling me she did what I suggested, what I was physically unable to do. She pushed Andy down the stairs.

"What?" I make sure I sound incredulous. "Why on earth would you think I suggested physically attacking the man?"

After J.T. regurgitates how I prodded her to do the deed, I deny everything. "Must have been that horrible identity thief. I'd never condone violence."

I stop short of hinting J.T. could make the whole mess go away by committing suicide. Postpone that for another installment.

Next, I contact Bubba, posing as his nativist gal pal, the one who provided details for his successful attack on Steph. Important to keep tabs on this nut job.

Finally, I spend a bit of time monitoring what these two minions have been blabbing about in their *private* social groups. J.T.'s been silent, incommunicado. Remorse? Hope so. I can work on that.

Bubba's a different story. He never knows when to shut his trap. He's bragged to his RebSocial buddies about shooting down a drone flying in the vicinity of his dock—a federal offense.

Bubba seems clueless about potential criminal charges, but knowing the penalties wouldn't faze him. He's certain no one can prove he did it. If he hadn't bragged online, he might be right.

My guess is the drone's owner—whoever that might be—was trying to locate Bubba's damaged motorboat. Bubba thinks he can play hide-and-seek until the authorities lose interest. With help from his pals, the simpleton believes he can make needed repairs without visiting a shop. Maybe yes, maybe no.

I'd sure like to know who owns the downed drone. The Coast Guard? The Sheriff's Office? A private citizen?

I shut down my laptop and make a packing list. Can't afford to forget some tech necessity. Hullis Island sits over twenty miles from what passes for Lowcountry civilization—primarily grocery stores, gift shops crammed with tourist trinkets, and restaurants.

When I left my Manhattan loft, I had to adjust to my diminished dining and entertainment options. In New York City, my friends and I could dine in a five-star restaurant at midnight after a Broadway show.

Friends...ha. They're gone, too.

Think I'll pick up some takeout en route to Hullis Island. While Beaufort may not have Manhattan's rich culinary variety, the locals do excel at shrimp and grits. True, the grits part sounds God-awful, but sufficient cheese camouflages the peasant fare.

Chapter Thirty-Two

Grant

Saturday, July 1, early evening

"About time you got here," Grandma Kane scolds. "Everyone's hungry. Even caught Frank sneaking into the kitchen to forage. You'd think I'm starving our dinner guests to death. A dozen deviled eggs have disappeared."

I laugh. "You'd have been down a dozen deviled eggs by now if we'd gotten here at six. I'd have disappeared six all by myself."

"Be that as it may, go wash up. It's time to ring the dinner bell."

I don't argue about washing up, even though Mimi, Aunt Kylee, and I all took turns below the River Rat's deck scrubbing off sweat and sunscreen and putting on clean clothes. I notice Aunt Kylee hustling down the hall to the bathroom in Frank's master bedroom. If she's reluctant to protest her mom's wash-up command, I figure it's not worth it. I do notice that Mimi somehow escaped Grandma Myrtle's decree.

Hands washed, I head back toward the chatter. Apparently, we're eating on Frank's screened porch. While there's a nice ocean breeze, I sort of hate to leave the air-conditioning after spending the day in the sun. Usually, it's my job to carry dishes to the table, but tonight, others have taken up the slack. Maybe Grandma wasn't kidding about people complaining they were on the edge of starvation.

This is the summer's second Welch company dinner. Since Mimi and Robin are the only extras, it's not all that different from a family meal. With Grandma Kane and Frank living together, he counts as family.

The food smells fantastic. When Grandma Kane announced she was planning an early July 4 celebration for the whole crew at Welch HOA Management, she said it would be an informal grab and growl. I'm happy to see how much there is to grab—deviled eggs, barbecue, potato and pasta salads, baked beans, and coleslaw. Pitchers of iced tea for everyone. Unsweetened, since that's what Grandma grew up with in Iowa.

I know there's dessert, too. Spied it on my way to the table—cheesecake with strawberries and blueberries, Grandma's annual salute to the patriotic red, white, and blue.

Aunt Kylee and I are the last to sit down. I'm seated between Mimi and Robin and across the table from Dad and Aunt Kylee. As soon as our butts touch the chairs, Grandma clears her throat and raises her iced tea glass. "To a happy Fourth of July—dig in!"

I smile, thinking she sounds like she's ordering race car drivers to start their engines.

I'm not surprised that Grandma forgoes saying grace, a practice she usually reserves for Thanksgiving and Christmas. When she does say grace, it's a simple "Thank you, Lord, for this food and our loved ones."

As a hostess, Grandma never calls on someone else to offer thanks. "Makes some folks feel like they've been ambushed," she told me.

"I know you phoned Myrt to say you were sailing and would be a little late," Dad says as folks start passing the dishes. "What prompted the impromptu sail?"

I look at Aunt Kylee and hope my expression says, "You're up!" I'm not eager to tell him I've lost another very expensive drone.

Kylee grins at me. Challenge accepted.

"Before I go into detail, I want to say Grant, Mimi, and I were never in danger," Kylee begins as she holds up her hands, asking for patience. "I made sure we were out of Bubba's shooting range."

Dad's eyebrows shoot up, and Grandma scowls. Frank returns a fully loaded fork to his plate, and Robin's blinks signal an "uh, oh, maybe I shoulda stayed home" unease. Mimi and I chuckle.

The table remains quiet, and Dad's raised fork hovers above his plate as Kylee speeds through her report on our mission and the drone's untimely demise.

When she finishes, Grandma says, "Eat up. We've got all night to interrogate these gung-ho investigators."

Interrogation is the right name for it, and my aunt's not the only one challenged for details.

"Why did you fly the drone so close to Bubba's dock?" Dad asks me.

"Wanted a wide angle shot to show how easy it would be for Bubba to stow his motorboat in the marsh and row back to his dock in a dinghy. Also thought it might help whoever tries to salvage the boat figure out the best route to reach it. Unfortunately, the drone flew a little closer to Bubba's dock than I imagined. Even so, I can't believe he shot it down. That's illegal."

Dad rolls his eyes. "And you thought breaking the law to shoot at a big plastic object would bother a man suspected of murdering someone with his motorboat?"

"I'll buy a replacement drone," Kylee jumps in. "I realize our little excursion wasn't to further security for any HOA client. True, Donna asked us for help, but I don't believe the circumstances of Steph's death pose an ongoing threat to owners in Satin Sands.

"While Bubba definitely appears to be the prime suspect in the homicide, there's no evidence he bears a grudge against anyone else in the HOA."

I add my two cents. "However, Bubba does seem to hate drones and rowers who come anywhere near his property."

Dad looks at me, then focuses his attention on Aunt Kylee. "I hope your next move is to give the GPS coordinates of the abandoned boat to the authorities," he says.

"Already done," Kylee answers. "Phoned a Coast Guard friend, who'll take a skiff out to the site on the morning's high tide. The plan is to tow the motorboat to a facility where it can be put on a lift and examined for evidence it rammed Steph's scull. If there's sufficient proof, the Coast Guard will coordinate Bubba's arrest with the Sheriff's Department."

"What about the drone?" I interrupt.

Kylee shakes her head. "The downed drone isn't a Coast Guard priority. We'll have to wait on Bubba's arrest before we attempt recovery. Can't ask any of Steph's fellow rowers to risk getting shot. Since the drone was in range of Bubba's gun when it went down, anyone attempting recovery would be in danger, too."

Dad turns to me. "Did you finish the drone photography at Rand Creek? Or do we need to replace the drone this weekend?"

"I finished. Unless Jocelyn doesn't like what we turn in."

Mimi chuckles. "Uh, oh. You know Jocelyn will nitpick all the photography, since we had the nerve to picture Rand Creek residents who actually look like the people who live there."

Dad sighs. "Let's sit down tomorrow afternoon and order a drone." He thumps Kylee's head. "And we'll discuss later who gets docked for the cost."

Sometimes, Dad acts like a kid when he's with Kylee. Doesn't bother me. After Mom left us, he hardly ever laughed. Okay, even during the years Mom stuck around, there wasn't much laughter. Glad to see him lighten up.

Grandma taps her iced tea glass with a knife to get everyone's attention. "Okay, young'uns, clear the table and bring in dessert plates and the cheesecake. If I say so myself, it's a masterpiece. And we need to enjoy something sweet before we get to the remaining company business— the upcoming Hullis Island owners' meeting, featuring a horde of angry residents ready to lynch yours truly over a ridiculous rumor tsunami."

Oh, yeah. With today's excitement, I almost forgot Grandma and her fellow Hullis Island board members stand accused of plotting to enact rules to outlaw everything from Christmas lights to garden flags. Wonder if I'll have an assignment.

Mimi nudges my knee under the table. "Robin and I are excused from tomorrow's yell-a-thon, right?" she whispers.

"I'm pretty sure you are," I whisper back. "You'll just have to listen to all the stories about it Wednesday. Dad promised you and Robin are on vacation until then."

Mimi swipes her forehead. "Whew. Have had enough drama for a couple of days. Must say this job is more exciting than last summer's waitressing gig."

Chapter Thirty-Three

The Chameleon

Saturday, July 1, early evening

I cross the street to reach a leisure path that winds past homes on this stretch of Hullis Island. Frank Donahue's house is one door down and catty-corner from my rental.

Voices and laughter. A party?

I glance around. Two teens are rollerblading half a block away, moving away from me. In the opposite direction, a dog walker watches while his poodle takes a crap. He's too busy preparing the plastic poop bag to pay me any mind.

An opportunity to cut through the side yard of a nearby house and reach the golf course. The tree-lined third fairway doubles as a backyard for Frank's house. Thank goodness for the trees. They let me blend with the shadows.

With sunset approaching, there shouldn't be much traffic on the front nine. Still, can't rule out tubby golfers trying to squeeze in a few more holes before they start knocking back martinis. Even duffers who can barely bend over to pick up their balls can bend their elbows to hoist nineteenth-hole beers.

Wish I had a golf cart or golf clubs. I'd look less suspicious if someone catches me lurking in the rough. Got it. If I'm spotted, I'll bat my eyes and claim I had to see if a puppy was in distress.

"Oh, dear, I heard what sounded like a little dog whimpering. Just had to make sure a darling little puppy wasn't injured."

Such simpering claptrap from women placates most men. They'd believe rescuing a puppy would be reason enough for a woman to risk getting conked by an errant drive.

I inch along the tree line until I reach the side yard of the house next to Frank's. The house is dark, silent. No worry occupants will alert island security about a prowler huddling in the shadows.

Looks like Frank Donahue and Myrtle Kane are hosting a dinner party on Frank's conveniently-lit screened porch. From the mug shots featured in the "Who We Are" section of the Welch HOA Management website, I recognize everyone at the table.

Kylee and Ted are easy. Frank's the old gent, Welch's construction and maintenance guy. He's seated next to Myrtle, Kylee's mother, who plays part-time receptionist for the Welch company.

The Gen Z summer interns—Ted's son, Grant, and Mimi—look very cozy. I watch as the young man whispers in Mimi's ear. Grant and the curvy redhead have definitely hooked up.

The other young chick has to be Robin, the company's IT person. God, she doesn't look old enough to vote. Can't believe Satin Sands is trusting her to do the software overhaul I volunteered to do for a song. At least Steph won't be opening his big mouth to interfere with any of my other plans.

No one at the dinner table seems to consider someone could be eaves-dropping on their chatter. What a break. The sun's low on the horizon now, and I'm totally hidden in long shadows cast by the trees.

Unfortunately, that means squadrons of mosquitoes are on the attack, intent on extracting a quart of my blood. I can't slap at them for fear the motion or noise will register with one of the Welch crew. Neither can I abandon my listening post. I'm picking up too much intel.

I set the video feature on my cellphone to record. While I'll have no problem remembering the salient points without a recording, the voice samples may prove useful if I want to script deepfake dialogue for one of the dinner guests.

Tomorrow should offer an even better chance to record voices, facial expressions, and telltale tics. I assume both Ted and Myrtle will address the HOA owners in the Hullis Island audience. If I'm lucky, Kylee will pipe up, too.

Dammit! I'm not happy to hear Kylee report that Satin Sands' president has asked her to look into Steph's motorboat fatality. In turn, Kylee roped Grant into flying a drone to locate Bubba's missing motorboat.

Wait, that's the drone Bubba shot down?

Shit! Bubba's anti-aircraft stunt didn't stop Kylee from reporting the boat's coordinates to old Coast Guard buddies. That boat needs to be moved tonight before it can be recovered.

Can't have Bubba arrested and interrogated just yet. If riled, he'd spout off about Steph snitching to the county that he violated outdoor burning regs. Then he'd finish with a tale about Steph suing to steal his land.

Of course, even if the authorities were to tell Bubba that Steph made no such report and never contemplated a lawsuit, Bubba would decide they're lying—like all government stooges.

Still, no sense raising inconvenient questions about how Bubba got word of Steph's misdeeds.

* * *

Back in my rental, I fume at my shortsightedness. While I loaded my BMW with computer gear, I failed to pack the oily Skin So Soft to deter mosquitoes. Also didn't bring AfterBite to ease the subsequent itching.

I abandoned my hideaway in that freaking mosquito incubator once the Welch crowd finished dinner and moved inside. It sounded as if Mimi, Grant, and Robin planned to escape their elders as quickly as possible. Imagine Grant and Mimi hope to satisfy their youthful lust. Not sure about the IT kid since she appeared to come solo.

After dark, I'll take another stroll—wearing a long-sleeved shirt and pants. Guess it's worth risking a few more mosquito bites to see if the older folks head back to the screened porch for after-dinner drinks and more interesting chitchat.

Maybe something a little stronger than iced tea will loosen their lips.

Chapter Thirty-Four

Kylee

Saturday, July 1, evening

After Grant, Mimi and Robin leave, Ted and I clean up the kitchen. Only fair since Mom did all the cooking. Once we finish, Ted suggests we go for a walk. I know he means go for a "talk" beyond Mom's and Frank's hearing range.

We've barely made it to the leisure path when Ted says, "Let's take Frank up on the offer of a guest bedroom tonight. Saves us a drive back to Beaufort, especially since we'll just need to turn around and head back to Hullis Island in the morning to set up for the one p.m. owners' meeting."

Having guessed what topic Ted wanted to discuss in private, I have an answer ready. "For starters, how about clothes for tomorrow's meeting? Won't you have to go back to Beaufort come morning, regardless? Then there's the fact that the bedroom Frank offered us shares a very thin wall with the one Grant occupies. You know I feel queasy about us sleeping together when your son's under the same roof."

"Kylee, it's time to get over this hang-up. You know I keep a duffel bag in the car with spare clothes in case I get called to deal with some HOA mess and need to change. And you have a stash of clothes in your mom's closet for the times you spend the night."

Ted pauses, takes a deep breath. "And here's a news flash. Grant doesn't think we're fifty-year-old virgins. For heaven's sake, he knows you had the bad judgment to sleep with the idiot deputy. Yet, he still loves you and calls you Aunt Kylee. Do you think his opinion of you will slide if you share a bedroom with his dad?"

Throwing up my brief and sorry affair with Nick Ibsen makes me angry. "That's a low blow," I say. "Mentioning Ibsen. You know I rate that short fling as one of the biggest mistakes of my life. One that's earned both of us the hatred of a sheriff's deputy."

Ted hangs his head. "I'm sorry. Mentioning Ibsen was uncalled for. But I get so frustrated by your ridiculous worries about Grant. You need to quit acting like some Victorian spinster throwback when he's around. He knows we're lovers, and he approves. He's a big boy who knows all about the birds and the bees. At this very moment, I'd hazard a guess that he and Mimi aren't looking at the sky, identifying constellations."

My anger fades. Why can't I adjust?

I stop walking and point overhead. "Speaking of constellations, there's the Big Dipper. One of the great things about Hullis Island is the chance to see the moon and the stars. No street lights to ruin the view."

Ted sighs, seizes my shoulders, and turns me to face him. "You can't sidetrack me that easily. What's your answer?"

"You win. But you'd better be quiet."

Ted laughs. "You're noisier than me!"

He takes my hand in his as we stroll down the path.

"See the house with the BMW in the driveway?" I ask. "Amanda Holder bought it six months ago. It's one of two Hullis Island houses in her rental portfolio."

"Dr. Holder? Right, you mentioned some of Andy Fyke's friends nominated her as one of his enemies. I gather that prompted you to check out her real estate holdings."

"Did more than that. My favorite chef and I called on the doc today."

I tell Ted about our chilly reception and the fact that Dr. Holder pretended to search her memory to place who Andy Fyke might be when she knew darn well that he'd filed complaints against her for damage caused by her renters and age-restriction violations."

"Sounds like you took an instant dislike to the woman," Ted says.

"Have to admit I did, and I'm not the Lone Ranger," I add, filling Ted in on why Donna and the Satin Sands board decided to award Welch HOA the contract to update its software instead of accepting the doctor's offer to do the work for half the price.

"Donna said Steph Cloyd was adamant that the woman shouldn't be trusted."

"Did Steph say why? Share any specifics?" Ted asks. "Would love to know why he felt so strongly. He was always so cost-conscious. Too bad we can't ask him. Did your research suggest any possible reason for his unease?"

I share the theory that a professor would only leave a university in the middle of an academic term if she's either sick or asked to leave.

"While Holder's mother died around that time, the doc could easily have taken a short leave and returned to her classes. And I doubt a serious illness caused the professor's sudden departure. Not as fit as she seems. Holder looks like she could bench press her weight and then compete in a triathlon.

"So, I'm guessing the good doctor did something university higher-ups couldn't forgive and forget. Haven't the foggiest notion what that might have been. There's a possibility it's related to Artificial Intelligence—AI is her field of expertise. Maybe she used AI to write articles she published as her own compositions. Or maybe she used AI to read and grade student papers without actually giving them a glance."

"Are you saying you actually suspect this woman of pushing Andy Fyke down the stairs?" Ted asks.

I shrug. "No. Not exactly. I called Lighthouse Cove security and had an off-the-record chat to find out if they'd had any interactions with the woman. Turns out, Holder called security right about the time Andy was pushed. She asked them to check out an attempted break-in at her home. Since she answered the door, she was ensconced in her Lighthouse Cove mansion when the deed was done."

Ted chuckles. "Your tone and your 'not exactly' tell me the doctor's alibi isn't enough to erase her from your suspect list."

"You're right. My gut tells me she knows something about Fyke's attack, something she's hiding. Could be she's covering for an ally who's equally opposed to Andy's anti-rental crusade."

I shiver. Just thinking about Dr. Holder and her cold, penetrating glare gives me the willies. "Let's go back to Frank's. I'll see if Mom will lend me a nightgown."

"Not that you'll be wearing it for long."

Despite the darkness, I imagine I can see Ted's grin shining through.

Chapter Thirty-Five

The Chameleon

Saturday, July 1, evening

I leave all the lights on in my rental and exit through the back door so it looks like whoever is renting this week is tucked in for the night. Though I'm fairly confident the Kane woman doesn't know I've become her mother's across-the-street neighbor, I don't believe in taking chances.

My rental has no garage, and my BMW is sitting in the driveway. There's a remote possibility the snoop took down my license plate when she foraged for online data. If she noticed my Beemer, Kylee might surmise I've camped out nearby.

Since my first eavesdropping foray proved so fruitful, I'm giving it another shot before settling in at the computer for serious AI work. All this personal turmoil is putting me behind schedule on my killer app's production.

As I walk down the rental's rear stairs, I hear people on the leisure path across the street. I freeze, then carefully slink around the corner of the house.

Can't believe my luck. How convenient. The Kane woman and Ted Welch are delivering their conversation to my door. They pause on the path directly across from my house for a little chat. All I have to do is listen.

Interesting.

Wasn't aware these two were lovers, or that Kylee and Deputy Ibsen did the nasty at some point in the past. I reread all of last year's newspaper articles with mentions of Kylee Kane. Ibsen's quotes clearly communicated the deputy was no fan of Kylee or Welch HOA Management. Nice to know it's personal.

Something I can use?

As the couple turns back toward Frank Donahue's house, the conversation pivots to my rental property and ME. *Shit!*

Well, at least Kylee hasn't figured out the BMW in the driveway belongs to yours truly. I move quietly in the shadows to stay within earshot.

My alarm increases as Kylee confides she still suspects me—even though Lighthouse Cove security verified my alibi for the morning Fyke took his toboggan-less slide down the stairs. What does she want a polygraph? That woman's far too curious about my abrupt departure from the university, too.

Dammit all to hell!

Okay, Kylee, if you won't leave me be, I won't leave you—or your loved ones—alone.

Count on it.

* * *

Sitting at my computer, I study my new to-do list, with priorities based on when goals need to be accomplished.

Motivate Bubba or one of his cronies to relocate—or, better yet, destroy—the damaged motorboat before Coast Guard investigators get their hands on it.

Prompt J.T. to commit suicide and leave a confession, admitting she attacked Fyke for reasons that have zip to do with rental properties.

Hack into Frank Donahue's Wi-Fi and poke around for info on his roommate, Myrtle, and her extended family.

Attend tomorrow afternoon's Hullis Island owners' meeting to watch and learn. Then, develop a strategy to cause maximum HOA upheaval and trouble for the Welch men and the Kane women. Would be especially delicious if Kylee decides to go a round with another irate homeowner. Edited videos could make her look like a deranged bully.

Invent reasons for Deputy Ibsen to harass Kylee, her mother, or the Welch men. I have a hunch he's aching for any excuse.

Create AI voice messages and deepfake videos to stir up crises and turn HOA boards against Welch management.

Chaos is my friend.

I go back to the first item on my list: the motorboat.

Afraid I can't count on addle-brained Bubba to keep shuffling the motorboat hither and yon to keep it away from the Coast Guard. I have no doubt forensic tests can prove the boat rammed Steph's scull. Techs might even find bits of the man's flesh in the propellers.

While I don't care if Bubba ultimately goes to jail—he seems preordained to do so without my whisperings—I don't want him incarcerated just yet. I may require the services of an easily-motivated homicidal extremist in the days to come.

Got it.

Bubba—okay, me acting as Bubba's deepfake stand-in—will reach out to one of his buddies. And I know just the one. In Bubba's private RebSocial group, a mechanic buddy bragged he knew how to blow away any government lackey who threatened him or his. Boasted his work on demolition jobs made him quite handy with explosives.

I've recorded Bubba's voice. Shouldn't be hard to convince Mr. Dynamite that I'm Bubba. I used to be terrified of using AI to engage in actual conversations. It's always been a piece of cake to sit in isolation and script a deepfake voice message or video when you could spend as much time as you needed. But responding to questions on the fly proved an entirely different matter.

Thankfully, AI advances now simplify the process. If Mr. Dynamite asks a question, I type in a desired response and command my bot to verbally spit out the reply in Bubba's voice and vernacular. I just need to decide in advance on my core message and anticipate any arguments.

How can my deepfake Bubba instill a sense of urgency in Mr. Dynamite? He can't procrastinate. He must act tonight before the Coast Guard begins a salvage operation early tomorrow. *Think.*

First, poor old Bubba needs to explain why he's calling on a burner phone and not from his usual number. That's easy. He's sure his regular phone's tapped, and he's being watched. That also explains why Bubba can't do the deed himself. The deed being blowing his motorboat to smithereens in the dead of night.

Will it fly?

Almost certainly. These paranoids always believe someone's watching them, yet they're stupid enough to brag about illegal activities on the internet. Go figure?

While I might have urged Bubba to blow up his own boat to avoid involving another whacko, my psychological persuasions do have their limits. Bubba would resist or stall. He'd be far more reticent to destroy his pride-and-joy water toy than he was to murder Steph.

My to-do list is a good start. I hope to tick off all the items as quickly as possible. Don't want to waste more time than need be on these pissant headaches. I need to focus my creative energy on my killer app. That's my pot of gold—my future.

With my strategy set, I get to work on convincing J.T. to exit this world and prepare for my phone call to Mr. Dynamite.

I chuckle. *I do have some dynamite ideas.*

Chapter Thirty-Six

Grant

Sunday, July 1, three-thirty a.m.

I use my GPS watch to guide me in the dark. With a new moon, the night's as black as Grandma Myrt's cats. Good for not being seen, but I hope I can find my drone without damaging my borrowed kayak in the process.

Once I dropped Mimi at her home, I texted a fellow cadet who lives in Beaufort, and asked to borrow his kayak. Then, I tied it to the roof of my Jeep, drove to the Satin Sands launch site, and dropped it off. That was nine o'clock, almost seven hours ago.

I didn't stay at Satin Sands. I first had to return to Hullis Island. If I hadn't, Dad, Grandma, and everyone else would have worried. Dad didn't ask why it had taken me so long to take Mimi home. Her house isn't that far away. Imagine he figured Mimi and I spent the extra hour making out. Would have been a good bet if Mimi's aunt and uncle weren't visiting. She'd promised to spend time with them this evening.

Once I said goodnight to Dad, Grandma, Frank, and Aunt Kylee, I closed the door to my bedroom, climbed in bed, and set an alarm in case I dozed off. Didn't need it. Never went to sleep. Thoughts of my salvage operation had me keyed up. Plus, the muffled giggling coming through the walls kept me amused.

145

Wonder when Dad and Aunt Kylee will quit acting like naughty little kids, playing "I'll show you mine, if you'll show me yours."

I feel kind of bad about sneaking out in the middle of the night. Unfortunately, I know Dad, Aunt Kylee, and Grandma would stroke out if they knew my plans.

True, Mimi and I did wind up kidnapped last Thanksgiving when I tried sleuthing on my own. But this is different. The water route I mapped out to reach my drone's last GPS location doesn't go anywhere near Bubba's dock. Even if it did, he'd never spot me in the dark.

Kayaks are quiet, too. Rustling palm fronds and croaking tree frogs make lots more noise. Besides, the only folks out this time of night are fisher folk gigging for flounder. They don't care squat about some crazy-ass nighttime kayaker.

Waiting till morning to try and retrieve my drone is a no-go. If it landed in marsh grass, I need to rescue it before it's dislodged and sinks in the salty drink. The incoming tide, winds, and waves from a Coast Guard skiff are equal dangers. The friends Aunt Kylee tapped to salvage the motorboat will arrive shortly after dawn. I need to beat them.

As I creep along, my eyes adjust enough to hint at hazards in the inky night. Still, I'm startled every few minutes when my kayak nudges a submerged log or becomes temporarily mired in quicksand-like pluff mud.

I did bring thick-soled waders in case I'm forced to get out of the kayak and push off a muddy bank. I know first-hand how oyster shells can shred sneakers and cut feet to ribbons if you're stupid enough to hop out unprepared.

The LED headband lamp Dad bought me for hiking is another precaution. I leave it switched off. Will only turn it on if I really need it. The sky seems lighter. Wonder what time it is?

I push a button on my watch to light the face. It's four a.m.; guess the change in the sky is my imagination. I checked the charts online before I left. Astronomical twilight doesn't start until 5:45 a.m.

The clock is ticking. I decide to risk paddling faster, even if it means I chance putting some dents in my borrowed kayak. My little excursion's taking longer than I hoped. Want to beach the kayak at Satin Sands by five a.m. and return to Hullis Island by seven.

I left a note on the fridge that I'd had trouble sleeping and decided to go for a drive. Told them I'd pick up donuts for everyone at our favorite Beaufort bakeshop. Since old folks tend to be early risers, I didn't want them panicking. If they got up before I returned, they'd notice my Jeep missing from the driveway.

I check my GPS. Good, I'm in the vicinity of my drone. Time to risk switching on my headlamp. Dad bought me a top-of-the-line model that offers white, red, and green light. Plus, with a flick of the dial, I can switch from a focused spotlight to a broad beam or even a pulsing strobe if I'm in trouble and want to be found.

I turn on the bright white, focused spotlight to search. While the beam's real narrow, it can spotlight objects up to two hundred feet away.

Come on, do your job. Bounce off my drone's white skin.

I slowly pivot a few degrees at a time. See nothing but marsh grass.

Wait! Something white, resting at an angle in a clump of high grass. Definitely man-made. I paddle toward it.

I smile as I tug my damaged drone from its resting place and horse it into the kayak. Looks like the memory stick stayed dry. If saltwater didn't get in, maybe we can save all the images. Including the last picture of old Bubba raising his gun.

The spotlight has ruined my night vision. I fumble with the switch to turn it off. I close my eyes to try and re-acclimate for my return paddle. Suddenly, an ear-splitting boom deafens me. The whoosh of pulsing air makes my eardrums vibrate. A blinding red and yellow fireball blossoms.

My kayak rocks wildly, and I grip the gunnels to steady it. If I could see my knuckles, they'd be white. I can't see 'cause I'm blind. All I see are yellow spots.

I hold tight as the nearby blast churns the shallow marsh into a foaming froth. Temporarily blind and deaf, my sense of smell seems to take over. The stench of decaying marsh grass mixes with the choking smoke.

Shit! What's happening?

I keep my eyes closed tight, hoping it will help me see something besides spots when I open them again. I count to sixty. Enough? My kayak begins to settle, and I loosen my hold on the gunnels. My pulse keeps racing. I take deep breaths.

I'm fine, I tell myself. *Kayak isn't damaged. Whatever the hell exploded, I'm okay.*

Despite the pep talk, my pulse ratchets back up as I realize the explosion wasn't some spontaneous combustion of marsh gas. Somebody blew up something, and the odor tells me whatever exploded had gasoline inside.

Bubba's boat! Of course, and whoever triggered that blast may be nearby.

Stay still. Don't move. Is it Bubba? Even he's not stupid enough to hang around and admire his work. He'll split as fast as he can.

I open my eyes, hoping I can see. Then I wish I hadn't. Somehow, I blew it when I tried to turn my headlamp off. Now, it spotlights a nightmarish face. In the focused beam, the man's brow ridge throws deep shadows over his eyes. It turns the sockets into black holes. He's standing, trying to steady himself on a greenish craft. He pivots, trying to pinpoint the location of my headlamp and me.

I once again fumble with the headlamp wheel to switch the light off. Great! I accidentally activate the strobe mode. The pulsing light advertises my exact location.

Way to go, Grant! Why don't you send him your GPS coordinates?

Afraid I'll screw up again if I try to switch the light off, I rip the headlamp band off and shove it beneath a thick towel. I can still see the red light's throbbing pulse through the terrycloth. At least the emergency signals are now nightlight dim. Hopefully, he can't see them any better than I can.

A shot rings out. It's loud. Uncomfortably close. I slouch down to make myself a smaller target. My forehead touches my knees. A few seconds pass. I no longer hear the tree frogs. Maybe they're holding their breath, too. A second shot rips the still night.

I try to picture the map I studied to plan my kayak route. The geography should be my friend. A wide stretch of grass-topped pluff mud separates the shooter's channel from my tributary. The two waterways don't intersect for miles.

A motor revs. Has he given up on shooting me?

The sound of his motor gradually recedes. I slowly sit up.

Maybe he thought his shots hit their target, and I'm dead. Or, he decided I was too far away to describe him. If so, he's right. I could barely tell he was a white man. Harsh shadows hid his features. The only thing I'm sure of is that he's astride what looks like a Jet Ski or WaveRunner. I've driven both and know you'd have to be insane to try zipping around the marsh at low tide when spots are often ankle-deep.

I hope his risk-taking eventually costs him. Pray he'll suck up debris and blow the motor before he leaves the marsh.

If it was Bubba, he must believe he can defy the odds and get away with anything he tries. Ramming sculls, blowing up boats, downing drones, hot-rodding on a Jet Ski.

I sit completely still. Don't put a paddle in the water. Minutes pass. The tree frogs are croaking again. No motor noise.

Damn. Bubba isn't the only one who takes stupid risks. At least this time, I didn't talk Mimi into joining me. Nonetheless, I can't simply buy donuts and show up at Hullis like nothing happened.

I know what I have to do. I take a deep breath and pull out my cellphone. Hope I can get a signal but, at the same time, I sort of hope I can't. Not anxious to hear the voice that picks up on the other end.

"Hello." Dad sounds groggy.

"It's me, Grant," I reply.

"Where are you? What's happened? Are you okay?"

"I'm okay. I'm just not sure who to call—the Sheriff or the Coast Guard."

Dad has a field day interrupting my story with his questions. Anger has crept into his tone. He's mad at me, disappointed, too.

"Hold on," he says.

I hear Kylee's voice, then Dad comes back on the phone.

"Call the Sheriff's Office and report what you saw," Dad barks. "Kylee will call the Coast Guard to give them an update on the boat. Then, you paddle back to Satin Sands, and don't you leave. We'll meet you there."

Chapter Thirty-Seven

The Chameleon

Sunday, July 2, pre-dawn

L oud voices jar me awake. Doors slam. A motor coughs. An engine
revs.
   What in blazes?

I rub my eyes and glance at the bedside clock. Not quite five. Hullis Island
is supposed to be a quiet, family-oriented resort. Who's making so much
racket before any decent rooster crows?

I'm in the master bedroom with the windows open wide. Something's
wrong with the freakin' heat pump. When it kept wheezing and clicking
on and off, I switched it off. Hoped the night air would be cool enough. So
much for hope. Sweat has practically glued my nightgown to my back and
thighs.

The window next to my bed overlooks the street with a perfect view of
Frank Donahue's house. A car's backing down his driveway. Not Kylee's
Camry. It's still parked. A Lexus. Must be Ted's car. Two people inside. As
the car turns in the street, I catch a glimpse of the person in the passenger
seat. White curly hair. The snoop.

Soon as the Lexus clears the drive and pivots past the mailbox, it rockets
away. Tires squealing.

Shame on you, Ted. You're violating the island's fifteen-mile-per-hour speed limit on residential side streets.

What's up? Some HOA client must have an emergency to prompt the lovers to leap from a cozy bed. The speedy departure's all the more curious given the day ahead. They'll want to prep carefully for the one p.m. Hullis owners' meeting. Won't want a blowup like the Marshview HOA fiasco.

Blow up? Oh, no!

Couldn't be. Who'd call Ted and Kylee about some explosion miles away in the swamp. Okay, Lowcountry folks prefer to call it marsh. It's not as if Ted and Kylee have the power to piece the humpty-dumpty motorboat back together again. So why are they fleeing like Satan himself is giving chase?

God, I hope my explosives nut didn't get caught.

I hop out of bed and start searching for the right burner phone. Brought along three dedicated burners. Guess I should attach easy-to-read labels to make sure I call the right stooge.

I power up my Bubba cell. Mr. Dynamite left me a text.

Boat is toast, but kayaker saw me. Shot at him. Ran.

I text back. *Where R U? Fuzz?*

No answer.

Great, just great. Another cock-up. Still, it doesn't explain why Ted and Kylee would be involved. Bubba's boat wasn't stashed inside an HOA client property. Maybe the kayaker is a friend, and Mr. Dynamite wounded him.

Wide awake, I start a pot of coffee and turn on the radio. Don't expect to hear a news bulletin for at least another hour. Given it's a holiday weekend and a Sunday, local stations are unlikely to have reporters pounding the payment this early.

Then again, maybe the explosion created a huge fireball, and a concussive whomp woke up folks demanding to know what happened.

Be patient. You'll hear soon enough. Too bad waiting isn't one of my strengths. I look out the window and stare at Frank Donahue's house. All the lights are on.

Kylee's Camry is the only car parked in the drive. I try to recall how many cars were there when I checked before I went to bed. Three. There were three cars. Kylee's Camry, Ted's Lexus, and an old Jeep. Imagine Myrtle and

Frank have first dibs on using the two-car garage, and their cars are inside.

The Jeep must belong to Ted's son. Maybe Grant's been in an accident. Perhaps the couple's hasty departure has nothing to do with Bubba's boat or me. Fingers crossed.

Since I'm up and wide awake, I might as well accomplish something. My cartoon idea excites me. It could give customers a way to ease their consciences—it's just cartoon fun—while they visit bloody wrath on their foes. Cartoons make violence socially acceptable.

What a hoot. I close my eyes and imagine a cartoon kangaroo (female, of course) kicking and pummeling some jerk like he's a piñata. When Kan-do Kangaroo's victim goes down for the count or breaks apart like a piñata, she can pick up souvenirs like watches or gold fillings. At the end, she tosses the mementos in her pouch and winks.

I'll direct my app to concoct a cartoon feline, too. A sexy one. She'll toy with her human mouse or birdie for hours before delivering a final coup de grace. Think I'll give users the option to blend their faces with their cartoon characters. I smile as I imagine my green eyes, slender nose, and high-boned cheeks welded onto a cartoon lioness.

Naturally, I'll have a magnificent mane and very long, sharp claws.

The visions make me chuckle. But first things first. It's time for a follow-up with J.T. Need to encourage the woman to bring down the curtain on her tear-jerker of a life.

Will keep trying to reconnect with Mr. Dynamite, too. May need him to blow town until I can make sure the kayaker he used for target practice can't identify him.

Chapter Thirty-Eight

Kylee

Sunday, July 2, dawn

As Ted pulls into the Satin Sands beach parking lot, I spot two sheriff's patrol cars haphazardly hogging multiple spaces. Twirling bubble lights atop the SUVs announce they're not on a coffee break. I cross my fingers that neither vehicle carried Nick Ibsen, Deputy Do-Wrong, to the scene.

Ted and I exit and walk toward the beach, figuring that's where we'll find Grant talking to the deputies. I spot the six-foot-three teen standing beside a kayak. His young athletic build is unmistakable. Grant's bookended by two deputies—a man and a woman. The male deputy is trying to crowd Grant. But it's hard to effectively get in someone's face if they're several inches taller than you. To compensate, the officer resorts to shouting as a means of intimidation.

"I don't believe you!" he roars.

Crapola. It's a voice I recognize. Nick's.

Thankfully, I haven't come face to face with Nick since late November. At the time, he was running for sheriff. Shortly after Thanksgiving, he withdrew from the race. Said he wasn't one-hundred-percent due to recent injuries. Nick said he wanted to fully recover before seeking the top office again in order "to best serve Beaufort County citizens."

In reality, Nick's primary injury was to his ego. A bomb fragment punctured his derriere. The deputy would never have been hurt if he hadn't arrogantly ignored multiple warnings from Ted and me. Nonetheless, Nick holds us responsible.

Not that we were Nick's favorites before Thanksgiving. I'm mortified I once had a brief fling with the deputy. It ended as soon as I discovered Nick was a misogynist bully. When I told him to take a hike, I did the unforgivable. Nick ditched women, not the other way around.

"Grant," Ted shouts as he rushes toward his son.

"Dad!" Grant's clearly relieved his father is here.

The woman deputy moves aside to give Ted room to hug his son.

"I'm sorry about slipping out last night," Grant says. "I just wanted to get my drone back before it sunk."

Nick glares at Ted. Since I'm trailing, the deputy hasn't noticed me yet.

"Go away, Mr. Welch," Nick snarls. "We're not done interviewing our suspect."

"Suspect?" Ted croaks. "He's a minor, and I'm his father. This interview is over, unless you're arresting Grant, in which case he won't say another word until he talks with a lawyer."

While it's not quite dawn, the sky has brightened, and halogen lamps on the Satin Sands pier provide sufficient garish light to watch Nick's face darken to a purplish red. Can't help but notice the man's chiseled good looks have begun to slide. The deputy's gained weight, not muscle. His face looks fleshy with the hint of approaching jowls.

"Let's not get excited." The female deputy attempts to calm things down. "We have no reason to suspect the kid of anything except bad judgment— kayaking in the middle of the night."

Nick responds to his fellow deputy's words with an icy stare. His jaw juts forward, and he clenches and unclenches his fists. The woman, an attractive lady, I guess to be in her mid-forties, ignores his aggressive posture.

"Mr. Welch, you're welcome to stay with your son," she adds. "While we do need to ask a few more questions, there's no need to take the young man into custody." She pauses. "Or delay matters by calling a lawyer."

Ted levies a hard look at Nick, then nods in agreement.

Grant clears his throat. "As I told you before, the man who shot at me and blew up the boat was white and male. That's about all I could tell. My headlamp only lit his face for a second. All I really saw was white skin and dark shadows. If you showed me his photo, I wouldn't be able to recognize him."

"Was he tall or short, big or small?" the woman deputy urges.

Grant closes his eyes. His forehead creases as he considers. "All I saw was a silhouette. He didn't seem real tall. I'd say under six feet. The guy looked kind of bulky, but maybe he was just wearing a puffy life jacket."

"Tell us about his boat?" the woman deputy continues.

"It wasn't a canoe, kayak, or flat boat," Grant says. "It was shorter than those with a high front end like a Jet Ski or WaveRunner. I remember shiny green metal, almost neon."

"You're full of it," Nick interrupts. "No Jet Ski or WaveRunner could make it through the channels where you claim you saw him buzzing about. Too shallow. Maybe there wasn't any man at all. Maybe you dynamited that boat to get revenge for someone shooting down your toy."

"We're done," Ted barks. "Arrest him or let us leave. Don't say another word, Grant."

"Dad, wait a second," Grant says. "I want to say something. The shooter's ride confused me, too. I couldn't believe someone was rocketing around the marsh in some version of a personal watercraft. Couldn't understand why he didn't get stuck in the mud. But that's what I saw."

"Think that'll do it," the female deputy jumps in before Nick can speak. "Thank you, Grant. You can go home with your father. We know how to reach you. Of course, we need to keep the drone until our techs can determine if the memory stick can be salvaged. Hopefully, it will still store whatever images were taken before it crashed.

"There's nothing more Deputy Ibsen and I can do here until dawn arrives and a high tide lets us get a look at the wreckage. We've arranged for a Sheriff's boat to collect whatever pieces are left. I'm not terribly optimistic. Plenty of folks reported the spectacular flames and the loud boom. I imagine the debris will be scattered over a wide area."

Though I realize speaking will up Nick's already sky-high blood pressure and possibly spark the night's second explosion, I edge closer.

"I'm Kylee Kane, a former Coast Guard investigator." I engage directly with the female officer, pointedly ignoring Nick. "Yesterday, I contacted Lt. Alysha Carter to suggest the Coast Guard scout this area for a missing motorboat. The Coast Guard will be eager to cooperate with you. They have plenty of experience with marine salvage operations, and they have excellent technical skills for image recovery from damaged devices.

"Could you please give the lieutenant a call? I've written her contact information on the back of my business card. The Coast Guard will be interested in potential federal crimes."

"Thank you, I'll call," the female deputy responds. "I'm Deputy Josie Muschel, by the way. Here's my card."

Nick snorts in disgust and stalks off.

Hallelujah. A deputy who isn't intimidated by Deputy Do-Wrong's bullying.

* * *

Even though Ted's now a couple inches shorter than his lanky son, he slings an arm around Grant's shoulders as we leave the officers and head toward Ted's Lexus. Grant's Jeep is parked right alongside it.

I glance back at the deputies. While I can't make out what Nick's mouthing off about, the man's finger-shaking and posture indicate he's quite displeased with Deputy Muschel's conduct.

Tough patooties.

When the tirade winds down, Deputy Muschel simply shrugs and turns her back on Nick. After a brief hesitation, she walks over, picks up Grant's drone, and secures it in the trunk of her patrol car. Nick expresses his ire by laying down some rubber as he peels out.

Must admit I'm downright gleeful to see Nick throw a temper tantrum and have zero to show for it. Too bad he holds so tight to his grudges. For months to come, I imagine Deputy Muschel will be a target of his wrathful, petty revenge.

Ted doesn't say anything until we reach his car.

"Are you hurt?" he asks Grant. "Yes, I'm angry. Don't think I'll forget tonight's stunt. There will be consequences. But first things first. Are you injured?"

Grant studies the ground at his feet and shakes his head. To his credit, he seems to regret what he's done.

"I'm okay. I know it was stupid, and I'm sorry. Before we head to Hullis, I do need to return the kayak. I borrowed it from a Beaufort buddy."

Ted nods and sucks in a deep breath. "Okay. "We'll put the kayak on the Jeep's rack, follow you to your friend's house, and unload it. Then we're heading straight to Hullis. It's going to be a busy day.

"We'll discuss your actions later. You scared all of us to death, including your Grandma Kane. It's pure luck that the shooter missed you. Pure luck. I'm not identifying your body at the morgue."

"Understood," Grant says. "I have no excuse."

Grant Welch, Citadel cadet, has re-appeared. He stands erect, ready to take his medicine.

I have no idea what consequences Ted plans to dish out. Hope he's not too tough on his son. Yes, Grant acted stupidly, but his motives were pure.

They say teen brains don't fully develop until age twenty-five. I believe it. We humans are supposed to be at our cognitive peak at thirty-five. Of course, once we reach forty-five, we begin a downhill slide.

That's me.

Hope to hell my experience can compensate for those brain cells intent on deserting me with every new year.

Chapter Thirty-Nine

Grant

Sunday, July 2, morning

I smell bacon, and the maple syrup Grandma Myrt warms in the microwave for French toast or pancakes. Last night, I thought I'd be passing out donuts this morning to celebrate my triumph.

Triumph, right? The cops are keeping my drone, and everyone's mad at me.

No doubt Grandma Myrt will still feed me breakfast. That's after she gives me a red-hot scolding. Whenever I cause her worry, she doesn't hold back.

I really am sorry. Didn't mean to cause her, Dad, or Aunt Kylee grief. 'Course, that's never a defense with Mighty Myrt. Grandma's sort of like Mighty Mouse. She may be tiny enough for a big wind to blow her away, but you better watch out when she blows her stack.

I trail Dad and Kylee into Frank's kitchen.

"Breakfast's almost ready," Grandma says. "Frank's setting the table. Is the nitwit reprobate dragging his tail behind you two? Come here, son."

I obey. She gives me the stink eye as I stand in front of her. Then Grandma's arm jumps up, and she thumps my head like she's testing a watermelon for ripeness.

Ouch.

I think it, don't say it. Don't dare utter a syllable.

Grandma grabs my upper arms. She's too short to shake me by the shoulders. "This day's going to be the pits. And what do you do to add to the fun? Wake us up before the dawn can crack. Then we find out you risked your life for an expensive flying eye in the sky. Someone shot at you!

"Sometimes I think all males should be locked away until they're at least thirty years old. You're no dummy, Grant. In fact, you're a lot smarter than me. What made you do something this dumb and give some maniac nighttime target practice?"

I know enough to look Grandma in the eye and stay mum. When she takes a deep breath, I hope she's winding down. Wrong again.

"Grant, THINK, son. Didn't you learn anything last Thanksgiving? The bad guys don't play by any rules of military engagement the Citadel might teach. They fight dirty, and they're unpredictable. Some are plain nutso. That means you need to THINK. You don't scare the folks who love you by sneaking out in the dark of night to retrieve a hunk of worthless plastic. Drones can be replaced. You can't."

Grandma thumps my head once more as an exclamation point.

Ouch.

"I'm sorry, Grandma. You're right. I didn't think it through."

"Of course, I'm right," she mumbles. "Now, everyone, go sit down and eat while the food's hot. I figure we need a hearty breakfast since we may not have time for lunch."

Once the plates of eggs, bacon, and French toast are passed, conversation resumes. Me? My mouth only opens for the bites my fork delivers. I'm starving and intelligent enough to let folks move onto topics that don't involve me.

"I take it no one went back to sleep after Ted and I left," Kylee begins. "Mom, what's the strategy for this afternoon's owners' meeting?"

"Strategy?" Grandma huffs. "You're talking about the Hullis Island board. I invited the directors here for a little pre-meeting confab. They're due to arrive an hour from now. Cliff Jackson, our hard-liner president, wants to open and close the owners' meeting with a two-sentence statement. No

159

audience questions. No discussion.

"As Cliff puts it, 'It's time to put the rabble-rousers in their place.' As a former—and probable future—rabble-rouser, I strongly disagree. The board owes these upset owners a chance to voice their concerns and get answers."

Dad frowns. "I don't get it. How does Cliff think a take-it-or-leave-it statement and shutting down all discussion will help? That won't put a lid on the angry speculation. The pot's already boiling."

Grandma Myrt shakes her head. "You'll have a chance to hear Cliff's words of *wisdom* when he and Bob arrive. Maybe you can talk some sense into the two of them. Cliff appointed the Covenant Review Committee members before last fall's board upheaval. That meant he didn't get any pushback from the three old biddies he now has as directors. Cliff wants Hullis to enact more rules and regulations. He'd love for the committee that started this mess to follow through and recommend lots of rule changes."

Aunt Kylee puts down her coffee cup. "I don't understand, Mom. Why can't you outvote Cliff? Won't it be a three-to-two vote? If so, you can run the owners' meeting however you see fit."

"Afraid not. Martha's on a cruise to the Galapagos and can't be reached, and Ruth's in the hospital for a hip replacement. That leaves Cliff, me, and Bob, who always sides with our president. Both men are angry about owners trashing them and the committee on Earful."

Dad sighs. "I sympathize with their consternation about the ridiculous rhetoric and misinformation on Earful. But, if the directors refuse to hear and answer questions, the board can expect more scorn to be heaped on them. Afraid that includes you, Myrt, and your two friends who will miss the meeting. What bad timing."

Frank clears his throat. "I decided to wade into the Earful madness and defend Myrt. In my post, I tried to invoke reason. Noted that just because a committee kicks around some new ideas for rules, it doesn't mean a majority of the board agrees with them. I also stressed that Myrt would make sure any proposed new rules would come up for a vote.

"Not sure if my comment helped or hurt. More than one reply noted anything I said couldn't be trusted since I was 'shacking up' with Myrt. Two posts kindly added that my wife must be turning over in her grave."

"Oh, Frank, I'm so sorry," Aunt Kylee says. "I never cease to be amazed at how cruel gossips can be—especially when they don't have to look whoever they're abusing in the eye."

Frank attempts a smile. "Hey, my wife would be spinning like a top in her grave if I paid any heed to the gossips. Jennifer never did."

Grandma reaches over and pats Frank's hand. When he looks at her, a genuine smile creases his face.

Glad they have each other.

Frank clears his throat. "The Earful insults petered out once a neighbor posted a rant about our utility company. His refrigerator went kaput, and he blamed the failure on frequent electrical surges. Said he planned to sue the electric company for a new fridge. That started an avalanche of blame-game posts.

"Several blamed the appliance manufacturer and our throw-away society. Another figured out a way for our HOA to be at fault. I award most creative to a claim the utility company intentionally creates electrical spikes so it can sell expensive whole-house surge protection for an add-on monthly fee."

Ted laughs. "Let's stop rehashing Earful nonsense and get the breakfast dishes cleared. Myrt, I assume you want your board quorum to meet at this table. Do Cliff and Bob expect me to attend?"

"Cliff probably suspects you'll be here, but didn't mention inviting our HOA manager," Grandma answers. "Doubt he'll object to you attending, though. Cliff thinks of himself as your boss and knows he can ignore you as long as the board votes with him. Today, there are three directors—a quorum—and Bob always votes with him. So, he'll have a two-to-one decision on anything he favors."

Kylee stands up and starts stacking plates. She shoos Dad with a wave of her hand.

"Since your presence is anticipated, you get first chance at a shower," she says. "Fortunately, I can think of no reason for Frank, Grant, and me to get yelled at. So, I plan to disappear. While I'd rather swim laps, the island pools will be too crowded this holiday weekend. Think I'll go for a run. Grant, want to join me? Imagine your Dad will let you leave the house if you have a chaperone."

"No, thanks. May take a short nap."

When I see Grandma's scowl, I quickly add, "After I clean up the kitchen."

* * *

Despite the bed's strong pull, I postpone shut-eye for a web search. I can't stop thinking about the neon green machine the shooter maneuvered through the shallow marshlands at high speed. Actually, I can't blame Deputy Ibsen for ridiculing my insistence that it looked like a WaveRunner or a Jet Ski.

It doesn't take long for my Google search to pay off. There are dozens of articles about rescue and research groups using a customized flat-bottomed, high-speed watercraft. The articles say it can skim over water that's only two-to-three inches deep. Speed? Sixty- to sixty-five miles per hour. Price? The specs on the manufacturer's website mention everything but the price.

Okay, whenever Grandma Kane sees an item missing a price tag, she jokes, "Guess if you have to ask, you can't afford it."

Huh. Can't imagine Bubba or any of his friends has sufficient bread to afford one. Then, again, maybe Bubba or a friend "borrowed" one. Need to find out if any Lowcountry groups own one of these nifty machines. I check the websites of government agencies and nonprofits with water-related missions that could use this kind of watercraft.

My first hit comes on the URL for Friends of the Atlantic Coast Environment—FACE. A recent FACE news release thanks a generous (anonymous) donor for buying FACE a next-generation watercraft. The news release says it's being used to conduct research in coastal wetlands and to aid in the rescue of injured marsh birds, aquatic mammals, and fish.

Everything points to Bubba being the one who killed Steph Cloyd, a FACE director. It would be horribly ironic if someone used a FACE-owned watercraft to reach Bubba's motorboat and blow it up. I'm afraid the explosion could have destroyed the evidence needed to prove Bubba rammed Steph's scull and fled the scene.

I shake my head. In what world would Bubba or any of his climate-change-denier pals have access to a FACE watercraft?

Maybe someone stole the craft from FACE. Okay, I know who would know. Kylee's BFF, Kay Barrett. She's a FACE director. Hope Kay's not too busy with her B&B guests to pick up the phone.

Chapter Forty

Kylee

Sunday, July 2, morning

A sudden wind gust whips sand in my face. I blink furiously and raise a hand to shield my eyes. Black clouds boil on the horizon as the temperature plummets. Time to pick up the pace. Probably two miles from Frank's house.

While I've yet to hear thunder, that doesn't mean lightning won't streak across the sky in the next five minutes. Didn't expect this pop-up thunderstorm. I don't mind rain. I'm drenched in sweat anyway. The dip in temperature is also welcome. It's typical July weather. Hot. Hot. Hot. Before the cool-down, the temperatures were goose-stepping their way up to a predicted high near one hundred degrees.

I run a little faster. I'm not a running addict who regularly punishes her knees and feet to seek an endorphin high. Swimming is my go-to exercise. However, I'll lace up my running shoes if I can't dive into a pool or lake. I'm not a fan of ocean swimming. If I'm trying to get real exercise, I end up swallowing a quart of saltwater. Can't seem to break the habit of swiveling my head for a breath, and it's often when a wave crests.

On days like this, when I'm frustrated and need alone time to think, I don't care whether I run or swim to get the needed release. Not even sure why I asked Grant if he wanted to join me. Guess I wanted him to know he was still loved despite his bone-headed escapade.

Lightning flashes, and the thunder claps that follow say the storm's close. Too close. I run faster. The black clouds on the horizon minutes ago are now overhead. A driving rain pelts me. Whipped by a fierce wind, the rain appears to be falling horizontally. Directly in my face.

My heart's pounding as I race up the stairs to the welcome shelter of Frank's front porch. I'm dripping wet. Figure I should ring the bell and ask whoever answers to bring me a towel. I don't want to barge inside and leave puddles on Frank's polished oak floors.

My finger's on the bell, ready to press down, when I realize the impromptu board meeting may still be underway. Don't want to interrupt that.

Wait. Don't see any golf carts or extra cars in the drive. Can't imagine Cliff or Bob walked over, though they might have shared a ride.

Once again, I hesitate as I debate pressing the doorbell. When the door swings open, it startles the heck out of me.

Frank chuckles as he steps out on the porch and hands me a towel. "Was looking out the window when I saw a tall drowned rat scurry up my porch stairs. This downpour caught everyone by surprise. But the radar shows it'll probably be over before you can dry that wild mop of hair."

"Thanks, Frank." I take the towel and vigorously rub my unruly curls. "You're just jealous you don't have a wild mop of hair."

"A low blow," Frank replies. "I'm wild about every strand of hair that's stuck by me."

I nod toward the door. "Is it safe to enter? Has any interior stormfront come and gone?"

"Yep," he answers. "Ted arm-twisted Cliff into opening the meeting with a brief summary of facts. He'll report that some members of a committee— one lacking any power—have been yapping publicly about rule changes they'd like to see. Cliff will add that the board hasn't approved—or even seen—a single committee recommendation.

"After that, Ted will take the mic and confirm the process required by our covenants to enact any rule change. Nothing happens unless a majority of owners vote in favor. Ted will then open the floor to owner questions and comments. Speakers will be limited to three minutes max. To win Cliff's agreement, Ted promised to warn the audience he'd immediately adjourn the meeting if folks started shouting over one another. Anyone who starts a disturbance will be escorted outside by a security officer, and there will be several officers in the hall. Guess that means you might be able to avoid any new bruises."

"Sounds like fun. Can't wait." I slip off the shoes that squish with every step and leave them on the porch. Then I follow Frank inside.

"Where is everybody?" I ask.

"Myrt's using my office desktop. She's looking at Earful posts to see if there are any new accusations she needs to be ready to parry," Frank answers. "Ted went to the community center to check on the setup and talk with security. He wants to make sure there are enough chairs and two or three roving mics. Also plans to check the audio system. He asked Chief O'Rourke to assign at least three security officers to help with traffic before the meeting. Then, once it gets underway, the officers will head inside and stand ready to boot loudmouths."

"Think I'll say hi to Mom and see if she needs anything before I hog the guest bathroom for a leisurely shower."

I knock on the doorframe to get Mom's attention. Hunched over Frank's desktop computer, she looks completely focused. Did she even hear my knock?

"Mom, I'm back from my run. Thought I'd check in with you before I clean up for the meeting."

Mom swivels the office chair to face me. No smile. Her expression isn't angry. It's troubled. Why? Ted convinced the board to engage in a dialogue with the owners and be open about the committee's misunderstanding. She should be relieved.

"You need to read these Earful posts about Andy Fyke," Mom says. "Some Rand Creek woman committed suicide, and she left a confession by her empty pill bottle. Says she pushed Andy down the stairs because she believed he was a child molester."

"What?" I explode. "No way that nice old man's a child molester. No way."

166

"Well, even old men can and do abuse children," Mom says. "As a nurse, I learned evil deeds have no upper age limits. But, toward the end of the suicide note, she mentions that the video that convinced her Fyke was a pedophile might have been a fake. Not wanting to go to jail or put her family through a trial, she took her own life."

I sink into a recliner in the cozy office. "God, one person dead and another severely injured. All because of malicious rumors. Gossip. What's the world coming to?"

Mom shrugs. "Hate to tell you, but the human race hasn't changed all that much since the Salem witch trials. Now whisper campaigns just fly farther and faster with apps like Earful. If a lie's repeated often enough, people believe it."

I share Mom's sorrow. "How sad. The dead woman's confession may actually make matters worse for Andy. He has enough on his plate, trying to recover from broken bones and internal injuries.

'I hate to think it, but I know some Earful regulars will decide something suspicious must have triggered the speculation about Andy being a pervert. For believers of 'where there's smoke, there's fire,' the whispers will haunt Andy for a very long time."

Mom shuts down the computer. "Nothing you can do about it. At least not now," she says as she shoos me away. "Go take your shower, get dressed. I want you at the owners' meeting. Not in an official capacity but as an observer. And certainly not as a punching bag. Just observe. You're good at reading people. See if you can tell which owners seem eager to carry torches and light more Hullis Island fires."

Chapter Forty-One

The Chameleon

Sunday, July 2, afternoon

Must say today's start has been dandy. Early news reports confirmed one or more unknown suspects blew up an unidentified vessel mired in the marsh. The reports breathlessly described the middle-of-the-night fireball that awakened and alarmed dozens of marshside residents. Lots of 911 calls. The Sheriff's Department is asking for leads.

Good. Must not have an ID on Mr. Dynamite. Still think it would be wise to remove his piece from the chessboard.

The second item of welcome news arrived when I visited the Earful gossip app. Rand Creek residents were all atwitter about the discovery of a suicide. The body of Jane Tina Landreth, nicknamed J.T., was found by a friend who decided it was just fine to share J.T.'s suicide note online. In her exit message, J.T. said she attacked Andy Fyke because she thought he was a child molester.

Hot diggity. The Earful post by J.T.'s friend is long and rambling. She waits until the last paragraph to mention J.T. eventually had misgivings, that maybe Andy wasn't a pedophile. That revelation will be lost in the verbal hand-wringing.

It's 12:45 as I slip into an aisle seat at the back of the Hullis Island

Community Center. I'm about to follow meeting protocol and turn off my cellphone's ringer when I get an alert from my Ring doorbell. It's detected motion—a pint-size moving van is using my driveway to turn around and back into Leona Grimm's drive. Looks like she's quickly moving out essentials, probably including Ginger's doggy bed. Hallelujah. My haunting-by-dead-husband ploy worked.

Wish I could have seen old Leona when she heard her dead hubby's plea. Bet she sobbed and crouched by one of her digital ask-me-anything spheres, praying her husband would tell her the secrets of the afterlife.

Sorry, Leona, I only had time to dream up a few chilling warnings. No insights beyond the veil.

Man, the good news just keeps coming.

Good thing I arrived fifteen minutes before the fireworks are due to start. Not many seats left. I'm guessing at least one-hundred-fifty fellow owners occupy the available chairs. Another twenty or so lean against the back wall. A fire marshal by the door counts heads. Imagine Hullis stormtroopers—three of the uniformed posse are inside—will bar entrance once the two-hundred-person occupancy limit's reached.

Good show. Turning people away should ratchet up the anger among the folks who arrive late.

Three people sit at a front table, facing the crowd. The middle man with a gavel at the ready must be the president, Cliff Jackson. A matching male sourpuss sits to his right. Both men studiously examine papers, avoiding eye contact with the crowd. To the president's left, Myrtle Kane proves an exception. She looks directly at the audience and attempts a pleasant expression.

Where are Kylee, Ted, and his son?

I scan the room. Ted's near the front wall, speaking with a security officer. I don't spot Kylee or Grant till I crane around to check out the wallflowers. Both of them are loitering near the back wall. Interesting. Would have thought Kylee would position herself up front. Especially since her back-of-the-room post at Marshview ended with a solid punch to the cheek. Had I arrived earlier, I'd have sat up front. Then I could swivel to see the faces of any members who pipe up. Hard to judge a person's mood, staring at the back of a neck.

Oh, crap, Kylee just recognized me.

Bad timing. Didn't want Kylee to catch me staring at her. Actually, I hoped my presence would go unnoticed. I don't plan to say a peep. Just gather intel and video of Ted and Myrtle, people I may need to spoof.

Ted walks to the podium and taps the mic, igniting an irritating feedback screech that sets my teeth on edge. I switch my cellphone to record to capture whatever he plans to say.

"Could I please have your attention for a moment. For those of you who haven't met me, I'm Ted Welch. Our company manages your Hullis Island Owners Association. Today, I'll serve as meeting facilitator. While it's not quite one o'clock, the fire marshal is closing the doors since we've reached this room's occupancy limit. But don't worry, new arrivals won't be shut out of the proceedings. We're piping the audio outdoors so everyone on the grounds can hear."

He pauses a moment for audience murmurs to subside.

"Grant Welch, one of our company's summer interns, will take a roving microphone outside. When the public comment period begins, everyone who wants to speak will have an opportunity. If you're outdoors, just raise your hand, and Grant will bring the mic to you."

Not bad.

The Welch website bio and mug shot don't do Ted justice. It should have included a video. He comes across as patient, sincere. Guess that's his State Department background. He's smart and savvy, too. He anticipated the overcrowding and took measures to prevent a furious mob from storming the castle.

The man isn't hurting in the looks department either. About my age—late forties to early fifties. At least six feet and trim. His thick black hair is threaded with a few distinguishing strands of silver at the temples. Winning smile.

Can't blame Kylee for jumping his bones. Just not sure what Ted sees in her. The woman could do herself a favor if she applied a little makeup.

Can't believe she hasn't even tried to hide the bruises on her cheek. Her clothes scream thrift shop. And what's with that mop of white hair? Can she even get a comb through it?

I return my attention to the fidgeting audience. The clock is set to strike one. Ted clears his throat. Let's see how he keeps all these Earful complainers in line.

* * *

The meeting ends with Ted's promise to create a portal on the Hullis Island website to let individuals comment about their desire for—or opposition to—new rules or regulations. The meeting's a major disappointment for me. The only bright spots were provided by the few full-throated militants who demanded the entire board resign.

For the most part, Ted kept it orderly and civil. I didn't say a word. However, I videoed several minutes of Ted and Myrtle speaking and gesturing. Plenty of material for AI training. Should be able to produce footage capable of fooling even the people who know them best. If the content is sufficiently frightening, Kylee won't stop to question if the speaker is REALLY her lover or her mom. No, she'll spring into action.

I also identified a few Myrtle Kane foes. Most promising is Byron Kisker, a former cowardly director. He deserted the board during last fall's mass resignation. Byron strongly disagrees with Myrt's belief that owners should be allowed to participate in board meetings and have input when prospective rule changes are drafted. In the meeting, Byron took pains to stress Myrt was *appointed* to the board, not elected.

He added people *elect* directors to act on their behalf and argued Hullis Island should be run like a corporation. Byron also insisted the board's failure to punish each and every rules infraction could result in the loss of all enforcement powers.

Hmm. I have the feeling Byron has a specific, existing infraction in mind. What is it? Can it be used against Myrtle?

I have high hopes for my new friend Byron. My enemy's enemy is my pal.

Chapter Forty-Two

Kylee

Sunday, July 2, afternoon

Once the meeting starts, I turn my cellphone to vibrate. Despite my antipathy to the intrusive hunks of plastic, I told Grant I'd keep my smartphone on. That way he can reach me if he needs any help with the crowd outside.

Toward the end of the meeting, the pocketed cell's gentle massage of my thigh startles me. Some last-minute trouble outside? Hope Grant's okay.

Surprise. The text message is from Sherry LeRoy, not Grant.

Need U come here. Urgent. Have info Andy's attack.

Grrr. This is why I hate texting. If we were talking on the phone, I'd ask questions. Find out why Sherry thinks it's urgent. Probably something that can easily wait until tomorrow. Today has enough headaches.

I type. *"Can do tomorrow."*

"Must be 2day. Can U get here by 4?"

"Will do best," I answer.

It's 1:55, and the meeting's winding down. Four o'clock should be doable. Since I've heard every word uttered in the meeting, it won't hurt to skip the family's follow-up rehash. I text Ted, knowing he won't look at his phone until after the meeting ends and people quit tugging on his sleeve.

I've seen the phenomenon plenty of times. If they get a chance for a private word, owners are eager to subject Ted to misgivings about their neighbors. 'Watch out for Eric or ignore Linda,' they whisper. Of course, they would never publicly voice their ill will.

My text tells Ted I plan to leave for Rand Creek as soon as the Hullis meeting concludes. Sherry LeRoy says we need to meet pronto. I add I'll call when I know more.

The minute the meeting adjourns, I circle around back of the Hullis Island Community Center to avoid the crush of people spilling out the front door. Don't want to be pigeonholed by any of Mom's friends eager to share their critiques of the meeting.

To avoid post-meeting traffic jams, I parked my Camry on a side street two blocks from the Community Center. I don't encounter a single person as I speedwalk to the car.

On my drive to Rand Creek, I can't stop thinking about Amanda Holder. She was staring a hole through my forehead when I spotted her in the back row. The sighting was unexpected. Thought she'd be too busy creating whatever computer app she's working on to leave her self-imposed isolation in the Lighthouse Cove mansion she inherited from her mother.

Even more surprising than seeing the doc in attendance was her silence. Since she had to drive almost thirty miles from her Lighthouse Cove hideaway to attend the Hullis meeting, I imagined she'd come to add her two cents. She doesn't impress me as someone who's shy about voicing her opinion. Her grim countenance certainly didn't suggest her mood was any cheerier than when she gave Ed and me the bum's rush yesterday.

What did she hope to gain by showing up?

As I pass Beaufort Memorial Hospital, my mind turns to Andy Fyke. I'm almost sorry I delivered a loaner tablet to him. I'm afraid he's seen the Earful posts and read how a Rand Creek neighbor attacked him because she thought he was a child molester. Can't imagine what must be going through Andy's mind. Trying to think who hates him enough to make up the story? Wondering if it's possible he said or did something someone misinterpreted? Worrying the innuendoes will poison his relationships, cost him friends?

I sure hope whatever reason Sherry has for demanding this urgent meeting will help me answer Andy's most pressing concerns.

Chapter Forty-Three

Kylee

Sunday, July 2, afternoon

When the Rand Creek elevator doors slide open on the fourth floor, I find Sherry waiting to walk me to her condo.

She hugs me. "Sorry to pounce on you, but before we go inside, you need the skinny on the woman you'll be meeting. Jeannie Crooks had a conversation with J.T. shortly before she committed suicide. I want you to hear her story."

I assume Sherry is prepping me to go easy on the woman, given her highly emotional state. "I'll be nice," I promise. "I understand she's distraught."

"Wait." Sherry seizes my arm to anchor me. "I waylaid you to warn you about Jeannie's vindictiveness, not her grief. She belongs to Grannies for Safety, a vigilante group. The old ladies who belong—J.T. was a member, too—don't think police and the courts do enough to protect women and children from sexual abuse. So, the Grannies identify and out people they suspect may be perverts.

"They're all about reporting their suspicions to neighbors and authorities. They don't fret too much about someone being wrongly accused, and they're homophobic. They assume all male homosexuals are likely child molesters or will become ones if given the right opportunity."

Sherry snorts. "Yeah, hard to believe Jeannie came to me. She has to know I'm one of THEM. But, for whatever reason, the Grannies don't lump lesbians with their male counterparts as potential abusers of children. Sexist, right?"

Sherry's nervous titter betrays her discomfort.

I'm dumbfounded and annoyed.

"Please don't tell me you called me here to listen to Jeannie justify J.T.'s attack on Andy."

Sherry vigorously shakes her head. "No. No. Not at all. Just listen to *everything* Jeannie has to say. I knew if she wandered off on some perverse tangent, you'd get your panties in a twist and split. But, please, keep it together until Jeannie shares every last word of her conversation with J.T. Jeannie has clues about a real, continuing danger to our HOA. Someone out there is a hell of a lot scarier than J.T., Jeannie, or any of the Grannies."

While I can't imagine what that someone might look like, I sigh. "Okay. For you, I'll grit my teeth and stay put."

When we enter Sherry's condo, Jeannie doesn't rise to shake my hand. I can see why. Lifting what I imagine to be her three hundred pounds off the sofa is a big ask. The sturdy cane beside her speaks to her limited mobility. Wonder if it also comes in handy to beat the crap out of suspected gays.

As Sherry makes the introductions, I choose a club chair across from Jeannie. While there's not much room on the couch, I also want to read the vigilante's expressions. Once Jeannie and I decline Sherry's offer of refreshments, our hostess slips into the other club chair.

"Sherry tells me you were friends with J.T.," I open. "I'm sorry for your loss."

"J.T. was a very dear friend." Jeannie pauses to dab a handkerchief to her eyes. Her soft, extremely high-pitched, girly voice seems a mismatch with her massive body.

"I feel so guilty I didn't pick up on J.T.'s utter despair," she continues. "I knew she was upset, but I never dreamed she'd commit suicide."

"What made you think J.T. was upset?" I coax.

"I phoned her early last evening," she replies. "Normally, we talk every day, and I hadn't heard from her since Thursday. Since my last few calls had gone to voice mail, I was relieved when J.T. picked up. If she hadn't answered, I'd have gone to her house and pounded on her door. I feared she'd fallen and couldn't get up."

Jeannie glances at her cane. "J.T. doesn't have my weight problem, but she is—was—on the plump side. If you're old with bad knees, getting up off the floor is like climbing Mt. Everest."

"Did J.T. explain why she'd been out of touch?" I probe.

"Not exactly. Said she'd had a lot on her mind and didn't like to burden others when she was feeling low. J.T. often had nightmares. She was raped when she was nine years old. A miracle she didn't die. Her rapist was never caught. J.T. was sentenced to a lifetime of bad dreams."

Jeannie pauses to dab at her eyes again. I do feel for the woman—and J.T. "Did J.T. eventually tell you why she was depressed?"

"Not right away. Didn't feel I should press. If J.T. didn't want to relive some nightmare, I wouldn't ask her to describe it. I hoped chatting about regular neighborhood stuff would take her mind off her sorrows. So, I asked J.T. if she'd seen the news about Andy Fyke's fall and the Earful suggestions he'd been pushed."

"I could believe someone pushed him. Me and my friends didn't appreciate Andy knocking on our doors like some Fuller Brush salesman. Campaigning like that isn't seemly. Not what gentlemen do. I felt Andy was exaggerating the rental evils and was out to screw fellow retirees counting on rental income."

I'm practically grinding my teeth, waiting for Jeannie to quit dissing Andy and get to the point. "So, how did J.T. respond?"

Jeannie's breath hitches. "That's when she began sobbing."

The way Jeannie sucks in oxygen on that last word, I decide she's trying to forestall a new crying jag. It fails. The woman's entire body quivers as she sobs.

"Let me get you some water." Sherry jumps up and heads to the kitchen.

Me? I sit mute. Have no idea what to say. Don't know the woman, and I'm pretty sure I would actively dislike her if I did. Yet it's uncomfortable to watch anyone in such distress and do nothing. Jeannie just lost a friend. I know how much that hurts.

Sherry hands the glass of water to Jeannie, who gulps half of it down in seconds. Her hand trembles as she searches the side table for a coaster. Her sobs slowly subside.

Should I ask another question? Would it risk triggering more tears?

I decide to sit quietly, wait for Jeannie to decide when she can continue.

She clears her throat and blinks back tears. The look she gives me isn't exactly friendly.

"Guess I should skip to the part of J.T.'s conversation that Sherry wanted you to hear," she says. "J.T. told me a woman named Ann Rand befriended her online several weeks ago. This Ann person said she'd recently moved into Rand Creek. Since she was wheelchair-bound, she explained she relied on a live-in aide to help her with everything from eating to baths. Ann claimed her computer was her only window on the world. Said she never left her condo because she hated people staring at her and pitying her condition."

Ayn Rand? Living in Rand Creek? Really?

From Jeannie's nonchalant mention of the name, I figure she isn't acquainted with the famous author's novels, and didn't consider the name might be a pseudonym. I keep my mouth shut, hardly dare to blink. I don't want to distract Jeannie. Need her to keep talking.

"Anyway, J.T. felt she and Ann had a deep common bond, since they'd both been abused as children," Jeannie continues. "Ann spent all her waking hours on the internet, searching for perverts who'd escaped justice. She said her sole mission in life was to protect children, make sure they never suffered like she and J.T. had. To do so, Ann had learned how to plumb the secrets of the dark web."

Sherry shudders. "Mention of the dark web should have alarmed J.T."

Sherry's interruption surprises me. She was the one who'd told me to let J.T. ramble and keep my opinions to myself.

"So, this person shared information she claimed came from the dark web?" I ask.

"Yes. Ann said that's how she *knew* Andy was a child molester. In fact, she sent J.T. a video to prove it. It showed Andy talking with fellow pedophiles in a group chat, where he proclaimed child porn was a First Amendment right.

"Ann sent a second clip that showed Andy teetering at the top of the clubhouse stairs. Ann vowed if she weren't confined to a wheelchair, she'd push Andy down those stairs herself. Make sure he never abused a sweet young child again."

Jeannie stops, looks down, and shakes her head.

"When J.T. confessed she'd pushed Andy, I was shocked. But I absolutely understood. Felt I might have done the same. She acted to protect the kids visiting their Rand Creek grandparents from an evil festering in our community. It's clear we can't depend on cops or the courts. They let predators off on technicalities so they're free to rape again. How can prisons release these monsters for good behavior while their victims remain in therapy?"

I'm dying to interrupt. Scream. Call foul. Vigilantes. Self-appointed judges, juries, and executioners. A guarantee innocents will be persecuted. Sherry's admonition to hold my tongue keeps me silent.

Jeannie's rant has made her thirsty. She takes another sip of water.

"Anyway, J.T. became distraught when Ann, her dear friend, disappeared. The texts J.T. sent to Ann came back as undeliverable. Ann also didn't respond to direct messages on Facebook, either. J.T. was confused. Was Ann mad at her? Hadn't she urged her to attack Andy? Or had Ann succumbed to the severe illness that kept her wheelchair-bound?"

Jeannie bites her lip. "Then Ann reconnected with J.T., using a new phone. She apologized for being out of touch. Said someone had stolen her identity and, pretending to be her, contacted all her friends. Meanwhile, since the thief had changed Ann's passwords, she was locked out of her accounts and had no idea what this doppelganger might be telling people. Ann told J.T. that the video of Andy Fyke advocating for child porn was probably a deepfake. Said she had no clue why the thief sent it."

"Oh, my Lord."

The comment escapes before I can censor myself. Why didn't J.T. ask

179

questions? Like how the hell did Ann know about the Andy Fyke video if she was locked out of her accounts?

Jeannie chokes back a sob before she continues.

"Ann layered on more guilt. Said she hoped J.T. would realize she would never have suggested a violent act like pushing Andy down the stairs. She shamed J.T. for how her actions would impact her children. Said they would be horrified and embarrassed once they learned. With all the camera monitors around Rand Creek, Ann predicted J.T.'s arrest would happen quickly."

Wow. Ann sure knew how to wage psychological warfare.

"How did you respond when J.T. told you all of this?" I finally ask.

"I offered to come over to talk things through. Reminded her Andy was alive and would recover from his injuries. Told J.T. things weren't as bad as they seemed. I thought J.T. pulled herself together. She thanked me for my offer but said she was too exhausted to talk any longer. Said we'd talk in the morning.

"The next day, when she didn't answer her door, I used the spare key she'd given me to go inside. J.T. was in her bedroom, fully clothed, hands folded across her chest, like she was already in a coffin. J.T. lay atop the quilt on her bed. Everything neat as a pin. Her confession sat next to the empty bottle of sleeping pills."

"Did you call 911?"

"Yes, an ambulance came first. After J.T. was pronounced dead, a sheriff's deputy arrived and took her suicide note. He didn't tell me to keep quiet about J.T.'s last words. I felt it my duty to set the record straight. To end the finger-pointing at the rental property owners wrongly accused of attacking Andy."

I want to scream at Jeannie. To set the record straight, Jeannie told the world J.T.'s attack of Andy was justified because she thought he was a pedophile. Good job. God, sometimes I wish social media didn't exist.

Sherry jumps up and starts to pace.

"When Jeannie shared her story, I set out to find this Ann Rand person," Sherry says. "She orchestrated this tragedy. Even if she was an invalid, the woman bore responsibility for the vicious gossip that set the stage."

Sherry makes another agitated round trip across her living room before she stops and looks down at me.

"Imagine my surprise when I discovered there was no Ann Rand listed in the owner directory. In fact, not a single owner has Rand as a last name. So, I called everyone who owns Rand Creek rentals and asked if an Ann Rand might be among their tenants.

"Naturally, everyone said no. The last rental property owner I called was a retired librarian. My question made him laugh. 'Don't you know, Ayn Rand died in 1982. I don't rent to deadbeats.'"

My brain is speeding along at a hundred miles a minute but can't seem to stay on the tracks.

Who hated or feared Andy Fyke enough to come up with an elaborate scheme to urge another tortured soul to harm him?

* * *

After Jeannie leaves, Sherry insists we move to the kitchen for iced tea and cookies. Sherry's wife, Alice, who made herself scarce during Jeannie's visit, joins us.

"I don't trust myself around that woman," Alice explains. "I hate bigots, especially ones who profess to be morally superior Christians yet embrace hatred as a religious virtue. My wife's more soft-hearted. Sherry gives Jeannie a pass because she was traumatized by the rape and murder of a college friend. I'm not so magnanimous. The Grannies encourage their followers to hate all homosexuals. That hate is not Christianity."

I instantly like Alice, Sherry's wife. She doesn't beat around the bush. Tells it like she sees it. Not always the best way to make one's way in the world. But better than choking on your anger.

"I wanted you to hear Jeannie's story before I call the Sheriff's Office about this Ann Rand provocateur," Sherry adds. "Jeannie didn't say boo about her to the deputy at the suicide scene. She excuses the oversight by saying she was too upset. Maybe. But I think Jeannie wanted to protect this invalid

Ann, who shared her prejudices and feared backlash for the Grannies for Safety."

"You are going to call the Sheriff's Office, right?" I ask.

"Yes, once Jeannie learned Ann Rand wasn't a real person, she agreed we should contact the authorities. 'Course, I'd have done so with or without her permission. Whoever this Ann Rand is, she needs to be locked up before she does more harm. This imposter is a security threat to our entire Rand Creek community."

"Do you think she lives in Rand Creek? That she's an owner?" I ask.

Sherry's fingers trace a line through the moisture on her iced tea glass. "Maybe. This imposter knew plenty about Andy Fyke and J.T. She's smart and talented. She created a fake video to make Fyke look like a pedophile and provoke J.T. to act. What if this woman dislikes another Rand Creek owner? My biggest fear is her success will prompt her to use the same tactics again."

I nod. "Yes, the Sheriff's Office needs to know about this. I'd like to talk with Ted about the best way to warn Rand Creek owners. My first inclination is to send an alert that a scam artist may be trying to befriend owners online, and they should be wary of any new 'friends'—especially individuals they've never met in person...people eager to paint others as evil."

I pause, thinking about Andy's situation. "However, the community message shouldn't mention Andy. That could warn this fake Ann and interfere with the sheriff's investigation. God, I do hope the Sheriff's Office is actively investigating Andy's assault and J.T.'s suicide."

"Sounds sensible," Sherry agrees. "Talk with Ted about the warning's exact wording. As soon as you leave, I'll let Jocelyn know what's going on. I'll ask her to call a board meeting immediately. If we can't meet in person, we can do it by Zoom."

Alice harrumphs. "Jocelyn will love getting this news. Don't expect any help from her quarter. I seriously doubt that warning owners a malicious scammer may be focused on Rand Creek will fit into Jocelyn's marketing plans."

"Better bad PR than another attack or suicide," I comment.

Alice chuckles. "Not if Jocelyn thinks she can pick who gets attacked and who commits suicide. Hey, Jocelyn had ample motive to sideline Andy. And she's smart and computer savvy. Maybe she's our Ann Rand. Sorry, I can't always censor my dark humor."

Maybe Alice's jest has some merit.

Maybe Jocelyn should be a suspect.

Chapter Forty-Four

Grant

Sunday, July 2, afternoon

I dial the number for Hank's Marine Repair. Pays to have friends. I asked Kylee's pal Kay Barrett to phone a few of her fellow FACE directors. Didn't take Kay long to discover FACE sent its professional watercraft to Hank's for a tune-up last Wednesday.

When the phone stops ringing, I get the standard thanks-for-calling-but-you're-out-of-luck recording. Robo-voice instructs me to leave a message. Someone will call back—whenever. As expected.

As soon as I finish reciting my name and number, I hear a series of digital clicks. Sounds like someone's dialing out on a party line. *Weird.*

"Hello, is someone there?" I ask.

"Huh? Who's this? I just came in the office to catch up on paperwork. Was calling my wife to tell her I'll be home in half an hour. Guess the lines crossed. What do you need?"

I stammer. Stumped. Didn't think anyone would answer the phone on a Sunday. Just thought I'd get in the queue for a call back when the folks returned to work.

"Hello, this is Hank Mitchell. You still there?"

"Yes, sorry. Got tongue-tied for a moment. Couldn't figure out where to start."

Hank laughs. "The beginning is always good. You have a boat that needs repair?"

"Uh, no. Wondered if I could take a look at the FACE professional watercraft that's in your shop for a tune-up."

"Why? You thinking of buying one? Hell of a machine, but mighty pricey."

"No, I just want to see it. Did you hear about last night's explosion? I was kayaking nearby when it happened, and what looked like a Jet Ski rocketed past me. It was really dark. Only had a few seconds to look.

"When I told the cops about it, they mocked me. Said I couldn't have seen a Jet Ski or a WaveRunner. They'd have choked on mud and grass at low tide. I'm stubborn. I saw what I saw. Searching online, I read about a professional watercraft that can bomb around in shallow water. A friend on the FACE board told me they have one, and it's in your shop."

"I hope you're not suggesting whoever set off that marsh explosion used the FACE watercraft?" Hank challenges.

Crap. I've made him angry and defensive. Way to go, Grant.

"No, no. Please hear me out. I just want to see the FACE watercraft in person. It'll help me decide if the machine I saw is like it. I'm not saying I saw the FACE craft."

Hank doesn't respond. The silence drags on for several seconds. I begin to wonder if he hung up, and I didn't hear the click.

"Actually," Hank says, "if you saw a machine like this, odds are pretty good it belongs to FACE. Don't know of another watercraft like this within two hundred miles. Who'd you say pointed you our way? A FACE director?"

"Yes, Kay Barrett," I answer. "Call her. She'll tell you I'm not a crank."

At least, I hope she will.

"Give me your number," Hank says. "If Kay vouches for you, I'll call you back."

When the call ends, I knock my knuckles against my forehead. "Cool moves, Grant. You're a real slick operator."

I figure it's fifty-fifty that Hank will call back. For starters, he may be unable to reach Kay. The B&B has her hopping. He also may decide to go home as planned. Spend the rest of Sunday with his wife. On the other

185

hand, Hank may worry I actually did see the FACE craft. If so, ignoring me could make *him* look like the bomber or a collaborator.

In less than five minutes, my cell rings.

"Okay, kid," Hank says. "If you can get here within the hour, I'll hang until five. Can't stay longer. Big neighborhood cookout tonight. Wife will kill me if I'm any later."

Hank gives me the address.

"I'll be there," I promise.

Of course, that promise depends on transportation. Dad pocketed the keys to my Jeep when we got home from Satin Sands. Since then, I haven't left Frank's house without a chaperone/jailer.

Time to talk to Dad.

Chapter Forty-Five

The Chameleon

Sunday, July 2, afternoon

T he minute I walk in my rental, I use my designated burner phone to send another text to Mr. Dynamite. This time, I get a reply.

Well, I should say Bubba gets a reply. My bombardier still thinks he's texting back and forth with Bubba's new burner.

Turns out Mr. Dynamite has a tattletale pal in the Sheriff's Office. The informant passed along some key intel—the name of the kayaker witness Mr. Dynamite failed to hit with his bullets. It's none other than freakin' Grant Welch.

Now I get why Grant's Jeep was absent from Frank Donahue's driveway last night. It also explains why Ted and Kylee tore out of here at early-dark-thirty. Grant must have phoned in a panic. The snitch in the Sheriff's Office confided Grant was unharmed but worth squat as a witness. He could only tell the shooter was male and white.

Nonetheless, I suggest it would be prudent for Mr. Dynamite to take a short vacation. Of course, I use AI to compose all texts to Mr. D. in Bubba's vernacular. Words like "prudent" would never pass Bubba's lips.

AI peppers the Bubba texts with appropriate bad grammar and obscenities. Interesting that AI initially resisted spewing sentences that my third-grade teacher would label grammatical nightmares. AI has been taught to avoid run-on sentences, mangled tenses, and other grammar faux pas, unless it's commanded to mimic a real boob. Bubba qualifies.

Mr. Dynamite agrees that his temporary banishment is a good idea. He'll tell his employer, Hank's Marine Repair, some Upstate South Carolina relative kicked the bucket. He won't be back to Beaufort for a week or two.

Having satisfactorily completed that task, it's time to devote a few hours to crafting my killer app's cartoon modules. For grins, I'm casting Kylee as my victim in a Beta cartoon experiment. For AI training, I downloaded Kylee news clips from the web. Last year TV news programs featured interviews with Kylee, Ted, Myrtle, and Grant. Quite handy for me.

As a salute to Kylee's sailor days, I whisper a series of descriptive phrases— black cartoon skunk...white stripe up the back...wears a pirate sash, three-corner hat, eye patch...white whiskers combed into handlebar moustache... one peg leg...brandishes long curved sword...twitching nose...bushy tail. Ah, yes, and a big pink asshole for up-close shots when the skunk sprays.

I hold my breath while I await my creature's initial rendering. Fingers crossed. I hope Knave O'Stinker is hilarious.

Wow! I laugh at the result. Can't wait to add animation. O'Stinker's secret weapon? Poisonous lethal farts, of course.

* * *

My progress on the cartoon module feels sluggish. While I've used dozens of Looney Tunes to teach AI how cartoon characters move, Knave O'Stinker's gestures and gait seem stilted and jerky. No worries. I'll solve this.

The reward's too great not to.

After two hours, I stand. While I do my stretches, I reflect on how I got here—excommunicated from academia. If I'd known what would happen, would I still have created that deepfake video featuring my esteemed colleagues?

I chuckle. Oh, yeah. In a heartbeat.

I deserved to be named head of my department. If I'd had a weenie between my legs, it would have happened years ago. The male tapped for the honor hadn't published nearly as many papers as me, hadn't been celebrated as an AI genius, hadn't had tech industry giants begging for consults.

I had to express my outrage and contempt. My gesture didn't harm a soul. Didn't tote an AR-15 to the university to riddle a dozen colleagues with lead. My response was really quite measured and, if I must say, a work of art.

I simply created a deepfake video. It showed my undeserving colleague in full doctoral regalia kneeling before our pompous university president. Of course, the new department head didn't kneel to be in position to kiss the president's ring. No, the video showed him sucking up in a more telling manner.

After my video made its circuit, I got anonymous hate mail—undoubtedly from our new department head's male pals. Made me glad I carry a gun. Started doing that once school shootings surged. Wasn't about to get bumped off by some pimply retard I flunked. How I wished one of the cowards who mailed in their hate would have given me a shove or provided some other excuse for me to play Dirty Harriette.

While the university destroyed all copies of my deepfake masterpiece on its servers and workstations, I still have the original. In fact, I call it up every now and then when I need a chuckle. Like now.

I smile as I play the thirty-second clip. I'm sure many of my female colleagues did the same when it arrived as an email attachment. Too bad none of them had the backbone to stand up for me. Their loss. My gain.

My dismissal may be the best thing that ever happened to me. I'm free to do whatever I please. Thank you, Ayn Rand, for removing my societal blinders. I'm strong, and very soon I will be very, very rich.

Refreshed by my short reverie, I revisit my to-do list. J.T.'s suicide should put an end to the snoop's attempts to tie Andy's attack to someone who rents Rand Creek real estate. Someone like me.

I'm a tad more queasy about Bubba and Mr. Dynamite, despite the descriptions of the sky-high fireball and Grant Welch's flop as a reliable witness. There's still reason to worry. I fear forensic experts will find enough uncharred fragments to prove Bubba's boat rammed Steph. Thank goodness, it'll be tougher to prove lethal intent.

Nonetheless, I want the entire Welch HOA Management team occupied with stamping out client and personal wildfires with zero time or energy to expend on yours truly.

First up?

Let's give Byron Kisker some ammunition to attack his enemy, Myrtle Kane.

Chapter Forty-Six

Grant

Sunday, July 2, afternoon

I find Dad sitting at the dining room table, typing away on his laptop.

"Do you have a minute?" I ask.

"Sure, I'm about finished. Wanted to type up meeting notes and action items while everything's fresh in my mind. Hope Robin can quickly add that public comment section to the Hullis website.

"I know the risks involved," he adds. "The website may get flooded with inflammatory posts and misinformation. Heaven forbid, it becomes indistinguishable from that God-awful Earful site. But we need a safety valve. The meeting made it quite evident owners doubt the board is hearing them. Public comments should let unhappy owners let off steam and help the board assess how to respond. Hate to ask Robin to monitor the posts, but not sure how else to keep comments focused and civil."

I laugh. "What, are you going to ask Robin to award color-coded check marks?"

"Very funny," Dad answers.

I glance around and realize Dad and I are alone. "Where did everyone go?"

"The minute the meeting adjourned, Kylee left for Rand Creek," Dad replies. "Sherry LeRoy texted about an emergency and the need to meet face-to-face. After Kylee leaves Sherry's, she's heading to the River Rat. Myrt and Frank are at an informal reception for the Owens' grandson and his new bride."

Dad shuts down his laptop and leans back in his chair. "Since we're alone, do you want to talk about last night?"

"Sort of." I hesitate.

How to begin?

"Can we maybe talk about last night on a drive to St. Helena. Do you know Hank's Marine Repair? The owner says he'll stay at the shop until five p.m. if we can get there before then."

Dad's eyebrows perform a high-jump maneuver. "Why do you need a repair shop? Did you damage your friend's kayak last night?"

"No." I quickly explain that a watercraft fitting the description of the one used by the boat bomber might be sitting on one of Hank's hoists.

Dad nods. "Okay. Let's go."

* * *

As expected, the car ride offers Dad ample opportunity to point out my intellectual shortcomings. He finds twenty different ways to tell me I do a piss poor job of weighing risks before I act.

When Dad finally wraps up, he asks, "Do you think there should be consequences for your actions—for sneaking out, risking your life? Not to mention scaring to death everyone who loves you?"

I'm not stupid. I answer yes.

Dad then outlines my penance options. My choice is a no-brainer. I agree to spend the remaining Saturdays of my summer vacation doing any yard or household repair chores that Grandma Myrt and Frank assign. Whatever those chores may be, I'm sure Grandma will insist I take rest breaks, complete with cookies and lemonade.

Despite the lecture, I'm glad Dad opted to come with me. I sense he's actually proud of my watercraft sleuthing efforts. Maybe this trip will let me prove I wasn't imagining things. Dad's presence will make Hank more comfortable, too. Someday I hope I have Dad's ability to put strangers at ease and coax information from them.

We see a sign for Hank's Marine Repair and bump down a rutted dirt road. It's not long before the rusty metal roofs of two oversized sheds appear. An adjacent graveled area provides parking for more than a dozen boats of varying sizes. They sit on trailers. Imagine some are waiting repair, while others are ready for pickup.

While the massive mechanic sheds have metal sides, they're open front and back to simplify rolling inventory in and out. Looking through the sheds, I see a sliver of choppy water beyond. The shop's piers and docks let customers steer or tow boats in for repair.

The nearest shed includes two bays. In the first, a sailboat that's even larger than Aunt Kylee's is hoisted on a lift. Its barnacle-pimpled hull is fully exposed. In the adjacent bay, a large pontoon boat awaits attention.

When we get closer to the second mechanic's shed, I count four smaller craft being dissected.

What I don't see are any signs of a human.

"Hope Hank hasn't left," I mutter as Dad and I near the sheds.

"I'm sure he hasn't," Dad responds. "I've been here before. Hank works out of a small office building behind the second shed. You can't see it from here."

As soon as Dad finishes his explanation, Hank appears around the shed's corner. He's middle-aged, wiry. Looks kind of like I expected based on his gravelly voice. He's not wearing the overalls I imagined, though. He's dressed in a neat polo shirt, khakis with a sharp crease, and boat deck shoes.

Duh, Hank mentioned he'd come in to tackle paperwork not grease gears.

Our respective paths intersect in front of the second shed. Dad handles the introductions and apologizes for inconveniencing Hank on a Sunday. He thanks him for meeting us.

"Not a problem," Hank replies and darts a look my way. "After I got your call, I gave the FACE craft paperwork a once-over. The tune-up is on our work schedule for tomorrow. So, it's still sitting in what we jokingly call our ER waiting room. Follow me."

When we arrive at the machine, Hank sucks in a deep breath. "This isn't where it was parked Friday when FACE trailered it in."

The minute I see the sleek craft's glossy green skin I flash back to my brief sighting. Can't swear I saw *this* machine, but if this isn't the one, it has to be its twin.

"Man, this looks exactly like the shooter's ride," I say.

"Shooter?" Hank's voice climbs an octave in alarm. "You told me you saw someone else near an explosion. Figured you were trying to find another witness. You didn't say nothing about some shooting."

"When he spotted me, the guy took a shot. Didn't hit me. Don't know if his aim was bad or if he just wanted to scare me. If that was his goal, he succeeded."

"Is it possible someone used this machine last night?" Dad asks.

Hank's discomfort is evident. "I want to say no. Whenever we're closed, the keys for all the boats in for repair hang on a pegboard in my office. I'm very careful about locking up. There was no sign of an office break-in."

Hank gives the craft a once-over, peering at its front, back, sides, and undercarriage. When he finishes, he shakes his head and scuffs the gravel with the toe of a shoe.

"The underside is muddy, and there's some marsh grass stuck to it. I'm almost certain that wasn't the case when it arrived."

"Hank, do your employees have keys to your office?" Dad asks.

"Not exactly," he replies. "But they all know where I hide the spare key. Can't afford to hold work up if I'm not around. Sometimes, if my guys have reason to take off early, they'll come in before we open. Don't have no time clocks. Pay good wages, and the honor system's always seemed to work."

"How many people work for you?" I ask.

Hank looks at me. "Five. What did this shooter of yours look like?"

I bite my lip, trying once more to remember any detail.

"Like I told the deputies. My light only swept over the man's face for a second or two. Mostly, I saw white skin and dark shadows. All I can be sure of is he was a white man. Had the impression he was medium-height. Not short, not tall. Under six feet."

"Well, that eliminates two of my guys—Gullah folk with real dark skins. Your description doesn't rule out the other three. Though it surely wasn't Lenny. He's been with me twenty years, celebrated his seventieth birthday a while back. Keeps working and swears he'll hang on till he croaks. Says his wife would drive him crazy with honey-do's if he stayed home."

"Can you tell us the names of the other two mechanics?" Dad asks.

Hank rakes his fingers through thinning dishwater-blond hair. "Geez, I don't know. It would be different if you were cops. Giving out names don't feel right. One—or maybe both of these fellas—haven't done a damn thing wrong. Could a been an innocent reason that FACE watercraft got moved. You admit you only had seconds to see whatever it is you saw."

Hank shakes his head again. "No. The answer is no. Not about to hand over information about my workers to strangers. If you come back with the sheriff, we can talk about it."

"I understand." Dad's voice is calm.

Me? I want to scream at Hank.

"If I were in your shoes, imagine I'd make the same call," Dad adds. "We'll share the information about the FACE craft with the sheriff."

Dad glances my way. Think he senses I'm ready to explode. He turns his head slightly so I can read his lips. "Don't," he mouths.

"Thanks again for meeting with us," Dad says as he turns back to Hank and shakes his hand.

Once we're in the car, I let Dad know I'm disappointed.

"You didn't even try to talk Hank into sharing those names. Now we're nowhere. Do you really think the Sheriff's Office will do anything? You saw how Deputy Ibsen discounted every word I said."

"Son, Hank was right. I would have done the same thing. I respect him for protecting the privacy of his employees. He doesn't know us from Adam. And I think you're wrong about the Sheriff's Department. That woman, Deputy Muschel, seemed to believe you. Let's contact her. If that doesn't work, there's more than one way to flush out a rat."

Chapter Forty-Seven

Kylee

Sunday, July 2, late afternoon

I 'm looking forward to spending at least an hour aboard the River Rat, my cozy sailboat home. Feel as if I've been awake for days, though it's not even twenty hours since Grant phoned and woke us in the middle of the night.

I've been running around like a headless chicken ever since. First, the scare that Grant might be injured, then the always unpleasant encounter with Deputy Ibsen. Next, I serve as an usher while an angry mob files into the Hullis Island community center.

Then comes the topper. Biting my tongue while I listen to a bigoted vigilante justify her friend's attack on Andy, a man offered no chance to dispute the malicious campaign that made him J.T.'s target.

Okay, I'm cranky.

It's danged hot, and my older Camry's air conditioner takes time to fire up. Trickles of sweat glue my blouse to my back. Have had no chance for a nap, let alone a shower. Can't wait to turn the water on full blast and wash my hair. I'll stand under the shower head and let the water massage my back and shoulders until the hot water supply totally peters out.

Next, I'll slip into clean jeans, a worn, super soft tee-shirt, and tennis shoes. I can't wait to discard my "professional" uniform—black pantsuit, blouse, and leather pumps. The dress shoes have thick two-inch heels, the most comfortable option I could find to wear with dress slacks.

At least, Welch HOA Management has no dress code. Wouldn't have stuck around this long if I had to don dresses, hose, and heels to represent Ted's company. I strictly reserve dresses for weddings and funerals.

When I see a sign for Beaufort Memorial Hospital, I suddenly feel guilty. Here I am bitching about my discomfort when Andy Fyke's stuck in a hospital bed. I need to stop and find out how he's holding up—mentally as well as physically.

I'm quite sure he hasn't been spared hearing his attacker thought he was a pedophile.

* * *

When Andy sees me in his doorway, he waves at me with his left, unbroken hand. Since his jaw's wired shut, he's unable to smile. Makes it kind of hard to tell if he's glad to see me.

"Thought I'd pop in for a minute to see how you're doing," I say. "See if there's anything else I can bring you?"

Andy dips his head toward the computer tablet Robin fixed for him. It's sitting closed on the stand beside his bed. His crabbing fingers motion that he wants me to come in and hand him the tablet. Not sure what Andy had been doing before I arrived. His TV was on, but the sound was muted. He seemed to be staring into space.

I wait while Andy pecks out a two-fingered message on the computer. Then he swivels the screen toward me.

"Spoke to this J.T. 1 x. Why she believe this crap?"

I watch Andy's eyes widen as I explain J.T. was sent a deepfake video that appeared to show him advocating for child pornography.

"Deepfake videos can be very convincing," I add. "People tend not to question what they see and hear. They don't ask 'Is this real?'—especially if a video reinforces their beliefs. J.T. belonged to a Grannies for Safety vigilante group. They suspect everyone outside their group of being a potential pervert."

Andy's eyes brim with unshed tears. My heart aches for him.

"Andy, I promise I'll make sure the truth gets out," I say. "And I swear we'll catch the monster who painted you as a child molester."

I don't tell Andy I already have two monster candidates—Jocelyn Waters and Amanda Holder.

Chapter Forty-Eight

The Chameleon

Sunday, July 2, afternoon

I go to the Earful app to start building a profile for Byron Kisker, the disgruntled former Hullis Island director. I hope he's a nutcase who thinks the government injected him with a tracking chip when he held out his arm for a Covid shot. Folks steeped in conspiracy theories are so easy to groom.

Before I start my Earful search, I spot a "trending" notification. The come-on is from an opportunist offering remedies to people with "Covid vaccine remorse."

Wonder what snake oil she's peddling?

Her *remedy* is probably a kit that lets customers defeat government tracking by duct-taping aluminum foil over vaccine injection sites. Imagine what a meeting of the "saved" would look like—a hundred people waving sparkling, tin-foil arms. The vision cracks me up.

More power to the entrepreneur. Nothing wrong with helping fools part with their money. They'll lose it anyway.

Now is not the time to get distracted. I don't care about the worldview of any of my recruits...not who they hate...not who they idolize. Don't need to know which aliens they think have landed. Just need to figure out how to manipulate their fevered brains.

Reading through Byron's posting history, I quickly discover the burr that's up his butt. A neighbor on his Hullis street lost a son to a drug overdose a little while back. To cope, the grieving mother created a memorial garden in her side yard. The memorial includes a polished bench where she meditates. Her special spot to commune with her lost boy.

The memorial's surrounded by a waist-high, black, wrought-iron fence. A decorative entry gate showcases a color photo of her dead son. Since her house is on the golf course, I get why the woman didn't opt for a backyard shrine. Tough to meditate if you're ducking shanked golf drives.

Ah, ha. Here's Byron's most telling harangue.

"I'm sorry that woman lost her son. Doesn't entitle her to break Hullis Island rules. Our covenants clearly prohibit ALL fences, including the wrought-iron one ringing her kitschy tribute. The whole mess, with the color photo, looks like some third-world shrine. Island visitors probably think her kid is buried there."

In another post, Byron complains his emails to the board have not yielded satisfactory replies. "They're stalling," he grouses. "If the board fails to act immediately, it will open up Pandora's Box. More people will break our rules and say—with justification—if so-and-so doesn't have to play by the rules, neither do I."

I wonder if the board has attempted to address the matter. Hard to say. I can't find any reference to it in the minutes of recent Hullis Island board meetings. But the directors did go into executive session last month. Maybe they contacted the woman privately and suggested a compromise.

Don't really care what the directors have or haven't done. With no official documents to contradict me, the doors are wide open to anonymously feed Byron "insider" information.

What insider information?

Think I'll concoct emails that "prove" Myrtle uses her close relationship with Ted Welch to influence when and if Hullis Island's management company enforces rules. The emails will suggest Myrtle regularly asks Welch HOA Management to ignore infractions by her friends and punish folks she dislikes by assessing fines.

Yes, Byron, Myrtle's out to get people like you!

Having plucked all the Earful intel needed to profile Byron, I open my backdoor to Rand Creek's software to scan for new board email traffic. Often, the emails contain nuggets about properties soon to come on the market.

What in blazes!

My anger boils as I read director Sherry LeRoy's email to President Jocelyn Waters and her fellow Rand Creek directors.

I can't believe it. Before J.T. committed suicide, the stupid cow blabbed to Jeannie, another blabbermouth, about Ann Rand and the fake Andy Fyke videos. And diarrhea mouth Jeannie, in turn, spilled to Sherry, who shared the story with Kylee Kane and the Sheriff's Office.

Shit!

I was already on the snoop's radar. Jeannie's talk of deepfakes—an AI specialty—will prompt Kylee to zero in on me. Will she share her suspicions with the Sheriff's Office?

No. I think not. Not yet.

Considering her bitter relationship with Deputy Ibsen, I imagine she'll dig for real proof before opening her big trap. Afraid it's time to abandon subtlety. Sure, I could use Byron to keep Kylee busy defending her mother's honor, but it would be better to permanently remove the snoop from the picture.

Erase Kylee, and her suspicions will vanish. But how?

I consider how easy it should be to lure Kylee to a spot where she's alone and vulnerable. With the audio and video samples of Myrtle and Ted, I can easily create deepfakes starring either her mom or her lover. Haven't a doubt Kylee would come if convinced either one is in peril.

My first hat trick will be inventing a believable peril. The second is to decide how to end the snoop's life once she responds and, more importantly, who I can call on to kill her.

The who is a major problem. I sent Mr. Dynamite to the Upstate. Unavailable. Bubba has proven himself capable of screwing the pooch no matter how simple the task he's assigned.

I mentally go through the list of minions in my reserve corps. Since moving to the Lowcountry, I've visited dozens of fringe groups looking for candidates.

I've only had time to groom six prospects. To win their trust, I begin by echoing and endorsing everything they believe. Then, once I understand how they think, I steadily increase my credibility. I push out deepfakes that serve to demonstrate my insider knowledge, my superiority. Each believes I have access to information that confirms their sacred conspiracies. They understand how privileged they are to be my vassals. They could never gain such information on their own.

Yeah, it would be hard to find, since it doesn't exist.

Of the six possibilities, three would balk at committing an act of violence— even though they'd cheer others who cross the line. Dismissing Bubba, only two assassin candidates remain, and one of them is on a trip to California.

That leaves Claude, a seventeen-year-old gamer. Like the kid who leaked top secret government documents to his online buddies, Claude is a gun nut, who considers himself a God-fearing patriot and great thinker. He's also a pimply incel—involuntary celibate—who despises women. He'd happily murder a woman, if given a righteous motive. However, he must believe he'll either get away with the killing or become a cult hero.

I need some time to dream up a perfect pretext, and time is a commodity in scarce supply. What would prompt Claude to borrow his daddy's AR-15 to blast umpteen rounds into Kylee? She's female. But something far more motivating is needed. It must be a mission. One that makes the seventeen-year-old believe he's serving as God's right hand and is a patriot worthy of being called George Washington's virtual son.

In Claude's mind, God is, of course, male, and the deity's worst screw-up was stealing that rib from Adam to create a female creature to ruin paradise.

A promised reward of receiving seventy-two virgins in heaven seems to convince some young boys to strap on explosives and accompany their victims to the hereafter. But I doubt that particular carrot would work on Claude. Raised by his father, an evangelical single parent, he's probably unfamiliar with the Koran. Need to do a little more in-depth study on incel culture.

Meanwhile, wonder if I can mine something of value from my hack of Frank Donahue's Wi-Fi. Since Myrtle Kane is staying at his house, I'm sure she uses it to communicate with her daughter and Ted. Maybe it can help me keep tabs on them without spending more evenings getting eaten by mosquitoes.

Chapter Forty-Nine

Kylee

Sunday, July 2, late afternoon

As soon as I board the River Rat, I decide to phone Ted. I owe him an update before my hot shower and clean clothes.

When I switch on my phone, there's a message from Lt. Alysha Carter, the young Coast Guard investigator I contacted with the GPS coordinates for Bubba's boat. Eager to see if she has an update, I decide to return her call before phoning Ted.

"So glad to hear from you," Lt. Carter says. "Hope you're free to join Deputy Muschel and me for dinner tonight. Six o'clock? The deputy and I believe an off-the-record, informal chat might help us make faster headway on the Steph Cloyd fatality."

"Um, I guess I can." The Coast Guard investigator's suggestion baffles me. While I've cooperated with Lt. Carter before, we're not exactly chums, and my introduction to Deputy Muschel is limited to the few minutes the deputies were questioning Grant.

"Great," the lieutenant says. "We're meeting at the Fishcamp on 11th Street, Port Royal. I'll explain everything then."

While Ted and I had planned a quiet dinner for two before the big Fourth of July festivities begin in earnest, Ted will understand.

When he answers my call, the background noise tells me Ted's on his hands-free Bluetooth and driving somewhere.

"Where are you?" I ask. "Sounds like you're on the road."

"I am," Ted answers. "Grant and I just paid a visit to Hank's Marine Repair on St. Helena Island, and I'm taking Grant back to Frank and Myrt's before I head to Beaufort. We still on for dinner?"

"Afraid not," I answer and tell him about my invitation to an informal roundtable with women officers of the Coast Guard and the Sheriff's Office.

"Understand," he says. "Need to give you an update on Bubba's boat explosion. It just might make you a star contributor to your dinner conversation."

I'm puzzled. "What are you talking about? Something to do with your visit to Hank's?"

Over the next several minutes, I get all the details from Ted—and Grant—since Ted's on his Bluetooth car speaker. Grant is more certain than ever that last night's bomber, the guy who fired at him, was astride a professional watercraft owned by FACE.

"You've told me the how but not the who. Did Hank say which employee might have borrowed the craft?"

Grant makes no secret of his disappointment in Hank's refusal to name names.

"Maybe Deputy Muschel can be persuaded to follow up on the lead."

Having received my briefing, I'm ready to hang up, when Ted calls foul.

"Hey, we've shared our afternoon's discoveries, but you haven't told us why Sherry wanted an emergency meeting."

Oh, right. I give a quick synopsis, reporting that a mystery provocateur first coaxed J.T. into attacking Andy and later hinted suicide was J.T.'s most noble exit from the stage. I promise to provide all the gory details later.

Before we disconnect, I tell Ted I'll come straight to his house after the dinner. "Want me to get takeout for you?"

"No. Love the Fishcamp, but am not about to count on your night out with the ladies wrapping up quickly. I'm already hungry."

* * *

I arrive at the Fishcamp at 5:45 p.m. and spot the lieutenant and deputy chatting on the restaurant's wide porch. The lieutenant would stand out in any crowd. She could easily be cast to play an African princess with her long, elegant neck and the close-cropped hair that shows off her perfectly-shaped head. Of course, the contrast between the passion pink of the investigator's blouse and her ebony skin also attracts the eye. The lieutenant definitely wants to appear off-duty. No sign of a uniform.

Same goes for Deputy Muschel. She's dressed in slim, hip-hugger jeans and a stretchy, form-fitting top. No bright colors. The top's beige; the jeans faded denim blue. Nonetheless, I notice her shapely figure is prompting an appreciative second glance from a gaggle of men climbing the porch stairs.

Comparing my wardrobe choices with those of my dinner companions, I land on the frumpy yet really comfy side. Since Ted and I eat at the Fishcamp at least twice a month, I know the dress code is anything goes. Actually, given the heat, I'd have worn shorts if I'd had time to shave my legs.

Since my personal hygiene has taken a backseat to snooping, I settled on the next best option—roomy pants that young'uns like Mimi call "Mommy" jeans, and a baggy cotton tee. A present from Ted on my last birthday, the tee sports a slogan in small print: "Underestimate me. That'll be fun."

The lieutenant, my fellow Coastie, spots me and waves. "Let's find a booth," she says as she leads the way into the big, wharf-front restaurant. The scent of fried food instantly reminds me I'm famished.

We find a booth near a back wall, and a waitress takes our drink order. *Hmm, we all order beer.* Not a wine snob in the bunch. A good omen?

"Well, Lieutenant," I begin.

The investigator immediately interrupts. "Hey, tonight I'm Alysha, the deputy here is Josie, and you're Kylee, okay? Josie and I talked this over. The old boys' network helps our male counterparts circumvent inconvenient bureaucracy. We figure what works for the gander should work for us female geese."

"And you included me to make it an *old* gals' network?" I kid.

Josie laughs. "Hey, I'm not much younger than you. Speeding toward the big 5-0, just a few years shy. Let's think of our triumvirate as the Smart Gals

Network."

Our beers arrive, and Alysha, in her mid-twenties, hoists her mug in a toast. "To the Smart Gals Network."

After we give the waitress our meal orders, Josie informally calls the meeting to order.

"Alysha phoned this afternoon to let me know the Coast Guard had processed enough debris from the explosion to unequivocally determine the fragments scattered across the marsh came from a boat owned by Bubba Quarles."

Alysha beams and picks up the narrative. "We were lucky. Found a hunk of hull with the boat registration number. I could have postponed reporting our findings to the Sheriff's Office until we called on Bubba, but I wanted to coordinate with Josie. A courtesy since she phoned me with the GPS coordinates for the explosion site and handed the drone over to us so our tech guys could try to recover images."

I interrupt. "Did they? Have any of the images survived?"

"Sure did," Alysha answers. "The last frame includes a nice shot of Bubba Quarles taking aim at an object in the sky."

"Hey, let's not get ahead of the story," Josie says. "Alysha has invited me to join her when she calls on Bubba. I figure we can play good cop, bad cop. Maybe get him to confess to ramming Steph's scull. That's why Alysha suggested we talk strategy with you. You have a reputation in the Coast Guard as one heck of an interrogator."

"Plus, since you're responsible for finding where Bubba stashed his boat, you probably have additional insights," Alysha adds.

I grin. "Just so happens that I do."

They're both surprised to learn an employee of Hank's Marine Repair may have borrowed a FACE craft to visit Bubba's boat and plant explosives inside it.

"Do you suppose Bubba asked a buddy to blow the boat up to destroy any proof that he rammed Steph?" Alysha asks.

Josie shakes her head. "I was one of the deputies who visited Bubba after Steph filed a complaint weeks back. That motorboat was the good ol' boy's most prized possession. I can't see him destroying it."

"But if Bubba didn't ask this guy from Hank's Marine to dynamite his boat, what possessed him to do it?" Alysha wonders.

That baffles me, too.

The women prompt me to provide background on Steph Cloyd. "Do you know if he had any Bubba interactions that weren't reported to the law?"

I share everything I know, mostly third-hand info. I repeat Chad's story that Bubba threatened to toss Steph like a piece of trash into his next burn pile. "Bubba raved that Steph was out to steal his property."

What else can I tell them about Steph?

"I admired Steph. He was a reasonable, level-headed member of the Satin Sands board. Everyone liked him. His FACE friends can't say enough about his dedication to protecting the Lowcountry environment. He'll be sorely missed."

When I finish, Alysha looks thoughtful. "Do you suppose Bubba's hatred of Steph wasn't entirely personal?" she asks. "Maybe Bubba decided to attack Steph as a strike against fuzzy-headed Yankee environmentalists?"

Josie chuckles. "No, you're crediting Bubba with too much cerebral capacity," she counters. "I met him. Bubba hates and distrusts all government on general principle. I'm sure he believes climate change is a hoax. But I can't see him targeting Steph as part of an ideological crusade. I'm certain it was personal."

For the next hour and a half—well, between bites of fried shrimp, deviled crab, and crispy French fries—we hash over a strategy that will help Josie and Alysha squeeze as much information as possible out of Bubba. We agree the approach has to avoid any hint he might soon face charges.

"Given his own run-ins with the law and his Daddy's history, Bubba will demand a lawyer if he thinks he's in custody and being questioned," Josie says. "Fortunately, there's no requirement to Mirandize someone if the 'interview' is voluntary and the subject's free to leave."

After batting around a number of ideas and finishing a second round of frosty beers, we arrive at a consensus approach. Alysha, representing the Coast Guard, and Josie, representing the Sheriff's Office, will visit Bubba early tomorrow morning—Monday, July 3.

Since there's no logical reason for my presence, I don't get to tag along. But Josie promises to switch on her bodycam to preserve the encounter for prosperity.

Alysha will begin with a "sorry-to-inform-you" gambit. She'll tell Bubba fragments recovered during a Coast Guard investigation of a recent explosion show his boat was destroyed. She'll commiserate, apologizing that the Coast Guard has no clue who could have done such a dastardly deed.

Next up, Josie will jump in, indicating the Sheriff's Office will vigorously pursue whoever stole Bubba's boat and later destroyed it. "No one thinks you're involved. Who would destroy his own valuable property?"

The hope is this will prompt Bubba to hardily agree. "Yes, some scumbag nicked my boat."

If so, Alysha will return to bat, asking if Bubba can name any enemies who might have stolen his motorboat.

We all chuckle at this feint, feeling it's certain to trigger an anti-government rant.

Once Bubba runs out of steam, Alysha will innocently ask, "Do you know anyone who works at Hank's Marine Repair?" Then, she'll reveal a witness saw one of Hank's workers speeding away from the explosion.

If the ploy works, the hope is Bubba will commence swearing and inadvertently name a prime suspect.

Finally, the two women plan to wind up their visit by apologizing to Bubba that some people initially suspected him of being involved in the boat collision that claimed Steph's life.

"Of course, that was before we realized your boat had been stolen," one of them will add. "Now, we need to determine if this Steph was the type of person who sought revenge on anyone he felt had crossed him. If so, it could open new avenues of investigation."

Josie shrugs. "It might work. Maybe it'll encourage Bubba to spill why he was convinced Steph wanted to steal his land and if that was his motive for targeting Steph."

Once we pay for our dinners and walk outside, I smile at my fellow plotters.

"I'm glad you reached out to me, and hope you'll keep me in the loop. If I discover any new information, I'll do likewise. Unfortunately, we all know interrogations—or, if you prefer, interviews—seldom turn out like we think they will."

Josie grins. "Too true. Have a good night. A pleasure getting to know you. And I won't bother to give your regards to my fellow deputy, Nick Ibsen.

"Girl, whatever you did to make Nick so angry, I applaud it."

Chapter Fifty

Kylee

Sunday, July 2, evening

I let myself into Ted's house. I'm ready to call out a greeting when I hear loud snores. Ted is tipped back in his recliner, feet up. His snores sound like he's sawing a cord of wood.

Lucky duck! I'm envious. Last night, we both got far less than forty winks and by middle age, we need at least forty-five winks. I don't feel "middle-aged," with its dowdy, past-your-prime connotation. Nonetheless, I doubt I'll live long enough to blow out one hundred and one candles. That makes my fifty-one years on the high side of middle age. Ted's forty-eight years are close behind.

I brush silky black hair back from Ted's forehead and settle a gentle kiss. He startles.

"Oh, you're home. What time is it?" He blinks as he shakes off sleep's remnants. "Must have dozed off for a minute."

"It's eight-thirty," I say, noticing congealed evidence of a lasagna meal on the plate beside his chair.

"Looks like you ate dinner a while back. How about I fix us a nightcap? Then we can catch each other up on the day's headlines and hit the sack before the clock strikes ten. I'm bushed. It looks like you are, too."

"It's a deal," he says. "Though your breath tells me you've already knocked back a few drinks. I'm behind the curve."

"Just a couple beers with my fellow Smart Gals Network members," I joke.

"So, that's what you're calling yourselves. Not Smarty Alecks?"

As Ted stands to take his dinner dishes to the sink—the one work area untouched by his kitchen renovation—I give Ted a half-hearted swat on his rump. "What's your poison? Schnapps?"

"Sure," he says. "The usual. One ice cube and a splash of water."

I fix his Schnapps and pour myself Kahlua over crushed ice. Hey, I refrained from ordering dessert.

We sit side-by-side on the couch. The best spot to catch the ceiling fan's anemic breeze.

"Before you tell me all about your Smarty Gals outing, I want to hear the details of your visit with Sherry," Ted says as I hand him his drink.

Though it was just a few hours ago, my Rand Creek sojourn seems like ancient history. I sip my Kahlua and share everything I can remember.

"It certainly sounds like the pretend Ann Rand knows how to create deepfakes," Ted says when I conclude. "I understand why your antennae are twitching in Dr. Amanda Holder's direction. But even if you're right, how would anyone ever prove it? If she's a computer science expert and smart enough to fool people with deepfakes, you can bet she knows all the hide-your-identity tricks, like using burner phones and VPN—Virtual Private Network—screens."

I frown. "I know. I know. Tomorrow, I'm meeting someone who may have some suggestions on that score—Aaron Cloyd, Steph's brother. Donna's picking Aaron up at the Hilton Head Airport early tomorrow morning. After leaving the Smarty Gals, I invited myself to ride along.

Aaron and the doc were faculty at the same university for at least a decade. Donna's sure Aaron knows why Steph warned the Satin Sands board against doing business with the doc. Maybe he can shed light on her methods and personality."

I remind Ted it's now his turn to talk. I want to know how he and Grant wound up at Hank's Marine Repair. Listening to his explanation, I sense he's proud of his son's determination to research watercraft and prove that his sighting of the shooter and bomb suspect wasn't some hallucination.

Ted then turns our discussion to the afternoon owners' meeting at Hullis Island. He's relatively pleased with the outcome, feeling it succeeded in dialing down the rhetoric and anger.

"Oh," I exclaim. "I forgot to tell you. Dr. Amanda Holder came to the meeting. Did you see her?"

"No," Ted answers. "Actually, I can't say yes or no. Remember, I've never met the woman. Wouldn't know her if I fell over her."

I provide as neutral a description as possible. About my age. Tall, maybe five-ten. Looks athletic. Short, dark hair streaked with blond. Green eyes. Might be attractive if she were capable of smiling.

"But I've only been treated to her glare. One she lasered me with when I caught her staring at me from a seat on the back row."

Ted shakes his head. "No, if I saw her, she didn't stand out in the crowd, and no one resembling the woman you describe talked to me after the meeting."

"Oh," I say, "that reminds me. Ed Hiller phoned to ask if we could join his family for dinner tomorrow night. He included Grant in the invitation. What do you say?"

"Why not? My dinner tonight came courtesy of Publix's freezer section, and it wasn't a great deal better than its cardboard wrapper. No one in his right mind would turn down a meal at Ed's table. What time?"

"Six o'clock," I answer.

"Should be fine. Let me check with Grant. Since I'm not returning the keys to his Jeep until Wednesday, Grant shouldn't have other plans. Besides, he seldom turns down good grub."

"Great," I say. "I'll email Mom. Let her know she'll be spared a dinner crowd tomorrow night. Imagine that may come as a relief. She loves company but, like me, savors personal time."

I smile, remembering how I got on Mom's nerves when she was going through chemo. As soon as Mom finished her cancer treatments, she practically ordered me out of her house. Told me to go live on my boat.

"It'll give Myrt a chance to rest up for the Fourth." Ted smiles. "I saw all the work she put in decorating Frank's extended, six-seater golf cart. Think it'll win a prize in the Hullis Island parade?"

"Doubt it, but that's not the point," I answer. "When people think of the military, too many think only of men. Mom's the one who suggested I invite Alysha and two other female Coasties to join in our island's little Independence Day salute. When the uniformed ladies wave to the little girls, maybe they'll realize military service is a career option for women, too. Besides, Alysha's bringing a ton of wrapped candy to toss to the kids. That's sure to get their attention."

Ted chuckles. "If the other Coast Guard ladies look anything like Lt. Carter, it'll get the attention of old boys, too. They'll want to sign up to be on the same boat."

* * *

After Ted confirms Grant will join us for dinner tomorrow at the Hiller home, I give Chef Ed a call to accept the invitation. He appears to be in a jovial mood.

"Before I decide on the menu, I should ask if any of you have allergies—nuts, shellfish, etc.?"

"I'm the only problem child," I answer. "Allergic to wine and champagne. So, don't be insulted if I turn down a glass with dinner. It's fine if you cook with it, though. Doesn't bother me a bit then."

"Whew," Ed answers. "I tend to improve many of my dishes with a dollop of sherry or, say, a cup of chardonnay. Hope you don't mind if the rest of us adults imbibe. My neighbor, Leona Grimm, gave me two bottles of Brunello di Montalcino for helping her with her hasty departure from Lighthouse Cove."

"Is this the neighbor with the yappy dog? I thought she was totally into your neighborhood and lobbying the HOA to add a dog park."

"She was. I was dumbfounded by her decision to move. Leona looked like she'd seen a ghost when she rang my doorbell. White as a sheet. Hair standing on end like she'd moused it to imitate a porcupine. While she didn't claim she'd seen a ghost, she did insist one chatted her up. Leona's convinced her dead husband came back from the other side to issue a warning. Told her to move out of her house immediately or else. The 'or else' wasn't exactly spelled out, but Leona was certain she and her dog would both perish.

"I didn't know what to say other than to ask if I could help. Leona handed me her house key. Said she hadn't stopped her mail yet, and wondered if I'd check her mailbox. Told me to just toss any mail inside her front door. Sounded as if she believed I might expire, too, if I stepped over the threshold."

"Wow. She believes her house is haunted. Are you worried Leona's having a mental breakdown? Does she seem to be hallucinating about other things?"

"No. She's a long-time believer in most things paranormal," Ed answers. "She's hosted seances at her house, consulted psychics. That type of thing. Leona seemed rational, coherent, to me, except when she repeated her husband's warnings. Leona was clearly spooked by her husband's voice, sounding clear as a bell through the speakers she's scattered about her house. She likes asking some computer app to play her favorite tunes and answer questions."

A chill runs down my spine. Computers, voices with alarming messages. *Is it a coincidence?*

Chapter Fifty-One

The Chameleon

Sunday, July 2, evening

Hacking into Frank Donahue's Wi-Fi was even easier than cracking Leona's worthless security. Yet, so far, I've only scored limited information from the couple's email traffic.

Good grief, Myrtle sounds like a kindergartner, proud as punch of her finger painting. She sent all her friends photos of the golf cart she helped Grant and Kylee decorate for the Fourth of July parade.

While I've never had the bad fortune of witnessing Hullis Island's PG event, the parade is apparently a lame collection of crepe-paper-swaddled golf carts, bicycles, and tricycles that toddle down the main thoroughfare. The route's lined with little kids in face paint, who wave flags at the mini-floats' occupants. Whoopee!

The floats promote various island clubs and civic organizations and salute the military. The golf cart Myrtle helped drape in reams of crepe streamers is supposed to resemble a Coast Guard cutter. Maybe, if you have cataracts and squint. Anyway, Kylee will drive it while three active-duty Coast Guard ladies throw candy at the kids.

Wonder if any of the little monsters get injured by gumballs to the eye?

After I finish poking fun at Myrtle's email, I realize it provides one valuable nugget of information. I know exactly where the snoop will be at ten o'clock

Tuesday morning, July 4.

Can it help? Maybe.

The second worthwhile piece of intel arrives as I'm about to abandon my Peeping-PC efforts. Kylee emailed Myrtle to tell her mother she, Ted, and Grant are dining with Ed Hiller and his family Monday night. Ted will pick Grant up about five o'clock. The dinner party starts at six. Now I know where Kylee will be tomorrow evening—right down the street from my Lighthouse Cove house.

Another opportunity?

Something's bothering me about the email. What is it? When I first skimmed Kylee's reported plans for Monday, she mentioned driving to the Hilton Head airport with Donna. Why?

Crap, I'll bet they're picking up Steph's brother.

This cannot be happening. Did I stop Steph from spreading gossip about me only to give his obnoxious brother a chance to slander me with first-person reports?

Kylee had to know Steph. After all, he was a director for an HOA that Welch manages. Maybe she's tagging along to express condolences.

But what if that's not the reason? What if she's smacking her lips in anticipation of grilling Aaron about me?

Calm down! No need to panic. Even if Aaron tells her how good I am at deepfakes and how I created one to humiliate two males who deserved it, doesn't prove a thing.

Nonetheless, I'm committed. I will put an end to the snoop's interference before it goes further. How? Duh, the Hullis Island parade. Claude would surely be offended by a bevy of women in uniform pretending to be patriots. Women who have no business in the military, wiggling their bottoms around, taunting men, distracting them from their duty.

Okay, I have a thread of a plan to activate Claude. But I'm a firm believer that software, including AI initiatives, should be backed up. I need to finish training AI to imitate Myrtle's voice and speech patterns. Will do the same using saved videos of Ted.

Should Claude resist my call to incel herodom, a deepfake of Ted or Myrtle pleading with Kylee to ride to the rescue will work. I'll find a nice isolated spot. If need be, I'll even do the wet work myself.

Interesting. The notion of killing the snoop with my own hands excites me. Though I need a murder method that lets me stay at a safe distance. I'm strong. Probably stronger than Kylee, but I saw how easily she handled the Marshview troublemaker who punched her.

Chapter Fifty-Two

Kylee

Monday, July 3, morning

It's nine a.m. when I see Donna's Prius pull to the curb in front of Ted's
house. Ready, I scurry outside before she has a chance to honk.

"You look a mite perkier than the last time I saw you." Donna lifts
an eyebrow. "Finally, get a good night's sleep? Or are you bright and bushy-
tailed due to other nocturnal activities?"

"Sleep," I say. "I think I fell asleep a second after my head hit the pillow.
Slept from nine p.m. until eight a.m. Heaven."

"Glad to hear it. You've certainly had enough late-night drama. What
with Grant out kayaking, witnessing the marsh explosion, and getting shot
at. It was Bubba's boat, right?"

Alysha and Josie made it clear I'm not free to share investigation details.
Especially the fact the women are visiting Bubba this very morning. Instead,
I assure Donna the authorities are making progress, and she needn't fret
about Deputy Do-Wrong throwing up investigative roadblocks.

"Glad to hear it," Donna says. "Now, tell me why you wanted to join me
on a round trip drive to Hilton Head's airport? We'll see more traffic than
scenery, and I doubt the joy my company brings is adequate incentive.

"That means you plan to pester Aaron for the lowdown on Dr. Holder.
The poor man's in mourning over his older brother's senseless death. Really

not a good time to be interrogated."

"Hey, Donna, I understand your concern about Aaron's emotional state," I say. "I promise I'll back off if it appears the conversation's upsetting him."

For most of our forty-five-minute drive, Donna and I share fond memories of Steph. Since he never married and his parents are gone, Aaron is Steph's closest relative and shoulders all the responsibilities that death sets in motion. Aaron has already arranged for Steph's remains to be cremated following the autopsy. Donna adds a memorial will be postponed until fall.

"That'll give the far-flung family a chance to gather. It would be very hard to arrange a service here at the height of the tourist season. Flights are packed, and most Lowcountry accommodations are booked."

I share an offer from our mutual friend, Kay Barrett, for Steph's family to stay at her B&B free-of-charge if they settle on a time she has vacancies.

Donna nods. "Kay told me how much she and the other FACE directors will miss Steph. His shoes will be equally hard for Satin Sands to fill. Don't want to think about finding someone to fill his board vacancy until our next election."

We pull into the Hilton Head Island Airport. It's located near the center of the boot-shaped island. The airport offers all the services of big-city airports with few of their vexing frustrations. Aaron's direct flight from New York City's LaGuardia is due to arrive on time. Having pre-arranged a parking permit, Donna sails directly into a convenient space only steps from the terminal.

Watching the arrivals, I spot Aaron with ease. He looks a lot like Steph, just a dozen years younger. Aaron wears wire-rimmed glasses, and his sandy hair's long enough to brush the edge of his collar. He also sports a trim goatee. Hand him a tweed coat and a pipe, and he'd be the image of the archetypical professor.

Once Donna and I introduce ourselves, we head straight to the car. Aaron only has a battered, leather carry-on. I try to convince Aaron to sit up front where he'll have more legroom. He insists on the back seat. That means I turn sideways to continue our conversation and meet his tired, sad eyes.

As one might expect, we devote our drive's first minutes to condolences.

Donna and I offer to help Aaron negotiate the bureaucratic obstacles he'll encounter as he settles his brother's estate. Given that government offices, insurance companies, and banks will be closed for Independence Day, he's likely to face longer than usual delays obtaining the death certificate, accessing Steph's safety deposit box and bank accounts, and contacting utilities, credit card providers, the Post Office, and others to pay bills, cancel services, and forward mail.

Condolences finished, Aaron asks me, "I'm sorry. What exactly is your connection to Steph? You introduced yourself as a security consultant for the company that manages Satin Sands' HOA. Are you involved in investigating Steph's death?"

Okay, time to explain my rather awkward motivation for meeting Aaron's flight. I'm here to ask questions, not simply spout sorry-for-your-loss platitudes.

"I'm hoping you can help me with a different investigation," I explain.

It takes several minutes for me to describe how an online provocateur egged J.T. into attacking Andy Fyke and then encouraged the attacker to end her own life. Finally, I share my rather flimsy rationale for suspecting Dr. Amanda Holder as the provocateur.

I tick off my reasons. She owns Rand Creek rental property, and Andy's spearheading a drive to end rentals. She and Andy had a nasty dispute over a claim her renters damaged common property. She pretended she was unsure who Andy Fyke might be when I mentioned his attack.

I shrug. "I know that amounts to a lot of nothing. A dozen other people own Rand Creek rental property, and the doctor may have implied she didn't know Andy to quickly get rid of me. But whoever was behind this scam has a talent for creating deepfakes. That seems to make her an interesting possibility.

"Aaron, you and the doctor taught at the same university for years," I comment. "So, here's what I'd like to know. Could Dr. Holder pull off a scam like this? Does she seem callous enough to precipitate events knowing they might result in a death?"

"Lord," he says. "Dr. Holder. Didn't see this one coming."

The professor doesn't say any more for a moment. I understand I've blindsided him. He probably needs time to put his thoughts together.

"I knew Amanda moved to the Lowcountry when she left the university. And Steph told me she bought rental property in his HOA. A couple months ago, Steph mentioned she offered her services on some HOA software project. He asked me why a hot-shot IT expert would make a low-ball bid on a project a student could handle. He wanted to know why Amanda left the university in the middle of a semester."

Aaron lapses into silence, tilts his head back, and closes his eyes. I hope he isn't through talking. Is he struggling with what to say? Or how to say it?

"I signed a pledge never to divulge the details of Dr. Holder's departure. I told Steph I couldn't comment on that. Instead, I warned my brother and Satin Sands to run, not walk, away from Amanda. Told him to flee like he was being chased by a crazed bull.

"Once again, I'm going to bend my promised silence about Amanda. I won't tell you why she left the university, but I feel morally obligated to answer your questions. Yes, I'm certain Dr. Holder has the knowledge and skills to pull off the horrifying deepfake con you describe. What's more, I don't think the idea of causing a death—other than her own—would bother the doctor one whit."

Not sure what I expected Aaron to say, but his vehement tone communicates far more than his words. He believes this woman is a monster.

"I haven't asked what you teach. Are you familiar with the doctor's field of expertise."

"Should be." Aaron chuckles. "I took over Amanda's AI/ML classes when she left. The course content was quite similar to what I was already teaching."

When I was in the Coast Guard, my graduate studies at the Naval Academy included classes in cyber warfare. Yet I don't have instant recall of all the acronyms involved. My blank look triggers the professor to explain the part of the abbreviation I can't place.

"AI/ML stands for Artificial Intelligence and Machine Learning. Our university's Computer Science curriculum is broad, and we offer numerous

Computer Science and Information Technology degrees. Computer Science courses focus on designing software and systems, while Information Technology—IT—courses focus on system maintenance and security. We were both tenured Computer Science professors, but Amanda had several years seniority. She also labored very successfully to build a high profile beyond academia."

"How good is she?" I ask. "Her mother bragged she was a genius."

"She's very, very smart," Aaron answers. "She knows the science, and AI's possibilities fascinated her. But she was no genius when it came to interacting with peers or students. She talked down to colleagues and treated students as if they were a human subspecies. While she didn't feel the need to be a team player, Amanda believed she should be our unanimous choice as team captain."

Aaron's description matches my impression of the doc. Arrogant, self-centered.

"I don't understand. How could someone so deficient in interpersonal skills successfully con people?"

"Your description of J.T. makes it sound like she had a poor self-image," Aaron answers. "Instead of pretending to be J.T.'s equal, Amanda may have portrayed herself as J.T.'s superior, a leader she could admire. One who generously shares pearls of wisdom with a lonely soul."

Aaron smiles. "Amanda would love playing a role like that. Couldn't work at the university. Her colleagues weren't looking for a savior to put on a pedestal or someone to make decisions for them."

Aaron's descriptions still leave me with questions about the Andy Fyke deepfakes.

"I haven't seen the deepfake video used to convince J.T. that Andy Fyke was a pedophile," I explain. "According to Andy, he never met Amanda in person. So, how could she create a deepfake good enough to fool J.T., who had met Andy face-to-face?"

"Easy. Want to hear Amanda's favorite classroom gambit? She'd research the students who signed up for her AI class and zero in on one poor slob. A kid she'd never met. In the middle of class—first day, mind you—she'd adopt an alarmed expression and tell students the university president had sent a text instructing her to broadcast a breaking news alert.

"On a big screen at the front of the classroom, she'd project the image of a well-known local reporter announcing a newsflash. What came next depended on what Amanda's research had unearthed. Usually, the breaking news featured a video of the targeted student's kidnapped boyfriend...girlfriend...sibling...or best friend pleading to be saved.

"Once in a blue moon, Amanda changed it up to portray the student's loved one as the hostage-taker. Think that gave her a special kick. Creating a deepfake of some innocent spouting demands that had to be met, or he'd kill multiple schmucks."

Aaron shakes his head. "Invariably, the student Amanda had targeted in her classroom became hysterical. He totally bought into the con and believed his loved one was in peril or had slipped into madness. Once her ruse succeeded, Amanda would chuckle and clap her hands. 'This is just make-believe,' she'd say. 'I made this little demonstration to prove AI's power to convince anyone of anything.'

"Amanda presented her cruel hoax as a teaching moment about the increasing use of Artificial Intelligence in virtual kidnappings, where con artists share deepfake pleas from supposed victims to prompt fast ransom payoffs. Amanda did include some helpful advice. Told students their families should adopt special words to prove they were really the ones making any emergency plea for money. Kidnap cons are just one possibility. The 'Grandma, I've been robbed, and I'm stranded' ploy works equally well."

Donna huffs, "I can't believe the university let Dr. Holder get away with targeting and terrorizing individual students. Didn't any of them file a complaint?"

"One did," Aaron answers. "Amanda defended her tactic as the most effective way to demonstrate a point. Said her cons made students safer. Stressed the real world held far worse surprises, and students weren't snowflakes. They wouldn't melt if she applied a little heat. Personally, I think Amanda got off on frightening kids while exhibiting her genius."

I glance over at Donna. Her tight grip on the wheel mimics how she'd like to squeeze the cruel professor's neck. "These scams are horrifying. Are deepfakes so perfect they always work?"

"They needn't be flawless," Aaron responds. "When someone's yelling fire, you don't study the person's diction or worry about how often he blinks. If the deepfakes are frightening enough, no one is going to stop and critique them. They don't wonder, 'Gee, I never heard Susie use that word before,'...or 'Susie's mouth looks a little strange when she calls my name.'"

I get that Amanda felt it was risk-free to create deepfakes that toyed with student emotions. But wouldn't she fear consequences for her actions outside the classroom?

"Let's say Amanda is guilty," I say. "If she manipulated J.T. using videos, texts, and emails, wouldn't she worry about computer and phone breadcrumbs leading back to her door?"

Aaron closes his eyes and massages his temples. "Yes, she'd worry, and she'd take precautions. Pay cash for burner phones to make her calls. Use a fake ID to pay for a year's worth of minutes from a service provider. Sign up for a VPN—Virtual Private Network—to hide the internet sites she visits and who she communicates with via encrypted texts or emails."

"If someone does all that, how can authorities catch them?" I ask. "If the doctor is truly behind J.T.'s attack on Andy, she isn't guilty of touching a hair on the man's head. Amanda simply activated her human robot. Are crimes scripted in the ether beyond the reach of the law?"

Aaron pauses and frowns.

Damn. I'm sorry my question appears to stump him.

"Law enforcement has some tools to identify burner phones, and it can obtain court orders to force VPN providers to reveal user data," Aaron says. "But these efforts take time and cost money. They're usually reserved for kidnapping or murder cases. But it is somewhat easier to catch a serial con artist—a repeat offender. A sting would work if the scammer can be tempted to target someone who is in on the game. The idea would be to lure the hacker to access a 'honeypot' of false info and act on it."

"Hey, maybe I can trick Amanda into targeting me," I say. "She clearly dislikes me."

Aaron shakes his head. "Not sure I'd recommend that. You may already be in her crosshairs. Give me your phone. I may be able to tell if it's been hacked or if anyone is tracking it."

I laugh. "Have to turn it on first. Leave it off unless I'm making a call or checking for messages. At my last Coast Guard post, security protocols prohibited cellphones inside our facility. Saved me from becoming addicted to all the apps."

Aaron's lips lift in a fleeting smile. "That does work in your favor. Less opportunity for hackers if your phone is mostly offline. Sounds like you don't download a lot of apps either, which makes you less likely to get sucked in by phishing scams offering free apps."

"Glad to hear my luddite tendencies have some advantages," I quip.

When I switch on my phone, there's a text from Alysha.

"Hold on a minute. A Coast Guard friend just texted me. Maybe there's been a breakthrough in one of her investigations."

While unlikely, I secretly pray Bubba has confessed to killing Steph and also given up the creep who dynamited the boat and shot at Grant. Not that such breakthroughs will do much to ease Aaron's pain.

I skim through Alysha's text, then read it again slowly, carefully.

What? Bubba said his jailbird dad borrowed a burner phone to tell his son all about Steph's vengeful plan to use his FACE influence to steal his land. Bubba Sr. supposedly learned of the plot while eavesdropping on a prison guard. An impossibility, Alysha reports. Bubba Sr. couldn't have phoned his son when Bubba said he did. The father's been hospitalized for weeks. Looks like someone impersonated Bubba Sr. to build Bubba Jr.'s murderous rage.

Is it possible? Another deepfake? Could Bubba be another J.T.? One of Dr. Amanda Holder's Frankensteins?

"What is it?" Donna risks a worried glance my way. "You look like you've been snake bit. Bad news?"

"Confusing news," I answer.

I pause. I need to know if the witch doctor might have considered Steph an enemy, but can't think of how to ask without prompting Aaron to jump to the same conclusion I've made. That Dr. Holder somehow used AI to engineer Steph's murder.

"Let's go back to Dr. Holder for a minute, Aaron. Do you think she considered you an enemy? Can you see her trying to punish people by hurting their relatives?"

Aaron stares at me. "You're asking about Steph, aren't you? As far as I know, my brother only met Amanda one time when he was visiting me. I took him to a faculty reception, where we chatted with Amanda for a couple minutes. Nothing controversial. Steph told me she'd volunteered to do work for Satin Sands. But I'm pretty sure he never met her in person."

"He didn't," Donna jumps in. "Amanda pitched her software services to the board a week before Steph joined. When he recommended the board find another vendor, I asked Steph how he knew the woman. Said he'd met her years back. Refused to explain why he felt so strongly. I didn't press him."

Aaron leans forward. He reaches over the car seat, and his fingers squeeze my shoulder in a viselike grip. "What did your Coast Guard friend text you? Are you now thinking the professor, that witch doctor, had a hand in Steph's death because of me...because she didn't win a software contract?"

I'm torn.

Nothing can derail an investigation faster than information leaked before charges are filed or arrests made. I bungled it when I asked Aaron if Dr. Holder considered him an enemy and hinted at the possibility she'd take vengeance on a loved one. I was rash and plain stupid. I need to put a lid back on Pandora's Box.

I shake my head. "I'm so sorry, Aaron. There isn't a shred of evidence to tie Amanda to Steph's death. All the talk of Dr. Holder's talents and callous mindset encouraged me to leap in a direction that's most likely one-hundred-eighty degrees off course. My outburst is unforgivable. I promise if any real connection is found, I'll tell you. Andy Fyke is in the hospital because J.T. believed an unfounded accusation. Please don't go there."

I study Aaron's face. Frustration? Anger? His grim expression doesn't radiate good cheer. Boy, have I botched our introduction.

Aaron sighs. "Still want me to see if your phone's been hacked? If so, whatever text you feel must be kept confidential is already compromised."

I nod. "Yes, please." I hand him the phone.

"There are a couple simple checks," he says. "Okay, since your phone is on a GSM—Global System for Mobiles—network, you can key in a code to see if unconditional data forwarding is relaying your information to another phone. It's not.

"You should tell folks you regularly phone or email to make similar checks," he adds.

After Aaron hands my phone back, Donna carries the conversation for the remainder of the trip. She praises Steph's efforts to protect the Lowcountry environment. She describes the beautiful makeshift memorial Steph's friends have created on the Satin Sands beach.

I stay quiet. My big mouth has landed me in enough trouble.

Chapter Fifty-Three

Kylee

Monday, July 3, afternoon

Worried by Aaron's dissertation on hacking and his recommendation that my regular contacts should check their phones and computers, I'm brooding about cyber security. Though Ted gave the whole Welch staff the day off, I decide to ask Robin, our IT expert, if she's willing to reap some freelance bonus pay. I'll offer vacation and holiday rates out of my own pocket.

While I had high-level cyber security training in the Coast Guard, it was theoretical and oriented toward high-ranking officers and division heads. No hands-on, here's-how-you-catch the-villains pointers.

I should get Ted's okay first—Robin's his employee, not mine. But he and Frank are tied up in follow-up Sea Bay meetings about the proposed plan to cure structural defects in the community's aging condos. I hope he won't mind my asking Robin if she's interested in a little freelance work.

Robin answers my call practically before her cell rings, and I quickly pitch my proposal.

"Hey, I never say no to extra money," she replies. "Got to stay indoors today anyway. Spent most of yesterday with friends on the Beaufort River and got burned to a crisp. Forgot to re-apply sunscreen. Actually, the catch-a-hacker hunt sounds kind of fun. Where do we start?"

* * *

.

Since Frank and Ted are at Sea Bay, I ask Mom if she knows how to open Frank's desktop PC. Don't want Robin and me to trek to Hullis for naught.

"Of course I can get on Frank's desktop," she huffs. "I live here, and we share his PC. Frank's password is Jennifer—his late wife's name. He leaves the PC on 24/7. It's an older desktop. Think he's afraid if he turns it off, it might not reboot. But some setting or other puts it to sleep if we don't use it for a while. Then, we have to enter the password to wake it up."

"Good," I say. "How about calling in a gate pass for Robin? We'll be there in half an hour to do a little computer security check."

Since I have my own let-me-in windshield sticker, I don't need Mom to tell security I'm coming. I beat Robin to Frank's house and sit on the front porch to watch for her.

Wow, she wasn't kidding about that sunburn.

"Your sunburn looks painful," I say. "Just wait. Mom is going to decorate your face with moist tea bags. That was always her remedy for me."

"If she's got a secret remedy, I'm not going to argue," Robin replies.

Mom indeed wants to treat Robin before we get down to business, but the young lady asks to wait till we're done. No dripping on the computer. Robin grins when Mom ushers us into Frank's office.

"Ooh, an antique. Are you running the old XP release of Windows?"

Mom gives Robin a playful swat. "Hush your mouth. Have you no respect for your elders? Actually, I kind of wish we were still running that release. Really liked that version. Why do software companies keep fiddling with things that work? Add features only one percent of users need and hide functions and shortcuts the other ninety-nine percent of us use."

I chuckle. "Mom didn't answer your question, so I will. It runs Windows 10. I occasionally use Frank's collectible."

"Huh. Didn't think a PC this age had the horsepower to run 10," Robin says.

"Think Frank took it into a computer shop for a brain transplant," Mom says.

Robin laughs. "Okay, let's wake her up and see what we have."

Ten minutes later, the IT guru isn't laughing.

"You've got problems. Frank's Wi-Fi is definitely compromised. The good news is I can fix it and add a utility to prevent any new intrusion. The bad news is whoever tapped into your Wi-Fi probably has a handy list of every password Frank uses. Yours, too, Myrt. They're all conveniently stored in a file labeled 'Passwords.' You need to change every single password. Does that file include passwords for your cellphones, online bank accounts, etc.?"

Mom looks simultaneously shame-faced and exasperated. "Guilty as charged. How else is a seventy-nine-year-old supposed to remember a zillion different letter, number, special-character combos? A lot of programs refuse to let me use plain old English phrases like Open Sesame. Frank and I had to store all those nonsense passwords somewhere handy. Who could remember them?"

Robin has the good sense—and instinct for self-preservation—to refrain from telling Mom that keeping such a list in a Word file labeled Passwords probably wasn't the smartest storage option.

"It's not the end of the world," Robin says. "We can start correcting the problem immediately. We'll change all the passwords, and we'll add protection to prevent another Wi-Fi network breach."

"No, I don't think so," I say. "Not just now."

"Are you nuts?" Mom asks. "Do you want to make it easy for some nerdy thief to steal our savings?"

Robin's wide-eyed look tells me she's equally aghast.

"I'm pretty sure I know who hacked Frank's computer," I explain. "And it wasn't to siphon off money. She wants a way to keep track of you, Frank, Grant, Ted, and me. She wants to see if we know or suspect anything that can cause her problems. Well, I say let the witch doctor have at it. She can peek all she wants. Bet we can come up with some mind-blowing surprises for her. A golden opportunity for a sting operation."

I jump when the backdoor bangs shut, then relax when Grant ambles inside. He's wearing grungy shorts and a ripped tee, and he's dripping sweat.

"Finished weeding the garden out back, Grandma," he says before he notices Robin and me. "Hey, Robin, Aunt Kylee. What's up? Thought we were all on vacation today."

"Have a seat," I answer. "We're about to do some collective brainstorming."

Mom shakes her head. "No way. First, Grant, you take a shower before you sit down on any surface in Frank's den. Second, I'm applying some wet tea bags to Robin's cheeks. Then we talk."

Fifteen minutes later, we're seated at Mom's kitchen table with icy glasses of lemonade and the requisite companion chocolate-chip cookies. Mom has secured the wet teabags to Robin's cheeks with the aid of a facemask she sewed during the pandemic.

"Before we start talking about a response, I'd like Robin to explain how Frank's Wi-Fi was hacked. Also, want to know if our hacker can now read every email or text Mom sends or receives."

Robin explains the hacker probably camped out in close proximity to Frank's Wi-Fi and searched for nearby networks. When she IDed her target, she most likely tried common passwords until she got a hit. Of course, it's even easier if she took the time beforehand to learn about the user—names of family members, birthdays, anniversaries, etc.

"If that's how the professor got into the computer, she'll only be able to rummage through emails and computer files if she remains in Wi-Fi range," Robin adds.

I silently swear. Mom's no stranger to cusswords, but she prefers we limit the use of obscenities when folks outside the immediate family can hear. Since Robin's present, I bite my tongue.

"If the witch doctor's rental unit across the street is vacant, she can camp out in comfort whenever she wants," I note. "Saw her at the Hullis Island meeting yesterday. Bet she's staying on the island."

Grant stops chewing on a cookie long enough to ask, "Why not do a hack-back? Robin, can't you hack the hacker and make a record of her computer logs to document what she's up to?"

"I'd need help," she admits. "But I'm not sure it would tell us anything. Not if she's primarily relying on burner phones to send her videos, texts, and emails. If so, none of them would show up in her computer logs. You also risk her realizing she's being hacked and destroying all the evidence."

"Thinking of cellphones, what about Grandma's? If the doc used Myrt's stored password to hack her cellphone and insert spyware, couldn't she redirect texts and messages to her own phone wherever she might be?"

"Yes, she could," Robin answers.

Mom rolls her eyes. "I limit my texting to young Grant here. I loathe texts. The keys on these cellphones are so tiny. Then there are all those abbreviations, using the letter 'U' for 'you.' Makes me worry that literacy and good grammar are doomed. At least with emails, people write complete sentences, even if they're run-on. If this geek's looking at my text exchanges to prepare some devious plot, she'll be sorely disappointed."

Mom makes a good point. If I need to tell her something, I usually phone or send an email. Knowing her preferences (and mine), our texts are few and far between. For starters, it may take her a week to check her phone for new text messages.

"Robin, can you go back to the den and print Mom's emails from the past week," I suggest. "Just want to verify we haven't shared any speculation about Dr. Holder, the investigations into J.T.'s attack, or Steph's death."

Mom sighs. "There's nothing there. I'm sure of it. You phoned to let me know Grant was okay, even though he'd been stupid."

Mom cuts Grant a stern look.

"I mean, what dimwit goes paddling around in the wee hours so someone can shoot at him."

I note Mom's scowl fails to cow Grant. Imagine he's already heard enough of her scolding on this subject that it now rolls off.

"Could the doc have overheard your call, Kylee?" Grant asks. "If so, she knows I was the witness. But that shouldn't worry her since I can't ID the shooter."

"But would Amanda know you can't ID him?" I interrupt. "How could she? I didn't know that when I phoned Mom. The witch doctor could assume you're a threat. If the explosives guy was following her orders, she wouldn't want him talking to the cops."

Robin returns to the kitchen with a complete list of emails Mom's sent and received. "I scanned all the emails. Not a single mention of J.T. or Steph. Not much worthwhile intel for the doc to chew on, unless she's concerned Myrt won't have any company for dinner tonight or wants a preview of your Fourth of July plans, from parade decorations to the beach picnic eats.

"By the way, wow," Robin says. "How can I score an invitation for a dinner cooked by the chef of *Eats with Ed*."

Grant gets up to refill his glass of lemonade. "Aunt Kylee, the emails do tell the witch doctor where you'll be tonight and tomorrow. Hope Chef Ed isn't borrowing a cup of sugar from his neighbor. She might add a pinch of arsenic."

I chuckle. "Wouldn't worry about that. Given the frosty reception the woman gave Ed and me, the chef's not likely to darken her door anytime soon."

"That leaves the parade and the afternoon picnic on the beach," Grant says. "But there'd be a lot of witnesses either place. Pretty high risk to try an attack there."

I shake my head. "You forget. The witch doctor's MO is to use other people. If they get caught or killed, she can just groom a replacement robot. But I agree. Doesn't look as if her hacking efforts have delivered great intel. Let's see about changing that. We need to put on our thinking caps and do as Aaron suggested. Create an information 'honeypot' our witch doctor will dive into with glee."

Chapter Fifty-Four

The Chameleon

Monday, July 3, afternoon

My research complete, I start composing my first entreaty to Claude. My small window of opportunity worries me. I only have a few hours to lather Claude into a homicidal frenzy. Possible? Not sure. It took weeks to condition J.T.

Claude thinks I'm a fellow incel. To call him to action, I need a logical reason I can't do the deed myself.

Danny, my fake persona who's befriended Claude, is an able-bodied, gun-savvy grunt in training at Fort Bragg in Fayetteville, North Carolina. That puts Danny close enough to go AWOL and drive to the Lowcountry if he believes he can make a statement on behalf of our nation's "real men." Danny has his very own M16. Doesn't need to borrow one of Daddy's guns. So, what's his excuse for punking out?

Geography.

The opportunity is on Hullis Island, and Danny's en route to Alaska for a survival training exercise.

From Myrtle's emails, I know the snoop talked three active-duty Coast Guard officers into riding the mini-float she's driving. Online photos of Lt. Alysha Carter and her friends Ellis and Flo are perfect. All three ladies represent the type of females incels like Claude lust after but have no prayer of bedding. Alysha is a knock-out.

Somehow, though, my messaging must emphasize it's essential for Claude to put his very first bullet in the snoop's brain. After all, she's the mentor, the one pushing women into the armed forces to displace men. Can't let the younger females distract Claude and cause him to neglect the white-haired Q-tip driving the golf cart.

Studying the parade route, I decide the Community Center roof is the ideal spot for my shooter. Behind the building, a massive live oak has branches that arc toward the ground before soaring skyward. Shinnying up that tree and accessing the roof should be easy for a fitness nut like Claude. On the roof, he'll be well above the flag-waving mob that gathers below.

My next problem?

Assuming Claude is eager to accept Danny's challenge, how do I get him past the Hullis Island security gate? He lives in Sea Bay with his divorced dad. True, since I'm a Hullis Island owner, I could simply call Claude in. Not going to happen. There will be no suggestion I'm involved.

I smile. The gate pass request that's emailed to Hullis Island security will appear to come from Frank Donahue's computer. Love the irony. Another small pleasure.

I decide Claude will be Frank's great-nephew visiting for a week. Of course, I'll use a fake name for Claude, and the last name will be Donohue. Good thing my minion is white. Tougher to pass off a Black as the old Irishman's relative.

A fake name matters. Assuming the incel's not nabbed or killed as soon as he finishes shooting—killed is my preference—I don't want authorities to ID Claude with ease. Though maybe that would be okay if he wants to leave a manifesto.

Chapter Fifty-Five

Kylee

Monday, July 3, afternoon

When Frank and Ted arrive, they're surprised to find a kitchen conference in process. I can't believe how badly I've lost track of the time. Need to go home and get cleaned up before our dinner with the Hiller family.

Ted says he'll wait for Grant to change clothes. We'll meet up at his house and drive to Lighthouse Cove together. While I imagine Grant will already have shared most of today's news, I promise to fill in any details and answer questions en route to the Hillers.

Aboard the River Rat, I take a hurried shower and get dressed. Thankfully, Ed said the evening was casual. "Shorts and flip-flops are fine. That's what my kids will be wearing."

I don't go quite that far, choosing feather-weight slacks, a loose top, and sneakers. A glance at the clock tells me I still have time to play catch-up with Alysha. Given Aaron's confidence my cellphone hasn't been hacked, I find my friend's name in my directory and call.

"Hey, girlfriend," Alysha answers. "Wondered when you'd get back to me. Thought you'd call as soon as you saw my text about Bubba. Insane how much he blabbed to Josie and me this morning. Come to think of it, insane is the perfect word for Bubba and his chums."

"I've had a crazy day, too," I respond. "Have some startling news of my own."

I share Aaron's insights into Dr. Holder's character as well as his confirmation the woman possesses enough talent to fake dialogue capable of convincing Bubba Jr., he was shooting the breeze with his dad. I add the doc may have held a grudge against Steph.

"Steph recommended that Satin Sands reject her offer to do software work on the cheap. Our witch doctor may have guessed he was the one who blackballed her. Though it's hard to believe losing chump change on a small coding job could matter to someone with her credentials. Certainly doesn't sound like enough motive to concoct an elaborate scheme to do Steph in."

"Maybe it wasn't losing the job that set the woman off," Alysha responds. "Perhaps it was knowing someone in her new playground had the goods on her. Perhaps Dr. Holder didn't want the news to spread."

A possibility.

"What are your next moves?" I ask. "When are you and Josie planning to arrest Bubba?"

"Not until we find Joe Wheeler. Thanks to your lead about Hank's Marine Repair, we startled an ID out of Bubba. When we hinted we were onto the guy who blew up his boat, we asked Bubba if he knew a mechanic who worked at Hank's. Bubba immediately blurted, 'Why would that summabitch Joe Wheeler do that to me?'

"Later, Hank told us Joe didn't show up for work today. Said he'd be out for at least a week due to a death of some Upstate family member. Strongly doubt anyone died. Josie's working on tracking Joe down through friends and relatives. Want to postpone arresting Bubba until we find Joe. If our explosives suspect hears Bubba is behind bars, he'll burrow deeper underground."

Suddenly, I realize Alysha doesn't know Frank's computer has been hacked or that I hope to set up a Dr. Holder sting.

Once I finish my update, I ask, "Any suggestions for conning the hacker?"

"Be very careful." Alysha's tone changes. The we're-closing-in-on these-scumbags cheer has been replaced with concern.

"I'm serious. This woman had no qualms about winding up two people to serve as her assassins by proxy over seemingly inconsequential slights. Imagine what she might plan if she thinks you're out to make her pay for her sins."

The Coastie's words give me a momentary chill. Still, I try to end the call on an upbeat note.

"Hey, no worries. You, Ellis, and Flo will provide me with Coast Guard Secret Service protection tomorrow. You'll be at the Hullis Island Marina by nine a.m., right? I made sure the harbormaster knows you're docking one of the USCG's retired SAFE boats for a show-and-tell after the parade.

"Should be a fun, relaxing day. Mom's preparing lots of goodies for a beach picnic to watch the afternoon's annual 'Salute from the Shore' flyover. If the weather cooperates, the military planes will be overhead around one-thirty, followed by a big contingent of civilian and antique aircraft."

"We'll be there," Alysha says. "Will talk over your idea of a sting operation with Josie. Maybe I'll have a brainstorm by then."

Chapter Fifty-Six

The Chameleon

Monday, July 3, evening

Sometimes I amaze myself. My Danny persona easily convinced Claude to shoulder his daddy's AR-15 and report for duty at Hullis Island early on the Fourth of July. I have high hopes Claude will do a better job of heeding my *(okay, Danny's)* detailed instructions than Bubba did.

Claude thinks of Danny as his incel commander-in-chief. That makes him more likely to salute and say, 'Yes, sir.' Since Danny is in the military, Claude considers him a trained man-killer, even though his hero's barely out of boot camp.

At seventeen, Claude thinks of Danny as a wizened senior, old enough to buy booze and vote. *(Lord, help us.)*

What is Danny instructing Claude to do tomorrow?

One, wear a ball cap, sunglasses, and a plain tee-shirt. Nothing memorable. Hide the AR-15 in a beach umbrella bag.

Two, arrive at the Hullis Island security gate around eight-thirty a.m. Smile and respond politely if the guard starts chatting while he scans the entry barcode I'll relay. *(Supposedly forwarded from Frank's computer.)*

Three, park on Birdwell Lane, which backs onto some undeveloped woods. The side street's relatively close to the Hullis Island Community Center and the Real Estate Sales Center. Casually walk to the Community Center. Make sure no one is around before shinnying up the live oak tree and swinging onto the roof.

Double-check the gun and make sure it's possible to get a clear, unobstructed shot of the mini-floats that go by.

When the Coast Guard float appears, immediately take out the golf cart's driver—the white-haired menace intent on upsetting the natural order and prompting women to reject the superiority of men. Once the driver's down, the golf cart will stop. Then it's fine to leisurely adorn the white dress uniforms of the three Coast Guard beauties with blooms of blood.

While panic ensues below, return the AR-15 to the beach umbrella bag, climb down from the roof, and mingle with the crowd.

Of course, Claude will not be apprised of *my* plans. Knowing the location of all my chess pieces, I'll pick out a great spot to monitor the action.

If Claude royally screws up, I have an excellent Plan B to salvage the situation.

Chapter Fifty-Seven

Kylee

Monday, July 3, evening

I 'm so happy we accepted Ed's dinner invitation. Ed's family is a delight. As soon as his first-grade son and second-grade daughter meet Grant, they form a hero worship club. Grant good-naturedly plays games with them before dinner.

The dinner is served family-style with paper napkins. Ed sees no need to artistically plate dishes with edible flowers. His five-plus star eats speak for themselves. I leave my dinner plate almost sparkling clean. Nary a leftover crumb in sight. Very happy my lightweight slacks have an elastic waistband.

Good thing Ed cooked up generous quantities. Grant isn't shy about taking up offers of second helpings of the chef's special version of a seafood paella, as well as his spinach and strawberry salad, and crunchy French bread.

When the crustless blueberry cheesecake arrives, I'm tempted to ask for seconds, too.

After dinner, it's bedtime for the Hiller young'uns, and they beg Grant to serve as their bedtime storyteller. He grins and sorts through a stack of children's books to pick one that'll let him ham it up.

Once the tucking-in-the-kids ritual begins, Ed ushers Ted and me into the living room and offers cordials.

"Grant's a terrific young man," Ed comments. "My compliments to your parenting, Ted. Hope my two are just as much fun to be around when they're nineteen."

Ted laughs. "Well, even with a terrific kid, the teen years can be challenging."

I know Ted's thinking about Grant's dangerous moonlight kayaking expedition. He discreetly refrains from spilling any teen trials-and-tribulations examples.

Ed swirls his brandy. "If it weren't still so blasted hot outside, I'd suggest sitting on our patio. One of the best things about leaving the city to spend time at Lighthouse Cove is the night sky. No street lights to spoil the view. Plus, now that Leona Grimm moved out—at least temporarily—it's very peaceful. No barking dog."

"Oh, you need to tell Ted about your neighbor's ghostly experience," I prompt.

Ed chuckles and proceeds to share Leona's middle-of-the-night visitation by her husband's ghost.

When he finishes, Ted asks, "You say you have a key to Leona's house?"

Ed laughs. "Yes, do you want to visit and see if the late Mr. Grimm is still in a haunting mood?"

"That's exactly what I'd like to do," Ted answers. "There's been a spate of hacking incidents lately in the HOAs we manage. I'm thinking this might be another one. You say Leona heard her dead husband's voice through computer-connected speakers?"

Ed tilts his head. "That's right. Guess hacking's more likely than a haunted house, though I don't get why a hacker would impersonate Leona's dead husband. Let's take a look."

Though I strongly suspected hacking, I hadn't considered taking advantage of a guided tour of the haunted house crime scene.

Ed calls to his wife and Grant, still cajoling the youngsters to close their eyes. "We're going to walk over to Leona's. Will be back in a few minutes."

Since the smallest Lighthouse Cove lots are at least an acre, our walk is long enough for my food to start settling. And Ed is correct. The clear night sky is magnificent. The heaven's twinkling stars defy count.

When we reach Leona's, Ed uses his key to open the door, then steps inside to enter a security code. "Leona gave me the code when she left," he says. "Not sure if she'll be back. She seemed awfully scared."

While Leona may have exited in a panic, her house looks like it was just tended by a large troop of cleaning elves. The scent of lemony furniture polish perfumes the air, and the old-fashioned mahogany tables and shelves gleam. Throw pillows are positioned just so on the couches. Even the magazines are fanned with precision, so each overlap is spaced the same number of millimeters. Not a speck of dust in sight.

"Quite a change from my house, huh?" Ed comments as he ushers us inside. "No worries here about stepping on a toy or discovering the chair you sat on last held a melted chocolate bar."

I smile. "Your house is much more to my liking. Give me lived-in charm over showroom sterility any day."

Ted glances around the living room. "So, where did Leona say her husband's voice came from?"

"Actually, she claimed it was like stereo." Ed points to a polished plastic sphere on the bookcase. "She'd fallen asleep on her couch and first heard the voice coming from that speaker. Scared her so badly she leaped up, ran to the master bedroom, and slammed the door shut. Then, she heard her late hubby's voice issuing from a twin speaker on her bedtable."

Ted nods. "Sounds right. All the speakers would be connected to Leona's computer network. If music is playing through one, it's playing through all of them. The devices respond to voice-activated commands, right?"

"Correct," the chef answers. "Leona really liked that instant gratification. She could say play Elvis Presley, and his hits would keep playing until she ordered it to play something else. Leona loves the ability to ask questions, too. When she couldn't recall something, all she needed to do was ask, 'Who starred in *North by Northwest*.'

"Oh, and our favorite doctor, Amanda Holder, recently emailed Leona a free weather app," he adds. "It let Leona request up-to-the-minute forecasts without logging onto her computer or looking at her cellphone. My neighbor decided Amanda's gift was a backhanded apology for her spiteful response to the dog park initiative."

"That's how she did it." Ted's words echo my conclusion.

"Who did what?" Ed asks, looking puzzled.

"You want to explain?" Ted asks me. "You just had the benefit of Aaron's hacking lecture."

"Ted and I believe the doc hacked Leona's Wi-Fi," I begin. "Then she gifted her with a weather application she'd doctored to include malware. The malware let Dr. Holder control the app, which she instructed to play a deepfake audio at a pre-set time. The audio featured a voice that was a dead ringer for Leona's late husband's voice.

"The witch doctor's motive? To get Leona and, more importantly, her dog, to abandon the neighborhood."

Ed's mouth falls open. "Wow. Who would think up such a thing? And how on earth could Amanda mimic the voice of someone who died two years ago?"

"Wouldn't be difficult if the late Mr. Grimm's voice was recorded and shared on the internet," Ted explains. "Seems like you can find voice samples for half the U.S. population on the web."

I give some examples. "Could have been a video of Mr. Grimm making a toast at a wedding or presenting a Kiwanis Club award. Aaron Cloyd tells me AI only needs a one- or two-minute voice training sample for it to create a near-perfect impersonation."

Ed shakes his head. "Unbelievable. Let's head back to my house. Now I can really use that after-dinner drink."

Chapter Fifty-Eight

Grant

Monday, July 3, evening

Once the Hiller kids quit fighting the Sandman and fall asleep, Mrs. Hiller—Lydia—and I return to the living room. We've barely sat down when Dad, Aunt Kylee, and Ed burst in with tales of the neighbor's not-so-haunted house.

"What a cruel hoax," Lydia comments. "The poor woman must have been terrified. Ed, are you going to call Leona? Let her know she's not in danger, that her ghostly visit was just a sick prank?"

Before Ed can reply, Dad jumps in. "I hope you two can keep that secret for a few days. It has a tangential relationship to a much more serious criminal investigation. I'd really appreciate it, if you'd let us talk with the authorities first. We need to follow their lead."

"Of course," Ed says, and Lydia nods her agreement.

No surprise. Dad's good at persuading most folks to do whatever he suggests. Grandma Myrt and Aunt Kylee being frequent exceptions. Sometimes, he wins them over, but it's never a sure thing. I've heard Dad grumble more than once about the "stubborn" Kane women. Maybe he views winning debates with them as an ongoing challenge.

When we leave the Hiller house, I open the front passenger door for my aunt, then slide my butt into the backseat. My preference. If Dad and Aunt

Kylee talk about something interesting, I can eavesdrop or join in. If not, I'll pull out my cellphone and text Mimi.

Dad's barely put the car in gear for our drive to his *This Old House* renovation project when Aunt Kylee wants to brainstorm ways to lure the vile professor out of her cyber hideaway. Her idea is to install an info honeypot on Frank's computer. One with a powerful fiction the witch doctor can't resist.

I mostly listen as Dad and Kylee catalog the types of information ineligible for the honeypot. Can't mention anything that connects the doc to J.T., Fyke, Bubba, Steph, and/or Leona. Their worry? Compromising the investigation or unintentionally making the doc decide it's time for a new attack.

Have to agree. Imagine what the doc might do to Bubba, if she learned he blabbed his *dad* provided the "insider" dope about Steph plotting to steal his land.

I smile, thinking the witch doctor would be plain out of luck trying to guilt Bubba into committing suicide.

I tune back in as my aunt and Dad rule out any reference to Steph's brother, Aaron. "The doc may already have guessed her former colleague has come to the Lowcountry to settle Steph's estate," Aunt Kylee says. "If she suspects Aaron is providing added intel about her, he'll be the doc's next target."

When quiet descends for a couple minutes, I throw in a thought. "Wouldn't try to fool the professor with some digital fabrication. She'd use AI or hack to make your efforts boomerang and bite you in the butt."

"Good point, Grant," Kylee says. "We need to send the witch doctor on a treasure hunt for something that can't be found by hacking computers, cellphones, or any other cyber device. How about a handwritten note?"

I'm puzzled. "Not sure I get how a paper note helps. Where would you hide this note? And couldn't the doc just destroy it, if she finds it?"

"I'd hide the note on the River Rat. Can't compete with our villain in AI and hacking realms, but I know security cameras and how to hide them. Two spy cams I ordered for Kay's B&B arrived yesterday. Planned to test them before installing them for Kay anyway. I can set them up to record the good doctor when she snoops on board the River Rat."

"Do they connect to Wi-Fi?" Dad asks. "If so, the professor will probably hack your Wi-Fi while she's aboard, find the videos, and erase them."

Aunt Kylee shakes her head. "No. To allow Kay's guests to connect to the internet, her Wi-Fi is public. That's why she wanted wireless, motion-activated spy cams that don't connect to Wi-Fi. The cams are for the B&B's common dining and living rooms. With guests constantly coming and going, her doors are only locked at night. Practically invites thieves to walk in and steal, either from Kay or guests who leave valuables unguarded while they're getting coffee refills. If something goes missing, Kay can physically download videos stored on the cam cards to her computer."

"What kind of note would entice the doc to risk coming aboard your boat to grab it?" Dad asks. "We've ruled out disclosing anything that might compromise the J.T. and Steph investigations. What else is there?"

"It appears the former professor is very protective of her reputation. Wouldn't want it tarnished by having her old, dirty laundry washed in public. If she feared her university misdeeds were about to come back to haunt her, I bet she'd react.

"How about learning there's a new initiative to dig up dirt at her university? I could say I'm flying to New York to interview the woman's former colleagues and students."

"How does a document fit in with that, Aunt Kylee?" I ask. "Just gives the doc more incentive to take you out of the picture."

Before I think better of it, I inject a little sarcasm. "Sounds riskier than taking a kayak for a spin at four a.m."

"Smartass," Aunt Kylee snips. "But you have a point, Grant.

"How about this? I email Mom. Let her know I'm flying to New York City Wednesday morning, July 5, to get the doc's former colleagues and students on the record. They've promised to deliver some very juicy details.

"I've jotted down all their names and why they despise the ex-professor in my spiral notebook. Too bad I haven't had a free minute to transfer my notes to my computer. I put my notebook in my carry-on so I can update my laptop on the plane ride. Put the carry-on where I'll trip over it, if I try leaving the River Rat without it."

Dad groans. "Not one of your better ideas. Yes, the doc might be curious about who's stabbing her in the back at the university, and what they're prepared to share. But it still makes you, Kylee, not the notebook, the primary target. If she finds a willing proxy to kill you, problem solved. Your little notebook won't matter."

"You're wrong there," Kylee argues. "She'll want to destroy the notebook. Otherwise, someone investigating my...let's call it disappearance...might look into the possibility my notebook holds clues about why I was disappeared."

Dad's voice gets a little louder, always does when he's frustrated. "That only means she'll want to do away with both you AND the notebook. Doesn't make me feel any better. The doc's prior actions suggest she'll trick someone into doing her dirty work.

"How can we protect you if we haven't a clue who might be coming after you? Bubba and J.T. aren't exactly likely assassin choices. Those two have zero in common. There's no way to predict who the witch doctor's next proxy might be."

While I agree with Dad, I have a hunch Aunt Kylee won't give in.

"Let's back up," she replies. "From her prior hacks, the woman knows I'll be on Hullis Island all day tomorrow, the Fourth of July. That means she also knows where I won't be—aboard the River Rat.

"With no one aboard, she has a perfect no-risk window to visit the River Rat and take a peek at the notebook. She'd want to know what's in it to plan her next moves. If she decides the university stoolies are just gossips with no first-hand knowledge, she can let me go merrily on my wild-goose chase. If not, she can then destroy the notebook and figure out how to get rid of me."

"There's a big flaw in your supposed logic," Dad complains. "What makes you think the doc won't decide to get rid of you *first* and the notebook second."

"Hey, I thought we agreed she's unlikely to try anything during Hullis Island's Fourth of July festivities," Kylee counters. "Too many witnesses. She's arranged her other attacks to take place in deserted spots with no witnesses. Plus, I'll have three armed Coast Guard ladies in my posse."

Dad shakes his head. "If we've learned anything about Dr. Holder, it's that she doesn't lack imagination. The attacks on J.T. and Steph had nothing in common. Maybe this time she'll decide big crowds will work in her favor."

Dad looks at Kylee and sighs. "Not going to change your mind about this proposed treasure hunt, am I?

"Nope," Kylee says. "I appreciate your concern, but you're exaggerating the risks. If she's not stopped—trapped—soon, the danger will be even greater."

I kind of agree with Dad. Aunt Kylee's plan seems mighty risky. But I see my aunt's point, too. Who knows what the woman might do next, if she's not caught.

It just dawned on me how different it is to hear Dad and Kylee argue. With them, it's give and take. Nothing like Dad's and Mom's scorched-earth fights before the divorce. At least, Dad and Kylee bother to listen to each other.

I think Mom had zero interest in what Dad did for a living or any concerns he might have beyond their social calendar. And Dad felt the frequently required State Department social appearances deserved combat pay. They're both happier now.

When Dad parks at the house, he kisses Aunt Kylee. "Please be careful," he says. "Send me a draft of that honeypot email tonight. Maybe I'll have suggestions to finetune it."

"I will. Promise."

Dad touches Kylee's cheek before she exits the car. "Just in case the good doctor might plan some Fourth of July surprise on Hullis, I'll talk with Chief O'Rourke about his security plans first thing tomorrow. Grant, how about helping out the guards on gate duty? If it's anything like last year, residents will call in gate passes for half of Beaufort County."

I shrug. "Sure. I can help. As long as Kylee saves me some of the candy her Coast Guard buddies are bringing for the kids."

Kylee laughs. "Not a problem. See you, gentlemen, bright and early tomorrow."

We exit Dad's car. As Aunt Kylee heads to her Camry, Dad's shoulders slump. Kylee hasn't convinced him, and he's plenty worried. Have to admit I am, too.

Chapter Fifty-Nine

Kylee

Tuesday, July 3, evening

Aboard the River Rat, I take out the two spy cams I purchased for Kay's B&B. One looks like an ordinary picture frame, the other a clothes hook. When motion activates the cameras, they record videos that are stored on a card for later download to a computer. When the motion stops, the recording stops.

Just need to decide the best places to position the cameras. Want them to capture the witch doctor's face when she picks up my carry-on and starts rummaging around for the notebook. I smile, imagining what her angry puss will look like when there's no notebook to find.

But what if she wears a mask? Might make the videos worthless.

No. She's not going to wear a mask if she visits in broad daylight. The marina has security cameras of its own, and folks manning the Ship's Store would certainly call the police if they saw a masked visitor poking around the marina boat slips.

Might she come at night?

Certainly not tonight. I won't send Mom the treasure hunt email until I leave for Hullis Island in the morning. One worry is how Mom might reply to the email. When she's not working, Mom usually checks her emails first thing each morning, then doesn't bother with the computer the rest of the day. I can't phone Mom to warn her the email is bogus since the wicked professor might be across the street and has found a way to eavesdrop.

Why didn't I think of this before? What a dummy.

I phone Ted. "Hope I'm not getting you out of bed."

"No, I'm waiting to see the draft of your email. Besides, I don't know if I'll ever get to sleep tonight. I'm really worried this sting strategy will backfire. And I don't know how to keep you safe."

"Yeah, well, I just realized another way the sting could backfire."

I explain my concern that Mom might inadvertently give the game away. Yes, my mother knows she's been hacked. But I'm afraid an alarming email might prompt Mom to phone me before she remembers her daughter may not be the only person on the line.

Ted offers to roust Grant super early so they're on Frank's doorstep by six-thirty, about the time Mom and Frank usually get up. I agree to wait until seven a.m. to send the email. Plenty of time for Ted to give Mom an in-person heads-up.

"Still wish I could talk you out of this," Ted says. "That woman's smart, unhinged, and arrogant. A very frightening and dangerous combination. There's no telling what she'll pull next."

Though I agree, I don't comment.

I try to sound upbeat. "Hey, don't want to keep you up all night, since you have to get up before the roosters start to crow. I'll send you that draft email in half an hour or less. Better say goodbye so I can finish it. I love you, Ted."

"Love you, too." Ted sounds worried and sad.

Makes me feel bad. Yet I don't see another way to stop the woman. If we get video of her aboard my boat, searching my carry-on, the authorities will have something to take to a judge. The only way the doc would know to search my carry-on is by hacking. I suspect that would provide sufficient cause for a search warrant. One that should turn up evidence of her crimes.

Can't imagine she's discarded all of her burner phones. And, if the authorities could get hold of one of them, they could contact her service provider, even if she used a fake ID to pay for it. Knowing the provider, authorities could request records of all her texts and calls.

For twenty minutes, I fiddle with the email before sending the draft to Ted. Five minutes later, he's suggested some minor tweaks.

"Thanks," I reply. "See you tomorrow morning."

Chapter Sixty

Grant

Wednesday, July 4, morning

At least Dad has coffee made when he shakes me awake. I can smell it.

When I open my eyes, my bedroom is dark. Means the sun isn't up yet, though there's a pre-dawn hint the sun will rise soon.

My bedroom has temporary window shades. Dad duct-taped old, so-thin-they're-practically-transparent sheets to the window frames. Far as I can tell, my shades only serve to prevent Peeping Toms from taking mug shots suitable for facial recognition. However, I'm sure a peeper could catalog my silhouette's every move.

Like if I yawn and scratch whatever. My current activities.

Dad returns to my doorway to see if I'm actually out of bed. "Hurry," he says. "Sorry to wake you so early, but I promised Kylee we'd get to Frank's by six-thirty. Have to warn Myrt in person about the sting email Kylee's sending at seven. Don't want Myrt to freak out. You can take a shower at Frank's once we get there."

When Dad leaves, I throw on shorts and a tee-shirt, and pound down the stairs.

Dad hands me an insulated to-go mug of coffee and gives me a once-over.

"Uh, run back upstairs and grab a polo shirt and long pants to wear when you help at the security gate. Even if the help is gratis, Chief O'Rourke would frown on anyone wearing shorts."

I sigh. "Okay, today's gonna be another hot one. Hope O'Rourke doesn't mind residents seeing sweat rings under my armpits."

I think about trying to sleep on the drive to Hullis, but once I drink the coffee, I'm wide awake. Dad doesn't say much. Too worried, I guess. So, I just zone out and watch the Lowcountry scenery slide by. The sunrise paints the clouds in pinks and purples. Since there isn't a breeze, the watery marsh acts as a mirror, painting a watercolor in soft pastels.

Mimi would love to get a shot of this. Especially if a blue heron or flock of egrets would happen by.

Hope she's still planning to join our family's Salute from the Shore picnic this afternoon. Will text her after I finish my security gate shift.

* * *

It's eight o'clock as I walk toward the security gate. Took a shower at Frank's and Grandma Myrt fixed me up with eggs, sausage, and biscuits. Dad wants me to help the guards on duty until ten a.m. That's when the parade starts. By then, he figures most folks coming from off-island for the Fourth celebrations will already have arrived.

I'm glad to see Bill Clark's on duty. He's leaning out the door, chatting with the newest arrival. Bill's one of the younger Hullis Island officers, and he has a good sense of humor.

Not too fond of some of the old farts. When we visited Grandma Myrt back when I was fifteen and sixteen, they hassled me plenty. If Myrt sent me to the convenience store in a golf cart, they'd pull me over and ask to see my driver's license. If I was in a car, they'd claim I was exceeding the fifteen-mile-per-hour-speed limit on Grandma Myrt's road. Like adults drive thirteen miles per hour. You have to coast and keep one foot on the brake to stay under fifteen.

What Dad calls the Hullis Island security gate is actually a guardhouse. Kind of looks like one of the tiny homes going up outside Charleston. The guard house sits on a traffic island between entry and exit roads.

A barrier arm on the exit side raises automatically when cars approach. On the entry side, a security officer lifts the arm in advance if he sees a car approaching with a Hullis decal sticker on the windshield. That lets owners roll through without coming to a full stop. Cars without decals must stop, and the drivers have to show QR—Quick Response—barcodes on their cellphones or hand printouts to the guard. The codes are scanned to verify they're pre-approved guests.

Of course, guests sometimes forget to bring codes or owners forget to call ahead for guests. That's one reason I'm here. When it's super busy, cars start stacking up behind the gate, and the officers get real harried. During prime times, there are two officers on duty. I'll probably help out by scanning the QR codes and checking them off the pre-approved list while Bill and the other officer answer questions, phone owners, and work the barrier arms.

Bill grins when he spots me. "Glad to see you, Grant. You just missed your Aunt Kylee. She came through maybe five minutes ago. Your dad told us you're gonna help Pete and me out for a couple of hours."

Anyone who's ever spent any time on Hullis Island quickly learns everybody seems to know everybody else's business. If a strange car remains parked in Frank's driveway for more than an hour, someone will call Frank or Myrt asking who's visiting them. Kinda glad Frank has more than old sheets up on his windows, or someone might ask why I don't wear PJs.

As expected, Bill tells me to scan QR codes and check them off on a printout. That means I'm tucked out of sight in the back of the very hot, non-air-conditioned tiny house. I understand why the air-conditioner isn't on. Pointless with Bill and Pete constantly leaning out the open top half of Dutch doors to gab and hand out passes. Means I sit on a high stool and sweat.

Coulda worn shorts. Nobody would know.

I've been at it about half an hour when Bill mentions Frank Donahue's name as he greets a guest. Bill hands me the printed QR code to scan. When I go to put a check beside the address requesting the pass, Frank's address comes up. Huh? Frank didn't mention calling in any guests. The name of

257

the guest is listed as Curtis Donahue. I lean forward to hear what Curtis and Bill are saying.

"So, are you a relative of Frank's?" Bill asks.

"Uh, yeah," a young man answers. "His nephew. Here to spend the week."

Nephew? I've met both of Frank's nephews. They're around Dad's age, and neither is named Curtis.

"You probably know Grant then," Bill says to the unseen Curtis.

I shove Bill hard while trying to remain out of sight. When the annoyed officer turns around, I shake my head and put my fingers to my lips. Then, I whisper, "Don't say anything else."

"Well, you have a good day now," Bill says as he hands Curtis the guest pass to display on his dash. "Happy Fourth of July."

Bill turns to me. "What in the devil is your problem?" he begins.

"Frank doesn't have a nephew named Curtis."

I practically knock Pete over as I bolt past him and out the guard house door on the exit side. Want to see the car Curtis is driving, and get his license plate number.

As I burst back inside the guard house, Bill's already on the phone. "Yeah, I let a kid through the gate before I found out he had a fake QR code. He's a teenager. Could be a pickpocket hoping to work the crowds. He's driving a gray 1998 Chevy Malibu."

I grab Bill's arm. "Wait, don't let anyone stop that kid, thinking he's some purse snatcher. I think he's armed, and he's come to kill Aunt Kylee."

"Hang on a minute," Bill tells the caller and clamps a hand over the phone to hear what I have to say. His look says he thinks I'm off my rocker.

I tighten my grip on Bill's arm. "I'm serious. Let me call Dad. He'll explain. You have to believe me."

Bill returns to the officer he's put on hold. "Seems there may be more to this story. The kid could be armed and dangerous. Until we get this sorted out, see if you can spot his car and shadow him. Watch where he goes. But don't approach until we know more."

My heart's beating a mile a minute. I pull out my cellphone. For a second, I wonder if my first call should be to Dad or Aunt Kylee, but Dad's more likely to pick up. Maybe this Curtis is just some juvenile delinquent. Yet, the fact his pass supposedly came from Frank's computer strongly suggests he's one of the foul professor's creatures. Not likely two people have hacked Frank's computer. The scary part is not knowing what the puppet master told this Curtis to do. Whatever the orders, I'm sure they include killing Aunt Kylee.

Dad answers immediately, and I curb the urge to start screaming long enough to share the gist of the story.

"Grant, I want you to call Kylee," Dad orders, his voice steady. "If she doesn't answer her phone, find her. If she's not at Frank's, she's already left for the marina to meet her Coast Guard friends. They're arriving by boat. Do you have a description of this kid?"

"No, but Bill saw him. He's right here."

I hand the phone to the security officer.

"Hey, Ted, I heard what Grant told you. You really think this kid has a gun? That he aims to kill Kylee?"

I can't hear Dad's answer, but watch as Bill's eyes widen.

"Okay, I agree," Bill replies. "No point taking chances. You want to know what he looks like, right? He's white. My guess is sixteen, seventeen. Young enough to still have lots of zits. On the skinny side. Had on a blue ball cap so only saw some shaved light brown stubble below it. Looked like a buzz cut, but some kids today grow it long up top and shave it below. Wore sunglasses, so couldn't say what eye color. Not much to go on."

Bill stops. Since he's nodding his head, I figure Dad's talking.

"He was wearing a light-colored tee-shirt," Bill adds. "Didn't notice a slogan. Have no idea what else he was wearing. Only saw him from the shoulders up. He was driving a gray 1998 Chevy Malibu."

I chime in with the license plate number. "The frame around the license advertised the Cole GM dealership," I add. "The car's local."

Bill looks at me. "Good catch. Go on, now, find Kylee. Your dad and I will get with Chief O'Rourke and figure out what's next."

I sprint from the guard house to my Jeep, parked in a visitor's lot by the convenience store. I call Aunt Kylee. No answer.

I jump in my Jeep and gun it toward Frank's house. The hell with the fifteen-mile-per-hour speed limit.

Chapter Sixty-One

Kylee

Wednesday, July 4, morning

"Hey, Mom, I'm heading to the marina. Want to be on the dock to greet Alysha, Flo, and Ellis when they arrive."

"What did you say?" Mom calls from the kitchen. "Couldn't hear you over the mixer."

I start toward the kitchen to tell Mom I'm leaving when the squeal of tires prompts a glance out the window. Grant's Jeep roars up the street and swings wildly into the driveway. For a second, I think he'll take out Mom's mailbox. In an uncontrolled slide, the Jeep slews to the left, toppling an oleander bush and churning a big swath of lawn.

"What in blazes?"

I run out on the porch.

Grant vaults from his Jeep. "Aunt Kylee, get back inside."

As he tears up the porch stairs, I jump backward to avoid a tackle.

"Grant!" I yell. "Stop. You're scaring me. What's happened?"

"Inside," he pants. "Then I'll tell you."

* * *

Once he's spilled his news, Grant calms down. Can't say the same for Mom and me. I take several deep breaths.

I'm responsible. I taunted her in person. Thought I could outsmart her.

I'm certain the witch doctor sent this kid to Hullis to murder me. Doubt she's fussy about who else might get killed in the process. I have to stop this kid. Who knows what mission she's given Curtis—or whatever his real name is.

The thought of Hullis security officers facing down this threat while I cower inside Frank's house doesn't sit well. Won't be able to live with myself if officers die trying to save my hide. I misjudged, underestimated the witch doctor, and I need to do something.

I call Ted. "Grant told me about the kid. Where are you? What's happening?"

"I'm with Chief O'Rourke. Officers found the kid's car parked on Birdwell Lane, a quiet side street. No sign of the boy. By now, he could be anywhere on the island. Finding the right kid in a light-colored tee shirt is like finding a needle in a haystack. Have to be dozens of tee-shirt-wearing teens scattered among the milling owners and tourists.

"The chief contacted the Sheriff's Office. They ran the license plate and reached Dirk Appleton, the kid's father. The boy's real name is Claude, and his father says the AR-15 he owns is missing. The sheriff is helicoptering Mr. Appleton to Hullis. If we find his son, we're hoping his father can talk him into surrendering before anyone gets hurt."

"Are you and the chief at his office?" I ask.

"Yes. The chief's assembling a team that's had some SWAT training. They're putting on protective gear. The Sheriff's SWAT team is en route."

"Man, this is bad." I sigh. "Families have already staked out prime parade viewing spots. If they see SWAT teams marching their way, they'll panic. Since victim counts from mass shootings are now reported as routinely as baseball scores, the crowd will assume the SWAT team has arrived to deal with an active shooter. That could cause a stampede. Lots of folks could get seriously injured, even if the kid never fires a shot."

"True, but what else can the chief and the sheriff do?" Ted asks. "Have to try and find the kid before he uses his AR-15 to mow down moms, dads, and little kids. And we can't ask officers to go hunting for a gunman without protective gear."

"I totally agree," I say. "But I can hunt for Claude without scaring anyone."

"What?" Ted barks. "You do realize his mission, whatever Claude thinks it may be, is to kill you. Stay at Frank's. Don't ask to be killed."

"Love you," I say a second before I end the call and turn off my cellphone.

Chapter Sixty-Two

The Chameleon

Wednesday, July 4, morning

E ight-thirty has come and gone. Haven't heard a single siren. Assume Claude made it on the island without incident and is perched on the Community Center roof with his daddy's AR-15. Though it's early, I'll head to the parade route in a few minutes. I've already scoped out spots near the Community Center where I can watch the action while staying beyond the range of any ricocheting gunfire.

First, however, I should check Frank's computer to confirm there's been no last-minute change in family plans. Would be very inconvenient if I've orchestrated all these arrangements, and Kylee has a bout of diarrhea and is skipping the parade.

I quickly scan Myrtle's inbox. Man, she gets a lot of junk email from politicians asking for campaign donations. Seems puzzling that the desperate I-need-money requests come from both Democrats and Republicans. At some time, Myrtle must have been foolish enough to shell out money for crooks in both parties.

Ah, finally. Here's an email from Kylee. Came in around seven a.m. Probably confirming when she'll arrive on Hullis. Yep, that's the news in her first line.

What?

I grind my teeth as I read and re-read what follows in the snoop's email. She's been phoning my old colleagues and students. The nerve. Who the hell implied they had enough startling revelations to prompt the pain-in-the-butt meddler to get on a plane to New York City? She leaves tomorrow morning?

I smile.

Well, of course, the snoop won't be leaving tomorrow morning. She'll be dead.

If Claude performs as ordered.

That leaves me with a decision. What to do about that notebook? Go to the meddler's boat and retrieve it, or leave it be. Do I care who's smearing me once the snoop is out of the way?

Would Myrtle raise a stink if she's unable to find her late daughter's notebook? Or would she be too consumed with grief to even remember her daughter mentioned a notebook? How soon after the murder would anyone visit the sneak's boat to search for clues or paw through what she left behind?

It's too early to settle on a plan. Not until I know if Claude is successful and escapes or gets killed by cops before he reaches his car. If Claude kills enough people, it won't appear as if his job was to commit a single murder.

I grab my purse, and double-check that my Sig Sauer's inside, easy to reach. No point having a concealed carry permit, if you leave your gun at home. Doubt I'll need it, but it could come in handy. Hey, if I spot a fleeing active shooter, I could take the opportunity to put him down. Kill the maniac before he murders more innocents.

Being the gun-toting, action heroine who saves countless lives by taking out a demented gunman could be a marketing coup. I smile, imagining a promo write-up.

"This killer app developed by a genius who witnessed mass murder and boldly acted to stop the carnage. Dr. Holder believes the best way to prevent such future horrors is to let people channel their violent fantasies into virtual violence. This killer app ensures actual blood is never spilled."

* * *

As I step out on my porch, a kamikaze driver careens down the street. Has to be going closer to fifty than fifteen miles per hour. The speeding Jeep doesn't slow quickly enough to handle the turn into Frank's driveway. It shimmies to a stop after skidding through a healthy patch of lawn and taking out an oleander.

Shit. It's the Welch boy.

I spot the snoop on the porch. Grant screams at her to get inside.

Why can't anything go according to plan?

Has Claude been caught? Why is Grant telling the meddler to hunker down inside and hide?

I'm not going to learn anything standing here with my mouth open. If nothing else, I can keep to my part of the plan. Find my spot on the parade route and check if Claude's where he's supposed to be. If I see officers searching for him, the game's up.

But maybe I can still be the heroine of the hour. Take out an active shooter before he can start telling tales.

Chapter Sixty-Three

Kylee

Wednesday, July 4, morning

"Mom, did you keep the wigs you bought when you started chemo and lost your hair?"

Mom grabs me by the shoulders. She's put back a few of the pounds she lost battling cancer, but she's still skinny. Doesn't seem to have lessened her steel grip.

"You're planning to go hunting for this deranged killer, aren't you? D'you think a wig will protect you from a bullet? Don't go. Let the security officers and sheriff's deputies deal with the situation. They have SWAT teams trained for this."

I cover her hands with my own and give them a gentle squeeze. "Can't just hide, Mom. He's after me. Not going to let other people lose their lives because of me."

"So, you're planning to sacrifice yourself?" Mom yells.

"No. I don't plan to paint a bullseye on my shirt for his bullets. What's the first thing most people notice about me? My curly white hair. It's the only thing that makes me stand out in a crowd. I'm sure that's what the doc told this kid to look for, how he could identify me. If his weapon is an AR-15, the boy doesn't plan to get up close and personal and verify my eye color.

"If you still have that Lucille Ball-style wig, the one you wore as a joke, it will do nicely," I say. "Please, Mom, go get it for me."

Mom shakes her head but heads toward a hallway storage closet.

I turn to Grant. "I want you to drive to the marina and meet Alysha, Ellis, and Flo. They're arriving in one of the Coast Guard's retired SAFE boats. Tell them to stay on the boat. Explain that a madwoman has persuaded a teenage shooter to believe he's been called to right some imagined wrong. My guess is his mission is to murder me and everyone else who happens to be riding the Coast Guard parade float.

"Go the back way," I add. "Don't go near the parade route. It's not safe. The witch doctor's car is gone from her rental house. No telling where she is. Since the doc thinks I'll be driving the golf cart float in the parade, she must have ordered her brainwashed recruit to hide in a nice hunter's blind somewhere along the route. Please, Grant, stay with my Coast Guard friends on the boat. Ted or I will call to let you and my friends know when the threat's over."

Mom's returned, holding the ratty wig between thumb and forefinger like she might be disposing of a dead mouse. If there were red-headed mice, the illusion would be perfect.

"I thought about telling you I couldn't find it," Mom says. "But you'd just run out with a headscarf or some other disguise that would be even worse. Still don't understand what you hope to accomplish. What makes you think you're better equipped to find the boy than all the security officers and deputies out looking for him?"

Grant frowns. "Grandma has a point. And, since the doc knows we're planning a beach picnic during the flyover, maybe she ordered the kid to take you out on the beach. Could be the idiot's nowhere near the parade route."

"True, but the Hullis Island beach is more than a mile long. She'd have no way to tell Claude where to look for us. No, it's the parade route. The professor wouldn't want the boy wandering around the beach with an AR-15.

"In orchestrating prior attacks, she's always tried to lessen the odds her humanoid commandos will be quickly captured and interrogated. Doubt she cares if they're killed. But I don't think she wants them caught in the act. Not while they're on adrenaline highs. They could say way too much about what drove them to act."

"The parade route's even longer than the beach," Grant points out. "He could be hiding anywhere along the way."

"She'll have scouted the route in advance for serviceable hunter blinds. Elevated spots where Claude would have an unobstructed sight-line and yet stay hidden until the Coast Guard mini-float appears. Only a couple of options fit the bill."

"If that's the case, have Ted tell the guys in SWAT gear to check them out," Mom pleads.

"I will. When I'm sure I'm right."

If I can't talk the kid down when I get there.

Chapter Sixty-Four

Kylee

Wednesday, July 4, morning

Taking off from Frank's house, I scrutinize the witch doctor's across-the-street rental. No car in the driveway. Has she left the island to ensure she's nowhere near the scene of the crime? Or did she drive her BMW and park near Claude's roost to watch the bloodbath?

God, I'm burning up!

The tight wig feels like a vice. Guess my noggin's bigger than Mom's. An opinion my mother would readily second at the moment, believing I have a swelled head and am overestimating my abilities.

I blow at one of the cheap wig's stray hairs tickling my cheek. Beads of perspiration pop on my forehead.

Can't blame all the sweat on my wig. Granted, it's hotter than Hades, but my jangling nerves are making me sweat, too. My Camry feels like a giant tin pressure cooker.

Where should I start my search?

At least three dozen tallish buildings line the parade route. Since flood insurance requires any houses built in the last few decades to elevate the first floor, the homes all sit on pilings. Many houses have a second story, making their roofs and balconies excellent options for would-be assassins.

Nonetheless, I rule out the houses. The professor's two rentals are on side streets and aren't options, and I doubt she'd risk choosing a house she doesn't own. Given the Independence Day crowds, she couldn't guarantee any house would be vacant.

Santa Claus isn't the only one who makes a clatter on the roof. Unless the doc has recruited a cat burglar, her proxy would likely make enough noise to get caught sneaking up on the roof of any house with people inside.

Ruling out houses leaves three commercial/public properties as candidates—the Real Estate Sales Center, the Fire Station, and the Community Center. I quickly discount the Fire Station. Folks are on duty there 24/7.

The Real Estate Sales Center has pros and cons. A fire escape at the back of the building would make it easy to climb to one of the second-story office balconies. The Real Estate parking lot is the designated assembly spot for everyone wanting to join the parade. As a result, the site will be mobbed. Since I volunteered to help last year, I know first-hand how the scene dissolves into chaos. Unless Claude's carrying his AR-15 out in the open, the bedlam could let him hide in plain sight.

The Community Center offers different advantages. Its flat roof is surrounded by a three-foot-tall decorative parapet. Perfect cover for a prone shooter.

It's doubtful anyone will be inside that building today. The parade ends at the children's playground and picnic area, more than a mile away. That's where the hawkers of kettle corn, fried Oreos, balloon animals, miniature U.S. flags, and assorted trinkets are set up.

Ted mentioned Claude's car was found on Birdwell Lane, a relatively short walk to either the Real Estate Sales Center or the Community Center. Since the main drag is already blocked off for the parade, I decide I'll park on Birdwell, too. If all else fails, maybe I can ambush Claude when he tries to make his getaway.

I speed walk toward the leisure path that borders the main drag. When I reach it, any thought of power walking or jogging to the Community Center or the Real Estate Sales Center becomes a joke. Walkers, bikers, and rollerbladers jam the walkway, and folks with their butts already parked in camp chairs make it impossible to leave the path to bypass the clogs. There's also the danger of getting tangled in leashes. Pet owners have brought their dogs, large and small, to the parade. Looks like half the pooches are outfitted in party hats and red, white, and blue tutus. How embarrassing.

I shoulder my way through the crowd, jumping off the path and onto vacant strips of grass wherever there's an opening. I'm slowly making headway. The good news is I've come nose to nose with several acquaintances, and no one has recognized me. The wig plus dark sunglasses with lenses the size of saucers appear to provide a decent disguise.

My clothes are nondescript, too. When Grant arrived with his possible shooter alert, I was ready to walk out the door in a tee-shirt that boasted a big Coast Guard logo. Not wanting to waste time changing, I threw a long-sleeved sun protection shirt over my tee. Since the puppet master probably told Claude to focus on a Coast Guard parade float, advertising my Coastie affiliation seems a bad idea.

When I reach the side street nearest the Community Center, I spot a Beemer snugged up to the curb in a prime getaway spot. It's the same model and color as the BMW recently parked in the driveway of the doc's rental house. Can't see the license plate and not sure I'd remember the number, even if I could. But my gut tells me it belongs to the witch doctor. I shiver. Maybe it's my imagination, but I sense her evil presence nearby.

Why? This isn't her usual modus operandi. No separation, no alibi.

Can't worry about the scheming witch now. Finding Claude is the priority. And I'm increasingly certain he's taken up a position on the Community Center roof. That's why the woman's close. She's come to watch the bloodbath.

Have seen no signs of the SWAT teams yet. Wish I had an idea where they are, and what's planned. Is the Hullis Island team waiting for the sheriff's larger SWAT contingent to join them?

If I'm right about the Community Center, I figure my best move is to leave the leisure path a half block away and slip into the surrounding woods. The stream that meanders through Hullis Island didn't leave developers enough room to build on this side of the center or behind it. The result is a short stretch of protected greenery. Another reason for the puppet master to have chosen this building for her proxy.

If Claude's instructions are to fire on one or more parade floats, he'll be scanning the road for signs of activity. No reason for him to pay attention to the woods behind and beside the building. I'm confident I can get very close without being seen.

I glance at my watch. Nine thirty. Half an hour until the parade is scheduled to start. However, I'm sure Chief O'Rourke has already called for a delay. I doubt he's shared the reason, though. Otherwise, the spectators' cellphones would be setting up an ear-splitting racket of high-pitched rings. No way would parade participants fail to phone friends along the parade route if they'd been warned about a possible active shooter situation. Talk about a phone tree.

The Real Estate Sales Center is close enough that I can hear the low hum of the hubbub as organizers try to herd golf carts, bicyclists, and walkers into some order. Equine whinnies tell me a few horses have been saddled up for the parade, too. As a former member of a high-school marching band, I pity all the folks assigned to follow the equestrians.

I take a calming breath. My brain is careening from thought to thought, too frightened to dwell on what comes next.

Do I attempt to sneak up on Claude? Would he hear me coming?

Or should I stay out of sight and call to him? Can I make a stab at what his mentor—whoever it may be—has persuaded him to do?

Chapter Sixty-Five

The Chameleon

Wednesday, July 4, morning

I carry my folding chair as I decide the perfect spot to watch the action. Might as well be comfortable. I decide against joining the throng packed on and beside the leisure path. I spot a family group camped on the opposite side of the street in front of a rambling vacation house. Assume the family's staked the claim to their own front yard.

I cross the street and approach the woman. Don't want her to think I have any designs on her man. Plus, I want to stay as far away from him as possible. Can't have some macho headcase interfere with any of my plans.

I smile. "Hi, I'm a little claustrophobic. Would you mind if I share your lawn? It's awfully crowded over there."

"Sure, you're welcome," the middle-aged woman answers.

A second later, she forgets all about me as she turns to swat the bottom of a prepubescent boy. "Quit pulling your sister's braids."

The frazzled woman is clearly the mother of this brood. Four kids, but—thankfully—no yipping dogs. Dad has a six-pack in a cooler next to his lawn chair, and he's tuned out the kids to stare at his cellphone. Probably live-streaming a sports program.

I find a spot of even ground and set my chair down. Once I'm seated, I take out my binoculars. Early on, I found equipping my rental units with binoculars wins really nice reviews, especially from bird- and dolphin-watching vacationers.

I scan the Community Center parapet. I think I detect the faint sound of scuffling feet atop the building. I check to see if any of my companions notice. No, too preoccupied. Good.

I bring the binoculars back up and am rewarded with a crystal-clear view of the AR-15's barrel. Luckily, the gun appears and disappears in the blink of an eye. Claude is performing according to my programming. He obviously made it through the security gate, parked, and reached his roost without being stopped.

Grant's reckless driving and his shouted warning for the snoop to get inside are clear signs something gave the game away. But what? And how will the security officers respond?

I assume they'll try to avoid panicking the crowd, but every minute they fail to find Claude, will wear on their nerves. What's the strategy for their search? There's been no announcement the parade will be canceled, but I expect that to come any second.

Then, what will Claude do? I didn't give him any bail-out options. If he's smart, once the parade's canceled, he'll leave his AR-15 on the roof, climb down, and hide. But he's not the brightest bulb. He'll probably head to his car and keep his AR-15 to defend himself.

If that's the case, I'll end Claude's nightmare for him. Having gotten a glimpse of his gun, I'll pull out my Sig Sauer and save all the lives this madman might otherwise have taken.

As soon as the parade's called off, I'll scoot over to the woods surrounding the Community Center. A good place to surprise a frightened, clueless Claude.

I virtually pat myself on the back for my forward thinking. Then, I train my binoculars on the woods to study my ambush options.

I see a flash of red. A figure weaving through the woods, furtively scurrying from trunk to trunk. A scout for a SWAT team? That's my first thought, but whoever it may be isn't dressed for the part. Nor is there any sign of officers amassed nearby for an assault. If a SWAT team had assembled anywhere close to the parade route, the spectators would react. They wouldn't just sit on their fannies and lick popsicles as officers in padded uniforms crept by.

So, who's in the woods? Does the person know Claude's location? If so, how? And what, if anything, should I do about it?

I train the binoculars back on the figure. A slight man or a woman. The silhouette and the clothing say woman. Could it be the snoop? The figure's no Q-tip with curly, white hair. But if I were trying to avoid notice, I'd do something about that hair, too.

The figure's face peeks out from behind a tree trunk. I double the binocular's magnification.

Shit! It's Kylee Kane. With the wig and oversized sunglasses, I'd never know, except for the red claw mark a recent HOA wrestling match left on her cheek.

The nosy woman's appearance presents some interesting possibilities. Wish I could phone Claude and tell him there's a change of plan. Then again, I could phone 911 and report seeing a figure with a gun sneaking through the woods.

The Hullis Island security force isn't used to dealing with gunmen. That heightens the odds some security guard with a nervous trigger finger may solve my problem by peppering the woods with bullets before the snoop can shout, "You want him, not me."

And once the first shot is fired, Claude is sure to join in. How could he not?

I turn to the harried mother seated near me. "Got a cramp in my leg. Need to walk it off."

I bring my purse with me as I retreat a safe distance from the family. Can't have any of them hear my call. Glad I brought a burner phone for just this sort of contingency.

I smile and dial 911.

Chapter Sixty-Six

Kylee

Wednesday, July 4, morning

The scrabbling sound is faint but distinctive. It's coming from the Community Center roof. And it's definitely not a squirrel. Not unless there's a one-hundred-fifty-pound mutant rodent dashing about.

I'm studying the roofline when a rifle barrel pops up above the parapet. A second later, it vanishes.

That's all the confirmation I need. Claude is on that roof, positioned in the northeast corner. The spot offers an excellent, unobstructed view of each approaching float.

I'm not stupid. I know whatever tactic I try may fail. I need to share what I know with Ted. I slip out my cellphone. While I may not answer my cell the moment it rings, Ted will pick up instantly, if he sees I'm calling.

As I power up my phone, one of the parade organizers loudly harangues a mischief-maker. Suddenly, I know how to improve the odds Claude can be captured without endangering any innocents.

"Ted, just listen," I whisper when he answers. "I'm in the woods beside the Community Center. Claude's up on the roof, northeast corner. Never would have spotted him, if his gun barrel hadn't appeared for a moment. Don't know where you are, but I assume the chief has at least one officer stationed at the parade assembly area.

"Ask the chief to have someone broadcast a last-minute change in the parade route. Say a detour will take the parade down side streets for the first four blocks. It will re-enter the main route at the Birdwell Lane intersection south of the Community Center. That will prompt all the spectators now gathered in harm's way to relocate beyond Claude's rooftop AR-15 range.

"When Claude hears the announcement, he'll have a decision to make. One not covered by his AI whisperer's instructions. Since the float or floats he's supposed to target won't parade past him, he has zero reason to stay on the roof."

I pause a second, considering his options. "Either he'll try to relocate where he can take a shot, or he'll run to fight another day. Either way, I can surprise Claude when he climbs down from the roof."

"Kylee—" Ted begins.

I don't hear another word as I switch off my cellphone. I trade the phone for my Glock. I'm ready even though I know I may have long minutes to wait. Claude will be angry, frustrated at being stymied.

What will he do?

Chapter Sixty-Seven

The Chameleon

Wednesday, July 4, morning

Waiting for the 911 operator to pick up, I pant like a dog that's just slipped his leash. My trick to instill the perfect amount of breathy panic into my voice.

"This is an emergency. There's a gunman lurking in the woods. Oh, my Lord, he's targeting the crowd. He'll kill dozens."

The operator overrides me. "Try to stay calm. Where are you, miss? What woods?"

"Hullis Island. Woods by the Community Center. Hundreds here for a parade. He'll kill us all. I have to go. I don't want to die."

I end the call. An excellent performance if I do say so, but I'll have to be satisfied imagining the applause. While I told the operator I was leaving, I have no intention of doing so. If things don't work out the way I envision, I may still play Dirty Harriette to ensure the proper outcome.

I'm walking back to my lawn chair when a man's voice booms. "Sorry folks, due to a small glitch, we're rerouting the parade."

For at least thirty minutes, all traffic has been banished from the main thoroughfare in advance of the parade. Barricades have stymied everyone trying to enter from a cross street. Now, an EMT vehicle toddles down the empty road. The voice announcing the route change blares through its speakers.

"The parade will leave the Real Estate Sales Center, turn left on Egret Lane, then right on Heron Street, and proceed three blocks before turning right on Birdwell. From Birdwell the parade will follow its usual route down our main street. We've delayed the parade's start until ten-thirty to give spectators along this portion of the route a chance to relocate."

The woman who welcomed me to share a patch of her lawn stands and sighs. "Well, I'll be. Why in heck are they changing the route? Not like there's an accident or a gas leak. Maybe we'll just skip the parade. I'd need a truck to move all our junk."

She glances over at her husband. His eyes are still on his phone. Hasn't heard a word. The woman marches over and yanks out an earbud. He jumps. "What!"

Where do I go?

Should have anticipated this. It's a smart move, prompting the crowd to vacate the area where someone has reported a figure with a gun creeping around the woods. Sound strategy to avoid panic.

Then I realize the timing's all wrong. No way could this be a reaction to my 911 call. Not possible in a few seconds.

This is the nosy snoop's doing.

She's giving Claude a reason to climb down from the roof. She thinks she can capture the gunman single-handedly.

We'll see about that.

I pick up my chair, cart it off the lawn, and stash it out of the irritated mother's sight. While I won't need the chair, I will need my shoulder bag. I zip it open and position it for easy access to my Sig Sauer.

Chapter Sixty-Eight

Kylee

Wednesday, July 4, morning

It's working! The EMT vehicle makes another pass through the sector, calmly announcing the route change. Spectators may be grumbling, but they're packing up their paraphernalia and moving. Not panicked, just pissed. Only a third of the original crowd remains, and they're busy pulling up stakes. The stragglers just need a little longer to gather coolers, kids, dogs, and camp chairs.

I listen for any rooftop noise. But, even if Claude's moving, it would be hard to make out any furtive movements over the racket associated with the shuffling crowd.

I scan activity up and down the street. A tall woman stands out. The loner strides purposely across the road. She's coming directly toward me and the Community Center. Absolutely, the wrong direction.

I can't see the woman's face. Her head's turned toward the Real Estate Sales Center, probably checking to see if the EMT vehicle is turning for a third pass. She glances behind her, where a family's carting drinks and toys back inside their house. Then, she turns toward me. Her attention zeroes in on the woods and me.

Dammit! It's Amanda Holder. What's her plan? Does she think she can issue new instructions to her young assassin on the fly? Have to assume she's spotted me. Making alternate plans for my disposal?

The professor's wearing her shoulder bag like a bandolier—over the shoulder, across the chest. It frees both of her hands while offering easy access to whatever's inside that bag. I have a feeling it's a gun, and, like me, she keeps it right beside her concealed carry permit.

Great. Now I have to divide my attention between Amanda the Anaconda and an unbalanced teen with an AR-15. Not sure which is the greater danger.

I thought I could ambush Claude and end this nightmare without endangering anyone else. What hubris. I'm as conceited as the witch doctor, imagining I can accurately predict what others will do and manage the scene like I'm directing a movie.

The SWAT team must be en route. I'm sure Ted and the chief have arranged for officers to burst on the scene as soon as the crowd has fully dispersed. They won't want to take any chance the shooter can escape. Not with all these people barely out of harm's way.

I track the puppet master's progress. Though sunglasses shield her eyes, she appears to be looking straight at me, until she veers right. I watch as she walks briskly into the woods and slips behind a tree. She's taken up a position between me and where I expect Claude to descend.

Dammit. Impossible to watch the doc and the section of roof nearest a massive live oak. Its branches arch near the roof. Easy for Claude to grab and climb down.

There's movement. Claude's head and shoulders pop up over the parapet right where I expected. God, the boy looks scrawny and oh so young.

"Claude," Amanda yells. 'Don't come down. A woman is waiting to kill you the minute you leave the roof. You have to take her out first."

Claude's head disappears as he drops behind the parapet. "Who are you? Why should I believe you?"

"I'm Danny's mother," Amanda calls. "He sent me to watch over you. To make sure you'd get away after completing your mission. There's a woman wearing a red wig, hiding behind a tree. About your ten o'clock. Just aim your AR-15 in that direction and let the bullets fly. Once she's dead, you're home free. I have your back."

So that's the vile woman's plan.

Once Claude kills me, she'll kill him and spin some story about being in the right place at the right time. Not going to happen.

Before Claude can aim, I abandon the cover of the woods and sprint in the witch doctor's direction. I slide into a spot behind a tree less than ten feet from the puppet master.

Want Claude to send bullets in my direction? Fine. I'll make sure the bullets find you as well.

My turn to talk to the teen. "Claude, the woman telling you to shoot me has no children. She's no one's mother. She used computer trickery to create Danny. He's a fake, like a cartoon character. Danny doesn't exist."

"Yes, he does!" Claude screams. "He's my friend, my hero."

"That's right," Amanda pipes up. "Don't listen to that bitch. She's the woman you were meant to kill all along. She's the woman who was supposed to drive the Coast Guard float. That red wig is hiding her white hair. She's trying to trick you."

I'm startled by the whir of a helicopter overhead. It circles the roof. Keeps moving. Doesn't hover. Must be hoping to dodge any bullets Claude might send its way.

"Claude, it's your father," a voice calls from the helicopter. "Please, son, throw down your weapon and put your hands in the air. No one will hurt you. It's going to be all right. I know someone has been trying to trick you. Please, Claude, don't throw your life away."

I hold my breath. Will the boy listen? And, if so, what's the puppet master's next play.

"Dad?" Claude sobs. "Don't let them shoot. Don't let them shoot. I'll throw the gun down."

As he stands and tosses the AR-15 off the roof, Amanda pulls a gun from her shoulder bag. She points it at the kid.

"Get down!" I scream at Claude.

He drops below the parapet. I look back at Amanda.

Oh, crap, now she's pointing her gun at me.

283

"You're coming with me, bitch," Amanda barks as she takes aim.

I dive for the ground as a bullet whizzes past my ear. Much too close. Realizing she'll keep firing till she hits me, I bring my legs up for a tuck and roll. I'm near the top of an embankment. My hope? To tumble quickly down the incline and into the stream-carved gulley. Fast enough that Amanda's next bullets miss.

My tumble isn't controlled. I grunt as I slam into the jagged edges of a fallen tree branch. My skull collides with a big rock.

I hear the report of a rifle, and a scream.

A woman's scream.

And it's not me.

"Subject down," comes a voice from the helicopter.

The next voice I hear projected from above is Ted's. "Kylee, careful. Can't tell how badly Amanda's injured. Stay down. A SWAT team is a minute out."

Okey, dokey.

Hope no one's recording video. I touch my forehead, and my fingers come away sticky. I'm bleeding. Pretty sure it's courtesy of those pointy branches, and not a bullet.

The branches must have torn the stupid wig loose. I want to brush its matted hair away from my face, but my wrist doesn't work.

Uh, oh, I feel lightheaded.

* * *

The helicopter lands in the Community Center parking lot as the SWAT team bursts on the scene. Then the world goes black.

When I wake, I know time has passed. How long was I out?

"The woman's dead," a baritone voice calls. "Danger's over."

A minute later, Ted scrambles down the embankment to my side.

"Are you okay? Have you been shot?"

"I'm okay," I answer. "Just a little banged up."

"I'll say." Ted shakes his head. "This time, you're going to need stitches.

That's a pretty big gash on your forehead."

He frees the wig that's somehow still attached to my ear and tosses it into the woods. "I prefer your curly white hair."

I'm still dizzy, a little woozy.

"What happened? Think I might have blacked out for a minute or two."

"The sharpshooter in the helicopter saw Amanda aim at you. He yelled at her to drop the weapon. She didn't, and he nailed her. That's all you need to know right now. The medics will be here in a second. They're taking you to Beaufort Memorial. I'll be there as soon as I can."

"I'm fine," I say. "Don't need an ambulance."

"You're going. These big guys are going to insist, and I don't think you're in any condition to argue with them. Take a little nap. I'll see you at the hospital."

Next thing I know, I'm strapped down, flat on my back, and bouncing up and down as the ambulance heads over a rough patch of road.

Guess that's why they strap you in.

Chapter Sixty-Nine

Kylee

Wednesday, July 4, evening

My eyes flutter open. I'm in a bed, and it's sure not my own. Starchy sheets.

"Welcome back to the world, Kylee," Mom says. "You have to quit scaring your old mother like this. You're going to be the death of me. A heart attack. Plus, we had to postpone our beach picnic because of you. Missed the Fourth of July flyover."

"Hey, Mom." I try to smile. "Sorry about that. I feel kind of groggy. Did they give me something?"

"Yeah, they usually give people something when they operate," she replies. "In addition to your concussion, you had a compound fracture of your left arm. You and Andy Fyke can compare injuries and incisions. They needed twenty-five stitches to close the gash on your forehead. I warned the doctor he'd better make them tiny, or he'd answer to me."

I see Ted lurking behind Mom, undoubtedly waiting his turn to scold me. Mom can tell I've seen Ted.

"I'll be back later," she says. "Need to give Ted his turn while you aren't prepared to sass back."

When Mom leaves, Ted sits on the edge of the bed.

"I brought you something," he says. "I've been waiting for the right moment. With you in a weakened state, I hope my chances are improved."

Ted holds out a small black jewelry box and opens the lid.

"You aren't the diamond type. I've never caught you looking longingly in jewelry store windows, and I've never seen you wear a ring. But I have seen you wear a necklace. So, I asked a friend to sculpt a gold piece showing a couple working together to sail a boat. Teamwork. Equal partners. It comes with a gold chain so you can wear it as a necklace.

"Consider it a gift to mark our engagement. And I'm hoping our engagement will be brief, with a wedding this fall or winter. Your choice." Ted grins. "I already warned the minister he hasn't a prayer of sneaking 'obey' into the vows. What do you say? Will you accept my engagement gift?"

To my surprise, my answer is no mystery.

"The sailboat is exquisite. Yes, I accept, Ted. I love you, too."

Chapter Seventy

Kylee

Wednesday, July 18, evening

As soon as I leave the car, I spot Josie and Alysha chatting on the Fishcamp restaurant's porch. It's the second meeting of our newly formed Smart Gals Network, and a lot has happened since we collaborated on a strategy to extract maximum intel from Bubba Quarles prior to his arrest.

"Hey, Kylee," Alysha calls. "You're looking a might better than the last time I saw you."

I smile as I walk up the stairs to give the Coast Guard lieutenant a one-armed hug. While my left arm is still in a cast, the bruises on my face are fading, leaving only the stitched-up gash on my forehead to attract stares.

"I know you visited me in the hospital, Alysha," I say. "Ted told me you kept him company while the doctor was operating on my arm. But I don't remember actually seeing you. Blame it on the drugs. I was a little loopy."

"Hey, I want a hug, too," Josie says. "Us Smart Gals stick together."

The deputy's hug, like Alysha's, is a careful one.

I must still look fragile, easy to break.

"I'll say you were loopy." Alysha chuckles. "The way I heard it, you said yes to an engagement before you had a chance to shake off the anesthesia."

"You heard right." I laugh. "But I haven't had a moment's regret. Figure if Ted wanted me when I was black-and-blue, concussed, and one-armed, he'll mean it when he vows to love me for better or worse."

Alysha holds the restaurant door open. "Let's get a table and order a first round of drinks. We've got plenty to celebrate besides your engagement. Lots of bad news for bad people, which is good news for us. Can't wait to catch you up."

As soon as we're seated, we each order a beer. "Let's start with Bubba Quarles," I say. "According to news reports, he's been arrested and charged with murdering Steph. One reporter also noted he'll stay behind bars until his trial. No bail."

Josie nods. "Correct. Alysha and I could prove Bubba's boat rammed Steph's scull. Despite Joe Wheeler dynamiting his souped-up toy, forensic experts found enough evidence in the debris. But it would have been much harder to prove Bubba was driving the boat. Even if we could have verified Bubba was at the helm, it would have been impossible to prove intent. The defense would have claimed it was an accident, and he panicked."

Alysha grins. "That's why Dr. Amanda Holder's death proved a godsend. Authorities searching her house and Hullis Island rental found a mother lode for prosecutors. The high-tech witch was so confident she couldn't be detected that she didn't bother to toss her burner phones after they served their purpose. Once we subpoenaed the service provider, we got all the phone records."

I smile. "So, her calls and texts showed the witch doctor was the puppet master, directing not only Bubba, but the dynamite patsy, the woman who pushed Andy down the stairs, and that confused incel teen, Claude Appleton?"

"Yes," Josie agrees. "The phone records plus her computer files. She'd kept all of the deepfake videos and audio recordings she created to groom her dupes. The forensic team also found bonuses like the X-marks-the-spot map created to show Bubba where to ram Steph. Discovering she had a backdoor into the Rand Creek software was another plus. The doc used it to peruse board emails and financial information so she could snap up distressed properties and quickly contact heirs about buying their parents' houses."

"Sounds like her dupes—at least the live ones—are all headed to jail. I have no pity for any of the adults. But what will happen to the seventeen-year-old? Would he ever have embraced violence if the witch doctor hadn't egged him on? And he gave up without hurting a soul."

Before my friends can share their thoughts, the waitress sets down three frosty beers and takes our dinner orders. When she leaves, we clink mugs and toast our luck in stopping Dr. Holder before she could recruit more brain-addled assassins to do her wicked work.

After the toast, Josie shares her thoughts about the incel teen. "Back to the question about what will happen to Claude. He's a minor, who was conned by an adult, and the boy didn't actually shoot anyone. My guess is his attorney will ask for a deal that will require time in a psychiatric hospital."

"I have no complaints about the outcomes," I add. "Not the least being my ability to keep on breathing. Yet with the explosion in Artificial Intelligence applications, I worry we'll see more Dr. Holders using deepfakes to deceive and exploit people."

"I worry about that, too," Alysha says. "But we can't stuff the genie back in the bottle. Guess it's more important than ever for our Smart Gals Network to live on."

"Hey, we've shared our updates, let's hear yours," Josie nudges. "You told us how the doc terrified that woman Leona Grimm into moving out of her home. Did she move back once she learned her dead husband hadn't been chatting her up?"

I smile. "No. My friend Ed Hiller asked to break the news to her. Leona sure didn't react like Ed expected. She remained confident her late husband *had* reached out to her—he just used Dr. Holder as his unwitting intermediary. Leona believed her late husband knew Dr. Holder would have harmed her and her pup if she hadn't left and put the idea of mimicking his voice in the doc's head. Leona's not planning to return to Lighthouse Cove. She found a subdivision that's only a short walk from a Dairy Queen and a dog park."

Alysha and Josie both laugh.

"Some people do manage to make lemonade when they're handed lemons," Alysha says.

I hold up my hand. "Wait, there's more good news—well, at least for some of my Rand Creek friends. Jocelyn Waters, the board president, resigned. While she didn't sanction Dr. Holder's plan to attack Andy Fyke, she was in regular contact with Dr. Holder, discussing ways to thwart Andy's petition drive and sharing information on the folks opposing rentals.

"Jocelyn knew she was in trouble when a board member, Sherry LeRoy, suggested hiring Welch HOA Management to review email archives to determine what information had been compromised by the doc's backdoor access to HOA software. When the motion was approved despite the president's objection, Jocelyn realized her unethical email exchanges would turn up, and she resigned."

Our dinners arrive as soon as I finish my update. I've just taken a big bite of my fried flounder when Alysha waves a fork at me.

"I do have one more question that's much more pressing," she says. "What color bridesmaid dresses will you want us to wear?'

Alysha's question is followed by uproarious laughter from my supposed friends.

I almost choke, trying to swallow fast enough to respond. Yeah, they're kidding, but it does raise an issue I hadn't considered. The idea of being married to Ted doesn't scare me. Unfortunately, it just dawned on me that marriage begins with a wedding.

Good grief. I hope no one expects a big to-do.

A Note from the Author

My love affair with the South Carolina Lowcountry made it a no-brainer to pick this location for my retired Coast Guard heroine's home. The dozen years we lived in the Lowcountry are chockful of fond memories. My biggest challenge has been inventing names for fictional HOAs, since most of my original ideas were already taken.

While I'm positive Beaufort County has no more homeowner association (HOA) feuds than other regions, the number and diversity of single-family home and condo communities make it perfect for this series. I also should note that Nick, my fictional deputy sheriff nemesis, is not meant to reflect on the competence of any law enforcement officer or the professionalism of the Beaufort County Sheriff's Office. However, if I let my fictional LEOs promptly solve local mysteries, my heroine would have nothing to do.

How do I feel about HOAs? Like all human collectives, their potential for good or harm depends on the ethics, personalities, and agendas of those in power. I admire the vast majority of individuals who volunteer for HOA boards and committees. I've met many wonderful people while serving as an HOA secretary, vice president, and president. Fortunately, for my series, I've also come across a few less than altruistic owners who are quite adept at generating the conflict every mystery novel needs.

Acknowledgements

Thanks to Peter Kristian, General Manager, Hilton Head Plantation Property Owners Association, and Kevin McCracken, General Manager, Keowee Key Property Owners Association, for their input on large homeowner association management issues. I really appreciate Jim Mann's help in steering my Artificial Intelligence and digital security research. Any technology mistakes are mine alone.

Congrats to Martha Steele, who attended my book launch for *Neighbors To Die For* and won a drawing to name a character in this book. Martha chose to gift the option to her granddaughter, who now shares a name with Deputy Sheriff Josie Muschel. My friend Kay Barrett, who won an earlier character-name chance, continues to pop up in my HOA Mysteries as Kylee's friend and go-to legal advisor.

I can't say enough about my faithful newsletter and Facebook friends who join in my book-related contests. My latest "Takes the Cake" contest asked people to nominate outrageous HOA restrictions. The contest netted 23 real and fictional entries. The laughable submissions will provide fodder for future fictional tales of neighborhood feuds. Would you like to get in on the next contest? Visit my website: https://lindalovely.com and click on the Contact Me tab to subscribe to my newsletter.

As always, I'm indebted to fellow authors, friends, and family who serve as critique partners and Beta readers. Their input and encouragement is invaluable. Hats off this time to Judy Ellis, Tammy Nowling, Howard Lewis, Robin Weaver, Lorraine Quinn, and Ann Chaney.

Level Best Books, my publisher, and editors Harriette Sackler and Shawn Simmons also deserve credit for excellent suggestions that improved the final copy.

Finally, thanks to my husband, Tom Hooker. Our multi-mile walks often include "what if" plot and character discussions with Tom serving as an honest sounding board. Thank heaven for a husband who shares my love of reading!

About the Author

A Killer App is Linda Lovely's eleventh mystery/suspense novel. Whether she's writing cozy mysteries, historical suspense or contemporary thrillers, her novels share one common element—smart, independent heroines. Humor and romance also sneak into every manuscript. Her work has been recognized as a finalist by such prestigious awards as RWA's Golden Heart for Romantic Suspense and Killer Nashville's Silver Falchion for Best Cozy Mystery.

A long-time member of Sisters in Crime and former chapter president, Lovely also belongs to Mystery Writers of America and International Thriller Writers. She lives on a lake in Upstate South Carolina with her husband, and enjoys swimming, tennis, gardening, long walks, and, of course, reading.

Look for Linda Lovely's next HOA Mystery, coming Fall 2024

SOCIAL MEDIA HANDLES:
Facebook: https://facebook.com/LindaLovelyAuthor/
Goodreads:

https://goodreads.com/author/show/4884053.Linda_Lovely
Amazon: https://amazon.com/author/lindalovely
Barnes & Noble: http://www.barnesandnoble.com/s/Linda+Lovely
BookBub: https://bookbub.com/authors/linda-lovely

AUTHOR WEBSITE:
https://lindalovely.com

Also by Linda Lovely

HOA Mysteries:
  With Neighbors Like These
  Neighbors To Die For

Marley Clark Mysteries:
  Dear Killer
  No Wake Zone

Brie Hooker Mysteries:
  Bones to Pick
  Picked Off
  Bad Pick

Historical Romantic Suspense:
  Lies—Secrets Can Kill

Smart Women, Dumb Luck Romantic Thrillers:
  Dead Line
  Dead Hunt

Printed in the USA
CPSIA information can be obtained
at www.ICGtesting.com
LVHW052017171023
761376LV00005B/45